P9-CRL-048

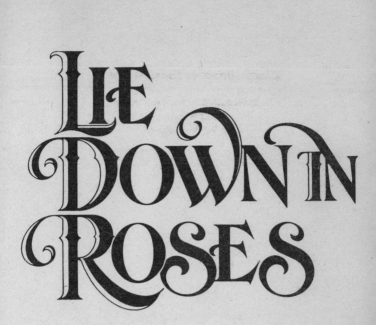

LIE DOWN IN ROSES

SHANNON DRAKE

CHARTER BOOKS, NEW YORK

LIE DOWN IN ROSES

A Charter Book/published by arrangement with
the author

PRINTING HISTORY
Charter edition/December 1988

ISBN: 1-55773-116-0

Charter Books are published by The Berkley Publishing Group,
200 Madison Avenue, New York, N.Y. 10016.
The name "CHARTER" and the "C"
logo are trademarks belonging to
Charter Communications, Inc.

PRINTED IN THE UNITED STATES OF AMERICA

10 9 8 7 6 5 4 3 2 1

Dedicated with all my love
and best wishes to my mother,
Violet Graham,
and to William Sherman,
on the occasion of their marriage,
July 23, 1988.

Bill, we are so very happy to have you!

Prologue

October 15th, 1483

"Needs must a maid be fair of face?
Needs must a maid be full of grace?
Way!
Ah, but a man's cares she must erase,
And, ah! her . . . limbs!—his love embrace!"

It was Sir Thomas Tidewell singing the boisterous ballad, loud and clear against the cool, darkening horizon. Sir Thomas was deep in his cups and he laughed so hard that he rocked sideways upon his mount. But for the fact that Jon of Pleasance rode next to him to right him, Sir Thomas would have crashed to the ground.

Jon was nearly as inebriated as Thomas; he threw an arm around his friend's shoulder, and thus they balanced on their horses to sing the ribald refrain together.

"Nay, she needn't have a face!
Be slim, be witty, or of noble grace.
She needs but love a man's embrace,
Embrace in turn! His sword . . . encase!"

As Jon righted himself, Thomas nearly fell again; he was steadied that time by the hereditary leader of their grouping, Tristan de la Tere, second son of the Earl of Bedford Heath. Jon grinned engagingly at Tristan, and Tristan arched a dark brow and grinned in return, shaking his head with resigned patience. The three had come from London, where Tristan had been embroiled in lengthy discussions of Richard III's accession to the throne. Did Richard's action constitute a seizure? Or was it a legitimate deed, made necessary because the rightful heir was but a boy of twelve—too weak to manage a countryside ravaged by what poets were calling the "Wars of the Roses"?

The difficulty did not end there. For years different factions of the Yorkist branch of the family had been scrambling for power—petty wars within the larger wars. Tristan de la Tere's family had managed to stay out of the internal conflicts. Tristan, barely into his teens, had battled for King Edward IV against Warwick the Kingmaker. Edward's reign had then witnessed a certain quiet. But with the death of Edward IV in 1483, Richard, Duke of Gloucester, took the crown from his nephew, Edward's son and heir. Tristan knew that there was trouble to come. Moreover this was trouble in which Tristan could not remain unaligned.

"Sing, Tristan!" Jon demanded. "You know the words!"

"He knows the words," Thomas agreed, adjusting his cap upon his head, "but he does not know the feeling. Ah, those fine ladies, that fine, sweet flesh we enjoyed so at Mr. Walcox's tavern!" He jabbed a finger accusingly at Tristan. "And you would not touch a one of them. Fie, my liege, my lord! You were the devil himself before marriage overtook you! No man knew better how to drain his ale and send the most seasoned fine young thing swooning—lady or slut!"

Tristan arched a brow once again at his friends in silence, his mouth curled slightly into a smile. These were young men—young and in their prime; hard and muscled from endless days in the saddle, from battles waged, from tournaments. Born into the fratricidal struggle for the crown between the houses of York and Lancaster, they had unwittingly been bred and tuned like soldiers—for survival.

And it was to Tristan that this heavy responsibility fell. He was the second son of the Earl Eustace of Bedford Heath; the land from which they all sprung was his father's domain. Eustace could call forth a thousand retainers at any time; his farms stretched across the horizon farther than the eye could see, and the wool that his farm manufactured was famous by name across the Channel. Tristan's elder brother would some-day take his father's place and title; but Tristan—unlike many younger sons—had not turned to the Church. Instead he had been granted large tracts of family land. Eustace had freed all of his bondsmen, but Tristan held loyalty from hundreds of tenants, yeomen, and the nearly noble gentry such as Thomas and Jon. From the time he had been a lad Tristan had been imbued with the weight of responsibility that would come his way. He could drink with his friends, but he never allowed himself to reach their stage of drunkenness. Nor could he ever stay free of politics. Tristan could not forget that loyalties were sometimes forced upon men, sometimes chosen—but always demanded a high price.

On this fall day, as the three young friends made their way home, things seemed quiet enough. But Tristan suspected that his countrymen would soon be fighting once more. Richard had deposed his nephew and taken the Crown, and in London the move had been accepted; the Crown needed strength. Tristan had reserved judgment on the undertaking. He felt that perhaps it was better for Richard—older, skilled, a grown man—to take the reins of the country, at least until the heir, a bookish, petulant boy, should reach maturity.

But then that boy and his younger brother had disappeared from their Tower prison. And the rumor was heard that Richard had ordered the murder of his own nephews.

Tristan, as son of a noted peer of the realm, had voiced a demand that the boys be shown. Richard had been evasive, but Tristan had not backed down. Then Buckingham, who had been Richard's staunchest supporter when he reached for the throne, had turned traitor and was causing insurrection in the south. Tristan had refused to become involved, telling Richard he would not take up arms on his behalf until the king proved himself innocent of the children's deaths.

So matters stood as they rode north from London that evening, Thomas and Jon sodden, Tristan amused but quietly thoughtful. He was anxious to reach the grand castle he had just completed building, a place that was modern, built for comfort rather than defense. It was a beautiful home, and more beautiful still was the thought that his wife, Lisette, awaited him there.

"Ah, look at that, will you, Jon?" Thomas demanded disgustedly. "Look at his face! The man has no sense of debauchery left! He is thinking of *her*."

Jon laughed. "Well, I might think of her, too—were she mine to dwell on."

"But she's his wife!" Thomas complained. "Wives, bah! They are delicate little things of fine family who bring in wealth and property. Tristan, dear, dear friend, my dear Lord Tristan! You're not supposed to enjoy her, you know! The good wenches at the taverns are put there just for enjoyment!"

Tristan laughed out loud and drew his horse close to Thomas'. He set an arm about the young man's shoulders and shook his head sadly. "Thomas, Thomas! Son, boy, child! You are wrong. A whore is but love that is purchased, and never could love that is bought be so exquisite as that which is freely given and shared! Think of your song, Thomas! My wife loves me. Never once has she been less than eager to greet me. And yet her face is the fairest ever: a face that shines, eyes that sparkle into mine. . . . Nay, Thomas, how could I ever want another? Her scent is sweet, the taste of her flesh is as clean as spring air—while your whores smell like a sow pen!"

"Marriage has ruined him," Thomas told Jon ruefully.

Tristan cast back his head and laughed, and Jon looked at his dancing eyes—eyes so dark they seemed like night and ink when indigo was their true color—and grinned along with him. Tristan and Lisette were indeed a happy couple. Their marriage had been arranged but in six months they found themselves more content with each other than either could have hoped. Tristan was tall as an oak and muscled like a thoroughbred stallion; Lisette was a glorious beauty, with an abundance of dark shimmering hair, an ever-gentle manner, a musical voice, and the face of an angel. A marriage like theirs so seldom happened; it was a union made in heaven. And to complete that happiness, Lisette now carried Tristan's heir.

Thomas glanced wryly at Jon. "My God—he sounds like a poet!" Then he smiled at the man to whom he owed his allegiance, "Ah, she's fair, m'lord! Like the angels are fair, and blessed and beautiful. And sweet—too sweet and good for you, oh roughened knight! But, sir! 'Tis sport of which we speak here—"

Jon interrupted laughing.

"Thomas! You were married off to a rich *widow* with a most luxurious *mustache!* What could you know of Tristan's happiness!"

Tristan couldn't help laughing aloud at that. True, indeed, Thomas' wife was wealthy, the daughter of a merchant in gold; and although she was nearly as ugly as a hag, her wit was quick and Tristan was quite fond of her. Also in one year of marriage she had produced a lusty, healthy baby boy for Thomas, and therefore he could find little to complain about.

"A pox upon upon you, Jon!" Thomas cried in mock horror. "If you marry—if ever you find a woman to bear the sight of that pretty face on a man!—may your wife be as frigid as a nun!"

Jon was about to answer Thomas, but his words died in his throat: for the frown on Tristan's face was so severe that Jon was taken aback. Tristan was a tall, good-looking man— handsome when he laughed, but frightening when he did not. There had been many times when Jon had counted his blessings for being on Tristan's side, for the young lord was a lethal foe.

He wore that lethal expression now, as if night's shadow had cast itself over his features: troubled, wary, dangerous.

"Tristan, what . . . ?" Jon followed his superior's gaze focused some way distant.

And then Jon saw. They had come upon a cottage on the outskirts of Tristan's lands. Darkness was falling quickly and it was not easy to see, but even in the shadow it was apparent that the cottage had been burned. Smoke still drifted up on the night air.

Tristan urged his mount forward at a gallop. Jon and Thomas, instantly sober, followed. Tristan leapt from his horse before the stone cottage, bending low to the ground over an old farmer. He touched the man's throat and drew back, studying the blood that bathed his fingers. It was still warm.

Jon and Thomas dismounted and were at Tristan's side. Tristan stood again quickly. With long strides he headed for the smoking cottage and entered through the burned-out doorway. Jon stood with Tristan before the door. In amazement they saw that someone had savagely destroyed the contents of the little house before setting it afire.

Behind them, Thomas inhaled sharply. They all saw the woman's body at the same time. Tristan strode to her and knelt beside her in unspeakable horror. She had been stripped naked and brutally assaulted, and then left to die in the burning house.

"My God," Tristan cried out. "Why? Ned was just a farmer, tilling his fields; Edith but a simple farmer's wife . . ."

His voice trailed away and then he straightened suddenly, rigid with terror.

"My God," he gasped again. Jon and Thomas could read the ragged fear on his features, hear the panic in his voice. He said nothing else but crossed swiftly to his horse and remounted in a blur of movement. Jon and Thomas raced behind him and mounted, both struck dumb with the horror of their friend's fear.

Murder, heinous murder, committed here on poor, harmless peasants. What then awaited them at their grand manors?

They galloped, madly, down the road, the horses tearing up the turf of autumn. Before they had journeyed far, they again saw smoke against the night sky. All around them the land lay devastated. Cottages were burned to the ground, gardens trampled, fences broken.

And the landscape was a wasteland of corpses.

At last Tristan came by the road of his castle—a castle built for a life of peace. With an unbelieving dismay he saw the bodies of his men-at-arms upon the ground here and there, on the bridge before the moat, the moat with the swans that Lisette loved so dearly.

As if the carnage he had seen on the road had not been enough of a portent! Lisette's beautiful long-necked swans, floated dismally in pools of blood—no longer the embodiment of grace, but decapitated, ugly carcasses.

Jon watched as Tristan dismounted, his face drawn into a horrible mask of fear. Tristan came to the first of his retainers, the captain of his home guard; that stalwart and loyal man lay bleeding where he had fallen at the door—defending until the end. Tristan fell to his knees, lifting the fellow's bloody head into his arms. "Sir Fielding! 'Tis I, Tristan. Can you see me? Can you speak?"

"Ah, lord!" The man found strength to clasp his hand. "Forgive us," he gasped weakly, "we failed you. . . . We knew not what came! Men . . . men in armor, with no badges . . . no pennants. They stormed upon us . . . we would have greeted them in the King's name! They ravaged . . . they murdered—but said not why. My lord . . ."

There were tears in his eyes. Tristan reassured him hastily, and in greater haste demanded, "My lady, Sir Fielding? My lady wife?"

Tears flowed more freely from Fielding's eyes.

"I know not," he said simply.

Jon came to Tristan's side, and the two raced across the bridge and into the hall. All was silence.

And all was death.

He stepped over one of Lisette's maids, a young girl who had been brutally slain and left with her skirts about her throat. Had another horror preceded her dying? More of the guard lay dead and dying, in pools of blood upon the floor.

"Lisette!"

Tristan screamed out her name, in prayer, in hope, in grave and horrible fear. His footsteps took him to the stairway as he desperately raced that distance. He searched from chamber to chamber, screaming her name again and again. There was no answer.

He came to the nursery. A small chamber beside his own,

where already a cradle, woolen garments, and fine small silks and linens awaited his child.

And there he found Lisette.

She leaned over the cradle, her head bowed within it, her hand trailed over it. Almost as if she were reaching to touch a child.

"Lisette!" He shouted no longer. There was no more need. It was a whispered prayer, a plea, a dread beseechment on the air. Tristan quailed inside, and he could not move. He froze, his hands clenched rigidly at his side.

He rushed forward.

She looked so peaceful there. Perhaps . . . and fell to his knees, taking her into his arms. Her head fell back and he saw the bruises at her throat, the trail of blood.

Like the swans, she had been butchered. Blood, blood, so much blood . . .

"Lisette!"

Now it was again a scream, a shriek of agony so deep that it burned his soul. Tristan held her, then clasped his poor dead wife to him, rocking her, rocking the tattered remnants of her youth and beauty.

Jon came upon him there. He watched in horror as his friend held Lisette, smoothed her hair, rocked her, as if she lived. Blood covered Tristan's tunic and his cloak with its white ermine. Jon had never seen a man so demented with grief.

He was afraid to speak; and there was even more to tell Tristan.

And then Tristan spoke. Like a rasp, like the sound of steel against stone.

"What happened?"

"Tristan—"

"What happened here?"

Jon swallowed and spoke as evenly as he could. "Geoffrey Menteith lies wounded by the fire. They were attacked for no reason, with no warning. By men with no mercy. Our soldiers fought, well and bravely, yet they were overrun." He couldn't go on. He couldn't tell Tristan the rest.

"Tell me what else was said!" Tristan roared. God in heaven, he sounded like a lion—wounded, vicious, terrible.

"Your father is also dead, Tristan. And—your brother. His wife. His . . . infant son. All are . . . slain."

Tristan did not move; he did not blink. Warmth swamped him—sticky, horrible warmth. Lisette's warmth, Lisette's blood, her life. The life of their child not yet born, lost before she had succumbed to death herself.

There was a whimpering in the corner. Jon moved, for Tristan could not. Beneath a fallen wardrobe Jon found a young girl, Lisette's handmaiden, cowering, sobbing now, eyes glazed with shock. Jon touched her, and she screamed and recoiled. Then she knew him as friend and flew into his arms, babbling incoherently. Before long, however, her sentences had become all too coherent.

"Oh, oh my lords! Dear God! How my mistress screamed and screamed, and begged and pleaded for mercy!" sobbed the maid. "They caught her in the hallway and took her . . . by force . . . but rape was not enough! She pleaded on her knees, in tears, for her own life and for the child. They . . . they chased her here . . ."

Tristan turned his attention fiercely on the girl, and then he paused, swallowing sharply, lowering Lisette gently to the floor. What he saw next nearly broke him.

His child lay on the floor. But six months in the womb, born dead and yet perfect. A perfect boy. Fingers, toes, limbs, all fully formed.

Jon followed Tristan's glance. "Oh, God," he cried out. "Oh, God most Holy . . ."

Tristan set his miscarried child upon his slain wife, and cradled both tenderly in his arms. The girl began to talk again, in great bursts of terror.

"Hush!" Jon commanded, lest Tristan hear more. Jon was afraid. Afraid further when Tristan lifted Lisette and carried her tenderly through to his own chamber, laying her on the bed, kissing her on the forehead, as if she lived, leaving the baby beside her.

Jon paused but a moment to assure the girl that the assailants were gone. Then he chased after Tristan, who, with deadly purpose, was heading back down the stairs, down to Fielding. Fielding, receiving water from a woman who had returned from the forests where she had hidden, talked to Tristan.

"One of them said that ye'd not demand again to know about the Princes in the Tower, Lord Tristan. That Richard would be pleased with this day's work."

"My God!" Jon cried out in heedless horror. "The King would not order this carnage!"

Fielding eyed him wearily. "Like as not, yet a man with an urge to please him . . ."

"When did they leave? Where did they ride?" Tristan demanded tersely.

Tristan should weep, Jon thought. No one can bear this grief. He should cry.

But the young widower—the new Earl of Bedford Heath— did not. He listened attentively to Fielding. And by then the men-at-arms from the northern boundaries of the property were flocking in, the wounded were beginning to walk about in their bandages. Tristan said nothing, but they were behind him when he turned. Outside, in the night air, more and more of the peasants and the craftsmen and the servants who had fled were returning. No order was given, for no words were needed. Horses and armaments began to appear in the court-yard, and in minutes a good-sized contingent,—including many wounded men, had formed. Tristan needed only lift a hand, and they followed.

They caught up with the murderers—having followed the trail of the troop of mounted men—at midnight. Tristan's forces were outnumbered, but this meant nothing. Tristan was an avenging angel; he was death incarnate. Sword and mace swung alike, in fury, with no fear. He had no care for personal safety, and men dropped in his path like felled trees.

At the end there were only prisoners, pathetic men who whined and cringed in fear, for in their hearts they knew they could ask no mercy. They refused to talk—until they saw Tristan's face—and then they hastened to speak, swearing they had not touched his wife, nor slain his father or his brother.

Tristan leaned over one saying, "Who did this? Who ordered this?"

The slightest hesitation brought the answer.

"Sir Martin Landry, dead there, Lord Tristan, slain by your hand. Please, for the love of God, have mercy! He claimed that we were blessed by the King!"

Even then Tristan did not believe that Richard had ordered the attack. Richard might have wanted him chastised or reproached in some way. But not this slaughter of women and children. Still, Richard might well have ordered his own nephews slain. And though he might not have said, "Go out and do murder," he might well have ordered the attack, and not have known what kind of scum he had sent to do his bidding.

Tristan turned his back on the men.

"What shall we do with them?" Jon asked. Thomas stood beside Jon, quiet, stiff. For with Tristan's sister-in-law and brother he had found his own wife, the dear and charmless hag, the witty young woman who had given him his beautiful son, butchered and slain.

"Mercy!" screamed one of the men.

Tristan spun about. He could not bear the word.

But he had no chance to take action; Thomas had slain the man, who died, choking upon his own blood. Two men remained living. Tristan could not find it in his heart to grant mercy.

He breathed in deeply. "We will keep them prisoners until—"

One suddenly came to his knees at Tristan's feet. "Slay me not! Drew there went into the house; Drew raped your wife! I ne'er touched her! He cast her over the cradle—"

The man broke off, noting something horrible in Tristan's face. Tristan had realized that blood soaked the man's front, and that he was not wounded. And if he had not attacked Lisette, how could he know that she lay over the cradle.

"I did not kill her, I did not kill her. Drew—"

Drew, the sniveling coward, cut in. "You liar, you were the first! The first to take her! Blame it on me! Nay, you—"

Tristan turned away; he wanted to disembowel them while

they lived, to torture them slowly and surely. He had never known a feeling of such rage and sickness.

"They're murderers, Tristan," Jon said quietly. "Death is the penalty."

Death was too easy, Tristan thought. But he swallowed and walked away, calling out over his shoulder, "Hang them."

He heard no more. No pleas, no accusations. He rode silently at the head of the men back to his home. Nay, manor, castle, property, holdings—but never *home* again.

Already the blood was being scoured away. The bodies of his kin were being cleaned by gentle hands, annointed by the priest. They would be laid to rest, masses would be said for their souls . . .

Jon and Thomas stayed with Tristan all night. He did not eat, he did not drink, he did not sleep, and he did not cry. The horror, the vengeance, brooded in him like a terrible storm.

At daybreak he kissed his father's proud old cheeks, the same to his brother, his brother's wife and child. He kissed poor Thomas' ugly wife.

And Lisette . . .

Lisette he took in his arms, holding her tenderly, rocking her. Commanding that she be buried with their son, the child who had not lived to know his love.

He did not remain for the funerals. He left the place in Thomas' hands; Jon would ride with him, Jon and his troops.

As day broke, Tristan had made a plan. He was going to Brittany, where Henry Tudor, the Lancastrian claimant, was gathering his forces and preparing to seize the Crown of England from Richard III.

Henry Tudor would be very glad to welcome him.

Chapter
One

August 15th, 1485

"GOD'S BLOOD!" EDGAR swore, hurtling the message from his hands into the fire, then turning his wrath on the herald who had brought it. "You wish me to feed and succor a regiment of an army advancing to do battle with my King? Nay, man! Not if every stone in this castle were overturned! I shall be among the men who fight that Tudor upstart from the land and sea, young man! You tell your commander, this—this Lord de la Tere—what I have said. Never! Unless this castle were razed to the ground and the vultures left to pick my eyes! Go now!"

The messenger, by now an ashy gray, turned quickly. As he exited the keep gates, Edgar Llewellyn, Lord of Edenby Castle, gave his daughter a satisfied grin.

"Pity, daughter, that one cannot take arms against a messenger!" he said with mock wistfulness.

Genevieve, sitting before the great hearth in the hall, stroking the long ears of a large hound, exhaled softly. She glanced at her aunt, Edwyna, and her betrothed, Axel, before returning her father's gaze.

"Father," she proclaimed firmly, "let's leave all as it is, shall we? The greatest dukes and earls and barons in the land are doing their best to remain uninvolved in this quarrel. 'Tis prudent, methinks, to keep quiet, and await—"

"Await!" Edgar cried, turning on her in passion. He was a tall man with blond hair barely graying and full of strength and vigor—but he knew his daughter would never tremble before him. Nor did she, as he ranted on. "What has become of loyalty? I swore an oath when Richard became King! I *swore* to support him at arms. And so, daughter, will I! In a few days' time we will ride to meet the King—and we will fight the Tudor beast!"

Genevieve smiled sweetly and continued to scratch the dog's ears, casting her fiancé a quick glance of amusement. The young couple were both aware that she loved to tease her father.

"Father! Henry carries the red dragon of Wales as his standard! We go against—"

"Nay! Not even the Welsh lords have all sworn their fealty as yet, girl. And you cease this taunting of yours!"

Axel, staring into the fire at Genevieve's side, caught her eye and winked, and she winked in turn. A tall, scholarly, beloved man, Axel spoke respectfully. "My Lord Edgar, your daughter, my fair betrothed, does have a wondrous point here. Why, sir! Think on Henry Percy, Earl of Northumbria! Great-grandfather slain in fighting against Henry IV. His father slain at Towton—and the earldom taken in attainder! In 1470 the property is restored. But, sir! Can you imagine why Percy is now for the *House of Percy,* no matter who should be King?"

"Percy will come to Richard's side!" Edgar stated.

"Ah, but will he fight?" Genevieve teased.

"God's blood, little girl, but I never should have taught you to speak of politics!" Edgar complained. But he gazed at his sister Edwyna with an apologetic smile that belied his words. He was proud of Genevieve, his daughter and his only heir.

Edwyna, who could not have cared less about politics,

smiled back vaguely and returned her attention to the tapestry she was weaving for her little daughter's bedroom.

Genevieve had always found her aunt exotically beautiful. Not quite ten years Genevieve's senior, she had been widowed young, and since the death of her husband had dwelt with her brother Edgar. Genevieve loved having Edwyna there; she was less a mother than a sister, a dear friend, and was always a bastion of peace.

"Hmmph!" Edgar snorted. "Henry Tudor my . . ."

"Edgar!" Edwyna remonstrated.

"Foot!" Edgar finished. He walked around to his daughter and patted her on the head; then he picked up a long tendril of her rich, golden hair, which was heavy and long enough to trail to the floor behind her when she sat. And her eyes . . . silver-blue like moonbeams, sparkling like stardust. His throat constricted, for she was so like her mother—the one woman he had ever loved, dead since Genevieve had been a child. Ah, and beauty is, he thought, as beauty does, for he knew she was all things he wished her to be—proud, kind, intelligent, and keenly aware of duty and loyalty.

He leaned over the back of her chair. "Genevieve," he reminded her, "you came with me when I traveled to London to swear my oath of allegiance to Richard. Would you have me betray my word?"

"Nay, father," Genevieve returned. "But 'tis true, most noble families mean to stay neutral in this battle. Father, should this thing continue many years more, there will be no nobility left!"

"That would be no problem to a new king," Axel said dryly, "for the king would create new nobles."

"The conversation," Edgar murmured suddenly, "is moot, daughter. I have sworn to bear arms in King Richard's defense. My word is given, and I mean to uphold it. Axel, when the time comes, I shall lead the men of Edenby to join Richard's service. You will, I assume, join me."

Axel bowed in acquiescence. Edgar muttered something about Henry Tudor's parentage that made them all grin, and then he quit the hall. Edwyna sighed and set her yarn upon the table to stretch, then announced that she was going to see to her five-year-old daughter, Anne. Thus were Axel and Genevieve smoothly given a few moments alone.

Genevieve watched her fiancé's face as he looked into the fire. She was fond of Axel, very fond. He tended to be soft-spoken and careful when he'd voice his views; Genevieve knew that he weighed matters with a grave intelligence. He was quick to smile, ready to listen to her and mull her opinions—a friend with whom she could well imagine it comfortable to spend her lifetime. And he was a handsome knight, too, she thought proudly. His eyes were hazel and warm, his hair a dusty blond like wheat. Tall and straight and fair in features, a gentle man, a scholar, good with figures, wonderful in his gift with languages.

"You're not easy with something," Genevieve observed, watching his expression.

He shrugged unhappily. "I don't like to say," he murmured, glancing at Griswald, who had come from the kitchen to light the tapers in the hall. Genevieve rose with a soft rustle of her silk skirts and hurried to old Griswald, asking that he bring them some wine, then whispering with a sly wink that she would like to be alone with Axel.

Griswald brought the wine and discreetly left them alone. Axel and Genevieve sat down to the table, and she softly stroked the bronzed flesh of his hand, waiting for him to speak.

"I shan't oppose your father, Genevieve," he told her at last, sipping the fine, rich wine. "I, too, swore loyalty to Richard. But this matter of the young Princes troubles me deeply. How can one honor a King who would murder his own kin—children at that?"

"Axel, it is not proved that Richard caused the boys' deaths," Genevieve said, "nor, for that matter, is there proof that they are even dead." She paused, remembering her meeting with Richard in London. She had been very impressed with him. Although a slight man, she'd found his face arresting, his eyes like magnets, reflecting the weight of the responsibility he carried. Richard, Genevieve was convinced, had not "seized" the throne. All of England had been up against the Woodvilles—the family of the "rightful" heir,

his brother's son. Men—including the merchants of England—
had come to Richard begging him to take power, to restore
law and order and commerce. Genevieve could not believe
the grave man she had met in London capable of murder.

And her father was right. Like him, she had sworn her
allegiance. She could not change that—not unless the King
were verily proven a murderer to her.

"I wonder if we will every know," she murmured.

Axel shrugged, then caught her hand and turned it palm
upward and drew a soft line upon it, smiling ruefully. "Nor
does any of it really matter. Richard will remain King. Henry
Tudor has landed, it is true, but not even the Welsh lords who
promised their loyalty have all flocked to his standard. Richard's forces will outnumber his nearly two to one." He
smiled. "We needn't really talk about this. I don't care to
bore you—"

"You know that I am never bored with such discussion,"
Genevieve corrected him primly, making him laugh.

"Neither am I, but as our banns have been cried and our
nuptials approach, I had rather hoped that you would be wont
to tease and taunt me with images of your gown. With—"

"It is silvery gray. And exquisite," Genevieve told him
simply, and added, "Edwyna has sewn in dozens and dozens
of pearls, and I am quite sure you will never see anything so
glorious in all your life."

"Nay, but that's a lie!"

"Most sincerely, it's—"

He kissed her hand. "I do not dispute that the gown will be
glorious. I say only that what lies beneath it will be far more
glorious than any fabric, fur, velvet, or silk."

Genevieve said softly "Oh!" then laughed, and kissed him
quickly, telling him that he was capable of saying the most
flattering things. They talked for several moments more, and
she found herself thinking that it really was going to be such a
good match. They liked one another, and he found it important to come to her with the things that weighed heavily on
his mind. He would, of course, gain not only a bride but
much property; yet Axel was a rich man himself. He approved of the fact that she knew the land so well—even

though she would never totally relinquish to him what was her inheritance. Axel expected that they would rule their little world together, and Genevieve was keenly aware that another man might not have been so farsighted.

In time he told her that he must join her father, for if they were to meet up with Richard's army in a few days' time, there were still many things to be seen to. Genevieve smiled a little dreamily and offered up her lips to him for a good-bye kiss. When he had stepped out into the daylight, she went back to the hearth and watched the fire burn, with a small smile curving her mouth. Ah, her father! He was so staunch in his beliefs! A good half of England would sit on its tail while Richard went off to fight the usurper, but not Edgar!

A little shiver touched her with sudden realization. Her father, beloved, the dearest man on earth, might be killed!

Nay, he will command younger men! she assured herself. Nor would the battle be drawn out. Surely Richard would quickly expel Henry Tudor, quickly send him running back across the Channel!

But if . . .

A flutter touched Genevieve's heart; she reached for the mantel to steady herself and she thought suddenly that if she were to lose her father she probably could not bear life. He was still young, he was still handsome; but more importantly he was gentle and kind. And when he talked about her mother in his soft and reverent tones, with love glowing in his eyes, she thought that that was how she wanted to be loved one day—that this was the kind of love that she wanted to elicit.

"Meditating? 'Tis not like you!"

Genevieve spun around at the sound of Edwyna's teasing voice.

"I was just thinking—that I was frightened," she answered honestly.

Edwyna shivered slightly, and Genevieve realized that her aunt had been quietly fearful since the first rumors of Henry's invasion had reached them.

Edwyna walked to the fire and, putting an arm about Genevieve's shoulders, pulled her close. "Edgar, Axel, Sir Guy, and Sir Humphrey are out there now, in the courtyard. Men! I watched them from my window. They have just sent two hundred men to Richard. If I know Edgar, he has sent promises that he will come in person soon.''

"It just never occurred to me before, Edwyna, that—that I could lose father. Oh, Edwyna! I love him so much! He has always been everything to me! If—''

Edwyna gave Genevieve's shoulder a little squeeze. ''Nothing will happen to your father; Richard will see to that. But, Genevieve, remember—if Edgar must fight, there is nothing that anyone can do. Men live by honor.''

''And don't women?'' Genevieve asked sharply.

Edwyna did not take offense. She smiled, lowered her eyes, and moved over to the great table, helping herself to a cup of the wine remaining there. ''Honor,'' she mused, ''is a very expensive commodity.''

''What are you saying?'' Genevieve cried hoarsely. ''Edwyna! You helped to teach me the meaning of honor!''

''Oh, aye—I do consider myself 'honorable'!'' Edwyna assured Genevieve, still smiling. She held up her chalice, in a toast to Genevieve, and to Edgar's picture above the fire. ''It's just that love is a far greater thing. I love my daughter dearly. And were Edgar's honor the price of my daughter's life or security, I would pay it gladly. When you have children, Genevieve, you will understand.''

Genevieve turned back to the fire. ''No matter,'' she said softly. ''I know what love is.''

''Ah yes, Axel! Did you enjoy your moments of privacy with the young swain?'' Edwyna changed her tone; she was teasing and light again. Had Genevieve imagined that grave, nearly bitter, side of her aunt? Probably.

''Swain?'' Genevieve laughed back. ''Axel is the dearest man, but no swain—and well you know it!''

''Spoken like a good fiancée!'' Edwyna returned cheerfully. ''Yours will be a beautiful wedding! Are you anxious, Genevieve?''

''Of—of course,'' Genevieve murmured.

''You're not feeling hesitant, are you?'' Edwyna asked. ''Oh, Genevieve! I was always so happy for you! Your father's choice being a man of whom were were so fond!''

"Nay, nay! I feel no reservations!" Genevieve protested. "It is simply—" She hesitated, and a flush suffused her cheeks. Then Genevieve laughed mischievously—for if she did not talk with Edwyna, with whom could she talk?

"Oh, Edwyna!"

Genevieve plucked up a chalice of wine and carried it with her in a little dance before the fire. "Axel and I shall make a brilliant match! Our cares are the same, our minds match, we've everything in common. He respects me, and I admire him! And more! Oh, I do love him, dearly. I imagine us sipping wine before the fire, laughing at the Christmas mummers, sitting down cheerfully to meals. It's just that . . ."

"Just what?" Edwyna prodded.

"Oh, I don't know, I don't know!" Genevieve wailed softly, spinning about, hair and gown trailing around her as she rushed to Edwyna. "Just—something! That something in all the sonnets, in all the beautiful poetry, in the French ballads, in Chaucer, in the Greek idylls. Edwyna, does it come, does it come with marriage? That wonder, that mystical feeling. That you'd die for his kiss, for his touch! That—"

"Genevieve," Edwyna said shrewdly, "you're in love with the idea of *being in love*! Love itself is different. It's quieter, it's deeper, and that's what can last forever. What you're talking about is—"

"What?" Genevieve asked wistfully.

"Well, passion," Edwyna murmured uneasily. She crossed to sit before her tapestry again, picking up her needle, looking into the distance, then pausing. "Genevieve, don't go looking for passion! Such a thing always hurts those who pursue it—even those who stumble upon it. Be glad that you and Axel are mature, that he is a gentle and considerate man, that—"

"Edwyna! Is that what it was for you?" Genevieve knelt at Edwyna's feet. Edwyna gazed into her niece's immense, beseeching eyes—eyes the color of silver, glittering now, beautiful, enchanting. She winced slightly, reflecting that Genevieve would never do things in half measures. She was reckless and filled with passion; and for a moment Edwyna worried that perhaps Axel had not been the right choice for

Genevieve. He was a fine man, but more the scholar than the knight; too gentle, perhaps, for this wild spirit, yearning to soar.

Edwyna forced herself to answer Genevieve's question.

"Was love passionate for me?" She laughed. "Genevieve, my first taste of grand passion left me wondering how on earth anyone had ever managed to write love poems. But then . . ."

"It did come to you! After marriage!" Genevieve persisted. "Oh, Edwyna! That's what I want! A man to love me like Lancelot loved Guinevere, as Paris loved Helen!"

"Destructive love," Edwyna warned.

"Romantic love!" Genevieve countered. "Oh, Edwyna, will it come? When we're married, will it come?"

What answer could Edwyna give? No, it had never come to her. Not the love that inspired the poets, that kept you from sleeping or eating, that made you shiver with anticipation.

Yet she had discovered a softer kind of love, and she had discovered that she wasn't at all a cold woman. Marriage had become fun; they had both been surprised—and pleased. But then Philip had died, and Edwyna had learned all about loneliness.

Edwyna looked away from Genevieve, feigning a pensive concentration on her skeins of yarn.

"I think that you care deeply for Axel, and that the two of you should do very well. Now—"

The door to the great hall suddenly flew open. Edgar burst in with Axel, Sir Guy, and Sir Humphrey on his heels.

"By God! It will not be borne!" Edgar thundered. His face was red with his rage; he slammed his gauntlets down on the table and started shouting for Griswald to bring meat and ale and plenty of both.

"Father, what is it?" Genevieve leapt to her feet and rushed over to him. She gazed at Sir Humphrey, an old and dear friend of her father, and on to young and handsome Sir Guy, Axel's close comrade.

"I tell you this Tristan de la Tere will sorely rue the day that he entered this world!" Edgar swore. "Daughter! Look at this! Just look at this message!"

Axel shrugged at her glance and indicated that she should read the letter. Genevieve gazed idly at the broken seal on the envelope and flipped it open. The handwriting was genteel enough, but the message itself was insolent and presumptuous, and—as her father had stated—not to be endured. It was addressed to Edgar Llewellyn, Duke of Edenby.

Dear Sir,
*   I, Tristan de la Tere, faithful retainer of Henry Tudor, do most solemnly beseech you to recant your stand, to uphold your title, lands, and honor, and to set your assets and energies toward the cause of said Henry Tudor. If, sir, you will, at this time, surrender the castle and your men, I swear that none in your domains will meet with harm, nor shall your people find themselves deprived of property, honor, or place.*
*   I cannot too greatly emphasize the importance of your friendly actions to Henry Tudor, Lancastrian heir to the Crown of England. I beseech you, sir, throw open your gates and welcome us to your table.*

Most cordially,
Tristan de la Tere
Earl of Bedford Heath
By order of Henry Tudor
The House of Lancaster

Genevieve stared up at her father. "How insolent!"

It was all she could think to say, yet even as she spoke a chill seized her—a chill, as if she had seen some figure rise from a grave.

"It's outrageous!" Edgar swore, "and this Tristan de la Tere shall have his answer most hastily! Axel! See that the messenger is shown out, that the gates are barred! Sir Guy, call the priest that he may come and bless our men and our efforts! Humphrey, you and I must see to the ammunition, quickly, for we shall stop this churlish agent of the devil where he stands, with pitch and hell's fire!"

"Father—" Genevieve began, but he was not listening. Sir

Edgar patted his daughter on the head and swept by her with long strides. Axel caught her eyes for one long moment.

She wanted to speak; she wanted to stop them. Too late. It was as if something unstoppable had whirled into motion. Axel's eyes were brooding and unhappy.

Genevieve lifted a hand to keep him from following her father, but he was already gone. She turned to stare at Edwyna. Edwyna returned her stare, stricken.

"What has happened?" Edwyna murmured. "What has happened? What have we begun here?"

By nightfall the answer was evident. Edenby had joined the battle for the English Crown before that battle had, in truth, begun. The castle of Edenby settled down for a siege; Henry's men, outside the gates, settled down to bombard the castle. They had cannons and catapults and rams; Edenby had walls that were as close to impregnable as walls could be. Throughout the first night, Edgar's longbows rained a shower of burning arrows down upon the invaders. Burning pitch and tar cascaded down the walls.

In turn, powder would flash, stone and rock would quiver and shudder. The smithy caught fire first and burned to the ground; the tannery was razed, and many other of the wooden outbuildings had caught fire. Edenby, though, was a very strong fortress, especially in a state of siege. Edgar could not believe that de la Tere's men could hold out against them long. Henry would need those men to fight Richard.

A second night passed in quiet, yet the dawn brought a new attack. In the afternoon came a request from de la Tere, asking Edgar to surrender.

Sir,

I should be most heartfully glad to hurry on from this place. But Henry is most offended by your stand, and has ordered that this castle be taken. Henry states that there is an ancient relationship existing between the Tudors and Llewellyns, and he is grossly wounded by your raising arms

*against him. Sir, again I beseech you, Surrender, for I have
been ordered to grant no quarter or mercy if we are obliged
to take the castle by force.*

Tristan de la Tere

"No quarter!" Edgar raged, tossing the letter aside. "He
shall see no quarter from us! Fool! Has he not yet seen that
this fortress is impregnable?"

Apparently he had not, for the cannons and catapults assaulted the walls the third day, and then a fourth.

On that night Genevieve climbed to the parapet with her
father and stared out to the fields, where a contingent of the
enemy slept, just beyond the walls. By their position, Edgar
judged that they intended to ram the gates and scale the walls
tomorrow. The infamy of it! Within the confines of the castle
walls, Genevieve could hear the cries of the wounded, the
sobs of the newly widowed and orphaned. Acrid smoke stung
her eyes as the outbuildings continued to smolder.

How she hated this Tristan de la Tere! How dare he come
here and make war against them? She hated him with a dread
fear—for although Edenby had withstood cannon fire again
and again, it would not stand forever against such stronger
forces. She wished that her father's army had not been sent
ahead to Richard.

"We could wait," Axel cautioned Edgar, knuckles white
as he gripped the stone to stare out at the campfires. "Wait—
and pray that Henry summons them away to battle Richard
before they can do further damage. With any luck, Richard—
who still commands so many of our men!—will beat back
Henry Tudor, and we will be saved."

But Edgar disagreed. He and Axel looked at the wall where
it grew weak—where the men would attempt to scale it.

"We must go out. We must go out this night in silence and
decrease these odds against us somewhat!"

"Father, no!" Genevieve cried heartily. "You cannot go!
You are the lord here, you cannot risk—"

"I cannot send men out to do battle in my name if I do not
lead them!" Edgar replied softly, and he hugged his daughter
to him, stroking her hair, smiling. He looked at Axel over her
head, and only when Axel was gone did Genevieve realize

that her father had already given the order for a host of his men to slip out the gate.

Edgar took her cheeks between his palms, and stared into her eyes with a gentle smile. "You musn't be afraid, my daughter," he told her. "God is my right, and I shall conquer my enemies!"

Genevieve tried to smile but she could not, and she clung to him again. They came back through the castle to the courtyard and the great gates. Then Genevieve was left to watch as her father lifted his hand, and the men followed in silence as they slipped over the wall to assault the enemy camp in darkness.

At the top of the wall she saw Axel pausing, looking down at her. She met his eyes with all her love in her own; she brought her fingers to her lips and let a kiss fly to him.

He ran back down. He drew her into his arms and his mouth fell upon hers with a hunger that sent fire cascading down into her. His arms were warm, his body hard against hers . . .

And then he was gone. Gone, just as she smiled and thought, this, then, is it. This is passion, this is love, this is the aching, this is the need to be touched again. Oh, Axel!

He had reached the wall, and disappeared over it.

The night wrapped around Genevieve, and she suddenly felt terribly alone in the silence. Edwyna had gone to lie with Anne, her arms hugging her daughter. The priest might have been company for Genevieve, but he could not be with her. He was too busy giving the last rites to so many.

She was alone in the silence . . .

And then the screams began to come, and the night erupted. But she was still alone when the men dragged the body of her fiancé back through the crack in the gate.

"Axel! Oh, God, oh, no!"

They hovered around her then, her father's men. Sir Humphrey cleared his throat to tell her that Axel had fought wisely and well. That he had been daring and courageous.

Genevieve could only stare down in horror. At his face, proud, scholarly, beautiful; his eyes, their hazel light put out forever. "Oh, Axel!" She strove to kiss him in disbelief, then stared at her hands where they had touched him and screamed, for they were covered in blood from the wound at his throat.

But further horror awaited her. Sir Guy, looking dismayed, told her the news.

Lord Edgar of Edenby had not returned from the foray. Guy and Humphrey meant to go in search of him, yet Genevieve would let no one stir but at her command—with her in the lead.

"I rank here in my father's absence," she told them coolly, and despite all protests it was Genevieve, finally, who slipped over the wall to search among the bodies at its base.

Thus it was she who stumbled upon Edgar—mortally wounded but still alive. She began to cry and sank to her knees, to sweep her arms about him and hold him to her breast, cleaning the blood from his face with her skirt, soothing, talking, swearing that all would be well.

"Dearest daughter, sweetest child, mine angel!" Edgar's words rasped against the heaving of his chest. His hand trembled and shook when he lifted it to touch her face.

"Child, it is yours—"

"Nay, father! I shall bathe your wounds, I shall—"

"You bathe them now with your tears," he told her gently. "I know that I am dying. Yet I leave all to you with the greatest pride! Our honor, our loyalty. Genevieve, you are ruler now! Be careful, be loyal, care for those who would serve you. Never, never surrender. And be of good cheer! Let not our people suffer in vain. Genevieve, Axel will guide you now. You will marry, Genevieve . . ."

A great convulsion shook Edgar; he did not speak again. Tears fell down Genevieve's cheeks in torrents as she rocked her father. He did not know that Axel had traveled the route to heaven before him; he had not known how horribly bereft she now found herself.

Sir Guy came upon her and lifted her to her feet. "Genevieve! In, we must come in! The enemy still lurks, hurry—"

"Nay, my father—my father's body! I'll not leave him to the carrion crows!"

So they carried Edgar back into his castle. Genevieve, wet

with blood, stood upon the parapets and would see no one. She felt the night air against her cheeks, and she vowed to her dead father's spirit that she would not surrender.

She vowed to Axel that their love would not have perished in vain.

"De la Tere!" she shouted to the night wind. "Tristan de la Tere! I will bring you down, I swear it!"

But that night, sobs of disbelieving grief belied her proud cry. She could not accept that her father was lost, that she would never call Axel husband, that her world as she had known and loved it could never be again.

Finally exhausted, Genevieve leaned her head against the stone wall and repeated her father's words.

"Never surrender."

De la Tere's forces would do battle against her again, she knew. And she had so few resources remaining! Ah, but some plan would come to her. Something.

Never surrender.

Chapter
Two

IT APPEARED AS if the sun itself flew, blazing, leaping in fiery splendor, high against the sky.

But then the huge stone—rolled in linen and soaked with oil and set to burn—fell, and screams of shrieking agony rose from beyond the stone walls and cliff barriers of Edenby Castle.

Tristan's cannon thundered and roared. But the stone walls were so thick that the ball had little effect, and soon the hastily constructed catapult loomed into action again. There was pandemonium. Between the fires arising and the gunpowder that blackened the air around them, it was difficult to tell who men were, or whom they followed. It was difficult even to make out their red rose crests, proclaiming the House of Lancaster.

Tristan de la Tere was seated upon his massive warhorse, in helmet and armor, bearing the emblem of the red rose on his mantle. All that could be seen of Tristan's face were his eyes, which were as dark as the night. His eyes narrowed as he sat there in silence. Not even his well-trained mount stirred.

Then he suddenly swore with an incredulous fury. "God

29

damn them! Haven't they the sense to surrender? I'd have no more of this senseless bloodshed!''

At his side, Jon, his second in command now, dared to speak. ''I'm afraid, Tristan, that they do not honor the Lancaster heir as we do. Nor, does it seem, that the Lord of Edenby is eager to hand over his castle.'' Like Tristan, he prayed that the bloodshed would end. Yet it was impossible not to admire a worthy foe, and even—in this particular battle—understand his position.

''Edgar of Edenby must understand that this is war.''

''Umm,'' Jon murmured, wincing silently for a moment as a horse went down, slain not by the enemy, but by the faulty firing of a cannon, which set ablaze the area not a hundred yards from where they stood to direct the battle. ''You were ordered to take this place as a conquered domain. By a king who does not yet sit upon a throne.''

''But will do so,'' Tristan said quietly and grimly. He shrugged. ''Jon, I tried everything. Now I have been ordered to give no mercy, but still I will try to do so. Yet if this keeps up, the men will be like lunatics when they go in.'' He fell silent for a moment. ''I will feel like a madman when I go in myself, yearning to destroy.''

''Looting, rape, and thievery! What a task we are set to!'' Jon mused. ''I've a mind for some fine silver plate myself. And once this ends,'' he paused, shrugging with a weary grin, ''the pleasure of fine wine, women, and song!''

Tristan grunted out an answer and spun about in his saddle, lifting a gauntleted hand. ''Damn the castle! And Edenby's pride! He had only to swear his loyalty.'' He turned back to the scene before him: the fire, blazing high against the wintry blue sky. The ramparts, where men could be seen racing along—awkward in their mail and helmets—and desperate to elude the flames and quench them. The castle sat on a bluff, a wall of sheer stone that rose from the sea at the left and protected the front. They had penetrated the fortress with their catapult, but there was still no hint that Edenby would capitulate.

Tristan grimly contemplated his own men—tired, filthy, and ragged. Blackened by soot, laden down by their shafts and arrows and spears and archers' armor and swords.

Fury soared in his heart again. By God, Edenby! he thought. Surrender! I have no wish to debase you, yet you give me no choice! I will win, Edenby! I will see that Henry Tudor ascends to his throne.

Tristan had become Henry's man himself, fiercely so. He could not forgive Richard. Perhaps Richard had not officially ordered murder, but he had made it clear that he was displeased with Tristan. Murder had ensued: the death of everything Tristan had loved. The King's displeasure had exacted a penalty that Tristan would never forgive; two years later, the wounds were still deep. The past was like a relentless knife in his heart, an agony that would not fade.

Henry Tudor—son of Owen and heir through his mother's branch of the family—was a man of stern and uncompromising judgment, but he was also determined to see the terror and bloodshed come to an end. Richard still claimed the throne, but Tristan believed fiercely that it was only a matter of time. The country was rising against his treachery and deceit.

Henry was, for some unfathomable reason, furious with Edgar Llewellyn. A curious fact, since he had known that few of the nobility would join the fight for the Crown this time. Neutrality not only was a wise course, but for many families it was the only way to survive.

But once Edgar had refused shelter to Henry's men, Henry had ordered the castle taken, Edgar demoralized. Perhaps it was Edgar's Welsh inheritance, but more likely it was personal between Henry and Edgar.

"I will get Edenby to surrender," Tristan had assured Henry; but the Lancastrian had laughed bitterly. Edgar had been proclaiming stalwartly for the Yorkists for the past thirty years. "He called me the 'Mad Bastard' once," Henry told Tristan. "He has not changed, and he will not surrender—not until every stone is overturned." Henry frowned darkly. "Go back, Tristan, and crush Edenby." And Henry had eyed Tristan with the shrewdness that was one of his greatest assets. "Give no quarter. Take Edenby, and Edenby is yours. Don't forget the heinous cruelties perpetrated on your family by the House of York."

Tristan had not forgotten. But despite Henry's words, Tristan knew that the man who would be king did not want endless fields of dead. Henry might bear a personal grudge against Edgar, but he possessed a certain avarice; he would want living subjects, men to till the fields and lords of the manors who were able to pay their taxes.

If Edgar only had honored their first request for food and hospitality! Tristan would never have sought Henry's advice, never received the severe and irrevocable answer.

"Damn them!" Tristan swore again furiously. When they did take the castle, he would not be able, in fairness, to deny his men any sort of plunder. You could not drag knights over a harsh, barren countryside and deny them the spoils of war. He could only pray for a minimum of bloodshed.

"So be it!" he muttered heatedly, and he lifted a hand to Tibald at the brace of a catapult. His hand fell; once again a soaring, flame-gold ball of death took flight.

The anguished screams rose from Edenby, loud and shrill. Smoke filled the air; people raced about, scurrying for cover, shrieking and gasping for water.

Tristan's eyes narrowed once again as he peered through the smoke and flame. The ramparts were empty now—his archers were assuring that those who dared to remain in sight would not do so for long. But then Tristan saw a lone figure, curiously tall and proud and apparently oblivious to the fire and cacophony. He blinked; the smoke was like a swirling fog, rising and misting. It seemed that the screams grew faint as he stared through the shield of smoke, almost as if he had entered another place and time.

It was a woman who stood there. Decked in white, in some snowy fabric that caught the breeze and floated and surrounded her. Reaching through the smoke-filled gray of the sky, the sunlight touched her long hair, which glittered like gold, curling in golden waves below her knees.

Her hands were on the walls; it seemed that she stared straight down at him. He could not see her face, and yet he sensed that she was not afraid, that she scorned their efforts completely. She stood so defiantly that he was shaken by her appearance.

What was she doing there? Where was her father, her husband, her brother, that they allowed her to stand there so! Defying danger . . .

Poor Lisette had begged for mercy, and found none. This woman stood there, daring death, and no harm came her way. Something simmered and scalded and roiled deep within Tristan's heart; he wanted to wrench her from that height and shake her and yell until she had some sense of danger . . .

"Milord Tristan!"

He started, and saw that Tibald was calling to him. "What order?"

"Do we give them another volley then?" Jon queried.

"Nay—we wait," Tristan said. He stared back to the ramparts; she was gone. "We leave them to ponder on our strength—and we send them another condition of surrender."

Suddenly, flying down from the ramparts, came a fluid stream of burning arrows. Screams rose again—this time from Tristan's men as they fell to the ground, beat at the flames, bled, and died. "Hold your shields!" Tristan commanded, his voice rising like thunder above the din about him. He did not move his position, but raised his shield—embossed with an intertwined hawk and tiger—high against the death rain. His men, in turn, did not panic, but raised their own shields, and those larger, wooden ones twined together for the siege so that they might drag away the wounded. The rain of arrows at last ceased. Furious, with his lips compressed grimly, Tristan spoke to Tibald. "They seek battle, and they shall receive battle! Another volley!"

Tibald nodded to the warrior with the fire taper; the flame was lit—and a burning ball sprang high to the heavens once again. Tristan did not hear the screams from beyond the wall. He was too busy commanding his own men to pull back the wounded. Even his great mount was prancing at the upheaval around them now; horses were down, and their agonized and eerie cries tore at the smoke-filled air.

At last Tristan looked back at the castle. Flames rose high, and smoke filled the sky. But no banner was raised to offer surrender.

Tristan ordered that they pull back to the tents. The same

bluff that shielded the castle had offered them a buffered camp in easy reach.

As litters were dragged along behind them with the giant catapult, Tristan rode grim-faced. When they reached camp and Tristan dismounted, not even Jon sought to talk to him. Tristan, who wore no beard, had harsh features to start with: a high forehead with winged, mocking brows, a long nose, cheekbones that rose high and stern, and a jawline that appeared sculpted of rock. His rich abundance of sable dark hair touched the collar of his tunic and fell almost to his brows in front, but was usually swept aside. His flesh was bronzed from many days spent outdoors. Although he had once smiled easily, Tristan rarely bore the look of amusement that had been so charming. For the last two years his wide mouth had been compressed with a severity that could cause the stoutest man to quake. His eyes were changeable and deep; they could rage with fire and threaten like the pits of hell. He could, by his mere presence, accomplish more with a word than many a man with a sword.

He rose high above other men, trim but with broad muscled shoulders that had been hardened by heavy practice with the weapons of war. He was a young man, not yet thirty, but the older barons never thought to question his command. He was always first beneath the fire; it seemed he could deny death.

He has become so hard, Jon thought, watching his friend.

Jon followed Tristan into his tent, and stood behind while he stripped away his helmet and mail, and washed his face furiously in cool water. "Call for Alaric," Tristan ordered shortly, and Jon moved to obey the summons.

Moments later the scribe, Alaric, was there. He was an old man, but one who had served Tristan's father faithfully. Tristan clasped his hands behind his back and paced the room. Alaric looked at Tristan calmly, awaiting the biting speech that would follow. Tristan's anger was evident in his carriage, in the smoldering flame of his eyes. His voice was calm, he was not shouting—and was therefore at his most dangerous stage.

"Tell them," Tristan said at last, pausing, "tell them no quarter. That we shall ram the gates tomorrow, and that they should pray for God to have mercy, for I—Tristan de la Tere, Earl and Lord in the service of Henry Tudor—shall have none.''

He paused again. He closed his eyes, and he could see his men, burning, shrieking, dying in agony in the streak of arrows. His was the stronger force; he would win.

Tristan opened his eyes and looked at the scribe. ''That is it, Alaric. See that it is brought to the gates under the proper banner. And see that it is understood. No mercy.''

Alaric nodded, bobbed, and left the tent. Tristan then turned calmly to Jon. ''Is there a meal that can be sent? I believe we've still a cache of Bordeaux. See to it, will you, Jon—and ask Tibald that I be given a report on the wounded.''

Not long after, they sat down to their meal. Tristan described the assault they would make in the morning. ''Before dawn, or just as the dawn arises,'' he said. And then he frowned, for Alaric burst in upon them. ''There was a reply to your message, milord. An urgent summons that you meet with the lord of the castle, this evening, alone, at a point that is too distant from the castle to be in range. A certain place upon the bluff.''

''Don't do it, Tristan!'' Jon declared warily. '' 'Tis surely a trick, and nothing more.''

''The request came out in the 'name of Christ's mercy.' ''

Tristan hesitated, drinking his cherished Bordeaux thoughtfully. ''Nay, I will go prepared for a trick. Solemn oath will be taken on both sides that there will be no interference.''

''Aye—that has been promised by the Yorkists.''

''And 'tis no better than the promise of dogs!'' Jon spat out.

Tristan clanked his goblet to the table. ''God's whit! But I've lost enough men! I will meet with this lord, and the surrender will be upon my terms, I swear it!''

Not an hour later, he was again mounted. He wore no helmet or mail, nor did he carry his sword. But he did have his knife in a sheath at his calf, ready to be drawn.

Jon accompanied Tristan to the bluff. Once there, he dismounted and gazed up at the maze of rock. He knew the appointed cove; he had been there when they had first started the siege.

"Go carefully, Tristan," Jon warned.

"I always move carefully," Tristan replied. He turned to the rock, and planted his boots against it to climb to the first plateau. Tossing his mantle over his shoulder, he continued along the harsh trail of boulders, a taper of fire high in his hand.

He approved the meeting place. No one could hide upon the windswept rock—the cove afforded the only privacy. Yet he moved cautiously, for he would never trust these Yorkists.

"Edenby!" He shouted when he reached the appointed cove. "Show yourself!"

There was a sound behind him and he turned, ever at the ready to draw his knife and strike. But he paused, startled. There was no man there—just the woman he had seen upon the ramparts. She was in white again, or was it the same white—somehow untouched by the smoke? Beneath the glow of the moon, her hair still seemed to hold sunlight. It was a rich and golden color, vivid and deep, and it framed a face that was finely sculpted, pale and rose, beautiful and young. The eyes that beheld him were silver with the moon, and as proudly defiant as her stance. She, too, held a taper; its blaze touched her eyes and set the sheen of pure gold to her hair.

Suddenly he found himself furious at her appearance—more furious still that she had stood like a fool upon the ramparts while the arrows flew. "Who are you?" he demanded harshly. "I came to meet the lord of the castle—not a girl."

She seemed to stiffen, then rich lashes fell over her eyes, and a disdainful smile curled the corners of her lips.

"The lord of the castle is quite dead, and has been since he was murdered on the fourth day of battle."

Tristan found a crevice in which to stash his torch. He walked slowly around her, hands on his hips. "So," he said at last, "the lord of the castle is dead. Where then, is his son, his brother, his cousin, or the man to take his place?"

There was such a calm about her that he longed to slap her, yet refrained. "I, sir, am the 'lord' of the castle."

"Then it is you who has caused these further days of needless and futile suffering and death!" Tristan spat out to her.

"I?" She raised a honey-colored brow. "Nay, sir, I did not set out to attack, to divest others of their home, to rape and pillage and murder. I have sought only to keep what is mine."

"I sought no pillage, no rape, no murder," Tristan muttered, "but my God, lady, now it shall be."

Her lashes lowered, and her head dipped just slightly. "Then there is no chance that I—might seek honorable surrender now?"

"You are late in asking, lady," Tristan said bitterly. "And there is nothing for me to gain. You seek to call my men animals—that is what you have made them."

She raised her head. "I asked you, milord, if there was no hope of mercy?" Her voice was soft, like velvet, drifting along his spine. He heard in it a plea, and more. Something that twisted inside of him, something that made him ache . . . burn . . .

Desire.

It was sudden, startling, stark, and painful. Love had died and been buried with Lisette and their child. But in the two years that had passed since then, Tristan had discovered that love and need were not the same. He had wanted many women since; he had easily had what he wanted. But this desire was unlike anything he had known.

It was like a fire burning, filling him. She was exquisite. Her hair . . . he could imagine it entangled about him, against him like silk. Skeins of gold. She was so fair. Her eyes were the most unusual color and shape he had ever seen. She had a strange power; she made a man want her with a shattering, reckless hunger; she made him burn, and throb, and long to take her on any level. She made him ache to forget all else, to reach for her, to strip her finery from her, and know right there, right then, upon the dirt and the rock, what mystery lay within her eyes, what passion shimmered there.

Yet as equally as he was drawn, she repelled him. She was cold and proud and stubborn. She held her head high; her eyes bore no light of pleading. Yet how had Lisette looked that night, meeting her butchers? Pleading for her life. Begging. Beseeching any small mercy. But finding none.

Tristan laughed harshly. He was the wrong man to be taken by any woman, no matter how fair. "Lady, just what is it you can offer?"

"Myself," she said simply.

"Yourself?" he queried, taking a few steps. Amusement twisted the hard line of his jaw; he stopped to face her again. "Lady, tomorrow we shall ram your gates, and take then what we wish."

He thought he saw a gleam as sharp as his sword in her eyes, but her lashes lowered quickly, and he was startled as she drew in a deep, shaky breath. A little sob escaped her. "There is nothing else I have to offer—except to end the bloodshed. And for tomorrow, milord, there is a portent for rivers of blood. You will come in to ravage, and so we will again be forced to fight. To the death. Yet if you were to take me as your wife, the castle would be yours in the eyes of all my men."

"Take you to wife, milady?" he queried incredulously, and he almost spat on the ground. She was a Yorkist. Smug, insolent little Yorkist, convinced of her own beauty and allure! Not to mention deadly. So she had carried on the battle! He could not forget the cries of his dying men. "I've no desire for a wife."

She did not raise her head, so he did not see the glint of fury that touched her eyes.

"I am the Lady of Edenby," she said coolly. "Nothing can change that—"

"I beg to differ," Tristan interrupted politely. "When the Tudor sits upon his throne, he shall do so with a stroke of a quill."

"Nay, only my head upon a block can do such a thing. Would your Tudor King dare go so far? Is he then determined to murder all who oppose him? The axmen and hangsmen of England will be busy, for a certainty!"

Tristan smiled slightly, crossing his arms over his chest. "This is war, my lady. I am but a soldier of the King—who will attaint your property and title. You are—no one, milady.'' He offered the last mockingly.

"You serve a pretender! Richard is King!"

"Have it as you will, my lady. We are remote here; there will be no clerics of the court to argue for you, no one left when it is over to come to your defense. I care not if you hold half of England; I will take this castle, and I will be its lord.'' He spoke lightly, then his voice deepened with a startling fury. "And I will take no woman as a wife, madam, no matter how rich, no matter how fine and fair. So barter yourself no further!"

Genevieve's head lowered quickly; about her the night seemed to seethe with friction. She appeared ready to pounce upon him, hawklike, with her nails for talons. As she waited the air was alive with a fascinating tension.

At last she spoke—but not with the venom he had expected.

"Then not as wife," she said softly. "As mistress, concubine, or whore." She stared at him, her smile as sweet as a summer rose. "You are the conquerors, are you not?"

Tristan arched a brow high, musing on this ploy of hers. What in God's name was she after? She feigned humility; there was none, in truth, about her. She was proud, yet she lowered her eyes from his. Ah, lady! he thought, were you but a tavern strumpet, I'd take your offer swift and sweet, for never have I known so quick and urgent and fierce a longing! It was as if the sight of her were a drug, a potent invader of the blood and soul. He would have to have her to ever forget her.

Yet she was the enemy, he reminded himself, and one whom he could not trust.

"Lady," he spoke harshly. "I'm not sure I want you. Perhaps there is someone more . . . alluring within the castle to be offered?"

"What?" she burst out. Her eyes were slivers of diamond-bright fury. Had they been lances, they'd have pierced his heart a thousand times.

"I don't find you particularly appealing."

"I find you loath—" she began, but she cut herself off, looking to the ground again. "Lord de la Tere, we talk of

peace. We talk of men who will defy you every step of the
way unless they believe that I have determined for peace!
Another fight within the walls, and Edenby will be nothing
but a sea of blood! Are you dim-witted? Don't you see why I
have come here tonight?''

"Magnanimous, aren't you?" he murmured. "The great
lady—so quick to shed the sanctity of marriage for the honorless position of whore."

She didn't flinch; she stared at him with the moon's silver
glitter in her eyes and allowed herself the pleasure of a cool,
scathing retort. "Lord Tristan, were circumstances different,
I would not sully my family lineage in marriage to you!"

He laughed, for his family name was a fine one, and the
superior claim of the lady of Edenby was rather amusing,
under the circumstances.

"That works out well then, does it not? You'd not wish to
sully your name. I've no wish to ever call a woman wife—
especially not an arrogant, foolish girl who cannot admit
defeat. But yet, I pray, explain why you would come to me
offering yourself even as a concubine, for surely such a thing
must be an abomination to your good name, too."

She paused slightly and raised a hand. She had dressed to
entrance him, he realized. The white garment moved with
her, flowing, and displaying a hint of the mounds of her
breasts, and the deep valley between them. The fabric clung
to her, and displayed all that was beautifully young and
beautifully female about her form.

Her hand fluttered back to her side. "I am desperate," she
said simply. It was, Tristan thought, the first honest statement
that she had given him.

He sighed. "To tell the truth, milady, I've little taste for
murder or plunder—or rape. I prefer my women willing and
tender. Passionate in their desire for me, as I for them.
Obviously you are aware of your beauty—else you would not
think to barter so. Yet, to me, it would mean little. There are
many beautiful women in the world. And among them are
those who who do not think of 'duty,' or of 'sacrifice,' but of
pleasure to be shared in the arms of a man."

At last, it seemed, he had drawn a flush from her. Scarlet

color stained her breast and cheeks. Yet, if she were angry, she did not display it. She gave him another smile, hesitant but full of sensual beauty.

"I've—I've watched you, Lord Tristan. From the ramparts. I'm quite certain that I can—be all that you wish."

"And not a despised enemy?" he queried skeptically.

"No."

He turned from her suddenly, flicking his mantle past his shoulder and staring out at the bluffs far below to the night-dark sea. Then he spun back to her.

"Keep yourself, lady. If peace can be arranged, it shall come to pass. Your coffers shall go to my men, and the castle will be mine, but no more will die. And I will hold my men in check. Your ladies will be pleased; your whores will be rich." He started down the bluff, and was stunned to hear her call him back. "Lord Tristan!"

He turned to her cry. She was following him, anxiety now in her eyes. Her breasts heaved with no thought of enticement; she touched his arm, then stared at her hand upon it and quickly drew away, panting slightly as she spoke.

"I—I—"

"What?" He demanded curtly. Damn you, leave me! he thought. Go away! You will quickly become an obsession with me. Something that I must have, even while I hate you and all that you stand for. Aye, hate even the fever, the feeling you create . . .

"It—it will not do! Not as you say! My people will protest if I am thrown from the castle. Please, for the love of God! I must greet you, and you—you must come to me! We . . . you and I . . . we must appear as friends. As more than friends."

He cocked his head, querying her. "Milady, spell it out. Clearly. What are you saying?"

"I beg you . . . to come to me."

"Clearer," he taunted her.

"As a lover!"

"I am the conqueror—but you'd have me be your lover—in what was your own castle?"

"Aye!"

For a moment he closed his eyes; he thought of his wife, so beautiful, so sweet, so loving.

Everything about him tensed in a fire-torn agony. He'd taken women since! Where was the difference here? Ah, but he had no interest in martyred virgins! Yet the sight of her had touched him fiercely; for all her golden beauty and cool elegance, there was also something raw and exciting about her. Something that hinted of a deep sensuality and a seething passion and spirit. He shrugged. Maybe she was no innocent virgin, maybe she had known numerous lovers. She was the strangest cross between angelic innocence, golden purity, and throbbing allure. If one were to touch her, she would come alive in tempest, great and startling in comparison to the restraint she feigned now.

The greatest ladies had been known to bed their own grooms. Perhaps it was easy for her to come to him because she was already well versed in the ways of the bedchamber.

Tristan felt the heat again, soaring. She did that. She beckoned, she seduced, on a level that was primal, where the body was scorched and no thought could take hold in the mind. She had invaded his senses. He could, perhaps, forget that she was a Yorkist. Whores, he had learned, were alike in the dark. "Please?" she whispered fervently, and again her tone entered him, and brought him to feel pity.

She made no sense. She must be watched, carefully and warily. Yet how could he, a man who still heard the echoes of screams for mercy in his dreams, refuse to grant a request that could lead to a peaceful negotiation? To . . . mercy.

And then there was the desire. The haunting desire that she created. He wanted no part of it! It was there, nonetheless.

He threw up his hands. "Lady, this is lunacy."

She did not reply.

"Did you hear?" he demanded harshly.

"I heard."

"I granted you mercy with no thought of barter!"

"Don't you understand? It would not be enough! Yet if they saw us together, they would know that I have surrendered completely, and thus they would surrender, too."

"Lady, then have it as you would! One whore is the same as another."

She surveyed him, regal and calm. He sighed.

"None will be harmed, no vengeance taken." His voice went suddenly ragged. "But I mean it—I do not want a wife! Nor will the cost be any less great to you; the castle is in my hands—gold and jewels and foodstuffs and land will be divided among my men."

"When will you come?" she asked him. She was relieved, he noted. Liar, witch—what are you planning? he wondered.

"At noon. And my men are hungry. If you would be the chatelaine, have a feast waiting—wine and food."

She nodded. "We will be waiting, Lord Tristan."

He started down the bluff again, but felt her watching him. He turned. The moon had caught her hair, and her eyes. A glitter, silver like that orb in the sky, touched them in a misted beauty. And yet he didn't trust her—he had caught her unaware, and he knew that she despised him with a vengeance.

No matter. She was welcome to despise him to his dying day.

"What is your name?" he called to her.

"Genevieve," she told him, "Lord Tristan."

It was that last retort which stopped him. Now, with her plea granted, her voice became so scathing and sarcastic that he thought at first he must have imagined the rich force of contempt that chilled its sweetness.

Anger raced through him, deep and dark and compelling. She played a dangerous game—and he knew it well.

And still . . . he wanted her. Despite it all, despite logic and sense, he wanted her. Knowing that she was treacherous, knowing that she was a lie.

He was suddenly back beside her, as contemptuous as she, and determined to shake her.

She did not fall back, though he thought that she longed to. He stood right before her, close enough to see those mauve and silver eyes in the moonlight, to feel her, the rush of her breath, the beat of her heart. And as she stared up at him he smiled, for he saw the furious pulse that strummed rampantly against the creamy length of her throat. He kept that smile in place, pleasant, easy, while cold and brutal anger held him.

She knew no humility, she would receive mercy when she did not know how to ask it. She played upon emotions and desires while . . .

Lisette had died.

Was it all anger? Was it something else? His heart felt frozen, his body ached and yearned. He was his own man, stronger than she. Stronger than the silken web she tried to weave about him. He would break her, break her web, and find the truth, he promised himself.

And so his mocking smile spread.

"I've never purchased without sampling the merchandise."

And then he seized her, holding her in anger, in pain; he was on fire and as cold as ice. He tilted her chin and seared her lips with his own.

He heard a sound deep in her throat, he felt her body stiffen, felt panic surge through her. Her heart took flight like a bird, her breath all but halted.

Her lips were as sweet as wine, but they hardened instinctively against his assault. No hungry lover here, he surmised, yet he gave no quarter, ignoring protest. Against his force her lips parted, and his tongue swept and ravaged and plundered the whole of her mouth with a blatant, searing intimacy.

She fought his touch. His hand was now cupped about her breast, and he could feel her panicked heartbeat. Further . . . he sampled and explored. And shuddered, heat coiling and sizzling inside of him. Her breast was full and firm, and she was beautifully formed, slim and curved, her waist a man's handspan, her hips seductive beneath.

A strangled cry escaped her at last. She stirred and tensed rigidly, as if she would spring on him, scratching, seething.

She did not. She remained rigid, but did not fight. The hand that moved to force his away fluttered and fell.

He pushed her away from him—to prove her lie, to save his own soul. She trembled visibly; her eyes were glazed and her lips damp and swollen. She stared at him, totally shaken.

"Second thoughts, milady?" He forced a chill into his voice.

She rallied quickly. "Nay, none at all, milord."

Still that pulse at her throat throbbed. Her fingers, laced before her, shook. Her eyes fell.

He stared at her for a moment in the moonlight, forcing himself to observe her with cold objectivity. Her hair was such a stunning, crowning glory, a cloak like a golden sunrise against the night. Yet if it were clipped away . . .

She would still possess an uncanny beauty. Her skin was unmarred, soft and fragrant as rose petals. Her features were delicate but majestic. Her mouth was finely shaped and defined, with a hint of fullness. And her eyes . . . They could not be described as blue or as gray. At times they had appeared the softest mauve; at times they had gleamed with the silver glint of a sword.

"Well, then . . . I suppose you shall do—as well as any."

Such a tremor rattled through her that he almost laughed. The lady was definitely outraged. But if she was outraged, he was afire.

He turned from her, convinced that at least for now she had no intent to stab him in the back.

"Good evening, Lady Genevieve," he said. Fifteen feet from her he stopped and turned around, unable to resist one final taunt.

"Milady?"

"Milord?"

"Your attitude . . . it isn't quite what I had in mind."

Even in the darkness he could see her furious blush.

"It will improve?" he asked mockingly.

She hesitated, then spoke softly. Like a whisper of silk on the breeze. Seductive. Her voice rising against him and inside of him.

Like an obsession.

"I promise, Lord Tristan," she returned with a whisper of husky silk, "that I will . . . please you."

She lifted a hand, then blended back into the night.

He watched her disappear and vowed silently that he would be both cautious and wary.

And that she would keep her promise—at all costs.

Chapter
Three

IN HER CHAMBER high above the great banqueting hall, Genevieve paced with a fury that sent her long white gown trailing like quicksilver and her hair like gold dust. Her hands rose and fell frequently, as did her voice.

"Oh, how *dare* he? How *dare* he! He was as cold as the rock, as casual—as despicable, as cruel as all his lot! I could barely stand there. I longed to rip his eyes out, to slit his throat then and there, to pitch him out upon the rocks. Oh, I could do it myself, Edwyna, I swear that I could! Skewer him straight through on a sword! We might well have been rid of him tonight, I was so—"

"Humiliated?" Edwyna suggested.

"And—degraded!" Genevieve clenched her fists tightly at her sides and swallowed sharply. Humiliated, degraded—and burning! She hadn't told Edwyna of his touch, of that last, acute misery! But she hadn't forgotten it! It would stay with her forever: the feel of his lips, the shock of his strength, the masculinity of his scent, the pressure of his large, powerful hand upon her. Each image was ingrained upon her memory. She would never forget his face as long as she lived. Handsome; cruel. Fire; ice.

Stop thinking about it, she told herself—but she couldn't; and when she remembered, she shivered, and felt like ice and fire herself. She longed to touch her lips, to rub them hard, to erase the deed, erase the memory.

"I could have slain him myself!" she swore again, but it was a whisper, desperate to her own ears. She was afraid of her enemy.

"And where would we have been then? Nay, this plan is frightening as it is. I'm worried. If he gave you decent terms—"

"Decent terms!" Genevieve flared with renewed fury. "Terms! He takes the castle, our land, and our people. And me. What 'terms' are those?"

Edwyna sighed with a small, soft shudder. "If only we had opened our gates to him that first day. If only Edgar—" A look at Genevieve's lovely, tormented features caused her to break off. Genevieve finished for her.

"If only father had let him in?" she demanded bitterly. "Well, father is dead and Axel is dead. And so many others!"

"We have fought, Genevieve. Every man and every woman here has supported the battle, from the tenants to the soldiers. We have tried valor, and we have tried tricks."

"But none so risky as this one," Genevieve said quietly. "Edwyna—this was not my idea!"

"Nay, it was Sir Guy's. Who supposedly adores you. Why he takes such chances, I cannot understand." She paused. "Unless he craves the castle—and you—for himself."

"Nay, nay! He cannot bear that my father's and Axel's deaths go unavenged, Edwyna! Shall we have lost all that in vain?"

"I don't know, I don't know!" Edwyna murmured. Miserably, she closed her eyes, shivering. She had expected the Lancastrians to break their gates that day, and to swarm the place, to butcher them all. They had not—and so she, with Genevieve and her council, had agreed to the plan set in motion this evening. She had been terrified since this thing had begun. The spoils did belong to the victor—and were often viciously claimed. In her short time on earth, the throne of England had changed hands so frequently that it had been hard to keep count. Henry VI had lost the Crown to the Earl of March, Edward VI. Edward lost the Crown to his own henchman, Warwick, and Warwick restored Henry. Then Edward had returned to the throne, and held it during comparative peace for fifteen years. But Edward had died, Richard had taken the throne, the Princes had disappeared to the Tower, and the rumor had begun that they were dead.

Edgar had always claimed Richard had had little choice; he had made his moves to bring peace to the country. The Lord of Edenby had remained fiercely loyal to Richard—so now they would be crushed in the war, while those with less honor remained unharmed. This internal war had always been a strange one; it affected the country only in spots. Commerce and farming went on, but where the warring parties struck their blows, there was devastation.

We will be that devastation! Edwyna realized. She wanted terms! No more tricks, fights, or games. No more death. The Lancastrian lord had said they all might live if the castle were turned over to him. What was territory and treasure compared to life?

"We should just surrender," Edwyna said hollowly.

Genevieve shivered, and for a moment Edwyna thought that her niece would agree with her. Genevieve gripped the bedpost for support; her face was drained of all color. She closed her eyes, shook her head, and spoke thinly.

"We cannot, Edwyna I swore, I gave a vow, that I would not."

"I know." Edwyna paused, bowing her head, forcing herself to accept the inevitable. Then she raised her head and smiled weakly at Genevieve. She sat at the foot of the bed. "I am frightened." She shivered convulsively. "His eyes are like a hawk's or a great cat's. He seems to see everything."

"Edwyna! Be sensible. He is a man, nothing more. A Lancastrian, sent to bring misery upon us. I swear I shall never fear him!" she added vehemently, then shivered slightly herself, aware that she lied but determined never to admit it. "Edwyna—he caused my father's death!" Genevieve went and knelt at Edwyna's feet. "We will not fail, Edwyna, we will not fail. How can we?"

"He has so many men, cannons, and fire power and guns—"

"There is no weapon like the good English crossbow—"

"He has those, too!"

"And we've guns!"

"That fire back upon our men!" Edwyna mourned.

"Would you spend your life as a servant to the very people who have butchered all whom you love?"

Edwyna looked at her steadily. "I have a daughter, Genevieve, and I would readily die to defend her. Aye! I would be their servant! I would shine their boots with my own hair to see her safe!"

Genevieve shook her head imploringly. "We will not fail—and the castle will remain ours." She laughed nervously then, rising to pace the room once more. "If I passed this evening, I will survive it all! Oh, vile bastard that he is! He did not wish to marry me! As if I would spend my life with him! Edwyna, it was strange, he was strange! I had to race after him to force the issue! But if I had not—"

"It might have been better!" Edwyna said with a shudder.

"What can go wrong?" Genevieve demanded sharply. "Tamkin and Michael will be in here—hidden behind the secret panel. Lord Tristan will already be drugged. Tamkin is huge and strong; Michael is built like a young bull. They will—"

"I've seen your Lord Tristan, too, Genevieve," Edwyna interrupted uncertainly. "No one can miss him, seated upon that mount of his, defying the arrows to strike him! Those eyes! He is no old man, Genevieve! He is alert and wary—and hates Yorkists, I hear, with a special vengeance. They say that he's never been nicked in sword play, and that his speed of movement is uncanny."

Genevieve sighed, "He is tall, Edwyna, and broad-shouldered. Perhaps . . ." She paused, willing herself not to shudder, imploring God that she cease to remember the man so clearly! Think of the death, the blood, the vengeance! she commanded herself. Learn to possess that cold and brutal determination that seems to rule him!

She stood and shrugged. "Aye, he is young, with muscles like rock—and wary. But he is a man, Edwyna, beneath that muscle, he bleeds. Like any other, when the heart is struck he will die!''

Edwyna looked down at her hands, clutching them together. "It is murder, Genevieve."

"Murder?" Now she felt the full force of her fury and agony again. "What has been done to us is murder! My father was murdered! Dear God in heaven, Edwyna, how can you forget? My father died in my arms! Axel's corpse was brought to me. Think on the widows here, the orphans! We were but in his path, Edwyna. We did no wrong! He was the murderer!"

"And we are going to kill all of his men?" Edwyna asked with pained sarcasm.

"No—he will not bring them all through the gates. I'd say no more than fifty tomorrow." She lifted her chin. "We won't kill anyone—unless we're forced to. Not even Tristan—if he can be subdued. If he cannot, then he will die. Those who give us trouble must die—what choice have we? Those who have had the sense to drink enough drugged wine will go to the dungeons."

Genevieve suddenly sank down beside her aunt. "Oh, Edwyna! I, too, am afraid. I don't think I've ever been so frightened as I was tonight when I had to face him. He is a hard man. And his eyes . . . they seem to pierce your body, like a knife. His touch . . ."

Genevieve broke off abruptly. She was shaking again. Hot and cold. She couldn't go on. She was trying to reassure Edwyna, but all that she did was to frighten herself.

She grinned, and hoped that Edwyna would not see how false her spirits were. "We will be all right, Edwyna."

Would they? Her fingers trembled even as she laced them together. How would she manage to sit beside him at a banquet tomorrow, smiling and welcoming, feeling his eyes upon her, knowing that he was every bit as alert and wary as Edwyna warned.

She breathed in a deep sigh. He had laughed, and almost been handsome. It had proved him flesh and blood. He could be taken.

Murdered, Edwyna called it. She was going to lure him to

his death. But what else could she do? Hand over all their lives—as servants and slaves? She could claim no one could take her title—but was that the truth? If Henry Tudor did indeed take the throne, he could attaint all her holdings at will.

Henry would not come to the throne! Richard had twice the forces of the Tudor upstart! She could not forget her father, the loving reality of her life. Nor Axel, her shimmering dream of the future. She touched her lips and thought of their last kiss. But treacherously that thought strayed. She was thinking of him again, of Tristan de la Tere. Thinking of the kiss he had pressed upon her lips, and the impact of heat and trembling that it had wrought . . .

"No!" she cried, horrified by her own thoughts.

"What? What?" Edwyna demanded, frightened anew.

Genevieve stared at her and shook her head in fierce denial, tense, frightened, angry. "I could!" she swore, a little hysterically. "Aye—I could kill him myself!"

Edwyna gazed at her sharply, her beautiful blue eyes narrowing. "Don't get any ideas."

Genevieve sighed. "I've no ideas, Edwyna. Tamkin is to strike the blow, as soon as possible after de la Tere and I have entered my chamber."

"What if they are not all drugged?"

"Then there will be scattered battle, but it can be easily quelled." She rose, trying to smile. Her bed stood on a low platform on a dais, surrounded by draperies. Next to it was a heavy wooden wardobe, surrounded by walls paneled in heavy oak. The paneling hid secret doorways and small closets where men might easily hide themselves. "Tamkin will be here, not four steps away. And to assure safety and success, Michael will be on the other side. Even if de la Tere searches the room, he will find nothing."

Edwyna was silent. "By our dear Lord!" Genevieve exclaimed. "This was not my plan, remember, even if I did agree. Sir Guy gave it birth, and my father's advisors eagerly seized upon it."

Edwyna rose, and came to Genevieve, hugging her quickly.

"I am just afraid." She tried to smile cheerfully. "I hope I do not falter or fail."

"You won't!"

"Good night, then. Shall I send Mary to you?"

"No—but tell her she must come early in the morning."

Edwyna kissed her, then left the chamber. Genevieve followed her to the door, rubbing her arms as if she were cold—though a fire burned brightly at her grate.

She suddenly felt very much alone, although the castle was still filled with people—her people. Downstairs, Michael, Tamkin, Sir Humphrey, and Sir Guy would be drinking ale, working out the details for the morrow. The soldiers within their homes would also be planning. Down to the last tenant, all would be nervously awaiting the morning.

And all would be prepared, ready to avenge the grief that had befallen them.

Genevieve shivered again, and hurried back to the dais. She disrobed quickly, not caring tonight that she threw the gown on the floor. She jumped quickly beneath the linen sheets and heavy furs on her bed, and held them closely to her breast. She was still shivering. Tomorrow night . . . tomorrow night, by this time, it would be over. They would have beaten back the Lancastrians.

"Oh, please God! Make it true!" she prayed aloud. She tried to sleep, but tossed about miserably. Each time she dozed, visions came to her. She saw her father staring at her, his eyes hazy, his blood seeping onto her lap; she screamed and screamed . . .

She saw Axel's body being brought to her. He looked so composed in death—the gentle scholar with too much honor to oppose her father's will. Gone forever . . .

"My love . . ." She whispered aloud, and she wanted to imagine him, to remember. Yet when she strained to see his features, she saw a different face instead. A face with eyes as dark as the night, eyes like a devil's. Eyes that burned fire and mirrored ice all in one. Hard and ruthless but fascinating for all that. A face not to be forgotten.

"Oh, God help me!" she moaned, sitting up to wrap her

arms around herself. "God help me, help me forget him, help me forget him!"

But her fingers were on her lips. She could feel his kiss, even now.

She bolted from the bed and raced to her washstand. She poured water nervously into her bowl and scrubbed her face again and again. Then she breathed deeply and returned to her bed.

She forced herself to lie down and try to sleep, but she dreamt again. She saw the man with the night-dark eyes towering over her with a mocking smile. She saw his face distinctly. The darkly tanned skin, the high cheekbones, dark arched brows that hiked in ridicule when he looked down upon her, hands arrogantly set upon his hips . . .

Touching her, covering her breast. A touch that even now came back to her so forcefully that the feeling it had evoked riddled her body.

"Damn him to a thousand hells!"

She woke with the cry on her lips, exhausted and haunted by Tristan de la Tere. By the memory of his face, the timbre of his deep, smooth voice.

Tomorrow he would be dead, and she would be able to sleep again without visions of him—and without visions of her father and Axel as they died, for they would be avenged.

A cock crowed then; the sun started a pink streak upward into the sky. Morning had come; it was today that he would die.

Mary, Genevieve's maidservant, came to her early. The girl was young, about her own age, with big bones, wide hips, and a customary cheerfulness that little could quell.

But even she was silent this morning, helping Genevieve from her bath, toweling dry the heavy length of her hair. When it was time to brush it, Genevieve gasped out with soft impatience, determined to take the task over herself rather than go bald.

"I'm sorry, oh, so sorry!" Mary cried, her freckled cheeks puckering as if she would cry.

"Don't be sorry—set out my green velvet!" Genevieve

commanded sharply. She had to be calm and completely controlled. It all depended on her. Mary scurried to do her bidding, and Genevieve relented. "Mary! We cannot falter—not one of us! Our very lives depend upon this day!"

Mary swallowed. "I'm just so frightened! What will they do when they come in? If we fail? We'd deserve their cruelty—"

"Mary! They are Englishmen."

Mary's lower lip jutted out. "Shouldn't we be nervous—with the Lancastrians vowing revenge?"

"It is our day to fight them," Genevieve said softly. "Be of good cheer, Mary! I must go down now, and prepare for our—guests."

She left the room, bracing herself only once for complete composure. Then she swept down the long stone stairway to the great banqueting hall. Sir Humphrey and Sir Guy were there, at the fire, along with Michael and Tamkin. Tamkin—a great brute of a man who had spent his life at her father's side—saw Genevieve enter. His grizzled head nodded in acknowledgment; he didn't try to talk. She swept across the room as if it were just another day of siege, kissing first Tamkin on the cheek, and then others. These were the men who had been her father's mainstays, and who had always had chambers in the keep.

"Are we ready then?" she inquired.

Sir Guy nodded gravely, his handsome features still set in a mask of concern. He rubbed his fingers over the fine ermine on his tunic. "We've ten boars roasting on spits in the yard, beef and kidney pies in the ovens, eels, and pike. There's food aplenty; each house is providing."

"And the—drink?" she asked, a little catch forming in her throat despite her composure.

"See that the lord drinks wine, and no ale," Sir Guy told her. "It is the wine that will do our bidding today."

Genevieve nodded, and found that her palms were damp. She turned around to survey the hall. In the old days ten servants had always been assigned to the kitchens and hall. Four of these had died during the siege, so Genevieve had made sure that four of the farm lads had been brought in to take their places. The table was set with what had been her mother's best plate—scrolled pewter with a pattern of lilies, from her native Brittany. It looked as if her father were about to return from a day's hawking with a goodly number of his friends.

Michael put a hand on her shoulder. "You mustn't worry, Genevieve. We will be with you."

And then Sir Humphrey—bearded and graying, and one of her father's dearest friends—took both of her hands, his blue eyes bright with sorrow. "I worry for you, Genevieve," he said sadly. "I believe I have come to detest this plan."

Sir Guy stepped up to her again.

"I will not let you be harmed by that lascivious monster," he assured her. Genevieve lowered her head with a little smile. She didn't bother to try to tell him that the lascivious monster had to be entreated into the agreement. They all knew that he was the key to their success; if the leader did not fall, men somehow continued to fight against all odds.

"I am not afraid," she said. But she was—because the trumpets already blared, announcing the arrival of the Lancastrians.

"Where is my aunt?" Genevieve asked quickly. Edwyna might be more nervous than she, but suddenly she felt she needed her at her side.

"Still with her child," Sir Guy told her.

"She must come down!" Genevieve said anxiously. "Sir Guy—no—I'll go myself!"

She turned and ran up the stairway. She was not surprised to find Edwyna and Mary together, playing with little Anne, who was holding a beautiful rag doll that had once been Genevieve's, brought from Brittany by her mother.

"Edwyna!" she called sharply. Edwyna looked up at her with an expression of dread.

"Already?"

"Aye, come now. Mary, I suppose it is best if you stay with Anne." Her little cousin was staring at her with wide blue eyes. Genevieve walked across the room and hugged the little girl. "Anne, it is very important that you stay in here today. Will you do that for me? You mustn't cry, and you mustn't come wandering out.''

For a moment Anne looked as if she would cry. Genevieve gave her a brilliant smile, and touched a finger to her lips. ''Please, Anne—it's a game, a very important game. Mary will be with you—you'll be all right.''

Anne nodded slowly. Genevieve gave her a quick hug, caught Edwyna's hand, and pulled her into the hall, and then quickly down the stairs. Sir Guy and Sir Humphrey were already at the door, beckoning to them. Protocol demanded that the victors be met at the door.

Already the Lancastrians had come through the outer gate— the one that they had planned to ram this day. Genevieve squared her shoulders as she moved out to the cold winter's day. Fifty men . . . it had not seemed like so many when she thought of it, but watching them come through, all helmeted and armored, bearing their swords and shields, they seemed like a hundred.

She knew Tristan immediately—she had been watching his movements beyond the gates long enough. He rode in front, on a curious piebald steed with heavily feathered hooves. She could never mistake his crest, nor the brilliant blue mantle he wore over his mail. She could not see his face—only his chilling eyes.

She felt his eyes on her, and felt as though the devil himself mocked her, read her thoughts, read her heart.

A great attack of trembling seized her. Her blood seemed to freeze and then to simmer and boil; she nearly could not stand. What if she could not deceive him? She was afraid. She would falter! She would fail!

''Genevieve!'' Sir Guy commanded.

They were all depending upon her; Genevieve would not let them down. Sir Guy prodded her gently and she stepped forward to bow gracefully and low.

Chapter Four

COURAGE CAME TO her then, when she needed it most. Courage—or a pretense of it, at least. She knew that she had to be sweet and poised and welcoming, or else doom them all.

"Edenby Castle and the estates of the Lord of Edenby," she told Tristan, not daring to look at him, "are now yours, Lord Tristan. It is your own hospitality we offer you today."

There was a sharp roar that went up among the Lancastrians, and they began to dismount. Still all she could see of Tristan were his piercing dark eyes, falling on her enigmatically. Then they left her as swiftly as they had touched her, and he called out orders to his men.

He had yet to say a word to her or to her party. Genevieve moistened her lips and took another step forward. "We've boar and pheasant, spiced eel, and casks of wine in the courtyard, milord. And an inner table that will accommodate fifteen of your number."

"Fifteen of my number, milady?" he inquired politely at last.

She dipped what she hoped was a very humble curtsy. "There are six of us, Lord Tristan. My aunt and myself—"

She paused for Edwyna to drop to a bow. "Sir Guy, Sir Humphrey, Michael, and Tamkin. Michael is—was—the head of my father's fighting men. Tamkin has handled the estates and tenants, and Sir Guy has long handled our accounts. Sir Humphrey knows our castle's strengths and weaknesses as no other man."

"Will I need a strong castle, do you think, milady?" Tristan inquired. He removed his helmet, then his gloves, and one of his men was quick to take them from him. She saw his face then: arresting, handsome—cold, proud. Watching him, she started to tremble.

She took a step backward. He seemed imposingly tall as he stood there; and his expression, despite his polite words that hummed with mockery, was icy. When he smiled it seemed that his lip merely curled.

He ran his fingers through his hair, pushing it away from his forehead. "Lady Genevieve? I'm not in the habit of repeating myself. Will I need a strong castle?"

"Any man craves a strong castle, does he not?"

"I shall rephrase it for you, milady. Is there a particular reason you feel I shall need a strong castle—soon?"

"There is always the threat of attack from the sea," she said demurely. "And I do believe Richard still sits upon the throne. I had thought you would want all the knowledge that we might give you."

"How kind of you. And perceptive."

"We seek peace."

"Ah. And mercy, I take it?"

"Mercy is a quality revered by the angels," she murmured sweetly in reply. "Why, a quality that you've already promised. Shall I show you the castle, milord?"

"By all means."

He nodded curtly to the others, barely glancing their way. And yet Genevieve had the feeling he had swiftly memorized them all, that he would know every name, and understand every nuance of expression and movement should he later be asked.

"The great hall, milord," said Genevieve, sweeping her arm in a graceful arc. "The lords of our vicinity have always met here; we are isolated, as you know, hence they've often conferred on rule and settled their own disorders." She smiled—hating it as she watched Tristan's men walk in and defile her father's hall. But as she watched them, free from helmets and face plates, she realized that they were men—young and old, handsome and scarred.

She felt suddenly dizzy, longing to sit. They were all—men. Flesh and blood and human, as she had reminded Edwyna. To someone, they were sons, husbands, fathers, lovers.

They should never have entered the castle. They had suddenly become real. It was best to fight an unknown enemy. Best when . . .

"Milady?"

Tristan was looking at her curiously. She realized suddenly that he was supporting her—her hand was held by his. He did not mock her for once, but watched her, curious but not condemning.

Real, the men were real—and so was this handsome, loathsome Tristan de la Tere. She looked down quickly. Aye, she hated him. Despised him. But it was a pity that he had not gone away and left them alone! He was young and strong, and it was a pity that he must die.

"Milady, are you ill?"

Of course I am ill! she longed to spit out. Ill to see your group of thieving cutthroats invade my home!

She smiled instead, withdrawing her hand quickly from his touch. "I am fine. If you'll excuse me . . . ?"

She turned.

"Sir Guy, will you be good enough to take my place? I'll see that the meal is served."

She left the hall behind, sweeping through the stone archway that separated the hall from the kitchen. Once there, she leaned against the wall. Griswald, the absurdly slim cook, looked at her over a massive cauldron of boiling stew. "Feed them!" Genevieve cried. "Bring the wine, we must get started."

"Aye, lady, aye." Griswald muttered. "The wine!" he called, passing down the order. He went for one of the great casks himself—then paused before passing her by. "We be with you, milady, you kin count on it." She nodded, and took another breath. The afternoon loomed long ahead of her. She turned, and returned to the hall.

A number of the Lancastrian knights had gathered around the fire, speaking in hushed tones. Genevieve could not follow all of the conversation, but she understood some to say that this was too polite a way to conquer an enemy. Others were commenting on the bounty of the table, and the value of property not destroyed.

Their eyes fell on her as she entered the room. One of them, a stout fellow with small, greedy eyes, murmured something. Another guffawed loudly, and a third man's speech told her that he thought they would have been better off to ram and raze the place—and share *all* of the bounty.

Human? Their insulting leers restored her feeling of righteousness. Her eyes narrowed as she watched them, and then she turned, warmed by an unfamiliar sensation.

Tristan was watching her. The servants were hurrying about, and he was already holding a cup. It dangled nonchalantly from his hand; his elbow leaned against the mantel and one foot rested on the stone below it. Sir Guy was talking to him. But he was watching her—and she had the uncanny feeling that he knew what she had heard, and what she was thinking.

For a disturbingly long moment, it seemed that his eyes held hers. He was starting to look less severe, she thought. His hair was slightly tousled, and he laughed openly at something Sir Guy said. Genevieve was startled to realize just how attractive a man he was when his smile was true, amused, and devilish.

Instinctively she touched her lips. Then she flushed furiously, remembering his words, his taunts.

He was responsible for her father's death. He had treated her atrociously, outrageously. This tall, arresting, laughing man deserved to be boiled in oil. He was autocratic, egotistical, and revoltingly arrogant. He had not really left behind the trappings of war: his sword was at his side, and he wore a dirk at his calf.

He smiled at her across the space that divided them.

Genevieve tore her eyes from his and walked toward the group. She noted that Edwyna was talking to one of the Lancastrians. A handsome young man—if an enemy could be called so—tall, trim, neatly dressed, and with a pleasant smile. So pleasant, Genevieve thought sickly, that he would be hard to kill. She closed her eyes quickly, and remembered the stout man who would have gladly ripped her to shreds, laughing all the while. How much better it was going to be to become the victors.

She interrrupted Sir Guy and his discourse on how to build stairways. "If you would care to sit, my lords, we may eat."

Very shortly they were arranged around the table. Genevieve was at the end—beside Tristan. Her people moved about the table serving; it might have been a party. Except that she couldn't eat a thing. Poor Genevieve wandered on in a monologue on the food, discussing the best season for eel, the best fish to be caught from the sea.

Tristan watched her, judging and absorbing. They were too close; his knee touched hers, and she felt feverish. And when his arm moved, she stared at the rippling muscle beneath his shirt; that, too, worked to unnerve her. She could see the pulse in his throat, and the skin of his cheek, just shaven and roughly masculine. She remembered his touch, no matter how hard she tried not to. Remembered . . . and knew that he knew what she was thinking, and tried not to blush, tried not to betray herself . . .

She was off-balance, she thought miserably, but not he. She was supposed to be charming the man. He had already seized an intimacy that had left her in ashes, and he had expressed disappointment.

Tristan wasn't drinking nearly as much wine as she would have hoped. His tastes seemed to be moderate.

"Boar," she heard herself say, "is best when roasted slowly for hours and hours and—" She broke off. His mouth had formed its twisted grin, and his eyes were on hers.

"You may cease your chattering, Lady Genevieve," he said. "When you've something of interest to say, please do so." He turned from her to address Sir Humphrey. "How many tenants have you, sir, to work the land? How many craftsmen?''

Sir Humphrey cleared his throat and began a dissertation on the farmers, the household workers, the smiths and potters and other tradesmen. Tristan listened to him carefully. He asked intelligent questions about the quality of their wool, the number of cattle and cottages.

Genevieve sipped her ale and pushed at the food on her plate. She jumped when she heard his voice again, close to her ear.

''This is quite a turnaround, wouldn't you say, Lady Genevieve?''

''What?''

''Several times, I offered you terms of surrender better than what you have received.'' He lifted a hand to encompass the table full of his men. ''Tomorrow I will disburse your jewels. I'll see the accounts. I'll take over residency here. You will have nothing, my lady. You might have spared yourself much pain had you surrendered earlier, but you chose to fight to the bitter end. Yet now you are the lady bountiful, insisting upon creeping into my bed, when most titled ladies go to sleep each night, praying for deliverance from the scourge of just such an infamous fate! I am curious, my lady. I would like some explanation.''

Genevieve tried hard to keep her eyes level with his. She failed. She folded her hands in her lap, and stared down at them. Vaguely she noted that one of the hounds had left the fire and was scrounging around the table for scraps.

''Given a choice between you and a number of your men, Lord Tristan, I find you—the lesser of evils. And as to the easier terms of surrender that I lost . . .'' she shrugged. ''I fought as long as I could. Before my surrender, I had not lost. But when there was no hope and you threatened no mercy, I thought that we should . . . try to make amends.''

''Ahh,'' he said slowly. ''Then you've not forgotten your promise?''

''My promise?'' she murmured.

''Aye. To be no victim—but as tender as a bride.''

She stiffened, shaken by the intimacy of his voice, which

left her breathless and weak. It was as if the strength in her had all faded to water, rippling away. She stared at him sharply, and she felt the intensity of his eyes, so dark—and mocking.

"Brides are not always tender, my lord," she said.

"A loving bride," he said, and she was stunned by the sudden bitterness in his tone. And then he turned again, as if he despised her, and made some joke to the young Lancastrian with the pleasant smile and laughing good looks.

She was shaking again. Her palms were wet, and she attempted to dry them on her skirt. What was it with this man? she wondered in dismay. He seemed to despise her; he denied that he found her even truly appealing . . .

And then he would tease her and laugh, and she would feel heat, a fire that arose, from him, igniting her. As if he would take her . . . more than take her.

She didn't need to understand him, she reminded herself sharply. She needed to entrap him.

As the meal progressed, voices started to rise. The men had been at war for a long time; the wine was sweet, the food good. They were growing raucous. Genevieve saw Griswald, and she lifted a hand to him. "Many goblets are empty," she warned him when he came to her service. "These men— celebrate their victory today," she said, aware that Tristan was watching her again. A flush warmed her cheek. "Call for the juggler now, too, I think." Griswald hurried away. The feel of Tristan's eyes upon her was a demand she discovered she could not deny. She turned to face him again.

"If there is some trick to this, lady," he said lightly, "you will live to regret it deeply. When I am served fairly, I deal fairly. When I am betrayed, I do not forgive or forget."

Genevieve lifted her goblet and eyed him over the rim, praying that she would not betray herself.

"Where could the trick be, my lord? You are the conqueror; you are the lord. All is yours to command."

"And you seem to accept it so . . . easily," Tristan murmured dryly. "Nor," he said, catching her eyes, "have I seen a single man here determined to protect your honor. That's strange, isn't it?"

Genevieve lowered her eyes, and used her elaborate three-pronged fork—another piece of her mother's dowry—to play with a piece of mutton upon her plate.

"Not so strange, milord," she replied with what she hoped was negligent acceptance. "We've old men here, now. Artisans and craftsmen and farmers. Who would protest?"

He raised a dark brow skeptically, and lifted his goblet toward Sir Guy. "Now there's a young man I would swear should be concerned. Lady, I did turn down your magnanimous offer of marriage. He should be outraged, since when he looks at you, his eyes are those of a young calf—smitten or bewitched, I'd say. Entangled in a skein of gold. Yet he smiles and clasps my hand. The situation is most peculiar."

Genevieve smiled at him sweetly, only the glitter in her eyes giving a hint of her sarcasm. "You speak of Sir Guy? He was but a friend to my betrothed, whom your men slew. I'm sure 'tis hard for him to accept Axel's death. Yet we are beaten. We would not see the people's homes razed and our harvests trampled. Our people butchered—our women so abused that they might wish for death. And so we accept defeat. But I must ask you this—what if your Henry Tudor never reaches the throne?"

"He will," Tristan said simply.

"Oh? Then we must assume he will defeat Richard in battle. And dispose of Richard. This succession is a tricky thing, isn't it? There are five daughters left to us by Edward IV—though his sons have disappeared—"

"Were murdered—by your Richard," Tristan interrupted calmly.

"No one is really sure that the boys are dead," Genevieve said coolly. "Let's do go on. King Edward also left a few nephews, I believe. Either could claim the throne. Edward, Earl of Warwick, might easily wear the Crown. Your Tudor's branch is a bastard one, Lord Tristan."

Tristan chuckled. "Piety! From the lady who offers her own services so easily! Madam, the bastard part of Henry's lineage is from a generation long past—and John of Gaunt married the lady who bore those Beaufort bastards. We who follow him are not bothered by the taint."

"But what if—Lord Tristan, I say only 'if'—your Tudor should not reach the throne?"

"Then, lady, I will hold this castle as you tried so hard to do. But I will not lose it." His assurance made Genevieve long to claw at his implacable features.

He caught her hand suddenly. She felt the power of his hold, and longed to break it. She felt the strange intensity of his eyes, and a quaking heat ripped through her.

She must not fail! Genevieve forced herself to cruel memories of the dead.

"All is mine to command?" he queried tersely.

She frowned and said slowly, "Aye."

He smiled, slowly touching her cheek with his knuckles. His voice was strange, cool, almost uninterested. But not his words.

"Then I command, Lady Genevieve, that you escort me to your chamber. It has been a long battle."

Her heart slammed hard against her chest, and panic filled her. "But my lord, I've entertainment planned. I—"

"I seek only one kind of entertainment," he told her. His eyes were upon her lazily, and he seemed to laugh inwardly at her panic. He leaned then to whisper to her, to watch her features. "That 'entertainment' which you were so insistent upon giving . . ."

She looked around the room. The winter's sun had fallen, but it was not yet dark. His men were drunk; but they were not yet disarmed. They were laughing heartily, demanding more wine, asking about sport.

"Oh! How distressing. What is that hesitance of yours, milady? Do you wish to renege on your proposal?"

"I—"

He stood, pulling her up with him. And to her horror, he intended to make his speech. He banged his tankard on the table. The room went silent. All eyes came to him.

"Good friends, we have sued for peace this day. It is not solved with a meal, nor shall you be denied the fruits of your valor. Tonight you may drink yourselves merry; what entertainment you may find is yours, but remember our agreement, and do not seek to take what is not offered." He lifted

Genevieve's hand. "The Lady Genevieve is mine—when I choose to claim her, and when I don't. She has . . ." he paused just slightly, with a cynical grin, "offered this arrangement. What is specifically mine, I do not share. Tibald, Jon, you are on guard. I bid you all good evening."

Sir Humphrey looked as if he would choke. Michael rose. Genevieve felt herself tugged firmly along.

"One moment!" she begged. He stopped instantly, looking at her with cool, cordial curiosity.

"Aye?"

"Let me see to the kitchen, that the evening goes on without us."

He released her hand and crossed his arms over his chest, smiling—or leering—she wasn't sure. The firelight cast a shadow over his features, and his eyes gleamed wickedly.

"Is that all? Then, most certainly, see to your duties. I'd not have my men deprived. I'd thought, perhaps, that you wished to back out—having seen that my men have no horns or talons and can be controlled."

She moistened her lips, but smiled easily and spoke with just a shade of huskiness. "No, no. I just wish—"

"Go on, then. It occurred to me that you might consider me responsible for your father's death. And sitting beside you, I had an odd feeling that you despised me. You are cold to my touch, my lady. But now that your offer has been accepted, I'd be highly disappointed should you change your mind."

How he mocked her! He knew that she despised him!

She said smoothly, "I've had no change of mind. Excuse me. I'll return straight away." She hurried past the table. Michael and Tamkin were rising, professing exhaustion. The Lancastrian knights seemed too far gone in their laughter to care.

Genevieve breathed a little sigh of relief and rushed through the archway, catching Griswald's arm as he lifted another cask of the wine. "Griswald! Stay with them, and let no goblet sit empty. They must drink, quickly—*now*!"

He nodded. She leaned against the wall again as he left the

kitchen. How much time could she take? Seconds ticked by, and then minutes.

Griswald came back in, looking anxious. "He is demanding to know where you are, milady."

She nodded and started back for the hall, squaring her shoulders, walking smoothly and assuredly. When she passed the table she again felt the stares of the men, and she flooded with color.

Tristan had been speaking with the man with the easy smile—Jon, she thought his name was—but when he saw her he came to the foot of the stairs to meet her. With curious, speculative eyes upon her, he lifted her hand and set it upon his arm, holding it there with his own.

It seemed that her vision blurred and all she saw was his hand, broad, strong with long fingers. She felt the warmth of his arm beneath his shirt sleeve, and the power of his muscle. She heard his even breathing—they were so close she even imagined that she could hear the beat of his heart.

A beat about to be stifled forever.

For a moment she thought of him as some sort of truly magnificent beast, like her father's stallions, born and bred for battle, sleek and powerful. To see such a stallion killed would have hurt her; she was seeking to kill a man in his prime, with a look about him that sent tremors like nothing she had ever known careening down her spine.

She shivered suddenly as they mounted the stairs.

"You're cold?" he asked her.

"Nay . ... aye. I am not certain," she murmured.

Even his voice touched her. Rich and husky when he spoke low; thundering when he raised it. Had things been different . . . had she met him as her father's friend—rather than his murderer!—she might well have found him appealing. She would have flirted with him, eager to tease Axel . . .

She glanced at his chiseled face.

But no. Somehow she knew that she would not have dared to tease with such a man. As friend or foe, he would have offered his strange sense of danger . . . and allure.

No! Oh, no! What was wrong with her . . .

She closed her eyes briefly. Thank heaven that the night would end it all! Tristan de la Tere would soon be dead.

And it was out of her hands. Everyone in the castle had agreed it was their only chance to wrest a victory from this defeat.

"Milady?" Tristan's tone was droll with cynical courtesy.

"Here . . ." she said, and stopped before the oaken door of her chamber.

She felt his eyes upon her as she pushed the door inward. Dark eyes, fire eyes. Eyes that reached into her and made her shiver with a fear she had never known, with more than fear, with . . . something that she could not understand. As elusive as the raging tension about him, whether he moved or stood still.

As unfathomable as the fire . . . the flame he created, the trembling heat that assailed her again with his touch . . .

With even the memory of that touch . . .

She closed her eyes and prayed fervently that she had given Michael and Tamkin time enough to arrive.

Chapter
Five

TRISTAN MADE NO effort at pretense when he entered the chamber. He searched it thoroughly, glancing her way only once. She had known that he would search her chamber. She was nervous, yet he caught her faint smile before she lowered her head when he was done. So there was no one here; still he expected a trick, and he had to discover it.

He clasped his hands idly behind his back as he regarded her private domain. It was impressive—as Edenby itself.

The bed on its dais was in the center of the huge chamber. The draperies, caught back at the finely hewn posters, were rich brocade in summer shades of green and yellow. The bed frame was elaborately carved, and the headboard was an elegant work of art. A hunting scene was chiseled there— great horses, men with flying mantles and epaulets, and hawks and falcons that flew high with widespread wings to sight wild boar.

Beyond the bed was a great hearth, pleasantly angled so that it formed a secluded corner in the room. It seemed an intimate, inviting place. Cross-legged chairs stood before the fireplace; here a lord might expound upon his thoughts to his lady, or merely enjoy a cup of mulled wine while gazing into the fire.

The chamber walls had been whitewashed, and scenes like those on the Bayeux tapestry had been painted on the far wall. The windows here were narrow archers' slits, but around them the stones were arched and fashioned to give an illusion of grace and beauty. Trunks lined the walls beneath the windows at various places, and there was a massive, carved oak wardrobe near the door. Near the wardrobe, at the center of the trunks that ranged along the wall, was a finely carved oak dressing table, neatly arrayed with silver combs, bone pins, and various attars. There was a washstand with a beautifully painted pitcher and bowl; the chairs about the room bore upholstered cushions.

It seemed, Tristan thought dryly, that Genevieve of Edenby was accustomed to splendor. But then all of Edenby had spoken of opulence, and power. From the huge jutting bluff of rock to the inner defenses of mortar and limestone, Edenby was built to withstand the heaviest blows. Having passed from the fortifications into the keep, Tristan could begin to understand the obstinacy of these people in their refusal to surrender. Edenby was self-sufficient. Why the gatehouse at the entryway had walls sixteen feet thick—a tough obstacle to overcome, long before the keep itself could be reached. Besides the gatehouse and the keep there were a number of wooden structures: living quarters for the soldiers, houses and shops for the smiths and craftsmen, kitchens, and huge wells, built upon high mottes. There were seven defense towers skirting the stone walls, and another wall—of another stone, from a different date, Tristan was certain—encompassed acres of cottages and farm dwellings. He hadn't seen much of the keep yet—just the great hall, and now the lady's chamber—but he had seen enough to realize that it was built for both comfort and defense. Old Sir Humphrey told him that the chapel, adjoined to the great hall, was a picture of superb craftsmanship and beauty with high mullioned windows, great rising arches, red velvet trailers, a marble altar, and a great pulpit carved from one block of wood to portray St. George slaying the dragon.

It was all his, Tristan thought suddenly. A feeling of incredible triumph coursed through his body. His reward, legally, when Henry ascended the throne.

And just as the sensation receded, he was assailed by raw pain, so strong that had he been alone, Tristan would have doubled over with the agony of it. How gladly he would have traded it all— Edenby and anything else that came his way—to go back in time! To be there to fight in defense of what had been his own, to save Lisette . . .

He didn't really want any of it. He hadn't wanted to subjugate these people, he hadn't wanted the death, he hadn't wanted the damn fight. And suddenly, in a way, he found that Edenby did appeal to him. He could never go back north to the estates at Bedford Heath. He could not return to the place where Lisette had died.

And so this fabulous fortress in the beautiful wilds, had become an enormous prize: a home, of sorts. He could live here. He could, perhaps, even find a certain peace here, eventually. Tristan had no doubt that Henry would win the coming battle. And he knew that the people would not hate him for long. People had an enormous capacity for adapting. He had not murdered Edgar—Edgar had died in battle, defending his beliefs. An honorable thing. And as to Edgar's daughter . . .

He clenched his teeth and turned to stare with sudden distaste at the woman who stood so quietly behind him. Her silver eyes promised battle and defiance, never tenderness; though her voice was laced with sweetness, her words had a biting edge. She was exceptionally beautiful; she moved with uncanny grace. She had not bound her hair, and it fell about her in a way that even now—when he was thinking that she could never be trusted—suggested the most delicious pleasure. She was nervous, he knew; for her fingers were clenched before her, the knuckles white. Yet her chin was high, and her pride appeared not at all touched, much less shattered. Smouldering fire lurked in the silver glitter of her long-lashed eyes. The cream of her alabaster complexion was touched with a high flame of color now; despite the defiance of her rigid stance, she was extremely self-conscious.

He wanted to strike her, to slap the cool defiance and arrogance from her eyes; yet he also wanted to touch her with tenderness and passion. To explore her exceptional beauty and lose the pain of his heart in the heat of base sexual sensation. He wanted to discover if what he sensed were true: if a rich, wild, and verdant passion lay in her, waiting to be touched.

It was a pity that he didn't trust her, he thought suddenly. A pity that there was something about her so dual-edged. He had warned Jon to be on guard, and to send half the captains back out to their troops should trouble ensue. She was lightning, a magic he longed to touch, and he wondered what he would feel once she had shown her hand. He would want her still; but whether he would take her, he did not know himself. Aye, he did, he decided.

Have you, milady—as *you* have so insisted—I will. One last chance I will give you now to renege and then our pact *is* sealed.

"Do you find the chamber . . . hospitable?" she inquired.

"Very," Tristan said curtly. He moved to one of the chairs before the hearth and sat, with his elbows upon the claw-curved armrests, his hands folded together prayer-fashion. He tapped his forefingers lightly to his lips. The hearth was behind him; from this position he could survey both her and the door. He had bolted it from the inside, but as the chamber was empty, any trouble had to be coming from beyond. Wary, he continued to sit there, merely watching her through narrowed dark eyes. The longer he sat, the more tightly her folded hands seemed to clench. At last it seemed that her composure broke, and she spoke to him.

"My Lord, surely you are eager to part with your vestments of war. How can you sit comfortably, with your sword still at your waist?"

"My sword?" he inquired politely. He was so accustomed to it that he barely noticed the steel and sheath jutting out along his leg. He smiled at her. "I am used to it."

"But . . ."

She paused, and he noted that she caught her lower lip between small pearly teeth, perplexed.

"Does it bother you?" he asked her conversationally.

"Aye," she returned his smile very sweetly, yet did not come near him. It was as if she longed to flirt—to ignite his fire—but not to come near the flame.

"Ummm . . . and why is that?"

"Well, Lord Tristan," she murmured lightly, her eyes wide with a guileless innocence, "a sword is a part of the battlefield; it speaks of blood and death and carnage. It's the very weapon which might have killed—"

"I did not kill your father, my lady," he interrupted her dryly. "I'd have known if I faced the Lord of the Castle—which I did not. Never did I see his crest, so I am quite free of his blood."

"You came to fight him—"

"Nay, I came for a meal! That would have been that! Then I but gave a request that he relinquish a worthless loyalty to a murderer of a king. He chose not to—and it was his choice. He was a knight who died in battle; that is the way of things, nothing more."

A flash of anger touched her eyes; the rose beauty of her lips was compressed to a white line. He raised a brow, wondering what had happened to the sweet humility she had been trying to offer him. He showed her a courteously questioning smile; her lashes fell, and when she spoke again it was in dulcet tones.

"Milord, the sword makes me uneasy. As if you would draw it against me."

"I don't make war against women."

"I am the Yorkist who carried on the battle," she reminded him, stepping toward him as if she pleaded.

"I do not intend to skewer you," he said.

"Then . . ." She paused again, drawing a deep breath, and a touch of impatience tinged her next query. "Why do you sit so? You dragged me up here—"

"Are you anxious, Lady Genevieve? Are you so very eager to give yourself to me?"

"I am eager to get it over with!" she snapped.

"Milady, I beg your pardon?" He feigned a note of hurt and shock.

"I—"

"If you are not eager, milady, you are free to go."

"What?" she gasped, stunned by his words. Then she murmured, "I meant only that . . . that I am, quite naturally, a little uneasy; I . . ." Her voice trailed away. Genevieve was more than a little uneasy. The more time that passed between them, the more terrified she became. She felt as if thunder rumbled around them, but the skies outside were entirely clear. He wasn't doing what had been expected, and she was failing miserably. He was supposed to be enchanted, eager to shed his sword, and so ardent that he would fail to pay attention to the things around him. She had feared defending herself until he could be brought down; but he was coming nowhere near her. He was so cool . . .

Yes, he was cool—while she felt that searing probe of his eyes in a thousand ways. They seemed to hold both humor and wariness—and a warning that raked along her spine and wound tightly like a coil in her abdomen. He was very real to her now: a hated enemy, but also a man. She was afraid that they would murder him, and equally afraid that they would not. She had to get him to disarm himself; the wounded who had regained the city after the battle had claimed that he could not be bested, that he was a winged Mercury with a sword.

He smiled at her again, a distant, mocking smile, as if he were totally indifferent to her. He despised her, she realized, with a dangerously controlled hatred, leashed beneath a cordial demeanor.

Yet it seemed he had not come with a destructive malice: he was giving her a chance to leave. She wished suddenly that he had been a monster, old and horrendous and cruel. She had to hate him. She wanted no decency from him, nor did she want to have to admit that he was enormously appealing.

His midnight eyes were far too shrewd at this moment. She swallowed, forcing herself to picture how her father had died in her arms. She could not lose her nerve; she could not go running from the room. If she did, she would have betrayed her most loyal supporters. If she left, this Tristan de la Tere would soon discover Michael and Tamkin, and if rumor were true, they would surely be slain.

"Where do those thoughts lead you?" he murmured suddenly. She realized that her face had given away her rapid flux of worry and emotion. He stood, and she stepped back slightly, shivering again at the ripple of muscle beneath his shirt.

He would come to her again! She thought in panic. He would reach for her and wrench her to his side, and she would feel those lips burn against hers. She would feel his hand upon her, and she would tremble and shake and seem to melt like boiling oil. She would be too weak to stand, unable to fight. And even when it was over she would be branded by that kiss, burned and branded for all time . . .

But he did not approach her; instead he walked around the chair to lean against the mantel and gaze into the fire. "You're a most intriguing character, Lady Genevieve," he told her, his dark eyes riveting hers again so quickly that she almost cried out. "What motive lurks in your heart, I wonder?"

She lowered her lashes. "Good will to my people, that is all," she lied.

He did move toward her then, and she had to steel herself. He touched her hair where it framed her cheek, and for a moment his eyes followed the movement of his fingers. He lifted a long lock of her hair and played it over his hand. And she somehow managed to remain still, though she thought she would go mad. His nearness sent great waves of heat to engulf her, as if her flesh and blood were seething with something explosive and disturbing. She noticed that his scent was clean and fresh, and that he was bathed and shaved. He stared into her eyes then, and for a moment she felt like his prisoner, as if his will alone could bind her.

And then he dropped her hair as if he had lost interest again, and casually sauntered back to the fire, resting one booted foot against the low stone fender and casting an arm idly against the mantel.

"So . . ." he murmured, staring at her quite frankly, "you intend to keep your promise?"

"Promise . . . ?" she murmured blankly, and again he hiked a dark brow, and his lip curled slightly with amusement.

"Your promise, Genevieve. To entertain and delight . . . and please me."

"Ah . . . of course," she murmured uneasily.

He smiled. "You should be warned, milady. Well and truly warned. You'll not break a promise to me, " he said softly.

She felt a terrible chill, a chill like death. What difference did it make that she lied? she asked herself furiously. In minutes it would be over; it was war, it was battle, and they were fighting the only way that they could.

"Genevieve?"

She couldn't speak; he didn't seem to notice.

"I swear to you, by God and all the saints, lady, that you'll keep whatever vows you make to me. Last chance, milady. Go now, or remember from here on out that I consider a promise a—most sacred vow. Do you intend this?" He spoke so softly. Oh, God, how long could this go on!

"Of course!" she cried out impatiently. He kept smiling.

A long silence ensued; like thick clouds, it seemed to fill the air with a tension that might forecast a storm. At last he spoke, still lightly.

"Well?"

"Yes, milord?"

"Start pleasing me."

"I—I don't—I mean—what do you—"

"I'd like to see this rare and unique gift I'm receiving."

"What?" she gasped.

He waved a hand in the air. "Surely that makes sense to you, milady. Ah, perhaps the request was stated with too great a complexity." He bowed slightly. "Disrobe, if you will, my lady."

A flicker of amusement crossed his features at the chagrin in her face. Genevieve, stunned, still had time to note that his eyes were not black at all. They were blue. The deepest, darkest blue she had even seen. She was frozen to the spot— but she wanted to run in sheer, blind panic. The situation had become desperate.

She had best do something quickly—something right, something that would convince him to shed the sword—and bare his back to the others.

Without daring to think long, Genevieve flew across the room, throwing herself to her knees at his feet, gripping the steel-hard muscle of his thigh, and casting her head back to plead. Surely she could plead well. Now—she was begging!

"Lord Tristan!" She implored, aware that she had startled him by the way he stared down at her, trying to catch her hands to drag her back to her feet. "Please, milord, I mean my promise. It is best to save my people. I give you my vow—but I beg of you! Cease with the weaponry of war, let us douse the lights—let me come gently to this!"

He cupped her chin, torn by pity. She was beautiful, Tristan thought, smoothing his thumb over her cheek. As beautiful as sunlight, as dazzling as gold, with her hair splayed now about the floor like a cloak of radiance, her eyes on his, naked with beseechment. They were not hard and silver; they were the lightest violet, the palest mauve. Her hands upon him were fragile and delicate, elegant and feminine. He felt a rush of desire that seemed to roar in his ears; the hunger raced through his body. He had nearly forgotten that she was the enemy—vanquished and dangerous. She would ease the hunger gnawing at him. She would be pure assuagement, raw and sweet, and he could take her and forget and fulfill the ravaging needs of his body, if not his heart.

"Stand up—" he started to tell her softly. But just then he heard something; a noise that should not have been. His eyes narrowed, focusing across the room.

He pushed her aside, striding angrily past her. He reached out a hand to the secret paneling that had just begun to open. He jerked at the oak; it gave like a thin branch. Michael was caught standing there, his sword in his hand.

"Michael!" she gasped out in warning—too late.

And Michael, too stunned to think clearly, backed away, raising his sword. Genevieve gasped out again as she saw Tristan's mouth compress grimly, his entire face darkening with rage.

"Drop it!" he warned. In terror, Michael raised his sword, and with a quick rasp of metal, Tristan reached for his.

Tristan's blow was so fast that Genevieve could not believe it had happened. She tried to scream, but could only gasp.

Michael—giant that he was—fell to the floor; his eyes were open, startled still, and a trail of blood dripped with a ridiculously slow tranquility from his neck and shoulder.

"No!" Genevieve protested insanely, and Tristan spun around to stare at her. Never had she felt such a furious look of scorn or hatred so intense. She backed toward the wall, grappling for a hold upon the stone to climb to her feet. He approached her slowly, and she wondered with a desperation akin to madness what had happened to Tamkin. She looked around wildly, and her eyes fell to the iron fire poker. But she shrank with horror from the possibility of using it against him—and failing.

She looked back to Tristan; he was approaching her with a hardened look of fury, stalking slowly—with his sword still in his hand. But even as she stared at him, he whipped about again, and following his movement, she saw that Tamkin had come from the other side of the wardrobe. Tamkin was more prepared; his sword was raised high—he was ready to do battle against the enemy.

The men came together and their swords clashed mightily, sending sparks shooting across the room. They backed away—and came toward one another again. "Genevieve!" Tamkin shouted as Tristan's next blow brought him to his knees.

He managed to stumble back to his feet. But he was barely able to catch Tristan's next thundering blow with his own weapon. Genevieve realized with a sinking heart that there was a deadly intent about Tristan; this was a fight that Tamkin would lose. Tamkin chanced a dazed and desperate glance in her direction; Tristan was totally oblivious to her. With a quick movement, she reached for the fire poker and hefted it carefully into her hand. She scurried away from the hearth and out to the center of the chamber where the men battled, edging behind Tristan, who still paid her no notice. He raised his sword high, cracking it down with another lightning jolt upon Tamkin's weapon.

But though he fought with such fury, Tristan was feeling a strange sapping of his strength. Something that wasn't quite right about him. As if a soft, warm tide were washing over his body and retreating, taking along with it his power and vitality. He almost wanted to lay his sword down . . .

He shook his head, to see, to clear his mind. And then he realized with painful alacrity—he had been drugged! Not heavily—subtly. Bit by bit, so that it had taken a long time for the substance to enter his body. Drugged—or poisoned. Whichever . . . He had been wary, but not wary enough. He hadn't trusted her—and yet he had not thought her so devious . . .

His sword was growing heavy; he could barely lift it. He had to end this clash of steel now, before he could no longer fight. He had warned Jon that he suspected a trick; he had to shout out to the men below that it was, indeed, a trick. He had to, had to . . .

One last time he raised his sword in a great flying arch. His enemy was a decent contestant at arms—weaker, but ready for defense. Tristan struck his blow, not catching the man, but succeeding in disarming him; with a last thunderous clash of steel, he sent his enemy's sword flying across the room. He might fall, but he would give his men a chance . . .

Genevieve knew that she had but one opportunity. She must seize it well, and with all her might. With both hands clenched tightly around the poker, she struck Tristan a desperate blow, hard against the base of his skull.

His sword fell; he held his head in his hands as he staggered. Terror-stricken and stunned, Genevieve backed away. He turned slightly, seeing her. His eyes were glazed with pain and bitter surprise.

She thought that he would attack her then; grab her and strangle the life out of her. But he didn't—he only touched her with his eyes for a second. Yet in that time, Genevieve thought that Tristan had seen her clearly—that he knew full well that she had deceived and betrayed him, and that she had struck the blow that was bringing him down.

She felt laughter and tears bubbling in her throat—he was going down, surely he was going down. She had heard the crack of the poker against his skull; she could see the blood . . .

His look swore revenge, bitter and powerful, as if even in

falling he could never really be vanquished. "Damn you," he muttered darkly. "Damn you, bitch of Edenby, to a thousand hells, treacherous . . . whore! Pray, lady, pray that I do die!"

"No . . ." She murmured, her hand coming to her mouth to choke back a cry.

But he had already turned from her, swivelling past Tamkin, who was also caught in a dead stupor, and lifting the bar on the door, he staggered into the hallway, and fell there.

"The others!" she cried. "We have to stop him—he'll warn them!" No longer immobile, Genevieve forced herself to follow behind him. She felt ill; oh, God, she could not hit him again! But she would have to, lest he issue a warning!

Tamkin—as if awakened by her words—grabbed his fallen sword and followed behind her. But it was too late.

"A trick!" Tristan bellowed out from the archway before the circular stone steps. The roar was like the throaty cry of a wolf beneath the moon. "Trick . . ."

He fell to his knees then, grasping his temples once again. An uproar began below, but Genevieve barely noticed. She was staring at Tristan, wobbling, still standing—but leaving a trail of blood along the stone hallway.

And then, to her great and numbing relief, he fell. Heavily, and completely—and with barely a sound except that of his muscled weight thudding hard against the cold stone of the floor.

For long seconds in which her heart seemed to beat a thousand times, Genevieve stood still, scarcely daring to breathe. Tamkin, too, remained silent and still. It seemed that neither of them could believe that Tristan was really down.

But he was. Genevieve took a step forward. Blood was oozing from his skull, matting his hair. His flesh was taking on a dingy pallor. His back did not rise and fall with his breath, for he had no breath left.

"I've killed him," Genevieve whispered, and it was half with horror. "Oh, my God!" She wailed, "I . . . I've killed him. I've killed a man!"

She was suddenly shaking so fiercely that she couldn't stand. Tamkin came to her, holding her shoulders fiercely, looking into her eyes. "You saved my life," he told her with a little shake. "Stay here, but be careful—I must get below."

Nodding but without comprehension, she felt only a stir of breeze as Tamkin left her, stepping over the fallen corpse of their enemy.

Genevieve just stood there shaking, unable to tear her eyes from the immobile, sinewy body of the Lancastrian knight. She tried to tell herself it was justice, but she felt his blood on her hands, and her soul.

Trembling so that she couldn't stand, she sank to the floor. And she did start to laugh then, and cry, threading her fingers through her hair, pressing against the sudden, throbbing pain in her temples. If she closed her eyes, it would all go away. The attack of the Lancastrians, the battle, the great body of the man she had slain.

But when she opened her eyes again, he was still there. Crumpled, lifeless, broken, on the top stair. His eyes were closed; she could see only the thick dark hair, clumped and matted now with blood . . .

And yet she thought that she saw his eyes. Dark and vengeful, furious, and promising all the fires of hell as he damned her and damned her . . .

She pressed more tightly against her temples. Noises drifted up the stairs and finally permeated the horrible numbness and hysteria that had gripped her. A great melee was taking place downstairs. Things had not gone as planned; this had been no smooth deceit, practiced wisely and well. Downstairs men were fighting, dying.

Genevieve could not move. The fate of Edenby—and of herself—was being decided in the great hall, but she could only stare at Tristan's body on the cold stone step, and pray that it would disappear.

The battle below was not as violent as Genevieve thought. Indeed had Tristan's warning not come, there would have been no clash of arms at all.

Yet Jon, alerted by Tristan earlier, had kept a wary eye on things from the moment Tristan had left the room. He had relaxed somewhat when a group of musicians had come to the gallery, playing gentle ballads and slightly bawdy tunes. Jon had been finding the great hall of Edenby Castle to be filled with many splendors—not the least of which was the Lady Edwyna.

She was not a girl. He assumed that she was a year or two older than himself. But there was a grace about her lacking in younger women, he thought, and the beauty of her face was enhanced by richness of character. She was slim and elegant and soft-spoken—and very nervous.

Jon had spent the majority of the afternoon and early evening at her side, trying to ease her fears. They had talked of little things, of the wonders of this castle of Edenby, where she had grown up. She told him of her marriage, sadly stating that no, her husband had not died in battle, but of disease, and that her brother, the late Lord of Edenby, had called her back from the north country, determined that she should be married again and form an advantageous alliance when the time was right.

"And you did not mind?" he asked her.

"Mind?" She asked him, her eyes curiously wide, as blue as the wildflowers that grew along the rocky coast.

"To be bartered twice?" he asked a little gruffly.

She merely smiled, lowering her eyes. "It is the way of things, isn't it?" she asked him dryly. "Shall I get you more wine?"

But he had chosen not to drink that day; in Tristan's absence, he was the captain in command, and Tristan had expected some treachery. The state of the men was making him a little uneasy. Too many were laughing now, heckling the minstrels at their bawdy songs. Forewarned, they were all drinking sparingly, yet they appeared drunk. Tibald, too, Jon noted, was uneasy. The middle-aged knight was still seated at the banquet table, frowning as if something wasn't quite right.

But what? The scene appeared most pleasant. Yorkists and Lancastrians talking, joking, drinking together. The peasant girls serving the wine now were young and buxom and earthy, laughing at the jests, seeming not to mind the lewd pinches they were receiving.

Maybe the tenants of Edenby did not care which royal heir received the crown; maybe it made little difference to them who ruled in the castle. But that wasn't consistent with the battle they had fought, holding out long and hard, against ridiculous odds.

It was as he looked around the great hall at this scene that Tristan's shout came to him, a gasping, thundering warning that emitted from the winding stairway toward the rear of the hall.

Jon's eyes fell on Edwyna. He saw the alarm in her face, and horror—and he knew that the entire day had been a trick. Still staring at her, stunned and furious, he backed away, drawing his sword. "To arms!" he cried.

But most of his knights paid him little heed; only Tibald arose, and Matthew of Wollingham, and two others.

Now the Yorkist guard of Edenby began to enter the room. Jon saw old Sir Humphrey with his sword raised.

And then one of the guards was upon him. He raised his sword and fought, catching the man off-guard, and striking a lethal blow hard across his midsection. The man slithered to the floor in a pool of blood.

Jon heard a sharp gasp and looked to see Edwyna, pressing her body against the stone archway and clinging there with horror as she stared down at the slain guard. Her eyes came to his, shocked and frightened. All around them, cries rose and fell; steel clashed—and the dying moaned.

Jon knew he had to get outside of the keep, to the men in the bailey. With whatever men he could salvage, he had to retreat.

But he never felt more bitter, more betrayed, and he smiled at Edwyna over hard-clenched teeth, and bowed slightly.

"My lady, pray that they kill me, for should I live . . ."

He did not finish his sentence. Another guard was upon him, and as he fought he backed his way to the door. "Tibald, Matthew! Lancastrians! We draw back!"

From the corner of his eye he saw that Tibald, at least, had understood. The older warrior was battling his way to Jon's side. And then Matthew was with him, too; they had formed the wall of their own defense. But with a heavy heart Jon realized that several of his men were already slain. Four others had not died; they had merely crashed face-first into the banqueting table. Of the fifteen men who had entered the great hall of the keep, only five were leaving the "hospitality" of Edenby Castle.

They finally reached the door; Jon kept their pursuers busy while Tibald lifted the heavy bar. And then they were in the daylight, freed to the realm of the inner bailey. But here, too, disaster had struck. Some men were engaged in battle; others, apparently unhurt, lay still, with their eyes closed and ridiculous grins upon their faces.

"Lancastrians, retreat!" Jon ordered, and he was sickened with the knowledge that each man must fend for himself, and that they would be leaving so many behind, to be cast to the dungeons—or hanged or slain.

"Jon!"

Tibald was at his side, mounted and leading Jon's steed. Jon leapt upon the beast, and fired out the order to retreat again.

They barely escaped before heavy steel bars of the inner portcullis fell at their heels. And again, as their horses' hooves clattered over stone to the drawbridge at the gatehouse, the heavy oaken gate was rising even as they traversed it; Jon's horse shied away from the widening gap. He slammed his heels against the great beast's side, and it leapt the distance to the rocky earth below.

Tibald cried out; Jon, hearing the shrill whining of Tibald's horse reined in. Tibald's mount seemed to have broken a leg in the fall.

Jon spun around to allow the older warrior to leap up behind him, then they raced heedlessly down the natural cliff defense wall, barely aware of the heavy rain of arrows that followed them.

Far down in the valley, Jon at last slowed in his horse and took stock of the situation. Of the fifty men who had entered the castle today, there were not twenty-five left—many of whom were bloodied and wounded, groaning and pitched forward upon their horses.

"To our camp," Jon said hoarsely, "we will regroup."

Of all that had been lost this day, Jon could think only of Tristan. Tristan shouting down the warning with fading breath. Tristan, who had been moved to offer Edenby mercy despite the honorless murder done at Bedford Heath to those he loved.

Betrayed here again. And Tristan was surely dead now, for the Yorkists would never let him live.

Jon thought of all the times his friend had saved him in battle. He sped ahead of his torn and weary men, for he was a valorous knight, and he mustn't let them see the tears that stung his eyes.

When his friend, his leader, his brother-at-arms had needed him, Jon hadn't been able to save him.

He pulled his mount to an abrupt halt and stared back at the castle, shaking with rage.

"By God and the saints most holy—I'll not leave this place without his body!"

The men, even those most painfully injured, fell silent.

"We will stay here!" Tibald cried.

"A thorn in their side—'til we've the strength to strike again, and throw them to their knees in the dirt!" roared Matthew.

"For Lord Tristan!" Tibald's voice rang out.

And the cry went up all around them. They all would gladly die in the effort, but they would have vengeance for the man they had served.

Jon nodded; the party trudged onward to their camp.

And as he rode now, Jon thought with a new fury of the ladies of Edenby—fighting their men's battles with beauty and treacherous wiles. He would like to see them both stripped and whipped and sport for every one of a hundred men—then left with their fine flesh bared for the buzzards.

It was a hard and bitter death to the gallantry he had been feeling.

When the noise died down, Genevieve still could not move. Huddled to the floor, she kept her palms pressed over her eyes.

There was a soft sound of footsteps coming up the stairs;

they were too light to be man's, but Genevieve was barely aware of the sound. Even when she heard a soft gasp, she could not look up. But when she heard Edwyna murmur, "Oh, dear God!" she at last looked up.

Edwyna was standing just below Tristan's body, afraid to walk around it. Genevieve tried to speak; sobs tore at her throat and her voice was shrill.

"He's dead, Edwyna. He's dead. I killed him, Edwyna!" And suddenly she was laughing again, and crying.

Edwyna stepped over the prone body and came to her, stooping down, putting her arms around her. The women hugged each other tightly, trying to comfort one another while they both were caught in a new wave of chills and sobs.

"It's over," Edwyna said, "it's over now, it's over now."

And then there was the clump of heavier feet upon the stairs. Sir Guy was there, with Tamkin behind him.

Sir Guy came to one knee beside Genevieve. "My lady, you are our heroine!" he told her. "You have prevailed; you brought down their lord, and they died and fled without him. You killed him, you are—"

"No, no, no *no!*" Genevieve cried. "I am no heroine! Please, please! Just get him out of here!"

Sir Guy nodded at Tamkin. Between them they strained to lift the muscular body of the fallen man, an incredible dead-weight now. "My lady," Tamkin murmured uneasily, with a glance at the body, "what arrangements—"

"Out, out!" Genevieve cried.

And so the men shrugged, and stumbled down the stairs with their burden.

In the great hall those Lancastrians who lived were being dragged down the dank corridor that led to the dungeons far below.

"Where do we take him, Sir Guy?" Tamkin asked.

"To the rear," Guy said after a moment. "To the seaside; we can bury him quickly there, beneath the rock and sand of the cliff."

"It will not be a Christian burial—" Tamkin said slowly and unhappily. The body of such a lord should be returned to his men, and given proper leave and interment.

"Nay—he goes to the rocks! You heard Lady Genevieve—she wants him out, now!"

Sir Guy was a knight; Tamkin was a guard, elevated by his lord to position of castle guard. He compressed his lips and held back his thoughts, and he and Sir Guy found a litter. They carried the corpse through the rear bailey, past the charred remains of cottages and craft houses that had been burned in the fighting, to the rear tower and gatehouse. This faced the sea, with the cliff itself forming the main wall.

"Here," said Sir Guy, panting when they neared the top of the crest that dropped to a small beach below, and the sea.

"Here? But I cannot dig a grave—"

"Cover him with stones," Sir Guy said. "If the buzzards do not take his eyes, he can, in death, survey his folly!"

Sir Guy dropped his end of the litter and dusted off his hands, as if they were filthy. Tamkin noted with a certain resentment that Sir Guy's fur-trimmed mantle, hose, and tunic were neatly in place, without a tear or a stain. Where had he been during the fight? Tamkin wondered with rancor. Or was Sir Guy so adept with his sword that he need not sweat to do battle?

"I leave you to it," Sir Guy said, and turned to head back to the rear gatehouse.

Tamkin looked down at the man who had almost slain him, and he shivered. Such a knight deserved more respect than this dismissive burial and the callow comments of a Sir Guy. But there would be much to do in Edenby. Walls and parapets to repair—in case the Lancastrians planned to try again. There would be new wounded to tend to, the hall to clear . . .

Tamkin hastily arranged stones over and around the body. It still wasn't right; a great lord fallen was still a great lord—even if he were the enemy.

Tamkin was no clergyman, nor did he often do more than daydream and mumble responses at Mass. But as the sky grew dark above him, he fell to his knees and muttered out a prayer for the soul of the lord who had been betrayed.

They had won today; they had been victorious. But Tamkin didn't feel triumphant; he just felt a little sick.

They had not defended their lady; their lady had defended them, and she had not appeared triumphant at all. It was a poor sort of victory, founded on deceit instead of honor.

Tamkin muttered out another prayer and very tiredly retraced his steps to the castle.

Chapter
Six

THAT NIGHT GENEVIEVE lay in the semidarkness, alone and safe in her own bed—but afraid to close her eyes. When she closed her eyes, she saw him, dark and burning and furious at her betrayal. She saw him fall again—and she saw the state of the hall once more when she had first descended the stairs. So many of her own guard strewn about the floor, intermingled with the invaders in death as they had never been in life.

She heard again the grief, saw the tears of mothers and children and young girls who found a husband or father slain, a lover lost forever.

There had been no reproach, no whispered words of condemnation from the people. Yet what could they really care who wore the Crown? Except for the minor lords and knights of the surrounding manors, these people lived out their lives on the land, and from the land. By ancient custom, banding together in hardship and in labor, paying their rents, surviving. They seldom journeyed to the next county, much less to London. After what had already passed, she owed them peace—not victory.

But how could she have handed over her father's holding—all that he had died for—without a fight? In all the days of

siege there had been ample bloodshed and agony; she had not
blanched, nor shrunk from the wounded. She had buried her
own dead and lamented with the others. But today something
had been different, something that weighed heavily on her
soul.

She was haunted, afraid to close her eyes. She was cold;
despite the fire in the hearth, and the warm fur bedspread
pulled tightly to her chin, she shivered. By God, she could
not forget his eyes, the smouldering, horrible fury in them . . .

She had killed him. Oh, God! She could not forget him!

Genevieve started suddenly at a rap at her door, where was
Tamkin? He should have been sleeping outside of her door.
There was always a guard at her door now when she slept,
and two massive wolfhounds.

"Genevieve!" It was her aunt's voice.

Glad of the company, Genevieve sprang from her bed and
raced barefoot to the door, throwing it open. Edwyna stood
there in a long nightgown, clutching a woolen blanket around
her shoulders, her eyes huge in the flickering firelight.

Genevieve noted that Tamkin was curled on the floor,
sound asleep—the hounds were curled beside him.

"Come in!" she told Edwyna, and pulled her into the
room.

"I couldn't sleep—"

"Neither could I—"

"We've won, and I'm more frightened than ever!"

Soothing Edwyna was always good for Genevieve. It forced
her to get a grip on her own emotions.

"It's all right, Edwyna—we really did win."

Edwyna ignored the bed and walked over to the mantel to
stare into the fire. "Did we?" she murmured, and then
shivered. "He'll come back."

Wild rampaging chills seized Genevieve, coursing along
her spine like the tip of a blade. She didn't have to close her
eyes to see Tristan then—her mind filled with him, blurring
the truth of her vision. She saw the fury in his eyes, heard the
reverberating power of his rage. But surely . . . surely, Edwyna
did not believe he could come back from the dead.

"Edwyna!" she murmured, approaching her aunt and lightly

placing a hand on her shoulder, hoping she had not become completely unhinged. "He—can't come back. He's dead. I—killed him. They took him out—and buried him somewhere. Edwyna—there are no ghosts. Men cannot rise from the grave to extract vengeance."

Edwyna was looking at her as if she were the one to have finally snapped from the events of the day.

"Dead—he's not dead at all!"

"Tristan is dead!" Genevieve almost shouted. "I did it myself, I saw it—oh, merciful heaven, it's true!".

Edwyna actually smiled a little. "I didn't mean Lord Tristan—I meant the other. His second in command. Jon of Pleasance."

"Oh," Genevieve murmured. Warmth seeped through her again. She sank into one of the chairs—then remembered that it was where *he* had been sitting and rose again. But Edwyna's smile had lightened her heart a bit. They had fought an enemy and won—and it was true: Tristan was not going to come from the dead to wreak vengeance.

"The man with the decent smile?" she queried.

Edwyna nodded. "But that smile was gone when he discovered himself trapped."

"Did he escape?" Genevieve asked.

Edwyna nodded.

"I—I think I'm glad," said Genevieve. "He appeared young and well-mannered and—"

"Until the end," Edwyna said a little bitterly. And then she flew into Genevieve's arms again. "Genevieve! Will it never end? I'm so afraid all over again! They will come back! They will slay us all and raze the castle to the ground for what was done!"

"Edwyna!" Genevieve said, trying to calm her. "You mustn't worry. Our masons will start at first light to repair the fortifications! The smiths will be busy forging new weapons and armor. And Sir Guy is going to leave with a few men to find the King and his forces, and see if our army cannot be replenished. We sent so many men to fight with the King. Sir Guy will apply for cannon and gunpowder and our men will be invincible again!"

"I wish that I believed that," Edwyna said mournfully.

"Believe it, for it will be true," Genevieve promised solemnly.

"Ah, Genevieve! What is it? You are so much younger than I—and so much stronger!"

I'm not stronger, Genevieve thought. I'm a true coward who is delighted to see you because I'm afraid to close my eyes! I keep remembering his touch, the fire . . . his eyes . . . his death!

"We need to get some sleep," was her only response.

"I don't want to be alone," Edwyna murmured, grimacing. "And I can't even crawl in with Anne because Mary has already done so."

Genevieve smiled weakly. "Well crawl in with me, then. This night will pass, and the horrors of today will begin to fade. You'll see."

They crawled into Genevieve's bed together and huddled close to one another like children. Genevieve shivered, thinking of what might have happened had Tristan not been killed.

And at last she began to reason and assure herself that the day had been a victory. The enemy would have vanquished her; she had vanquished the enemy instead.

Still it was almost dawn before she slept.

There was darkness—a great, endless pit of swirling darkness. A pit so dark that there wasn't any pain; there wasn't anything at all but darkness.

He could not see himself, but he could feel himself traversing that darkness. It seemed he walked for hours and hours and hours before the darkness began to lift—and then it was gray. Like the very worst fogs upon the moors and swampland. The gray came at him soaring and curling, enfolding him.

And then in the gray he began to see shapes. Bodies, fallen all around him. He paused and touched a shoulder to turn over the body. It was one of his men, a young squire from Northumbria, a man who had yet to achieve knighthood. He was dead.

And as Tristan stared at him he saw that the man had no

eyes, that the carrion had feasted upon them. A scream seemed to come from the gaping mouth; the blank eye sockets riveted upon him, accusing him, sending a soaring pain to his head so that he staggered back, clutching his temples.

And then he tripped—over another body. His own scream rose to his throat when saw that it was Lisette's. Her chestnut hair was matted and tangled about her. Her throat was black and blue; her flesh was gray. There was blood crusted to her skirts . . .

But her eyes, too, were gone. Black empty pools of reproach fell on him, touched him, tore into his soul. And then she moved, as if she handed him something; it was another corpse—a small corpse, so small that it could rest in his hand, and he saw that it was the child who had never lived . . .

Again he felt the soaring, stabbing, debilitating pain in his head, and he clutched his temples and started to scream . . .

And dirt fell into his mouth.

For long, long moments he lay there, completely dazed, remembering the dream—and wondering what grime filled his mouth and what cover shielded his eyes from sight.

His head . . . the pain in it was excruciating.

He tried to move; the earth seemed to shuffle and crumble around him, and he heard great, horrible rasping sounds, gasps . . .

And then he froze, chilled by the realization that he had been buried alive. The gasping was his breath in this tomb, where rock covered him and sand and dirt filled his mouth.

Anger gripped him in such great, shocking waves that he trembled, and the black fury caused the pain in his head to explode. Everything grew black again, and he knew he had to calm himself. He could not get enough air. He swallowed, forcing himself to breathe very slowly. Carefully, he warned himself, he must move very carefully . . .

It did not seem that he could move, at first. His arms were useless, his muscles were as weak as butter. He strained with the slim energy he could summon, and at last his fingers moved, ever so slightly. He began to sweat, fearful that he would panic again, and smother. He judged that this hasty grave was not a deep one—just a few layers of stone. He kept

moving his fingers, slowly, slowly against rock. He knew
that they bled. Earth and stone loosened; at last he felt cool
air on one hand, and he cautiously began to free the other.

This was harder than anything he had ever done. Over and
over his strength failed him; he tightened his jaw and strove
again.

His other hand fought free of the grave. Lord! He was not
deep! It was his weakened state that made such an effort of
moving pebbles and earth. He removed dirt and stones from
his head, and breathed in cool air.

He strained to sit up; he gave all his concentration to the
effort, and at last, he managed to force his torso upward.
But the pain in his head was fierce, and again he returned to a
world of darkness.

Even in that darkness, he knew that he was alive; and in
moments the darkness faded again. He opened his eyes to the
night around him, slowly ascertaining that he was upon a huge
clifftop. He coughed, suddenly, raggedly—air filled his lungs.
He wheezed, he breathed deeply, and then he could smell the
sea. Far away he could hear waves lashing the rocks and sand
below him.

He closed his eyes again, and inhaled deeply of the sweet
night air, pure and cleansed by the sea. The pain in his head
subsided to a steady throb. He willed vitality to his limbs
once again, and sat up.

He flexed his arms. There was a moon tonight, not bright,
not full, but he felt that his eyes would not have managed to
open in brilliant sunlight. Finding a large boulder in easy
reach, he set his hand upon it and willed himself to stand. But
once he had staggered to his feet, gray danced before him—he
fell. He sat, forcing himself to patience. He had to wait until
the spinning gray ceased to blur his vision.

And as he waited he remembered, with a keen clarity that
sent his temper soaring once again. The treachery of her
devious, treacherous, whorespun betrayal. He'd been drugged.
He had known she was a lie. Her act had been sweetly
staged, faultlessly performed.

And he was angrier still because he had known, and had
fallen prey to her spell in those moments. Genevieve of

Edenby . . . falling to her knees, pleading . . . promising, spinning her web of seduction, finally begging in earnest so that his heart was torn by her beauty and humility—so that she might set him up for an assassin's blow. And when that had failed, she had tried to slay him herself.

He was shaking in the moonlight, so close had death come to him.

"I *will* stand!" he swore suddenly, furiously to the night. "I will stand and I will live . . ." He continued to grate out, groping for the boulder once again and straining against it. ". . . if only for one purpose—to strip that daughter of hell of everything that she possesses . . . her castle, her lands, her honor—and every stitch of her pride!"

The swearing—weak and gasping as it was—seemed to help. Panting out the vow, he came slowly to his feet. Eventually he swallowed hard, let go of the boulder, and stood on his own.

And when he stood he could see Edenby Castle below the rise of this very rock.

His eyes began to blur. He swayed—and realized that he was about to lose consciousness again. He grabbed the boulder, leaned against it, and quickly surveyed his immediate surroundings. There was a mossy plain, sheltered by brush and an overhang not more than a stone's throw away. Staggering, blinking furiously, he tried to reach it. His legs began to wobble fiercely; he fell to his knees and crawled the rest of the way, then sighed deeply and lay down, closing his eyes and fighting nausea and the horrible drunken mists that clouded his vision even when his eyes were closed.

A drink . . . if he could only clear his parched throat with water! But there was no water, nothing to alleviate the thick, swollen feel of his tongue against his mouth. He could only pray that the pain and dizziness would clear if he rested.

He felt a night mist creep around him, and he opened his eyes once more to stare up at the half-moon in the velvet sky. All he need do was think of *her*. Genevieve of Edenby . . . clad in all the silken beauty of her golden tresses, at his knees . . . pleading. Her eyes such a lustre of mauve beauty that he had succumbed to her treachery.

He closed his eyes once again, feeling absurdly serene. Strength seemed even then to pour back into his limbs. He felt as if his heart had found a stronger beat, that he could sleep and wake again.

Because he would have his revenge. Just as surely as the tide would wash the rocks below him, and the sun would rise in the heavens with the morning, he would have his revenge.

The dawn woke Tristan. He opened his eyes carefully at first, and found that his vision seemed to be fine. He blinked against the rising sun, and then smiled slowly because it was perfect, a golden orb rising out of the pink and gray mists of the cliff.

He sat up carefully. He touched the wound at the base of his skull and winced; it hurt badly to touch. But though he was hungry and wretchedly thirsty and weak, he no longer had the horrible dizzying sensation that had kept him from standing last night. He carefully rose to his feet, and smiled. He could stand.

Tristan surveyed his position carefully. Before him was Edenby and the rear gatehouse. He noted that there was only one wall here—other than that of the cliff itself. And when he turned around there was the sea. No natural harbor here—it was rock-strewn and harsh. There was a small beach, but even that was rimmed by cliffs and caves and natural rock barriers. No large ship would dare sail close to shore—yet a small raft might well brave the obstacles. A small raft . . . or a swimmer.

It was certain that he could not escape through Edenby. He hadn't the strength to scale the walls, nor the agility to sneak through the place like a shadow. His only chance was the sea, and that was far below him.

But it was time to move, time to take action. His thirst had become desperate; he had never known before that it was possible to crave water so desperately. Reason was with him, though, and he used that reason to drive himself. If he could reach the sea, he could use the current and waves to carry him; he would round the great cliff, and, if God were with him, reach shore near the cove where his men were camped.

He closed his eyes for one brief moment. He had to get down the near-vertical cliff first.

The same moss that had given him a bed for the night grew over the rock, making the cliffside slick. Tristan went down on his hands and grasped for any hold that he could find—rocks and roots and the spidery branches of the tenacious wild ferns that grew here. At the end he lost his hold; a grunt escaped him as he began falling, rolling with increasing speed along the smooth stone. Then he was suddenly pitched into empty air—and hurtled down hard into a small spit of white sand.

For several seconds he lay there, stunned and breathless. Then he began to flex his muscles, and he laughed out loud. He was covered with scratches and bruises, but he had broken no bones. The sand beneath him was clean and soft, and the sound of the waves that came to him was like a potent wine to his blood—giving him hope and faith and renewed determination. A wave crashed, and seawater washed his body in a lazy embrace, cold and invigorating. He stood and rushed out to greet the water, stiffening as its coldness jolted his body. But he didn't think about it—he just began to swim.

It was not as easy as he had hoped; the tide was like an enemy that longed to dash him against the rock. His arms tired quickly; the icy water made him long to sleep again—to rest—to give up his hold on life and slip beneath the surface to an aquamarine paradise . . . .

Don't rest, don't pause, don't give up . . . he repeated to himself over and over. And though each and every one of his muscles ached with burning pain, he kept going.

Each time he was ready to give up, each time the salt so sorely stung his eyes that he was blinded, he thought of Lady Genevieve. The most beautiful, the most treacherous woman he had ever met. If he did not live, she would never be brought to justice. He would force her to pay in some earthly hell for trying to kill him for the casual, degrading, unholy burial that she had given him.

Anger gave him a burst of energy. Stroke, breathe, stroke, breathe. Again and again . . .

And suddenly the great rocks to his left disappeared. He

blinked furiously against the salt water that filled his eyes. There was land again—a strip of beach.

He kicked—and his foot touched rock. He tried for a foothold and managed to brace against the sand. The shore . . . the shore was before him! The cove . . . he could see tents and men and horses and cooking fires.

Staggering and floundering to avoid the rocks, he moved forward. At last he cleared the water—and pitched forward, blackness claiming him again in a burst of stars.

But voices tore at his oblivion. Arms tugged at his shoulders, lifting him, clearing him from the gentle lap of the sea.

"Tristan! By God and the Blessed Virgin—it is Lord Tristan!"

He opened his eyes. A man—a man with the red rose of Lancaster—was kneeled anxiously at his side.

Tristan smiled with parched lips.

"Water," he whispered hoarsely, and closed his eyes again. He could do that now—he had made it.

By midmorning Genevieve had such a headache that her images of yesterday had begun to blur.

Mary had been at her door early; it seemed that everyone in Edenby awaited her orders to begin the day. Genevieve had found herself at a loss; her father had seldom cared much about the running of his castle. He had often been called to court, and had spent years tenaciously clinging to his property with the continual change of the English monarchy. He had loved to hunt, and had spent numerous hours with friends on debates of philosophy and theology. He had been concerned only with his comfort—and his rents!—as far as the running of Edenby had gone.

Michael had acted as their steward. He had kept everything running smoothly, from the castle itself to the farms beyond. He had collected the rents, he had supervised the grain mill. He had, in short, done everything. And until this morning, Genevieve realized sadly, she had never known it.

When her father had died she had been ready to assume his command. Directing their defenses had been a balm to her soul. She hadn't had time to worry that she would fail; she had been in such emotional turmoil that she had expected no insurrection and received none.

But now she felt lost. Michael was dead. Her father was dead. Axel was dead, and Sir Guy was leaving soon. Half of Edenby lay in ruins, and danger still lurked beyond the walls.

Mary told Genevieve that Father Thomas and Sir Humphrey awaited her in Edgar's counting room. Edwyna was still sleeping; Genevieve decided to let her be, and dismissed Mary with the message that she would be down soon.

She dressed in a somber gray velvet that suited her mood, tied her hair into one long braid, and descended the stairs. Sir Humphrey and Father Thomas rose as soon as she entered. From behind her father's sturdy oak desk, Sir Humphrey cleared his throat; he offered her the chair, wishing her an awkward good-morning.

Genevieve took the chair there and watched Father Thomas a little uneasily. By choice, he had spent the day before in the chapel—on his hands and knees. He had not approved their plan—and had plainly said so—but he had acquiesced when it had been agreed upon by the others. He was a tall, slim man with a keen wit.

A commoner, he had chosen a life in the Church more from vocation than as a means to rise above the menial and hard labor of a tenant farmer. Genevieve had been pleased Father Thomas had come to Edenby; he was not so strict that she spent her life on her knees saying novenas, nor was he so lax that she felt she had no spiritual guidance at all. He was usually like a friend, slightly older, often very wise—and quietly in the background when she needed him. He was a very good-looking man, with tawny hair and dark green eyes, and Genevieve was certain that he kept discreet company with one of the craftsmen's daughters. He was a man of the Church, yet not entirely supportive of its rules for the clergy. But perhaps that was what she liked about him, Genevieve reflected: he lived by God—and by common sense.

"We've the dead to worry about, my lady," he told her now, wasting no time.

"They must be buried as their families choose," Genevieve replied. "Tell Jack, the stonemason, to carve their stones. Edenby will pay."

He nodded, bowing slightly, then asked. "And Michael?"

"Michael," she murmured softly. "Michael must be interred in the chapel, beside my father whom he served so well."

"That is well, Lady Genevieve," Father Thomas said. Genevieve didn't like the way that he was looking at her, or his tone. Both seemed disapproving, but even as she gazed at him a little rebelliously, Sir Humphrey began speaking. "The walls must be repaired, yet so many have been lost that the tenants are afraid to take the time from the fields to build. Some may surely be spared, yet who shall work and thus lose his income, and who should not be called? Also there is the matter of the guard. More men must be chosen, yet which families shall you honor?"

There was a quill sitting on the desk. Genevieve picked it up and idly tapped upon a parchment accounting for the rents. "As to the walls, Sir Humphrey, the able-bodied workers must be split in two groups. They shall alter their work each day, and no one shall lose out. I will have Tamkin advise me on who should be called to join the guard. Giles, from the kitchen, must be promoted to Michael's position, for his knowledge of the castle is great. Sir Humphrey, if you would be so good as to speak with him, I'll see him here now. And ask Tamkin to see to the division of men so that we waste no time, lest we find ourselves weakened against another attack."

Sir Humphrey seemed vastly relieved; he bowed to her and went in search of Giles. Genevieve watched his departure, then turned back to Father Thomas, aware that he was staring at her.

"What is it, Father?" she demanded curtly. "I feel your disapproval. How have I offended you?"

He walked toward the mullioned window that looked out upon the inner bailey. The sun was scarcely up, and the pink glow of morning was showing the ruin of the smithy. He turned again.

"My lady, I was distressed that you should use the promise of carnal delight to lure a man to his death, yet I was overwhelmed by the opposition. Now it has come to my attention that you struck the blow yourself, and ordered that a Christian knight should be denied a Christian burial.''

Genevieve felt a flush of annoyance. ''Father, I struck down the man who was about to kill Tamkin. It did not please me to do so; it was necessary. Perhaps I was wrong to allow his body to be so callously taken, but I was distressed when I gave the order. Is that all, Father? I will be at Mass; please understand that my prayers for my own shall precede those I would offer for an enemy.''

Father Thomas stiffened. ''My child—''

Genevieve tossed the pen onto the desk irritably. ''Please, Father! Don't 'my child' me! I am doing the best that I can!''

He smiled then and came to the desk, lifting her chin. ''I'm sorry. This has been quite difficult for you, hasn't it? A father lost, a betrothed slain. Responsibility resting upon shoulders too slim—''

''They are not too slim, Father Thomas,'' she said softly.

He smiled again, then moved away. ''I was worried, Genevieve. I prayed yesterday that you would not be injured. It was a risky plan. And now I pray that the murder will not live with you because I know your soul. I feel that we were not honorable, and that sits hard with my conscience.''

''What *is* honorable?'' she charged him heatedly. ''Were they honorable—attacking Edenby with no provocation?''

Father Thomas sighed. ''Your father was given the opportunity to surrender. To live, to maintain his position. All he had to do was capitulate to the demands of the Tudor.''

''Father, it would not have been honorable to betray a vow once made! My father was sworn to Richard—loyalty cannot shift with the wind.''

''Perhaps not—but the Lancastrians did battle fairly—and we did not.''

''There is never anything fair about battle, Father,'' Genevieve said stubbornly. ''It was not fair to see our buildings burn—with our people inside of them. It was not fair that I should watch my father die. We fight with what weapons we have, Father. There was no remorse among the Lancastrians when my father died; should we regret the death of their leader? Victory is costly—but not so costly as defeat.''

"Well spoken," Father Thomas murmured. He shrugged. "But I'd have your permission to see that Lord Tristan is brought down and returned to his men for proper interment. A messenger came early this morning requesting his remains.''

Genevieve waved a hand in the air. "Do what you will," she sighed softly. "Then I'd have you leave me be, for I wish to make a survey of the damage and see what state our defenses are in. And our fields—I'd not have us all starve this winter.''

"We've one more matter to discuss, my lady," Father Thomas said gravely.

"And that is?''

"Your marriage.''

She sat back, staring at him in stunned surprise, and feeling a pain she had not allowed herself before sting her eyes with the promise of tears. "Axel barely grows cold in his grave, and you would speak to me so?" she demanded harshly. She remembered him acutely then, young and handsome and gentle, and ever ready to smile; beloved.

"Genevieve, I do not speak so to hurt you," Father Thomas said quietly. "But you must guard your position. You are a woman alone now, with vast holdings. A tempting fruit for the plucking, and there are many less than noble knights about.''

"No one can force me into marriage, Father. Were I bound and gagged and dragged to an altar, I could not be forced to speak. I am, perhaps, as you say, a woman alone. Yet I shall remain so for the time being. Edenby is strong. We will make it stronger.''

Father Thomas still hesitated. "Sir Guy has approached me, as your spiritual advisor—since your father is dead—with a suggestion of a union between you two.''

Again Genevieve was startled. "Sir Guy?''

"Aye.''

He was strangely silent. Genevieve stood, smiling slightly, and moved around the desk. "You've an opinion, Father.

Give it to me, please. I've not the patience for innuendo this morning.''

He raised his brows and shrugged. "There is no reason to disapprove the match. He is young and spirited, of suitable family. But he reaches—for he is landless. I believe you could make a better match that would ally us with the lords of our coast.''

She frowned watching him. He still wasn't telling her what he was really thinking. "Father, I'm not really surprised by Sir Guy's approach. He was Axel's dear friend. He cares for me. And I do care for him. But I cannot think of making any marriage arrangements at this time. I have lost a betrothed and will not dishonor him so.'' She paused, then asked curiously, "Do you dislike Guy, Father?''

"Nay, I do not dislike him. I know little of him. But . . .''

"What?''

He straightened his shoulders and said, "If you truly wish my opinion, Genevieve, I will give it. It was wrong for that young knight to suggest that a high-born lady offer herself as whore to the enemy. A true knight goes to battle and lays down his own life first.''

Genevieve turned away from him, her interest in the conversation waning. "Oh, I daresay that the idea was rather clever—and he was terribly worried, Father.'' Her lower lip trembled slightly. "Had we not lost Michael after so many others . . .'' She paused. "Perhaps I will go on pilgrimage soon, Father. And pray for their souls—and my own. For now,'' she added brusquely, "I must tend to things here. You will tell Sir Guy only the truth—that I cannot speak of marriage now.''

"He will leave soon. You will offer him the stirrup cup?''

"Aye . . . Before Mass?''

"He leaves any moment.''

"To seek aid,'' she began to murmur, but broke off as there was a sharp rap at the door. She and Father Thomas gazed at one another, and both shrugged. Father Thomas moved to the door and opened it.

Sir Guy himself was standing there, his handsome face flushed and excited. "Genevieve!'' He rushed to the desk, then, as if remembering himself, paused to nod to Father Thomas, "Good-day, Father."

"Good-day."

"Genevieve, the guards in the northern tower recently spotted a party riding from the north. Riding—with banners flying high. It is a group of the knights displaying Richard's colors—and the white rose crest of York!"

"Bid them enter—"

"I did!"

She raised a brow slightly at such an assumption of privilege, but he was so excited that he didn't notice.

"They've come for men!"

"For men!" she cried with dismay.

"Aye. The troops are amassing. Henry Tudor has an invasion force ready to meet the King, and Richard is calling upon his loyalists. They say his troops will so far outnumber those of the invaders that the Tudor will not stand a chance!"

Genevieve stared blankly down at the parchment. So it was coming at last—the true battle for the Crown. With God's help, Henry Tudor would be defeated.

She should be glad. But she had hoped right now for the King's aid—not to have to help his cause.

She sighed. "Sir Humphrey is too old to go. Tamkin I cannot spare. Take ten of the guard, and see that they serve with their own horses and that we provide the armor. Also if any of the village youths wish to go as foot soldiers, they have my blessing—if they have that of their parents." And what shall I do? she wondered a little bitterly. Already we struggle . . .

"It will be over soon!" Sir Guy said joyously, and he leaned across the desk heavily to plant a kiss upon her forehead. "And when I return, Genevieve . . ."

Father Thomas cleared his throat. "If we have messengers from the King as our guests, perhaps we should be seeing to their comfort."

"I'll see to it—" Guy began. But Genevieve interrupted him.

"Aye, Father. As the Lady of Edenby, I shall see to it." She stood regally, squaring her shoulders. Responsibility had fallen upon her; she'd no choice but to take it. But it was something that she was determined not to relinquish. Father Thomas was worried that she was a woman alone; well, for the time being she would stand alone, and neither Guy, nor Father Thomas, nor anyone else would take what was hers by right. She had fought too hard to maintain it.

"Sir Guy?" she queried politely. "Would you see to the men and arms we offer the King?"

"Aye, Genevieve!" he agreed. He caught her hand and kissed it feverishly, then rushed out.

Father Thomas lifted a brow to her, smiling slightly. "I believe he feels he is the lord of the castle already."

"Perhaps he will be one day," Genevieve said. "And perhaps he will not. Father, I'm discovering that I enjoy my power. Perhaps I will do so all my days!"

Father Thomas started to frown disapprovingly, and she smiled. "Oh, Father, let's take this a step at a time, shall we? Right now we must go give food and drink to the King's men, and send them all on their way—although, God knows, surely I am needier than the King at this moment! And then . . ."

"And then?"

"Then we must have Mass for our dead," she said quietly. "Father?" She offered him her arm. "Will you stand with me now and serve as host in my father's place, since I would be wary of any other man?"

He smiled. "Aye, Genevieve. I'll stand at your side. And," he muttered, rolling his eyes towards heaven, "I will pray for your soul at Mass."

Chapter
Seven

"IF WE BROUGHT a party around so," Tristan said, making a diagram on the ground, "just a few men in small rafts, we could take the guards at the far tower by surprise. Following along these parapets, we can force those guards to open the gates—before anyone in the keep is even aware of danger. Meanwhile we can have two men assigned to reaching the dungeons and freeing our men there. Before any alarm can be raised at all, we will have subdued the castle."

Hunched down and balancing on the balls of his feet, Tristan looked from Jon to Tibald. Both were studying his drawing with frowns, as if they looked for a flaw in the plan. They could find none.

Jon spoke eagerly. "When?"

"Nightfall, I believe."

Tibald shook his great, shaggy head. "My Lord Tristan, you have only just begun to recover. It is a miracle that you live, when we had accepted your death."

Tristan grimaced, then grinned broadly and stood. He felt wonderful. The true miracle had been the effect of clean, fresh water, a hearty meal, and the physician's assurance that nothing had been so beneficial to his wound as the sea water that had cleansed it. He was still sore, but not plagued by dizziness or weakness. Having shaved and dressed in fresh garments, he felt as renewed as the ancient Phoenix of myth, rising from the ashes.

"Tibald, I have never felt so ripe for battle in my life. And," he added, a scowl darkening his features, "we've men imprisoned in their dungeons. I fear that we cannot waste time. Jon, you will accompany me—with a group of ten men—around the cliff by way of the sea. Tibald, you will lead the bulk of the men when the gates are opened."

"And what are the orders to the men—this time?" Jon asked thickly. Tristan gazed at Jon and saw in his eyes the same smouldering fury that he had felt himself.

Tristan walked around to his desk and sat, musing over the question. When he had awakened in his grave of rock, he would have gladly slain them all—every last inhabitant of Edenby, from soldiers to children—even dogs and cattle. But his temper was easing somewhat. His moral sense was returning, just as his health had been restored. He felt a needed distance from the event now; an objectivity toward all—but one woman.

"Jon, Tibald," he said at last, lightly drumming his fingers and staring beyond them. "We would gain nothing from mass slaughter. If we kill the masons, no one will rebuild the walls. If the farmers are gone, there will be no one to bring in the harvest. We will need wool for Flemish trade, so we will need shepherds to care for the sheep."

"You can't suggest that what was done to us go unpunished!" Jon said incredulously.

"Nay, I do not make that suggestion at all," Tristan said with a quiet vehemence that set Jon's mind to rest. "I found," Tristan continued dryly, "that the greatest torture I faced was not being struck down—it was wondering what my fate would be as I struggled to free myself from my grave and fight my way back to life. Uncertainty and fear are great weapons. The dungeons at Edenby will be full."

"If we don't do something more," Tibald reminded him, "they will not fear or respect us."

"Oh, we shall have floggings," Tristan murmured. "And

set up a court where the tenants and craftsmen may swear their new loyalties. Infractions will be brutally punished. There will be a steel band of authority that they will learn has no tolerance for anything other than strict adherence to orders.''

''And the night that we go in?'' Jon pressed. ''What do we tell the men?''

Tristan laughed bitterly. ''Tell them that the young women are fair game. We will not take the farmers' wives, but we will have their daughters.'' His eyes narrowed sharply. ''There is but one that I claim myself, and that is the Lady of Edenby. When she is discovered, she is to be brought to me.''

''I'd ask a boon,'' Jon said tensely.

''Which is?''

''The Lady Edwyna.''

Tristan remembered the aunt who resided in the castle. ''She is yours.'' He gazed at Tibald. ''And have you no requests, my friend?''

Tibald laughed. ''Nay—give me a score of broad-hipped farm girls, and I'll find myself happy. And give me a plot of land on which to build a manor. That is all I ask.''

''Done,'' Tristan said, then added dryly, ''Now we have naught to do but put our plans into action. And see that they are fulfilled this time. I warn you both, as I would warn the men—never turn your back upon those people. Take no chances. Trust no soft words or pleas for mercy or—''

He broke off with a frown. From beyond the tent came hoofbeats and an excited rise of voices. There was the blare of a trumpet and then the sound of footsteps racing toward the tent.

Tristan rose and strode the distance to the entrance, ducking beneath it to see the visitors. Jon and Tibald followed behind him.

His men were grouping around the newly arrived party on horseback, calling out greetings and shouting salutations. The newcomers bore banners with the colors of the Lancastrians; fresh red summer roses bedecked their mantles. It was a small group, dangerously small to roam the countryside at this time. Tristan recognized Sir Mark Taylor—one of Henry Tudor's greatest advocates—in the fore, and stepped forward to meet him, accepting the clamp of his arm as they met. "Lord Tristan!" Mark greeted him. "We've urgent matters to discuss!"

Sir Mark was slim and dark, of a strong and wiry build, a man who had spent all his years since childhood in battle. He was a decade Tristan's senior but neither landed nor titled, and Tristan knew that he sought Henry's kingship not only for the Lancastrian party, but for his own social rise. Yet there was honesty about him; and few men followed a would-be king without hope of their own gain.

Tristan raised a brow and directed Mark into his tent. The knight, heavily clad in armor, clumped his way in, idly observing Tristan's diagram upon the floor.

"You've not taken the castle of Edenby yet?" Mark inquired.

Tristan shrugged. "The castle will be mine now," he said flatly, "I've no doubt."

Sir Mark was not much interested in the diagram. Tristan was careful to walk over it; he was not having his conquest taken now by any other—not even a man of his own following.

"The castle of Edenby will have to wait."

"What?" Tristan demanded, frowning fiercely. "I am here—I need but a night—"

"The real and true battle for supremacy is upon us. Richard's troops are amassing—in greater number than ours. You and your men must come with me. By order of Henry Tudor. He needs every able-bodied fighting man that he can draw upon."

Tristan walked around his table and sank into his chair, compressing his lips, idly clenching his fists together. To have come so close . . . and find himself called away now! Ah, but the taste of revenge grew bitter on his lips. He could well fall on the battlefield and never return.

But the moment of true importance had come at last—the Yorkist King would meet the Lancastrian aspirant to the Crown. He had no choice.

"I will alert the men to break camp," Tristan said, rising again. Leaving Sir Mark behind him, he set out from his tent. From the entrance there he stared across the distance of field and cliff to Edenby Castle, rising out of rock and boulder, impregnable, taunting.

"I will return," he muttered darkly. "Lady, I will return."

He strode outward in the circle of tents, his mantle flowing behind him, his footsteps strong and sure.

"Break camp!" he called with a thundering conviction. "We ride for the House of Lancaster! The time has come to best a Yorkist King!"

Genevieve climbed to the ramparts by the main gatehouse and looked back over Edenby, sighing softly with a great deal of satisfaction. Her people were builders. Already the burned-out shops of the smiths and stonecarvers had been timbered, though it would take months to repair the damage done the walls by the Lancastrians' cannons, Edenby was again totally defendable. A second steel gate had been added behind the outer wall, and new "murder holes" had been added to the gatehouse. Should the enemy ram the heavy wooden gate of the outer wall, they could be trapped in the portcullis of the gatehouse—and men on the floor above could pour boiling oil upon them from comparative safety. Light arrows could also be used and any number of other techniques—or so Sir Humphrey had assured her.

But when she turned her sights the other way, looking southeastward, away from the coast, she saw nothing but total peace and tranquility. It would soon be autumn; the crops were beginning to come in, the grain was being milled. The sheep were beginning to grow their thick winter coats again. All appeared well and fine.

Hearing footsteps behind her, Genevieve started and swung about. She relaxed when she saw Father Thomas approaching her, and ridiculed herself for her nervousness. What had she to fear in her own castle?

Nightmares.

These nightly torments continued to plague her. Genevieve would have expected to dream of her father, of Axel, and of poor Michael. But it wasn't of them that she dreamed. It was of Tristan de la Tere.

She had been so very busy . . . trying to rebuild, struggling along with Tamkin and Giles to see that their food supplies and their defenses were brought back to survival levels. Perhaps the nightmares were natural. The day kept her too busy to remember the good about those she had loved; the night claimed her exhausted mind and sent it further terror instead.

In her dreams she walked the cliffs alone as around her the sky grew dark and stormy. Unable to find her way home, she would start to run—only to race into an implacable wall. Looking up, she would discover that she had run into a corpse—that of Tristan de la Tere. But he would be very much alive in death, as virile and powerful as ever; and he would laugh at her, reach for her, swear that she would pay, that she would join him in death. Genevieve would try to run, but his fingers would entwine in her hair and she would be forced to meet his deep, dark eyes, which fascinated and compelled her—and left her speechless, unable to fight. She would feel the fire those eyes kindled in her blood, a blaze that threatened to engulf her for eternity . . .

Then he would hold her tightly, and she would feel the strength of his arms; and his brutal, deep, and searing kiss would enflame her like burning oil. She could feel his hands on her, so intimately that she felt she would melt with the shame of it . . .

And then all would grow cold. His hand, his lips. He would smile at her and his features would take on an icy mask of cruel mockery, he would whisper that his kiss was the kiss of death.

"My Lady Genevieve!" Father Thomas called, interrupting her thoughts.

Genevieve turned to him. "Yes, Father?"

He smiled at her with his now customary concern and lifted his shoulders in a shrug. "There is nothing, really, that requires urgent attention. The Flemish merchant has arrived to pay for his wool. He and his party are in the hall, where the Lady Edwyna sees to their welfare."

"Perhaps I should go back," she murmured.

"There is no need," Father Thomas said.

She gazed at him curiously, with a little smile. "Then what is it you wish to speak about, Father?"

"I have no thought to speak at all. I thought that you might care to—as you have not been to the confessional lately."

Genevieve stared out at the land, then turned to face the westerly cliffs and the sea. "Father," she said, "would you accompany me out the rear gate? I've a sudden yearning to walk along the beach."

He arched a brow, then shrugged, somewhat disturbed by the silver and gray storms that seemed to rage in her eyes. "You should not venture out without the guard—"

"Then summon a member of the guard, will you, Father?"

He shrugged and did so. Moments later they followed the parapets and towers around until they came to the rear gatehouse. They did not traverse the cliffs; there was a slim path, overgrown with thistle and weeds, that led between bluffs to the scant area of beach. The guards positioned themselves discreetly. Father Thomas remained behind Genevieve as she laughed and ran to the water, shedding her shoes and heedless of her gown, to allow the tide to run over her feet. She turned back. "Father! Have you never run through the sea?"

"I was not born near the sea," he responded, but he smiled suddenly, and Genevieve returned his gaze, aware that he thought that she had been far too morose in the days past.

"You have missed much!" Genevieve told him. "Come and feel the water!"

He stepped forward skeptically. Genevieve was already sitting in the sand, so close to the water that the waves washed over her again and again, loving the water that rushed all around her. Father Thomas joined her, wincing as the cool water soaked through his frock to chill the flesh of his rump.

She was staring straight out at the sea. "Father, did you return the body of Lord Tristan to his men?" she asked him, sounding most casual.

He hesitated, having no desire to tell her that they had not been able to find the body. The entire cliff was rock—and Tamkin could not be blamed for forgetting such a burial place at such a tempestuous time. Nor had there been an odor to assist them; the sea here kept the rugged terrain fresh, and they had given up the search. It was likely that marauding wolves and buzzards had taken their toll.

"It is something you need not worry about," he told her.

She turned to him suddenly, fiercely. "Men truly do not come back from the grave, do they, Father?" she asked him.

He laughed. "Nay, that they do not. Is that what worries you?" he asked her.

She shook her head sheepishly. "Not really—I suppose I knew the truth. I have just been thinking . . . when I was young, my father used to bring me here. I was not a 'lady' then—not a grown one, at least—and he would allow me to swim and play by the shore. Edwyna used to come, too, and we brought food, and the sun shone. Those were the easiest, most delightful days." She sighed, drawing a pattern with her finger in the wet sand. "I wonder, Father, what it would be to live so again. What it might have been to live when the country was not in constant turmoil. I wish I could go back— such a little bit of time, really. Before my father's death. And Axel's, and Michael's. And before—"

She broke off abruptly, painfully.

"Before the . . . the . . . death of the Lancastrian?" Father Thomas could have bitten his tongue; the word had nearly tumbled out.

"Before his murder. Yes," she said softly. "I wish I could go back. Oh, God, it's horrible. I really couldn't have acted any differently. I had to—to do what I did. Sometimes I just wish—" She shook her head miserably, staring at the water, where the blue and gold sky and the indigo sea met to form the horizon. "I wish that my father had given Tristan de la Tere a single stupid meal. Then none of this had come to pass!"

"You wish that you hadn't been forced to do what you did," Father Thomas broke in gently, slipping an arm about her shoulders.

"Will I go to hell, do you think?"

He shook his head. "Genevieve, you did what you had to. You fought with what weapons you had. You fought in defense."

She nodded, swallowing unhappily. "I keep dreaming of hell. Are you so sure that I will not wind up there?"

"I am convinced that God knows the hearts of men—and women. And your heart, dear girl, is pure."

She didn't feel that her heart was very pure. Nor did she believe that God would be so forgiving of the fact that she had tried to use her physical beauty to lure a man to his death. Perhaps, though, he would understand that she'd had no choice.

"I worry, still."

"About the battle to come?"

"Aye. So much blood has been spilled! Do you believe that Richard will triumph? Then, at last, our wars will end, when the Tudor is defeated."

Again Father Thomas hesitated. He'd had a few strange dreams himself in which he had seen a country united, and peace and prosperity coming to the land. But in that picture, a dark spot blurred Edenby, as if it must endure some greater trial before finding peace.

"Peace is not achieved easily," he said, then added optimistically, "but you heard the King's messengers. Richard's forces far outnumber those of Henry Tudor!"

"Umm," Genevieve murmured, standing. "The last we heard from the traveling minstrel was that they all seem to be amassing at a town called Market Bosworth. Perhaps we shall hear soon that all is well."

"Perhaps," Father Thomas agreed.

Genevieve smiled impishly. The fresh sea air seemed to have cleared her soul of nightmare images. "Turn your back, will you, Father? I'd not have your sense of propriety upset. But I've the urge to take off my gown and swim again."

"My lady—"

"Please?" She laughed, and he was glad of her laugh. "Await me by the cliff—I shan't be long, I promise!"

Father Thomas did as she bade him. And Genevieve quickly forgot his presence. Leaving her velvet gown upon the sand, she took to the water in her linen shift, delighting in the chill, diving deep to enjoy the sense of freedom. She had not felt so young and easy in what seemed like forever; for these few minutes she could forget everything again. It was as if the sea could cleanse her of memories and the blood upon her hands.

When she emerged at last she felt lighthearted and very confident. Her hair was a soaking mantle around her, but she rejoined Father Thomas with a steady smile.

"Do you know, Father, I feel much better."

"Behaving like a fish is not truly considered proper behavior for a lady of your standing, Genevieve."

"But I had such a wonderful time."

"Then I am glad. A husband, though, might not approve."

She sobered suddenly, shuddering slightly. Again, Father Thomas was sorry he had spoken

"I believe, Father, that I prove myself daily. I do not need a husband."

"You are hurt now, you feel Axel's loss keenly. But you must marry one day, you know that."

She shook her head vehemently. "Perhaps I shall not. I have fought too hard and lost too much. Axel was rare. Husbands think to rule a wife's land—and the wife. I cannot be ruled, Father. I have come too far."

Father Thomas shivered slightly. She meant what she said. The dark pall that had blurred Edenby in his dreams seemed to fall about him now. He looked up at the cliffs and shivered again. He felt a sense of foreboding.

But Genevieve was hurrying on ahead of him, smiling again. "I think I shall order a holiday," she called back to him. "Surely we can find an appropriate saint's day, wouldn't you agree, Father? The people have worked hard. It isn't May, but we'll have a Maypole! We'll roast lamb and beef and dance beneath the moon!"

It was a good plan, Father Thomas admitted to himself. Genevieve had earned the loyalty of her tenants. To them she was young, and beautiful, and heroic. But she also needed the celebration herself. Something to appease her spirit and allow her to laugh again.

"Aye—we can find an appropriate saint," he agreed dryly. But even as spoke the sun seemed to fade. Storm clouds were encroaching upon them from the west.

From the area of Market Bosworth, Father Thomas thought a little dismally. What was happening out on that battlefield now?

*   *   *

On the night of August twenty-first, Tristan silently walked beneath the stars and stared out—at the hundreds and hundreds of campfires that could be seen blazing from all the many troops encircling Ambien Hill, awaiting the morrow.

Henry's scouts had been out all day. Tristan knew almost as much about the enemy's movements as their own. King Richard had ridden that morning from Leicester, trumpets resounding, his men-at-arms, archers, and cavalry before him. Even in his armor he was a slight figure. He wore a golden crown so that both his own men—and the enemy—would know him on sight.

Tristan stared at the campfires, then bowed his head. Richard was not without courage. Not without valor, not without his fine virtues. Yet too many sins lay upon his soul. His climb to power had been too careless.

Tomorrow, Tristan thought, God would choose the future king.

He fell to his knees, trying to pray. It seemed to him as if he had somehow forgotten how. The night seemed like pitch except for the campfires. Like my life, he thought—dark. But then he discovered that he was praying.

Let me live, Father. Let us be victorious. I do not fear death, but for all that has befallen me I fear my soul will never know peace until I have found vengeance. I do not seek to slay her in return. Only to take what was promised.

Was it wrong to pray for vengeance? Perhaps not. Perhaps God, too, was a warrior.

Tristan stood and stared up to heaven, grinning a little crookedly. "Tomorrow," he whispered softly to the night breeze, "will tell."

He started back to his tent. Sentries saluted and he saluted in return. Not far away Richard probably surveyed his own camp, as Henry Tudor was doing now.

Tristan slipped into his tent. He should have been thinking of battle, of strategy.

Not two feet away Jon was already asleep. Tristan laced his fingers behind his head and stared into the darkness of his tent. If he opened his eyes or if he closed them, he saw her.

He saw her in white, with mist around her; saw her hair, shimmering gold, saw her eyes, shimmering silver. The curl of her smile, the passion when she pleaded, when he had found pity . . .

"If I live tomorrow, Genevieve of Edenby, I swear I shall have that castle—and you—or die in the trying," he whispered out loud. And then he smiled. Heat, desire, and fever: to be fulfilled, and then purged, cleansed. Vengeance was perhaps a good thing. It had given him the will to live; now it would give him the will to triumph.

The battle would begin with the dawn.

August twenty-second, Year of our Lord Fourteen Hundred and Eighty Five . . .

The day had become gray, with storm clouds joining the mass of swirling black gunpowder that hovered near the ground. The heat was so great that Tristan had taken off his helmet. Beads of grime formed on his forehead, and filth blackened his face.

Long ago he had tossed away his pistol, finding it useless in the melee. He fought with his sword, on horseback, blindly slashing down those who sought to skewer or dismount him.

The tremendous odds hadn't dampened the heart of the Lancastrian forces. They fought with greater ferocity—for if they lost, they would be demolished.

Tristan fought near Henry Tudor, with a guard around their would-be king. Henry Tudor was no coward; he was a young man not yet thirty years—a man willing to fight for the Crown he sought. But his true talents lay in wit and strategy. He was of medium build and medium height, shrewd and determined, but not as powerful as many of those who would find great pride and glory in bringing him down.

Even as Tristan thought this, a great burly Yorkist broke through their ranks, wielding a pike. Tristan spurred his mount; the heavy beast reared and plunged toward this new threat. Tristan raised his sword and brought it down with all his strength against the pike, which snapped before the steel tip could reach Henry Tudor. The giant Yorkist roared out his rage and charged Tristan, unbalancing him from his mount.

Against the cries and shouting and running footsteps and the distant explosions of cannon and gunfire, they rolled together in the field that had become nothing but muck and blood amid the bodies of the dead and wounded, men and horses.

The Yorkist was on top of Tristan, striking at him with knotted fists. Tristan twisted, sending the Yorkist toppling forward, and Tristan used his momentum to rise. The shaft of the pike lay by him. He grabbed it hastily and brought it down upon the back of his enemy with such force that it snapped again. The Yorkist started to rise to his knees, but let out a grunt and fell forward into the mud.

Dazed, Tristan turned to find his mount and his sword before he could be attacked again. Henry was there, mounted, and leading Tristan's horse.

"You saved my life," Henry said briefly. Tristan accepted the reins of his horse without reply; Henry Tudor did not waste words, so he offered no denial. He glanced at the slim face of the man to whom he had given his allegiance and nodded. "We've still a battle to win," he replied.

How much longer could it go on? Tristan wondered. The sky grew darker and darker, and the dead were everywhere. White and red roses lay trampled in the filth. And still it went on.

In the end the battle was decided by Lord Stanley and his son—and his three thousand men. They were, for all intents and purposes, aligned with Richard. Yet when Richard charged upon his white horse for Henry, the Stanleys cast their powerful lot with Henry Tudor.

Tristan knew that Henry had met and negotiated with Sir William Stanley. But from that meeting Henry had learned that he would be supported only if he proved he could win the battle. Until the turning point the Stanleys had appeared to be with Richard. Clearly they meant to cast their lot with the winner, and in their movement then they did decide it all.

Richard was trapped—crushed between Henry's troops and the massive wing created by Lord Stanley's men. But he fought bravely until the end.

Finally Tristan heard a cry go up.

"He's dead! The King is dead! Richard III is slain—they've

seen him, the corpse stripped naked by our own and lain over his horse that all may see him!''

''The Yorkists are dispersing—and scattering! They are retreating from the field! The battle is won!''

And it was true, Tristan saw. Like a wave, the enemy was retreating. By narrowing his eyes, he could see a horse running wild, with a naked body cast over it.

A foot soldier ran forward, bearing the golden crown that Richard had worn. He fell to his knees before Henry, offering it up.

And Henry began to laugh, deeply, heartily. ''The battle, my friends, is indeed won!''

''Your Highness!'' the foot soldier called out reverently.

And Henry sobered, his pinched features now severe. ''I am not King—not until I am crowned so! But that, loyal servants, will be soon. To you all, my gratitude. Promised rewards are yours, and in turn I will have the promise that we will build this country and make her rich beyond imagination!'' He swiveled quickly in his saddle. ''Sir Mark, you will ride for Elizabeth of York. She will be brought to London.''

''You'll marry her, Sire, and the title will be secure—'' Sir Mark began, but Henry Tudor quickly cut him off.

''I marry for no title! All here know and history will tell that I negotiated for Elizabeth's hand long before this day! My title will be my own! Not until I am duly King will she be my bride. I marry for peace in this realm. The Houses of Lancaster and York will be united under one name. Tudor!''

Henry cast Tristan a glance. ''Well, Lord Tristan, what would you have? Do you come to London with me? To shake battle from your blood and bones in splendor? Come, speak to me, man, for I always pay my debts; and I owe you my life.''

Tristan shook his head, smiling dryly. ''I would return to Edenby and take the castle, Sir. I've a personal matter to clear there. If you would truly reward me, give over the castle—and its lady—to my keeping.''

Henry Tudor tightened his hold on his mount as the animal

belatedly sought to fight its bit. He raised a brow. "As you wish. Would you take more men and arms?"

"Nay—only those men who are mine. I believe I know how to take the castle with as little bloodshed as possible."

Henry watched him for a moment. "I mean what I say, Tristan, that I want peace. We were at war; there are nobles I will strip of power and some who will reside in the Tower. I dare say that some will eventually lose their heads, for if they oppose me now it will be treason. But I intend to extract no great revenge; only those who refuse to accept my claim need fear for their lives. Edenby is yours—but it has always been a prosperous place, and I want those taxes. Warfare has bled this country. See that you take the place in my name. I trust you to follow my policy."

"The Lady of Edenby—" Tristan began, but Henry interrupted him impatiently.

"The woman is your concern. Do with her what you will."

Tristan smiled slowly. "I'd like that as a promise, Your Grace."

"Why do you press me so?" Henry inquired irritably.

"Because she is young and very beautiful and of unimpeachable family line. Should another make a claim, I would have you remember that she is not to be a reward or a pawn in a marriage game. No matter what I choose to do, she is mine."

"The promise is yours!" Henry bellowed. "Good God! This over a woman! Leave me now for your Edenby. I've other requests to fill and the business of a kingdom to claim!"

Henry spun his mount about and rode off.

Tristan just sat still for a moment. It felt as if the sun had broken through the clouds, though it surely had not. Elation filled him like a rampaging fire, and he threw back his head to shout out his joy and triumph.

Jon, battle-grimed and weary, made his way toward his friend. He frowned as he gazed at Tristan. "Victory is one thing; you sound like a cock crowing in the morning."

Tristan laughed, but then his features tensed. "We've permission to take Edenby. With royal warning not to mar its value, but . . . with free leave and blessing!"

Jon smiled, too. A sweet breeze swept around them, cool with the promise of rain. It filled Tristan with a thunder of elation. After all that had been done to him, and all that he had fought for, resolution was near. He turned to Jon, his dark eyes glittering with a purposeful fire.

"Gather our forces—we ride hard tonight. We will waste no time."

The breeze was indeed sweet. As sweet as the long-awaited promise of revenge about to come their way.

Genevieve was in the counting room, looking at Tamkin's accounting of the rents. The paper was blurring before her a bit. They had celebrated their summer "May Day" the night before, and she had freely imbibed ale with the peasants, danced with them about their pole—and had altogether a far too enjoyable time to meet the morning with anything other than a headache.

She was fiercely startled when the door suddenly banged open and Sir Humphrey entered, white-faced and shaking. "It's over! The battle at Bosworth Field is over. Richard was killed."

"What?" she cried out with astonished alarm.

He nodded, swallowing sickly. "Henry Tudor goes to London, where he will be crowned King."

"How can you know?" Genevieve queried, fighting the nausea that rose in her. It couldn't be! Richard's forces had well outnumbered the invaders! How could it be?

"One of our men stumbled back to the gates. He is ill and wounded, but he says there is no doubt. He saw King Richard's body himself. The Yorkist forces were badly beaten and scattered. Henry Tudor is the victor."

"Oh, dear God!" Genevieve groaned, leaning an arm across the desk and resting her head upon it. "Perhaps . . . perhaps it will mean nothing. There are still others who could make a bid for the Crown. Perhaps this Tudor upstart will also be killed!"

She hadn't seen Edwyna enter the room, but now her aunt spoke, running to the desk to take Genevieve's hand and implore her.

"Genevieve! We must give it up now! We must! If we do not accept this man as King, he will send others out to crush us! Genevieve! Please, think of us all! If you go to this man, swear your loyalty—lay down our arms and our crest of white roses—he will perhaps let us be!"

Genevieve sat back in the chair, staring at Edwyna's huge, moist blue eyes. She gazed past her aunt to Sir Humphrey.

"Well?" she inquired wearily.

He shook his head unhappily. "I see no other way, my lady. Edwyna is right—we must swear our loyalty to this new King. And pray that he does not intend to punish the countryside."

"Please, Genevieve!" Edwyna implored once more.

Her head began to pound viciously. She pressed her temples between her thumbs and forefingers.

"Genevieve!"

"You are right. I must go to plead the favor of this upstart King!" She wished the pain would leave her head so that she could think. "If he does indeed become King, half of us could wind up in the Tower or on the block. I will go to him and swear our loyalty."

Edwyna was already on her feet. "I'll pack for you. He is a young King. If you wear your jewels and your finest gowns, he will not be able to refuse you."

"I hear that he is sly, shrewd, and cold—and far more concerned with pounds and shillings than he is with women. But do what you like." She paused again and added bitterly, "If I am to beg, I may as well be regally dressed for the occasion."

Edwyna was already gone. Genevieve rose wearily and gazed at Sir Humphrey. "You, sir, will accompany me. And Mary must come along. And an escort of five—"

"Ten, if I may suggest it, Lady Genevieve," Sir Humphrey interrupted her. "The countryside will be crawling with soldiers beaten and in need. We would be prime picking for attack."

"Ten then," Genevieve said. She sighed. "We might as well leave this afternoon; I'd have this over as soon as is possible."

Less than two hours later, Genevieve and her escorts were ready to ride out of the gates.

Father Thomas and Edwyna stood by to raise the stirrup cup and wish them a good journey.

"When our men return—those who do—care for them all. They were loyal to Edenby, and to the House of York."

Father Thomas nodded gravely.

"And if Sir Guy returns, see that he is made comfortable in the castle."

"I will," Edwyna murmured anxiously. Little Anne was at her mother's side, wide-eyed at the proceedings. Genevieve found herself leaping from her saddle to hug her little cousin.

"Annie—I'm going to the City! Be good now, and I will bring you back a lovely doll or a puppet! Would you like that?"

"A puppet?"

"Aye—a wonderful puppet!"

Anne smiled and kissed her. Genevieve tried to grin at Father Thomas and Edwyna.

"Don't fear—all will be well. I intend to practice my 'begging' all the way!"

Edwyna smiled, but Father Thomas frowned sternly. "Genevieve!" he implored. "Take care, for such words are treason now."

She sighed. "Father, I will take care. I have no thought to lose my holdings—or my neck! I will return with all haste, God willing. Be well."

"God bless you, child, you be well," he told her, holding her hands tightly. She looked so regal and so bold. Her words were so nonchalant—confident and proud.

He felt her fingers tremble slightly.

"Father, think on it! If only we had offered a meal to Tristan de la Tere and his troops, I should not be supplicant now!"

"Genevieve—"

"We would not have fought, nor seen so many die." She laughed wearily. "And I—I would not be guilty of—of treachery and murder. For nothing. For absolutely—nothing at all."

"Genevieve, you must not dwell on the past. Remember,

as I have told you, you could have done nothing differently. Not, and stayed true to your heart, to your people, to yourself."

She smiled. "Thank you, Father."

Then she drew her hands from him and waved gaily, "Father, all is well!"

The great gates opened, and Genevieve and her escort rode out from Edenby.

Chapter Eight

THE MOON HAD risen high; it was little more than a sliver, casting a quiet glow upon the fog and mist that covered the cliff and made intriguing secrets of the bracken that grew there.

The water had been very cold; Tristan and his group of twelve men who took the water route to the beach were shivering from their contact with the sea; their boots were wet and sodden, but they moved without complaint, ready next to tackle the cliffs and the sharp rocks that would lead to the wall and the rear gatehouse.

Tristan led, remembering the way well, a fierce, determined scowl imprinted upon his features the entire way. Jon was behind him, occasionally grunting softly, straining for the grasps and toeholds they needed to breach the cliff. But other than those straining gasps, and the sounds of heavy breathing and the sporadic noise of pebbles cascading downward, the party was silent.

At last they crested the top, and whatever exhaustion Tristan might have been feeling quickly evaporated as he saw the spot where the men of Edenby had sought to bury him with rock.

Jon stood beside him. Tristan lifted an arm to indicate the wall in the moonlight. "We can leap to the wall from the cliff there. You and I shall go first and overpower the guards. Then we shall signal the others with a light."

Jon nodded. The distance from the cliff to the wall seemed great. But Tristan was already motioning in the darkness. The others were scurrying around them silently. Tristan touched his scabbard, assuring himself that his sword was at his side. Then he started to move down the cliff. Jon watched him for a moment, catching his breath. He saw Tristan plant his feet squarely, bend his knees—and then leap. There was a slight thud as he landed on the center of the parapet. Jon released his pent-up breath and hurried to the spot where Tristan had been. He prayed silently for a second; then with his arms out for balance, he leapt.

He would have sprawled noisily, but Tristan was there to catch him.

"The guard will pass in another moment!" Tristan hissed. Jon nodded, his heart pounding.

It was not long. A guard—recklessly clad with no armor and carrying no weapon but a knife—sauntered into view. Perhaps it was not so reckless to be casual, Jon mused. Who would expect an attack from an unreachable shoreline scored with piercing rock?

The guard came closer. Tristan moved suddenly like a blur of motion in the night. He did not draw his sword; he used his fist with a sickening crunch to level the man.

"He will live," Tristan muttered, staring down at the guard, "And he'll have learned a good lesson—that of staying alert!"

Creeping along the parapet, they came upon a second guard on duty. That one was staring out at the night. Jon took that one, very simply tapping the man on the shoulder—and catching his jaw with his knuckles as he turned.

They ventured silently into the gatehouse. Three men were there loudly gambling at dice. Tristan drew his sword carefully and nodded for Jon to do likewise. They rushed into the room, swords drawn.

These guards started, and stood, ready to reach for their weapons.

"I think not, my friends," Tristan drawled slowly. "Touch your weapons and you die. Stay quiet and pray, and those prayers might well be answered. Jon! Take that lantern and signal the men."

Jon grabbed one candle with the tin holder about it and retreated from the post to the parapet. The guards eyed one another—weighing their chances of rushing Tristan.

He smiled slowly. "My reputation is well earned. There may be three of you, but my sword is in my hand, and it has had great experience of late!"

The guards were saved from a choice of honor or death. Jon came back in, with five of the men in tow.

"Now," Tristan said, "If you'll be good enough to escort yourselves to the dungeons . . ." He raised a brow, and smiled very politely once again.

A guard stepped forward. "We—surrender, Lord Tristan. But we cannot escort ourselves to the dungeons. They are beneath the main keep."

Tristan shrugged, musing over that knowledge. "You—what is your name, man?"

"Jack Higgen, my lord."

"Jack Higgen, you will accompany me alone to the dungeons. I'll take one of your friends' cloaks—hasn't anyone told you yet that these white roses must go?—and you and I will proceed to the dungeons alone. How many guards are on duty there?"

"Only two."

"Don't lie to me. It will cost you your life."

Jack Higgen was not yet twenty, Tristan ascertained quickly. He was a tall, slim youth, apparently determined to live. He swallowed, and his throat wobbled with the effort, and then he spoke again. "I swear by the Blessed Virgin there's none but two guards there." He shrugged uncomfortably. "There's no need for more. The place is made of stone and steel."

Tristan nodded. "Jon, await my return. Then young Jack here can escort us to the main gate."

Dressed in one of the guards' cloaks with the white rose

insignia and the crest of Edenby boldly upon it, Tristan
hurried young Jack down the gatehouse stairs to the outer
bailey. Jack, prodded by Tristan's knife at his spine, saluted a
guard at a wooden gate that led to the inner bailey. They
passed the frame structures of craftsmen and village traders,
quiet in the night, and approached the main keep with its high
towers and round of parapets. At the door with its massive
iron handles there stood two more guards.

"Is that the only entrance?" Tristan demanded, twisting
the knife closer to Jack's spine.

Jack shook his head. "It's . . . it's built on a motte. If we
veer around to the right, we'll come to a staircase that rounds
to the dungeons below."

"What else is below?" Tristan asked quietly.

"Only the tombs beneath the chapel," Jack said.

Tristan nodded. "And guards?"

"Only one at the foot of the steps."

"Fine. Smile as we approach."

Jack did so, though his smile wavered a little. The boy was
trying, Tristan decided.

"What are you doing there?" the guard rasped out in
challenge.

Tristan pushed Jack forward into the guard, forcing them
both to fall. He pulled off his cape quickly, throwing it over
the pair, then shoving them both to the stairs. They fell
heavily along the full, treacherous curve of the stairway.
Tristan heard every bang and thud clearly and hurried after
them. The other two guards were up, anxious as to the noise.
But by then Tristan had his sword drawn and was ready. He
eyed the startled men sternly and promised, "If you force me,
I'd lose no sleep by taking a life in Edenby."

They recognized him—he knew it by the horror in their
eyes. He inclined his head quickly to keys hooked to a peg in
the wall. "I want my men out—and you in."

With shaking fingers, the oldest guard, a graying man with
sad brown eyes, hurried to do as bidden. The dungeons were
cleared of Tristan's men—and filled with the guards except
for Jack.

"Lord Tristan!" called out one of his men with awe. "Ah, we'd given you up for dead—"

"We'd thought to spend our lives in here—"

"Bless you—"

"Shush!" Tristan warned them sharply. "We've still work to do this night!"

He instructed those who could to don the guards' cloaks and mantles, and warned them that they would be outnumbered until the main gates were opened.

Half of the men followed him and Jack; the other half returned to the rear gatehouse to round up what men they could pick off and haul them back to the dungeons. It was a huge place, Tristan realized. His plan had really been foolhardy—it was a miracle that it seemed to be working.

He tensed as he moved along the bailey again with Jack at his side—under knife point again. In moments he would have the castle. He would have . . . *her*. And though he still wasn't quite sure what kind of justice he intended to mete out, it would be sweet satisfaction to have her know that he lived—and that revenge was imminent. His heartbeat quickened with anticipation. He would not fail.

"Tell the guards on gate duty that a party of men, returned from Bosworth Field, seek sanctuary in Edenby," Tristan instructed Jack. Jack started swallowing again. Tristan edged his knife more closely against the youth's spine.

His words were ragged as he shouted up to the gatekeeper, and the gatekeeper scratched his head in confusion.

"I know them!" Tristan called out himself, strongly. If the gatekeeper knew his face, he could not see it in the darkness. "They are friends!"

To his great relief, the iron gates began to crank open. And behind them the great wooden drawbridge, too, began to fall. For seconds Tristan barely dared to breathe. Then he heard Tibald's wild war cry—and score upon score of horses thundered through the gate.

Too late Edenby's guards rushed forward in shock to attempt to defend the castle.

It was all over in seconds. The guard was surrounded and had no choice but surrender.

Tristan found Tibald, and clasped his arm. "I leave to you the business of prisoners—and our positions upon the guard towers." His eyes, dark and narrowed, turned to the keep. "The castle is mine. Send ten men for duty in the great hall tonight. I'll not have a repeat of treachery."

"As you say, my lord!" Tibald agreed heartily. Tristan started for the keep with his sword drawn. There was a rush of footsteps behind him. He whirled, ready for any attack. But it was only Jon.

"I've my own score to settle this night," Jon reminded him.

Tristan threw an arm around him. He smiled, but Jon sensed the contained fury within him. "Revenge is something necessary, isn't it, Jon? A man craves it—he feels that he will never be whole again without it. It is something that gnaws and tears at the insides until it feels as if it draws blood from the heart!"

Jon glanced at his friend. Aye, revenge was sweet. And he intended to have his share.

But he was heartily glad that he wasn't Genevieve of Edenby that night. He had never seen Tristan so implacable, nor had he ever sensed such burning tension from the other man.

Together they entered the keep.

Edwyna had been sleeping. Since the Lancastrians had first taken to assaulting their gates, she had found comfort in taking her daughter into her bed and holding her throughout the night.

She began to awake with the sound of noise in the bailey; but the sound had died down, and in the pleasant mists of drowsiness she assumed that the guards had handled the disturbance. She closed her eyes again, hugged Anne more tightly to her, and sighed lazily.

She was shocked to full awareness as her door burst open with a thunderous crash. There was a gleam of light from the hall, enough to show a tall figure silhouetted there, feet braced far apart, hands upon his hips.

Edwyna blinked and then gasped. As terror firmly clutched

her heart, she leapt from the bed to place herself between the horrible menace of the Lancastrian and her only child.

She could move no more. She stood there, her heart beating like a hare's as he took a step into the room. She remembered the eyes that had sparkled so brightly with laughter, the lips that had so easily twisted into a smile, the young, handsome face that had once spoken with gentleness and humor.

There was no humor about him now. His eyes glittered like hard gems, his smile was drawn and bitter.

"Lady Edwyna," he muttered, "we meet again at last."

He walked idly into the room. She discovered that she could only stare at him. He cast aside his mantle and calmly took off his sword.

"Have you no pleasant words of greeting this evening?" he taunted, with cruel mockery in his tone.

"I—" she began, and then her shaking knees gave way. She fell upon them to the floor, lowering her head. "I did not . . . I did not encourage the plan, Jon! I swear I did not. I did not wish to see you killed!" She could not raise her eyes, and she knew she couldn't let herself be the coward that she was; there was Anne to think of! Whatever he might choose to do to her, she had to beg that he spare her child.

Yet Edwyna was doing far better than she knew. Jon stared down at her, at her lowered head and her tawny chestnut hair caught by the firelight and spilling over the sheer white linen of her nightdress. The pale light reflected through that material, outlining the fullness of her breasts and the lithe beauty of her form.

He came to her and lifted her chin.

"Do you swear to me, Edwyna, that you were not part of that treachery?" he demanded harshly.

Her eyes filled with tears as she surveyed his harsh expression. She had no thought to fight him or to escape. She tried to speak but could not; she shook her head. Jon dropped her chin and moved away from her. She sobbed slightly, then found her voice. "I did not wish for your death! Yet whatever you would do, find mercy for my child, for I swear she is but five and could have no hand in treachery!"

She gazed at him imploringly, her heart beating murderously again, for not only was he fierce standing there, but he was young and striking—and he touched in her desires that she had never truly fulfilled in her brief marriage. She thought she had gone mad—and perhaps she had.

But before Jon could reply to her entreaty, she gasped again, for there was a furious thunder at the door

Tristan slammed open the door; he stood there, tall and powerful and enraged, his dark eyes gleaming, his strong features set like granite, and his lips compressed to disappear in a taunt line of fury.

He was alive! Edwyna was horrified. He had truly come back from the dead! She thought that she would faint. He gave Jon one brief glance and came to her, clutching her arms and shaking her.

"Where is she?" he demanded in a guttural voice. Edwyna's teeth chattered. "*Where is she?*"

Genevieve, he meant Genevieve, Edwyna thought sickly. She tried to force words from between her frozen teeth. "G-gone! Gone!"

"*Gone?*"

His rage seemed to encompass her. She had never known fear such as this or the power by which he held her. She had to speak, she knew. She moistened her lips, staring into the temptestuous darkness of his eyes.

"Genevieve . . . left today for London." She moistened her lips again. "She went to London to surrender Edenby to Henry Tudor and to swear an oath of loyalty."

He continued to hold her in a grip like steel, staring with disbelief and fury. Then he swore with such a vengeful fury that she shrank from him. "*Damn her!*"

And to Edwyna's stunned amazement, he released her almost gently, spun about, and stalked about the room with great striding steps. At length he paused before Jon.

"I head out tonight to retrieve my property," he said with a sudden and deathly quiet. "You'll see to the castle, and the arrangements as we've discussed them, in my absence. No one leaves, and no one is released from imprisonment until my return. You and Tibald are in charge.''

Jon nodded. Tristan strode from the room, his mantle flying behind him like a great banner of justice.

Edwyna gazed at Jon uneasily. He walked slowly to the door and closed it. She felt again the shivers that raked along her spine, and she could not tell if she were terrified or . . . merely waiting. She knew she should be worried for Genevieve; but tonight her own fate stood before her.

She closed her eyes briefly. Her fate was sealed: she knew from the anger, and the purpose in Jon's face, that this night was his.

And she was a little amazed at herself. She was almost glad of it. She was cornered, she had no recourse. She had been— whether willingly or no—a part of a great treachery. It was her turn to pay.

And yet she couldn't ignore his youth, his fine build, his solid muscles. She flushed; she almost longed to touch him; and feel his touch. She should have been ashamed, and perhaps she was. But she wasn't an innocent girl; she knew the duties of the marital bed, and if this wasn't marriage— neither was he the husband she had lost. He was younger, and more striking. He promised something . . . more.

Edwyna stood, suddenly calm. Her voice was still ragged, breathy when she beseeched him again.

''My daughter, she sleeps . . .''

Jon inclined his head toward the door and spoke harshly. ''Call a servant. See that she is sent to sleep in her own bed.''

Edwyna could scarcely believe him. She couldn't move. Impatiently he opened the door himself and shouted for a woman to come.

Old Meg, one of the kitchen help, came scurrying up, a look of terror on her face. ''Take the child,'' Jon said bluntly. ''Sleep by her side this night.''

Meg waddled past Edwyna, barely daring to glance her way. She picked Anne up with tenderness and relief that her chore should be so simple a one. She paused before Edwyna. ''Her own chamber, my lady?''

''Aye,'' Edwyna managed to whisper.

Meg exited with Anne. Jon, without taking his eyes from Edwyna, closed the door again and latched it.

He came slowly toward her. His hands touched her face, and it seemed that the tension fell from them as he held her cheeks and gazed into her eyes.

She didn't move. He smiled slightly, and his hands came to her breast. "Your heart beats like a bird's," he told her.

Still she could find no words. Her breath caught at the feel of his hand cupping her breast, strong and gentle. He smiled again and his fingers came to her throat, lightly stroking her flesh. Then his hands slipped beneath the fabric at her shoulders and pushed the gown downward until it fell from her, leaving her naked to his perusal. He stepped back, surveying her with a quick admiration, the speed of the pulse at his throat increasing with her own.

Then he took a step forward again, taking her into his arms. His kiss was hungry and deep, and the warm pressure of his mouth made her delirious. The kiss was good and exciting, as thrilling as the hardness of his body next to her own naked flesh. He stroked her back gently, and she put her arms around him, her fingers lacing at his neck as she choked out a little cry of surrender and . . . desire.

He lifted her and carried her to bed.

His lips and hands moved over her. He whispered things she did not understand, yet they enflamed her. She knew that she moaned softly, yet with no protest.

And by the time he came to her, divested of his own garments, naked and hard with his desire, she knew that this night would bring no punishment, and no pain.

Just a pleasure greater than anything she had never known before in her life. A pleasure so intense that it was a little like dying—and being born again.

Genevieve nervously paced the long hallway at Windsor, occasionally glancing at Sir Humphrey. They had been here three days already and were still waiting—with numerous other supplicants—for an audience with the new King.

It had taken long days and nights of hard travel to reach London, and they had difficulty finding lodgings. At last she had been given a room at Windsor with other ladies of family; Mary had been sent to share the servants' quarters, Sir Humphrey was staying with an old friend, and her guards were lodged in a horse barn.

London was full of refugees. The merchants were having a heyday, while King Henry VII, meantime, granted audiences with the generosity of a miser.

Sir Humphrey, behind her, cleared his throat. "You mustn't grow so distraught, Genevieve."

"Oh, I'm worried, Sir Humphrey!" she exclaimed, then lowered her voice so others about the hall wouldn't hear her. "Perhaps we should have stayed at Edenby. Perhaps we should have waited and sent only a letter, vowing our acceptance of his rule."

Sir Humphrey shook his head, clutched her hands, and stood back from her.

"Genevieve . . . were I but a few years younger!" He smiled sheepishly. "You will enchant the King when he sees you! He will forgive us all, and you will have saved Edenby!"

Genevieve truly was enchanting. She was dressed in silver satin today, a gown with fashionably puffed sleeves, and trimmed with exotic white fox. It had a graceful train and a low bodice. Her hair was free to float down her back like angels' wings, and the small headdress she had chosen was fragile, composed of semiprecious stones and gossamer silk that hid none of the luster of her hair.

If they could just get in to see the King!

As if called by Sir Humphrey's desperate prayer, a royal page came before them. "Lady Genevieve of Edenby?" he inquired, bowing slightly and precisely.

"Aye?"

"You may come before His Majesty now."

She smiled at Sir Humphrey, trying to wink with assurance, and started to follow the page. But a tap on the shoulder stopped her, and she turned around to cry out with startled surprise.

Sir Guy was standing there. Handsome and unharmed— and wearing a very red rose by the brooch of his mantle.

"Guy!" she gasped out.

"Shush!" he warned her, pulling her quickly aside. "It's a long story, Genevieve! But I had to see you, to tell you to take heart! I served Henry at the Battle of Bosworth Field."

"Henry!" she gasped out, stunned.

"I had to—I did it for Edenby!" he told her. "I know that your audience before the King is now. Whatever he should say, accept. If aught goes wrong, I will plead with him. He will know that I stand by your side," Guy grimaced, "and that I was loyal."

"Lady Genevieve!" The distraught voice of the page who had lost her called out. Guy gave her a quick kiss on the cheek, then hurried off into the crowd of milling supplicants.

"I'm . . . here," Genevieve said distractedly to the page. She smiled brilliantly, her poise somewhat collected but still shaken by Guy's appearance. She willed herself to stand straight. She would plead for Edenby—but she would plead with pride.

She was not alone before Henry. There were several other lords and ladies in the solar where he held his audiences. She was led to the back of the room, and from there surveyed the King.

He was young, not unhandsome, with a slim face. His nose was long and prominent, his eyes small, dark, and shrewd.

A council of ministers was ranged about him, and as people were introduced and brought before him, his counselors whispered, he weighed their words, and made judgments.

Genevieve began to breathe more easily as she saw that this new King seemed to be dealing lightly with his subjects. A noble of Cornwall—an old knight, long a Yorkist supporter—was brought before him. The old man spoke eloquently, telling Henry that he had fought only where his vows had lain. But Richard was dead now, and he was glad to see the end of the wars. He would swear his loyalty now to Henry Tudor and keep that oath as ever he had kept that which he had given before.

King Henry VII dealt gently with the old man, saying that his oath of allegiance and a "minor" fine—which seemed rather a large fine to Genevieve—would be necessary for peace to be sworn between them.

Others came forward and were dealt with. Then Genevieve's heart caught in her throat as she heard her own name called. She walked through the room to stand before the throne and the King, her chin held high. She knelt before him, then rose to meet his eyes, stunned by the interest and amusement she saw in them.

"So you are Genevieve of Edenby," he murmured. "Come to seek audience with us?"

She felt acutely uneasy. His eyes were skimming over her as if they shed her of all her clothing within his mind and mused over her assets and possible worth with a special intent.

"Aye, Your Grace," she murmured, smiling humbly. "As did many fine and valiant lords, my father had sworn his loyalty to Richard III. And a sworn oath, Sire, must in all honor be kept. Yet with Richard's death, so dies the oath. We of Edenby would gladly lay down our arms and sue for the peace that your Majesty so magnanimously seeks for his country."

Henry was smiling, as with some secret joke.

"Lady Genevieve, you are very beautiful—and most gracious before us," Henry said slowly, as she heaved a sigh of relief; things were going to go well. He smiled at her, and she felt a rush of release and joy. She would be hit with a great fine such as the Cornish lord had received, but Edenby could pay such a fine. And they would have peace.

"Very beautiful," he repeated, and she frowned as she noted that he glanced off into the crowd as a slightly lascivious smile crossed his lips.

He gazed back at her, his small eyes once again surveying her form with sly amusement. He was a man, she thought uncomfortably, with a sense of humor even his closest followers sometimes found appalling. He was clearly enjoying himself at this moment. She felt suddenly as if she were lost and groping, and she didn't understand why. Why didn't he demand a fine from her? Was she supposed to say more?

"Your Grace," Genevieve murmured, "we do swear our loyalty to your realm . . ."

"Yes," he said at last with a long sigh. "But I am afraid, my lady, that it is not your position to do so."

"Your pardon, Sire?" she said, puzzled.

He smiled. "Edenby laid down its arms days ago, Lady Genevieve."

"Pardon?" She gasped again, still confused, yet aware now that something was very wrong somewhere.

The King was gazing past her toward the crowd once again. She heard footsteps, light against the velvet sweep on the aisle. She turned, frowning.

Lightning swept through her—a firestorm of horror and disbelief.

Tristan!

She blinked. It could not be! Could not be! He was dead, dead and buried. She had slain him herself, she had seen the light go out of his eyes, out of his soul.

He strode slowly toward her, not dressed for battle as she had seen him last, but in fine and elegant attire. His hose was royal blue, his tunic a shade to match, trimmed in fine ermine. His mantle was a brilliant red, and caught at his shoulder with an emerald brooch. He was smiling pleasantly, yet there was no warmth, no humor in that smile. It was cold and chilling and deathly and mocking.

He towered before her, filling the whole room with his energy and power. Genevieve thought that she would faint.

He bowed low to her. He stared into her eyes. She could only stare back as molten lightning ripped through her again. Her knees shook.

Father Thomas had lied to her! Men could come back from the grave, for Lord Tristan had done so. As dark and vital as ever, as menacing, as strongly masculine and threatening. Staring at her, here, now. With those eyes dark as fire, blue as midnight. Eyes that taunted and reminded. She had forgotten nothing of him.

He had forgotten nothing of her.

"Lady," he murmured, smiling briefly; then he directed his gaze to the King. "Your Highness."

"Ah, Tristan! This is the lady you seek?"

"Aye, Your Grace. You've met, I see. Still I give you the Lady Genevieve, my sweet, beloved mistress." His gaze raked Genevieve once again and bowed once again, most mockingly, before directing his next dry remark to the King again.

"At the lady's request, I assure you."

The room started to spin before Genevieve's eyes. King Henry laughed as though he were part of a great and wonderful joke.

"We are glad to have seen her, Tristan. I understand your insistence on my promise, for I could well have been tempted . . ." His voice trailed away with insinuation. The room seemed incredibly quiet, as if all eyes and all thoughts were on Genevieve. She realized with sickening clarity that she had never had a chance here—that explained the King's bemused greeting.

Tristan had exacted some kind of promise regarding her from the new King.

She could barely breathe. How was it that even before Tristan had spoken, Edenby had no longer been hers?

"Take her," Henry said briefly, dismissing them.

A mist reeled around her. He was alive. Tristan was alive, and standing behind her, and ready to claim her! It was her nightmare, the worst of all nightmares, come to life! If he claimed her, it would surely be to kill her, to execute her slowly for the treachery she had wrought . . .

She felt his hand, like a hot iron shackle, wind about her arm. She gazed into his face, saw the chilling triumph and hatred in his eyes—and wrenched furiously from him, racing forward to kneel before the King.

"Your Grace!" she pleaded. "Place me in the Tower, if you would. Take me before your courts! Sire! Have mercy, for I offered no treason against you—only loyalty to the King my father had sworn allegiance to! Sire . . ."

She heard Tristan's soft laughter. He took a step forward, and tears of pain sprung to Genevieve's eyes; he had trodden—purposely, she was sure, upon her hair.

"She does this well, Sire, does she not? She pleads so

prettily. Why, this is the same position she took before me—just seconds before I was treacherously attacked by her men.''

"Your Grace!" Genevieve pleaded. "Surely you understand loyalty—"

"Ah, but not a knife in the back, lady!"

"Your Grace—"

"My lady," Henry interrupted her, bending low, and so fascinated by the silver beauty of her eyes and the golden flowing cloak of her hair that he would have gladly listened to her plea—and kept her at Court—had he not made a solemn vow to Tristan. "My lady, I fear that your fate is sealed. I, too, make promises and owe loyalty. You do understand. Now, go, lady. I have spoken. You are beneath the—guardianship?—of the Lord de la Tere.''

She shook her head, unable to believe that the King could refuse her. That he had handed her over to Tristan like property—to be owned, used, to be discarded, if he liked.

A heavy hand rested on her shoulder, and she heard a mocking whisper searing the flesh at her throat and sending shudders throughout her limbs.

"Genevieve, you make a fool of yourself before the multitude! Risc and walk out of here with me—or else you shall depart his Royal Grace and all this nobility like a wayward girl, cast over my shoulder with my handprint firmly established upon your treacherous but lovely and most noble derriere.''

"No!" she grated desperately. Panic had assailed her, stark, animal panic. She made her first serious mistake. She rose quickly, bowed to the King—and tried to run.

Laughter rose all around her.

She did not take five steps before she was jerked back by the hair. Barely aware of what happened, she was spun about so suddenly that her head reeled, and her feet flew out from under her.

Tears stung her eyes as she was crudely carried from the solar, jounced about like a sack of grain, with whispers and laughter surrounding her on all sides.

It must be a nightmare! And she *would* awake. Tristan was dead. Good God, hadn't his death haunted her again and again and again? He was dead!

But he was not. His hold upon her was like steel. She was his prisoner—by royal decree.

Chapter
Nine

GENEVIEVE OUGHT TO have passed out; she should have allowed her trembling legs to give way and her shock to take her into oblivion. She should have remained in a sea of gray where nothing was real.

Unfortunately, she was all too aware. And in those miserable moments, as she bounced along the halls of Windsor, Genevieve did not know if she were more mortified—or terrified. Great silences, followed by titters of uneasy laughter, followed them all the way. They approached a group of women, who stood gossiping, unaware of Tristan's long strides coming toward them; he made matters all the worse by bowing very politely, then speaking cordially, "Ladies, if you will excuse me . . . ?"

They parted swiftly. From her rear view Genevieve was able to see their mouths gaping—then shut to move with a wild speed again as they marveled over the form of their interruption.

Shock kept her from reacting at first. She was so horrified to realize that he was alive—alive and very healthy—that she did not resist at first, or even speculate upon their destination or her immediate fate.

But once they passed those gossiping ladies, something instinctive came to Genevieve's defense. She grasped his mantle, struggling to rise against his shoulder and face him.

He gazed at her, with sharp, narrowing eyes. For a moment her courage failed her. She would never forget the way he had looked at her the night she had struck the blow. Never forget the way that he had despised her and reviled her—and promised vengeance. Yet—there had to be some way to escape him. "Put me down," she begged, keeping wary eyes upon him and faltering again. "I'll—I'll walk." She hesitated. "Please."

She was somewhat startled when he stopped and allowed her to slide along his length until she was standing. She stared up into his eyes, and backed hurriedly away from him a step, trembling from that close contact. She lowered her eyes, then raised them again.

"Where are you taking me?" she asked him hoarsely.

He planted his hands on his hips and tilted his head slightly to regard her caustically. "That's it, my lady? 'Where are you taking me?' Not, 'Welcome back from the dead, Lord Tristan. It's a pleasure to see you alive'?"

"It most certainly isn't a pleasure!" she snapped back without thinking.

Pray . . . pray that I do die, he had warned her once.

He laughed, dryly and bitterly, and gripped her upper arm to drag her down yet another hall. There seemed to be no one in this part of the palace; she realized that they had come to living quarters and that only a stray guest or a servant might be wandering about here. There would be no help for her, she thought with a sinking heart. Indeed nowhere would she find help. No one would defy the direct order of the King—not in so paltry a thing as aiding a belligerent heiress against the man the King had chosen to hand her to.

Tristan walked very quickly, not releasing his hold. Genevieve gasped, hardly able to keep up with his long strides, especially while her mind and heart raced so desperately.

But, oh! She was so blank! She was afraid to think, afraid to wonder, and she had to think . . .

So far, think as she might, she had reached only one sure

conclusion—he was definitely alive and very real. He was enraged. And he had just been given leave to do with her what he would. She swallowed uneasily, jerking so hard upon his hold that he was forced to stop and stare at her again.

"Where are you taking me?" she demanded again.

"My quarters," he said briefly.

"What—are you going to do to me?"

He smiled slowly, raising a brow. "I haven't quite decided yet. I thought of boiling you in oil, then decided it would be too mild. Drawing and quartering occurred to me, but I dismissed that, too, as rather easy."

"You wouldn't dare!" she challenged him. "The King did not give you leave to murder me—"

" 'Execute,' is the term. And, aye, it usually requires a royal signature. But not in this case, I think. Then of course there is simple torture. Umm, let's see. Perhaps we could brand you, burn a warning of treachery onto one of those beautiful cheeks. Too quick! Let's see, we could rip out your nails, one by one . . ."

"Stop it!" she hissed.

Was he serious? she wondered sickly. She couldn't tell by the way he looked at her, eyes as hard and deep as dark fire again, his pleasant tone marked with an unmistakable edge.

"My people would revolt. They would find you—"

"They'll have no difficulty finding me. We are returning to Edenby. And I doubt that they'll ever rise against me again. They are nicely subdued at this point, I dare say."

"What . . . are you talking about?" she asked with dismay.

"Merely that Edenby is mine, Genevieve. We went in the night you left." He smiled and started walking again, dragging her along. Horrible images filled her mind; images of Edenby. Dear God! How many of her people still lived? What of poor Edwyna? Of Anne? Of Tamkin—who had been in the room with her that terrible night? Dearest God! She shuddered to think of Edwyna, gentle Edwyna who had wanted nothing to do with treachery, left to pay the price.

"Oh, God!" she wailed aloud, barely aware that the sound escaped her.

He stopped once again, looking down at her upturned face with another cordial—and deathly—smile.

"What now, my lady?" he mocked.

She wrenched her arm from his hold, trembling yet determined at all costs never to let him know her fear. "What did you do in Edenby?" she demanded furiously. "Slaughter innocents who had no part or parcel in the war fought against you?"

"Precisely," he said coolly. He waved an encompassing arm. "The people of Edenby line the great walls—they hang from them, they rot in gibbets from them! Not a one was spared, my lady!"

She backed away from him, again not knowing if he told the truth or not. He stepped forward, grasping her so tightly again that she cried out. He did not start walking but led her to one of the great mullioned windows that lined the wall.

"See below, my dear Lady Genevieve?" he taunted, and she did see below. In a sheltered courtyard a whipping post had been set. Men in shackles were being dragged to it—to face lashes for some infractions against the new Tudor King. Genevieve tried to turn away; he forced her to remain there, lifting her chin so that she could not hide her eyes.

"Tudor justice is careful—but strict. If you continue to plague me now, I might be tempted to see your garrulous spirit tamed a bit at the hands of these stout fellows before we take our leave!"

"What difference does it make?" she demanded coldly. "A lash in their hands or one in yours? I dare say that the blows would be softer from those men! I'd prefer justice here!"

"Really?" he inquired politely. "Just as you'd prefer the Tower—to being my prisoner."

"Aye, that I would!" she swore heatedly.

"You'd never leave the Tower alive," he warned her dryly.

"A good headsman can allow one to leave this life easily!" she exclaimed, and to her horror panic tinged her voice. Which brought an honest rumble of laughter from his chest.

"Ah, yes! I'd forgotten what an expert you were at death, Lady Genevieve!" he proclaimed.

She smoothed her hands over her skirt, lowering her head. "If I'm to die, Lord Tristan," she managed to say smoothly, "I'd do so here and now."

"Ah—but I've no intention of letting you die—yet," he informed her softly. "And if anyone is going to take a whip to your hide, I do reserve that pleasure for myself! Nor do I believe you're in any great hurry to depart this life. Let's go— you waste time."

Waste time! she thought, panic rising in her breast again. Oh, God, yes! She needed to waste time, she needed to play for all the time that she could get!

Did he intend to bring her to his quarters—and execute her? Or rape her first . . . No, he seemed to hate her too much to really want her—even in violence. Yet if he felt it would hurt her . . .

No, he wasn't going to murder her now. He could do many, many things to her before taking her life. He seemed to be in a great hurry to reach Edenby—perhaps part of his revenge was forcing her to see what he had done to her home!

She started to shiver as he pulled her along again. And then he stopped before a door, releasing his grip upon her arm to open it.

Genevieve panicked. She was free and young and agile— and the palace halls stretched forever; she turned to bolt away. But after one step she screamed out in pain. Tristan's other hand had been entangled in her hair all the while.

She stared at him, while he used his grip upon her hair to turn her back to him. Trembling and clamping her teeth together with all her might, she met his eyes, trying to pull her hair from his grasp. If only it were bound! He did not release her; he pulled her closer to him with that golden chain.

He didn't appear at all perturbed—merely amused.

"My lady," he mocked her softly, holding her so tight against him that his whisper touched her cheek, "bear in mind that I shall never, never trust you again. That I shall never turn my back on you."

He shoved her into the room, then entered behind her. She stood still, afraid to look at him, and afraid not to do so. She braced herself, determined to await with courage whatever would come.

But he totally ignored her, moving about the room, collecting his belongings. Genevieve continued to watch him, ready to spring away yet wondering dismally what good it would do her.

She vaguely noted that his quarters here were private and rather grand. He did indeed stand high in the Tudor King's eyes.

His scabbard and sword lay on the bed. When he reached for them, she instinctively flinched. He smiled as he strapped the scabbard about his waist.

"Dear, dear Lady Genevieve! You are jumpy, aren't you."

She disdained to give him a reply, raising her chin a shade higher even as her heart leapt.

He turned from her. She swallowed sharply and then lashed out at him.

"Tell me! Damn you, tell me! What do you intend to—to do!"

He paused, turned again, and stared at her, long and hard. And then he smiled, slowly. Shivers of remembrance tore at her. She remembered that smile so well, his wide, sensual mouth; his lips, hard upon hers—a brand she had already received, and not forgotten. That memory came to her now, robbing her of strength and courage.

"Tell me!" she cried out again, fighting for courage.

He shrugged. "Actually, milady, I'm not really quite sure yet—of everything, that is."

His tone froze any further words on her lips. He turned back and collected a slim leather satchel, then bowed slightly. "Shall we, my lady?"

"Shall we what?" she snapped out harshly.

"Why, take our leave, of course."

"Aye!" she whispered gladly, her heart racing again. They were going to leave this chamber, which his presence made so horribly small. There would be a modicum of safety for her again, for surely he would not dare harm her before a multi-tude of people!

But was that true? He had already dragged her from the King's solar . . .

He had her arm again as he opened the door this time. "My things are—" she began, but he interrupted her curtly.

"Mary will retrieve your belongings and come along at a later time."

"Mary?" she murmured nervously.

"Aye, Genevieve, I've seen your maid, of course. She is a gentle lass—not the type to anger the King. Or the new Lord of Edenby, for that matter. She'll be along."

They were in the hallway again. Genevieve spun on him the best that she could. "What of Sir Humphrey?" she demanded, her voice growing a little shrill. "You didn't—"

"Slay him in the audience chamber?" Tristan suggested. "Nay—I did not."

"Then—"

"Last answer to a question, Genevieve," Tristan warned her, his eyes narrowing to truly advise her that his patience had come to an end. "He is an old knight, very loyal. And though he played a great part in it all, he touched something in my heart—aye, Genevieve, even that organ of ice within me can be touched! Sir Humphrey has been warned that if he comes to Edenby, he will reside in the dungeons. He is a free man if he chooses to stay in London."

Genevieve lowered her head and followed him meekly for several moments as she absorbed the fact that at least Sir Humphrey would be allowed to live free and well. Tristan moved quickly, so quickly that before she was truly aware again they were outside in bright daylight. She saw a group of his men, easily recognizable by their crests and armor. They were mounted and waiting.

Mounted! She thought with renewed hope. She could ride as well as she could walk! Once they entered the part of the country that she surely knew better than they, she could escape.

"Where is my horse?" she asked, trying to make her voice sound bitterly resigned, and kept her head lowered.

But he didn't reply, and eventually she raised her eyes to him, startled to discover him watching her with a dry trace of amusement curling his lip and sparking his eyes.

"Ah, lady! It is poor reasoning to attack a man and bury him—and then take him for a fool as well! Your horse, like your things, will come later. For this journey you will travel in a very certain style!"

Before she knew it, she was off her feet again. He was carrying her down the muddy road—to deposit her ungraciously in a rickety carriage. She struggled for balance, to sit up. "Wait! I cannot ride in such a thing! It will make me ill! Let me out!" She pounded against the door and fought with the handle. It would not budge. Even as she bitterly banged against it, she heard the sharp crack of a whip. The carriage bolted, sending her flying against the other side. Her temple slammed hard against the opposing seat, and she cried out, rubbing it as she tried to right herself.

It was ridiculous to attempt to stay upright. Tristan intended to waste no time again. The wheels of the carriage careened over every rock and gouge in the muddy road.

And the pace continued, forcing Genevieve to think of nothing but the preservation of her flesh. It seemed forever before the carriage slowed somewhat, and then the journey became a monotonous one. Now she had time to speculate on her fate.

Wretchedly, she pulled off the torn remnants of the headdress that had been so beautiful and elegant only that morning. He was going to take his time killing her, she thought dismally. He was waiting, moving slowly to assure himself that she would die a dozen times over before it really came to pass . . .

No! She would never give him that satisfaction. She would never let him see her frightened. Never! Though terror fills me! she vowed to herself, I will never let that Lancastrian son of Satan see that I am afraid.

She clenched her fists. Believe it, with all your faith, and you will stay proud and untouched! she promised herself. The thought helped to calm her.

Night had fallen, she realized at some point. Yet still they did not stop. Did his sense of fury extend to horses? she wondered acidly. And then she wondered what difference any of it made at all. Worn and exhausted, she curled herself in the far corner of the carriage and eventually fell into a fitful slumber.

She awoke slowly, with a horrible sense of confusion. At first she thought that she had been dreaming again. Dreaming that she had been running and had run straight into Tristan, and found herself sinking, falling, unable to run again, unable to fight against the dark, compelling magnetism of his eyes . . .

And then she started, realizing that the horror was no dream, but truth. She was stuffed into a carriage, stiff and cramped. Light seeped in; it was morning again. The carriage had stopped.

Genevieve suddenly realized that she very badly needed to take care of certain personal necessities. Just then the carriage door swung open. The bright light flooding in blinded her, and she put a hand over her eyes.

"Good morning, Lady Genevieve," Tristan greeted her with a low bow. "I do trust that you slept well?"

She was so miserable that she couldn't even rise to his taunt. "I *have* to get out, my lord," she murmured bitterly.

"Indeed you do," he said simply, offering her a hand. She hesitated, then seeing little choice, accepted it. When her feet were on the ground, she almost fell, her legs were so cramped. His hands around her waist steadied her and sent warm currents of awareness through her limbs. She quickly stepped from his hold, eager to see what was around them.

It seemed that they were passing through one of the great forests, filled with oaks and misted, secretive beauty. All was quiet except for the occasional cry of a morning bird—and the laughter of his men, who were ranged around a carefully laid fire and eating something that gave off a wonderful aroma.

Was Tristan going to feed her, she wondered? Or was starving her to death part of his plan.

"Let's go, shall we?" he suggested.

"Let's go?" she repeated. "I have to be *alone*!"

He shook his head. "Never."

"But . . ." She stared at him with her dismay evident. Perhaps he had found one of the most cruel ways to torment her. Genevieve was both private and fastidious. She certainly could bear no one with her . . . now!

"Please?" she whispered miserably.

"The last time you said that, my lady," Tristan reminded her coolly, "I awoke to find myself buried in rock."

"Where can I go? What could I possibly do to you?" she asked a little desperately.

"I'm sure that you are full of vast resources!" he told her dryly. His dark gaze was unfathomable and his jaw was set so tightly that she was certain he meant to continue to refuse her. But then he sighed and said, "Come. We'll go to the stream. But I warn you most strictly, make no attempt to run or disappear into the trees. Or you'll never have a moment's privacy again."

They started together through the forest for the stream. A morning mist still lay heavily upon the ground, and the sensation of walking here was a strange one, made stranger still by the touch of his hand upon her arm. She chanced a quick glance up at him, wondering if he had softened toward her at all. But when his eyes met hers they were sharp and dark; he smiled slowly, and she realized that he had lost none of the intensity of his feelings. Rather he was like a hawk, knowing that he circled his prey—and awaited the moment of final attack with a wicked satisfaction.

The stream was a cool brook that rippled like a melody through the trees; its peace was oddly discordant with the leashed tension of his gaze. He released her. "There's brush just ahead," he told her curtly. "Return here immediately—or forever pay the price," he warned softly.

Moments later she looked forlornly about her. The forest was so rich and thick! It would be so easy to slip away!

With her head bowed and her teeth clenched tightly together, she returned to him. He awaited her, a foot angled idly against a tree stump, his arms crossed over his chest. She ignored him and lowered herself to the edge of the water, anxious to wash her face and rinse her teeth.

She was startled at his touch—then filled with alarm, certain that he meant to force her face into the stream and drown her there. Her eyes must have betrayed her emotion, for he laughed when he saw them and said, "I'm only trying to salvage this tangled mane here that you call hair! That's all—for the time being at least."

"You needn't!" she retorted. She didn't want his touch; she didn't want him so close beside her, she didn't want to feel the strength that emanated from his hands, or to be aware of his clean, bracing, masculine scent.

But she was very thirsty and so she forced herself to forget him and drink. After several moments she felt a tug on her hair.

"That's enough."

Tristan practically dragged her to her feet and back through the trees to the carriage. She stared down at the men by the fire with longing. Her stomach was knotted with hunger—and nauseated at the prospect of reentering the rickety carriage.

"Couldn't I stay out a moment longer?" she asked him, drawing herself up straight to ask the favor.

He shook his head. He seemed very irritated at that moment—as if she were a game of which he had suddenly grown bored. "I'll bring you something to eat."

He lifted her back into the carriage and closed the door. A moment later he returned with a wooden trencher—wild boar roasted upon the fire. It proved a little stringy and tough, but Genevieve was too hungry to care much.

The carriage rolled into action while she was still eating, and their hard ride of the day before was repeated.

Genevieve spent a long day with her own thoughts again, alternately wondering when he would pounce upon her and when and how she could possibly escape him. In the late afternoon she was brought some ale, not by Tristan, but by one of his men, a handsome polite lad named Roger de Treyne. He gave her renewed hope, as he seemed to feel some sympathy for her plight.

It was Roger who came for her the next morning. She smiled sorrowfully at him and begged him to leave when he brought her to a stream again, telling him that she needed to bathe. She pleaded so prettily that he agreed, and when he was some distance away she stripped to her shift and moved into the water to enjoy it—and survey the opposite shore.

The opposite shore . . .

She could easily swim the distance. And Tristan would not be expecting such a move on her part. The trees were thick and dense, and one could hide within their shelter for hours. For days. For months, even.

Genevieve turned around carefully. Roger was a fair distance from her; his back was most respectfully turned. Quietly she slipped beneath the water. She swam under its surface lest he hear her movements. Only when she saw the bank before her did she rise to gasp for breath and steal quietly up to the bank.

But when she reached the top she let go a cry of shock. Tristan awaited her there, leaning comfortably and silently against a large oak.

Surprise held her immobile as his dark eyes traveled slowly over her. She felt suddenly naked and very heated, aware that her linen shift was stuck to her body like a second skin, molding over her breasts and hips. Her hair was soaked and plastered all about her, and she knew she must surely look a little like some wild thing of the forest.

But he was curiously aloof—and merely tossed her his mantle to cover herself as she shivered beneath his stare.

"Don't think to seduce my men into aiding you in an escape, Genevieve," he said coolly. "I selected those who came with me on this ride very carefully. They all spent time in the dungeons at Edenby—at your command."

"You're—you're dry," she commented, her teeth chattering.

He smiled and directed her vision to a small raft drawn up to the shore down the bank. "Shall we go back?" he asked her.

A few thrusts of the single oar brought them back. Tristan reached for his mantle and tossed Genevieve the gown she had abandoned.

Genevieve struggled back into her gown. He waited, then took her arm again to propel her toward the road and her rickety carriage. She felt his touch like a chain about her. Dismay and discouragement settled over her, and a rising sense of panic. Oh, God, he was like a hawk, like a great cat, playing so skillfully with his prey!

She spun on him, finding that all her courage and poise were about to break.

"Do it!" she charged him. "Do it! Strangle me, shoot me, rip my flesh ragged! Get it over with!"

He smiled rather pleasantly. "And deny myself the ultimate joy of waiting? Nay, my lady, Edenby was my downfall. It will be yours."

"It won't!" she seethed, crossing her arms over her chest. "I'll not move! I'll—"

He shrugged, and dipped to pitch her over his shoulder. She pounded against him with a wild fury, clawing and scratching—at that moment determined to hurt him, to force him into action.

She had no effect upon him. Moments later she was being tossed back into the carriage. Like a captured wild animal, she dove for the floor. He was there. "Haven't you anything better to do than torment a woman!" she demanded, in scathing tones that she was sure would offend his pride.

"Actually, at this moment, my time is quite free," he assured her. "And of course, you, Lady Genevieve, are certainly not just any woman."

The carriage closed despite her shrill protests.

The next day, it was Tristan who came for her. She didn't say a word to him and moved along stiffly.

But after she had washed her face, she felt a new rising of alarm again, for when she turned to him he hoarsely ordered her to get to her knees.

This was it . . .

Whatever it was. Would he slay her, maim her, cut her?

"No . . ." she gasped out. She didn't want to be afraid. She didn't want to falter.

He made an impatient sound and his hands came to her shoulders forcing her down. It was horrible . . . she couldn't see him, she didn't know . . . She braced herself—waiting a knife to slit through her throat. She was stunned to feel his thighs, hard and heated beneath his hose, at her back.

And his fingers—pulling at her hair with little gentleness as he raked a comb through it.

Kneeling there and shaking, she couldn't protest the treatment, but remained as still as she could. No words passed between them for the long time he took, and when he was done with the mass of tresses, he curtly told her that she could rise.

She rose and stared at him. He returned her gaze. She was still trembling so that she was afraid that she would fall. He reached for her and seemed startled at the way she shook. He arched a brow with interest and she lowered her eyes quickly.

"I—I thought . . ." she began.

"You thought what?"

"That you were going to—to—"

"Slay you—from behind?"

"I—yes."

He was silent for a moment. More weary than taunting when he murmured, "Nay, lady, knives in the back are your field of expertise, not mine."

"Sir, I did not expect you to care about the state of a captive enemy's hair."

"Then you were gravely mistaken. That hair is a treasure, and it is mine."

She didn't know what to think or feel; she fled from him toward the carriage. For once, she entered that particular prison without his help.

They reached Edenby in the late afternoon of the next day, when the sun was falling and shadows were long and all was still bathed in a glow of softest crimson and gold.

Roused from lethargy in her continual habitat in the corner of the carriage, Genevieve started, aware that they were there as she heard Tristan shouting to the man at the gatehouse.

Her heart sank with fresh despair. It was true: he had taken Edenby. Somehow, her heart had fought against that reality. She could not see out of the carriage, but images filled her eyes of her people, her guards, her farmers and craftsmen, hanging from ropes and gibbets from the castle walls. With dark despair, she began to wonder about Edwyna again. And

Tamkin. And little Anne! Surely not even Tristan would have hurt a child . . .

The carriage moved past the gates. She could feel the direction. Then it came to a halt. The door was opened, and Tristan was there. Smiling with vast amusement, his eyes deep and dark with the fire of the lanterns about them.

"Edenby, Genevieve." He reached for her and lifted her high, whispering as she slid against the length of his body to stand. "Your time has indeed come, my lady."

She wrenched away from his hold, watching him in dismay. He chuckled devilishly and caught her wrist with a grip that brought her spinning back to him.

"Have you no pleas tonight, my lady?" he mocked. "Aren't you going to beg mercy—or better yet, to amuse me—and save your poor people from my wrath—and the horror of a Lancastrian rule?"

"I'll never plead!" she snapped to him, but her knees were shaking. The men who had ridden with them were fading away through the bailey; she looked about herself, wondering if there wasn't some help somewhere . . .

There was not. They were alone before the doors to the great hall. What lay within? Lancastrian louts, defiling all that had been hers?

"Will you walk in? Or shall I carry you? I'm very sorry, but our business will have to wait awhile as I've pressing affairs to attend to here."

She turned and headed for the doors, then paused.

"Oh, excuse me. Am I going the right way? Or should I be heading for the dungeons?"

"Later, perhaps," he replied idly. Then she saw his white smile slash across the hard bronze contours of his face again. "I've waited for tonight for a long time. Eons, milady." He bowed, the knight, the master of chivalry. He spat out an order from between clenched teeth. "Move!"

God, what his voice could do to her! Soft, harsh, soft again. What fear it could elicit; and a liquid heat that made her feel she would, at last, faint and take her refuge in oblivion!

She turned and bolted. If she could reach the rear gate, she could climb to the cliff and escape—either across the rocks or by the sea.

It was a futile attempt and she had known it would be—but what could she do but fight it out?

He caught her by the train of her dress this time and merely sighed as he tossed her over his shoulder. She twisted furiously, trying to bite and kick and claw. It was useless. She was almost in tears as they entered the keep. For herself—and for the horror she was convinced she would find inside the banqueting hall.

"Tristan!" a voice interrupted Genevieve's desperate thoughts.

It was the young and handsome Lancastrian who greeted him, grinning his amusement at the wild burden his friend carried. With a struggle, Genevieve at last wound herself in a position to see his face; he threw her an amused glance, then addressed his leader.

"All's well enough here—"

"What have you done with my aunt?" Genevieve cried angrily.

"Let me deposit the lady," Tristan said dryly, "and I'll meet with you in the counting room."

"Wait!" Genevieve shouted. Perhaps she had betrayed this man, but he seemed to have a semblance of a heart. "Please! What has happened to—"

"Edwyna sits by the fire," he told her gently, and they entered the hall. And sure enough, Edwyna was there—very pale and with a look of misery in her eyes. She appeared otherwise very well and healthy; regally attired and as elegant as ever.

"Edwyna!" Genevieve gasped.

Edwyna started to race for her. She was caught by Tristan's young friend—gently secured by his arms about her waist. "No, Edwyna," he told her very softly. "You cannot interfere."

Stunned, Genevieve continued to stare at her aunt while Tristan headed for the winding stairway. Edwyna's eyes followed her as far as possible—large and blue and liquid with concern.

"She alive!" Genevieve gasped out.

"Of course she's alive," Tristan said irritably. "Your aunt is no back-biting tigress!"

Did that mean that Edwyna was alive, while she, Genevieve, would not be? Genevieve started to struggle again. He swore softly and set her to her feet, winding his hand into her hair to keep her immobile. They reached the door to her chamber and she realized dismally that he was lifting an outer bolt that had never been there before.

Tristan pushed her inside, and she staggered to keep her balance. Then he stood, towering, at the door, and addressed her sarcastically.

"I truly am sorry to leave you so, but alas! There are things that must be attended to! Bathe, my lady, at your leisure—find comfort, for I swear I will return at the first available moment."

Smiling, bowing, he left her.

She heard the bolt slide tight across the door.

Jon and Tibald awaited Tristan in the counting room. Both appeared pleasantly relaxed—and quite happy with life, which pleased Tristan because he knew it meant that the takeover had indeed been smooth.

He took the seat behind the desk to listen to their reports. Tibald told him that the majority of the old guard remained in the dungeons—they couldn't yet risk releasing them. But the farmers and craftsmen were at their work; the servants were at times a little sullen, but no one had offered a protest against the new order.

"I had the man Tamkin in the dungeon," Jon informed Tristan dryly. "But I have him sequestered here now in one of the towers. He knows the rents and the land allotments, and is most capable with the grain and mill reports. I know that he battled with you that night, yet it was not my place to take measures against him." Jon shrugged. "He trembles daily as it is—awaiting your return."

"Umm," Tristan murmured dryly, taking a long draught of the ale that had been brought him.

"What will you do?" Jon asked curiously.

"I don't know yet," Tristan replied thoughtfully. "Something must be done to instill a respect for authority. I don't know . . . perhaps a flogging. The man will live—yet the people will see that they cannot oppose us." He exhaled, and flexed and unflexed his fingers. They had ridden hard and he was tired—and he still had Genevieve to deal with.

Nor did he quite know yet what he wanted from her—or what he intended to do with her. He was sure of only one thing: in the long days of travel he had become aware, with a damning need, of the desire she created in him, a hunger like nothing he had known before, taunting his flesh, filling his soul. She is just a woman! he told himself now, as he had many times before.

Yet that only increased his bitterness at her betrayal. Had she been a man, he would have given her a sword with which to fight—and by God, she would have lain dead when it was over. That justice was not to be, for she was a woman—one he desired with a heady fascination.

She was his right, he thought dryly. And this night she would come to know it. Whatever the future held was to be seen. This night, this night was black and white. She had invited him to her bedchamber. She had begged that he come there. Well, by God, tonight she would have him there—welcome or no.

"I believe anything else can wait until morning," he said with a long sigh. "Jon, is there a chamber where I might sleep?"

Jon gazed at him quizzically. "I had thought—"

"Oh, I plan to visit the Lady Genevieve," he said dryly. "But I'd never sleep beside her! My life would be worthless!"

Jon grinned. "The master chamber is down the hall. I'll see that it is quickly prepared."

Jon and Tibald rose. But before they could leave the room, there was a flurry at the door. Tristan had begun to stand, but he was knocked back to his chair by the Lady Edwyna, who was now placing her slender hands upon his knees and beseeching him with tear-stained eyes.

"Don't slay her! My lord, I beg you! She is young—she had no choice! Oh, I swear it distressed her so—she had no choice, can't you see? She but fought an enemy! I know . . . I—Jon has told me about your wife. But surely, Lord Tristan, you are above such atrocities yourself! Please, Lord Tristan—''

"Edwyna!" He caught her face between his hands and stared into her huge, brilliant blue eyes, aware then of what so entranced Jon. He was angry with Jon for having spoken of his tragedy. "I have no intention of slaying a woman, Lady Edwyna," he said a little harshly. His glance flew to Jon, who looked uneasy. "But I warn you that the story of my life is not to be the stuff of idle chatter!" He stared again at Edwyna. "You may rest easy— she will not die. But she is a prisoner in this castle and will remain so. That no amount of tender tears can change.''

Edwyna lowered her head. Her voice trembled. "I thank you," she murmured.

"Edwyna!" Jon said sharply. She rose and joined him at the door, looking back to Tristan. "My lord, I have not been a prisoner here. Why should—"

"You are not a prisoner, my lady," Tristan said flatly, "because you have apparently proven yourself quite resigned to the situation—and trustworthy now. Demonstrate otherwise and you will find your life quite different.''

"But, my Lord, surely—" Edwyna began.

"Jon, Tibald, Lady Edwyna, good-night," Tristan said firmly. He raised a brow to Jon.

Jon clamped a tight arm about Edwyna and led her quickly from the room. Tibald grinned, shaking his head, and left the counting room.

Tristan thoughtfully finished his ale, then decided that he had indeed waited long enough. The longer he sat here, the more his anger flared. He closed his eyes and called to mind a vision of her at his knees, begging; then another vision of Genevieve standing before him with the poker dripping his blood.

He stood resolutely.

It was time to remind the lady of the warning he'd given her—not to make a promise that she didn't fully intend to keep.

Chapter
Ten

GENEVIEVE PACED ABOUT her chamber, near panic. Once—it seemed a lifetime ago!—she had vowed that she would never be afraid of a Lancastrian whether peasant or king.

But that was before she had seen Tristan at court. So deadly calm, his eyes black glittering pits of burning hell, his soft words carrying a threat that made her shiver even now with the memory.

Wildly, for the hundreth time, she tried the door; tears of weary frustration rose to her eyes. It did not budge.

She moved back into the chamber, stepping up to the dais and regarding the tub of bathwater before the fire. The tub had been there, hot and steamy and awaiting her, as if someone had known they would arrive that night. Maybe someone had known. Perhaps Tristan had sent a rider on ahead.

She had bathed quickly, with terror gripping her at any sound from below. She had not intended to be caught by him in the tub. So she had washed in a frenzy.

But—as he had so curtly told her—he had been busy. He had *not* come. She had leapt from the tub and dressed in the fine blue velvet that someone had left out for her. And now she paced, barely conscious that she continually pulled at the strings of her low-cut bodice, trying to cover herself more effectively.

She paused, closing her eyes, praying for courage. Did he intend to murder her himself tonight? Perhaps with the very poker she had used against him?

Oh, damn him! He truly knew how to draw out torture and vengeance. Better that he had claimed her head at Court, when she retained some semblance of fatalistic courage, than to drag her back all that distance and leave her to these hours of gnawing fear.

Genevieve opened her eyes, and they fell on the tapestry across the room that covered the windows—merely archers' slits, and very narrow. She was slim and agile; it was possible that she could squeeze through and leap to the parapet beneath. She could also break a leg, she reminded herself. But what was the threat of a broken leg in comparison to the vengeance that awaited at the hands of Tristan de la Tere?

She crossed the room to the windows, tearing desperately at the tapestry of her father's hunt. It fell to the ground, and she looked at the slit with rising dismay. It was higher from the ground than she had thought, and narrower. But still . . . if she twisted and flattened herself, clearing her shoulders and then her hips . . .

She turned around again and spotted the stool before her dressing table. She raced for it, and breathing raggedly, she dragged it to the wall beneath the window. She hopped up on it and pulled herself up, shivering as she looked below. The parapet seemed a long distance away.

It was then that the door to the chamber slammed inward. The sound itself churned new terror in Genevieve's heart; the stool beneath her fell away, but she hung on to the window. She twisted instinctively and saw Tristan, implacable, observing her efforts from the doorway. His sword was at his side, as always, and his hands were upon his hips. His silhouette nearly filled the doorway; the arch barely seemed to top his head, and his mantle floated about him. He appeared majestic— and totally ruthless.

Genevieve let out a moan and clawed desperately at the stone. Her moment of reckoning had come.

She pushed herself frantically—she was almost through!

But hands like steel clamped her around the waist; she was dragged down and cast to the floor. She landed hard and gasped for breath, brushing the hair from her eyes.

Genevieve's terrified vision fell upon Tristan's boots, planted wide apart. She scooted backward, then along the wall, to put distance between them. Then she forced her eyes to move upward, to the tops of his boots, to his thigh muscles bulging against the tight leather of his breeches, to the hem of his tunic. Clenching her teeth and swallowing briefly—and offering up a last plaintive prayer—she forced her eyes up the lean sector of his hips and the forbidding breadth of his chest to meet his eyes, willing her own to be wide and defiant and scornful.

"That was rather foolish, don't you think?" he inquired politely, reaching down a hand to help her rise. She stared at it, but did not take it, preferring to rise by her own power.

"No," she said flatly. Her back was to the wall as he took a step closer, not touching her but not freeing her from the deadly dark heat of his eyes. She shuddered, holding the stone behind her with her palms for support. His words were smooth and coolly spoken, but his fury was so tangible it smouldered in the very air, like dry lightning cracking the sky on a summer's night.

Tristan smiled slowly, a dry, twisted, humorless grin, and walked away from her, unbuckling his scabbard, dropping it on one of the chairs before the fire.

"Was that an escape attempt—or a wish for suicide?" he asked her casually.

"Does it matter?" she replied.

He shrugged, walked over to the bed, and sat. "Not particularly," he told her. He kept watching her as he pulled off his boots, and his face was an enigma. A slight trace of amusement suddenly seemed to touch his features, but his eyes were still brilliant with a smouldering, deep-seated rage.

Her eyes fell inadvertently to his scabbard and his sword. He followed her gaze and smiled more fully. "Were you thinking of turning my own sword against me?"

She lifted her chin. "The thought had crossed my mind."

He raised a brow slightly. Suddenly panic and desperation

took over in Genevieve. With a sharp cry, she pushed herself away from the wall and raced desperately to the door. As she lifted the bar, it was slammed back into place. She turned; he was behind her. Tears began to blur her vision, but she would not let him see them. She would not be humbled; she had *sworn* not to cower.

She spun on him, lashing out with desperate hands. He made no comment but his face was set grimly as he secured her wrists. Genevieve brought her knee against his groin with a vengeance, and he swore, momentarily losing his hold upon her. Like a gazelle, she leapt past him, plunging over the bed and making a desperate dive for his sword. It came free in her hand, and she rolled to her back to raise it against him. He stood over her now, but paused warily as he looked from her eyes to the glinting steel of the blade. He smiled, backed up a shade, and bowed. "Would you come and get me then, lady? I'd see you try."

"I will!" she cried out. "I will skewer you through, I'll lay you open!" Bracing herself with one hand against the chair, she carefully rose, inching toward him with the threat. His smile seemed almost real then, youthful and truly amused. He certainly wasn't frightened.

"I swear," she repeated, "I'll kill you!"

"Oh, I've no doubt you'll try!" he said dryly. "Believe me, Genevieve—I've not forgotten your last attempt! Yet, I'm not as easy to kill as you may have hoped."

"I don't want to—"

Her words were broken by a cry of dismay as he kicked out, his foot rising with a sure, stunning swiftness to send the blade flying, like a silver bird of the night, over his shoulder, far from her hand.

Genevieve gasped. Tristan casually retrieved the blade from the floor. She dared not move, could not move, when he turned with it, and brought the tip of the cold steel to her throat.

"Lady," he said softly, "you do taunt death."

"Then kill me!" she retorted, "and have done with it!" But the words were a lie; she knew it. Her voice wavered as she spoke them.

He smiled slightly, and his gaze moved over her. A muscle rippled against his shirt, and the breath left her as the point of his sword fell against the soft flesh at her throat. She thought he meant to slay her then, for he dexterously moved the sword against her. But he drew no blood. The blade clipped away the ties that held her bodice together, and left the material gaping her breasts freed.

She did not move; she froze, paralyzed. She looked at him, and he shrugged and walked to the mantel. He twisted the sword in the firelight. "I've no intention to kill you, Genevieve," he said at last. "God knows, it would be my right. But I have a knight's code of honor. Yet," he turned to her, speaking in a slow drawl, "I've no compunction about seeing you beaten at a whipping post. A rather easy punishment, really for a murdering, lying, traitorous little bitch."

Genevieve trembled. "I was never a traitor to the Crown I recognized," she murmured, turning away and staring at the floor.

She heard a movement behind her, and the sound of something falling. Surreptitiously she looked out from the corner of her eyes. Tristan had taken off his leather tunic and tossed it onto the chair over his sword. Genevieve drew in a sharp breath as he removed his fine white linen shirt. Uneasily aware of the fascinating bare chest and shoulders, of his hard, muscular build, she forced her glance elsewhere.

"Well?" he said impatiently. "I am waiting."

The warning demand in his voice caused her to turn uneasily. "For what?"

"The fulfillment of a promise."

Firelight touched his shoulders and chest, gleaming golden against them, and delineating all the line of sinew and tendon and muscle. His eyes, too, had caught the fire. He looked like a devil standing there, hands impatiently on his hips, tall and tense and powerful.

Then he smiled slowly, mockingly. "This is—approximately, I believe—where we started out, isn't it? Actually, I'm mistaken. I was here by the fire. And you were kneeling at my feet, begging that I take you, in this very bed. Have you forgotten your promise? To please me? To come to me like a tender bride? I have not," he said very coldly. "I gave you every chance to back out—but you were so very insistent, lady! Of course I didn't know what you had in mind. I did warn you, Genevieve, that if you made a promise to me, you would keep it. And by God, lady, you shall."

An hysterical little laugh escaped Genevieve. She quickly stilled it. "You . . . despise me!"

"Aye, that I do!" he said bitterly.

"Then . . ." she managed to whisper.

"I have decided that I do *want* you, Genevieve. And the one has very little to do with the other."

"Where is your fine, Lancastrian gallantry?" she demanded sharply.

"It was buried alive on a clifftop," he replied curtly.

"You said that you did not make war upon women!"

"Lady, you gave up any concessions that might be made to your fair sex when you tricked me. Your promise will be fulfilled—with or without your cooperation. It is the one thing that I have vowed. A promise I made to myself, Genevieve, while I lay dying in a rocky grave." He tilted his head slightly, and his bitter smile was back in place. "Come here, milady. We begin now."

She shook her head. "I'll never come to you—never!"

"Then, Genevieve," with a slight mocking bow, "I will come to you."

"No. *No!*" she choked out in rage and desperation. He strode calmly toward her, and she spun blindly about to run— anywhere. But his hands were entwined in her hair, and as she tried to bolt he dragged her back. A cry of pain and frustration escaped her. She was spun into his arms, her golden web of hair tangling about his shoulders and chest.

Now his hands began to move with purpose, touching her throat, easing down it and slipping to her bare shoulders. An impatient flick of his fingers sent her torn gown sliding to her feet. Genevieve gasped out in horror as her naked breasts came in contact with the hairy roughness of his bare chest. She tried to raise her fists against him, but he pinned them in a steely grasp. She tried to kick him again, and instantly found herself off her feet and in his arms. His hold was like rock around her; no matter how she choked and tried to tear at his flesh, she was imprisoned. She raised her eyes to his and saw no sign of mercy; the grim line of his mouth showed no pity. "No!" she shrieked.

But he was oblivious to her cry, and terribly purposeful. He walked to the bed and tore back draperies as he tossed her on it. "I've yet," he told her quite calmly, "to really see this great bounty I've been—promised."

She tried to roll off the bed. He was beside her, leaning on an elbow and pinning her by the hair. He reached serenely for the bedside candle, brought it high above her, and surveyed her as she lay there—trapped, exhausted, spent, gasping, and trembling. Then he sniffed with disdain, blew out the candle and returned it to his post.

He rose, and for a moment she was free. She could not look at him. She heard his breeches drop to the floor, and then a lighter sound, that of his hose falling.

Like a wounded animal, Genevieve kept fighting. She rolled from the bed and sprang to her feet, but in the darkened room she could see nothing. She stumbled at the edge of the dais, and cried out when she felt Tristan's hands on her naked flesh, his rough palms, his long and powerful fingers. He lifted her, and in the pale ghost of moonlight she met his eyes, feeling tears rise to hers in earnest now. "You are a beast, an animal of the lowest form!" she cried. "Never have I met a man so atrociously cruel!"

He went deathly still for a moment. She felt all the tension in him like a great wall of heat.

"Cruel, lady?" he snapped back to her. "You know nothing of cruelty! Cruelty is a knife in the belly, a line of blood about the throat, the murder of an unborn infant!"

He moved again, with erratic steps now. He tore at the draperies and ripped them from the canopy. Clinging to him, Genevieve knew a whole new terror—and remorse.

What had she said to him? Why had his face taken on such heedless menace, such a threat of ruthlessness? She shivered furiously, suddenly aware that he was completely naked, as was she. That his hands were on her flesh, hot burning brands. That his body was hard like rock, and that it was heated, explosive power where it touched hers.

Dazed and newly terrified by the change in him, Genevieve could fight no longer. He tossed her down onto the mattress. And then he was beside her, on her; she felt his masculinity against her thigh, and it caused within her great heaving shudders—for his huge sheath pulsed like thunder against her naked flesh. He was one length of muscle, hard and unrelenting. As hard as the hell's fire promise of his eyes. No weakness, no vulnerability: his hatred of her was now fully unleashed. Genevieve was too stunned by the primitive, raw maleness of him, taut and rugged and overwhelming, to even move.

He raised himself over her, that fire in his eyes, a ruthless clench to his jaw, and at last she cried out; she had failed, she was a coward—but she was ready to cry for mercy.

"Please!" she whispered raggedly. "Please!" His knee had wedged between her own; she felt him against her inner thigh, hot against the portals of her virginity. Tears sprang to her eyes, and she hated herself, but she had to plead. "I fought the only way I could. I—please—I never really wished to kill! Don't you understand? I was desperate. You had the strength . . . you still have the strength! I had to use what weaponry I had. I—" Her voice trailed away in a whisper as she stared at him, with naked beseechment softening her eyes to crystal mauve.

Again her words seemed to strike a chord. His determination remained, and he did not shift from her. But his lashes lowered warily, and it seemed that the line of his mouth softened.

"Please what?" he asked her hoarsely. "Do you still think that men line the chamber, my lady? That they will come to your rescue at any time? They will not, I assure you. Tonight is it, my lady. The fulfillment of your promise. So tell me—honestly, if you are capable of honesty—what it is you seek."

She closed her eyes, shuddering, and her voice came out as nothing more than a whisper. "Please—don't hurt me."

"Then remember your promise, Genevieve. Your vow that

night, to come to me as tenderly as a bride. Seek to hurt me no longer. I have borne the brunt not only of a poker well wielded in your hands, but the rage of your fists, your nails, your teeth—and your knee.''

She didn't dare open her eyes or trust the hint of amusement in his tone. But she could feel him with all of her being, with the length of her body and flesh. She was acutely sensitive to him, aware of him; his hair-covered legs and chest; his lean hips—corded, hard muscles; his pulsing . . . masculinity.

He was still above her, very still for a long, long time. Then his weight eased beside her. She could not open her eyes.

Then he touched her again, but now his touch was so light that she almost arched instinctively to feel it more. His palm grazed over her, over her midriff, over her hip, in a slow, stroking motion. It moved and moved . . . His palm came to rest on her breast, and his fingers closed gently there, testing the weight, coursing over her nipple. She made a little sound, a ragged gasp of protest, and he whispered something that she did not hear, and yet the spell of it caused her to remain still, trembling beneath his touch.

''Be still . . . lie easy.''

It seemed that she lay there forever, trembling, taut, as he stroked her, whispering. She had fought; she had lost. She could fight no more. She could only close her eyes to his touch.

He was gentle and patient; in time she ceased to tremble. He lulled her, bound her by a certain spell. It was not acquiescence, and yet . . . the fear slowly drained from her. The feel of his hands was not hurtful . . . but soothing. As if it played upon something deep inside of her, something that could not help softly responding . . .

In the pale moonlight his magic played on. His patience was endless. She vaguely realized that she was surrendering on a level far different than merely succumbing to his overwhelming strength.

His touch . . . she became achingly alive. Her body was cool, yet where he touched she felt heat, and where he did not touch she began to long for him. Not for Tristan de la Tere, her enemy, but for the male force beside her. In a corner of her mind she knew who he was, but that corner began to recede, pushed there by the rising sensations that left room for nothing else. Genevieve was alive as she had never been before.

She whimpered again when he shifted, lowering his dark head against her, taking her breast into his mouth, and playing the nipple subtly with his tongue. The pressure of his mouth increased, then he was tugging slightly, surrounding, and just touching the nipple again.

She couldn't remember now they got here, but her fingers were entwined in his hair. Unconsciously she raised her knee slightly, angling one leg slightly over the other as a sweetness suddenly grew inside of her. She inhaled the rich scent of him, clean and musky and male, and the sweetness increased, seeping like a slow fog throughout her, but most intense at some secret, intimate center.

His lips moved to the valley of her breasts, hovered there, then he nursed the other. She gasped. Her hands fell to his shoulder and she trembled at the feel of muscles beneath his skin, at the strength under her fingers. As a man, he was beautiful: strong and hard and lean; healthy and virile. And . . .

At last his mouth came to hers. He stared at her just a moment in the darkness, then took her cheeks between his hands and touched his lips to hers. He moistened her lips with his tongue, then with a gentle force parted her lips. The kiss was deep, his mouth open wide, his tongue plunging ever deeper; and in the moist heat and intimacy, Genevieve found the same invading sweetness. She should be hating him, but she could not hate the sensation; and in his spell sensation was all that the night had become.

Instinctively she gasped as his hands roamed her body again, sliding, stroking her thighs, forcing her knees apart. She whimpered a protest against his mouth and he slowly broke the kiss, whispering to her with lips just above her own. "Easy . . . easy . . . let me touch you." She clung to his shoulders, trying not to jerk or protest, and his mouth met hers again, hungry and fusing, distracting and not distracting her from the movement of his hand along the flesh of her thigh at the juncture of her legs. Her nails dug into his back at the searing sensation and the shock of the intimacy. He looked at her and smiled slightly—still a demon's grin, still mocking, yet he looked so much gentler than the man she had thought would kill her earlier. "Easy," was all that he murmured to her again.

He touched her lips lightly, and then she felt a delicious shudder, filled with that sweetness as the heated length of his flesh rubbed against hers slowly. Again her breasts felt the touch of his tongue, her belly was teased by it, and then her legs were parted—and he touched her with an intimate caress of his mouth that shot through her like wildfire, causing her to shake and cry out. She wriggled; his hands caught hers and clenched them tightly, and the delving of his kiss and the play of his tongue caused lightning to cascade all through her. She tossed her head back and forth, whimpering that she hated him, then whimpering that . . . she could bear no more. She heard him chuckle; at last he rose above her, his hands still laced with hers, and for a moment she did hate him for the look of triumph on his face. Still she felt a surge, like molten lava, where he had been. He pressed her hands beside her head and lowered his face to hers, kissing her mouth again, slowly, slowly lowering the weight of his body over hers, spreading her legs still farther with his own. She was shaking, twisting; wanting him, and wanting to free herself from him; and yet she could not even unwind her fingers from his—she clung to them desperately.

"Is this your first time?" he muttered to her.

She bit her lip and answered hoarsely, furious, insulted, that he should ask. "Aye!" She hated him for speaking; his words broke the spell she had woven.

"Then I cannot ease it completely," he told her. She felt her dislike of him deepen. It was a night's worry for him; but for her it was a moment in life that would never come again.

"I do hate you!" she whispered harshly. His smile was bitter as he took her lips again. He freed her hands, and she wrapped her arms around his back, to steady herself against his kiss—demanding and plundering, somehow still coercive, sweeping her again into the realm of sensation. He shifted, and his fingers played intimately with her again, bringing a fresh rise of whimpers from her throat.

But when next he shifted the pain was a shock; choking and gasping, she longed to wrench him from her, but he held her steady. His voice held no trace of mockery.

''Be calm, be easy . . .'' he repeated the words, remaining still, allowing her to adjust to the burning shaft of himself inside her. Hot tears stung her eyes, but he continued to whisper little things, and he moved his palm over her breast again, then suckled it with his mouth, then kissed her lips with an all-consuming passion as he began to move slowly, fluidly.

She would never know where the pain ended—and the sweet, driving rapture began. At first he seemed so alien—a presence that split her asunder, too hot, too thrusting, too deep and hard, to ever be absorbed. But her body did absorb him, melded and fused and writhed to his rhythm. His movements were at first long and slow, and then sped up, with a wild and wanton eroticism. The dulcet tones of a melody seemed to streak through her. She shivered and quaked, and felt the fluid motion of his body, its hardness next to hers, the bunch and tremor and play of his muscles, the pressure of his lean hips. A throbbing started in her, the thunder of his thrust increased, and she pressed her face against his shoulder, crying out. The throbbing, hungry need within her soared. A blinding, reckless beat swept through and around her, and she spun on clouds, tempestuously thrown to the heavens by the relentless crashing waves of the cliffside sea. Something seemed to ignite and explode, and for one glorious moment nothing else existed except for the sunsweet beauty of the sensation, drenching her and filling her. She was barely aware as he drove into her one last time with a shattering force; he groaned and relaxed as his seed spilled into her.

Staring blankly into the darkness, Genevieve realized with a sudden and painful clarity that she had totally capitulated to him. Her pride, her fear—all seemed to crumble about her like a shower of broken glass. Here, tonight, she had lost the one real battle she had been given to fight.

She turned from him, her shoulders covered in a fine sheen

of sweat, and pressed her face into the pillow. A ragged sob escaped her and she tried to pull further away; she could not, her hair was splayed beneath his body.

She felt his thumb, grazing over her cheek.

"You're crying now?" he asked her.

Careless of her hair, she wrenched furiously from his touch. "I believe that mine is quite a customary reaction to rape!"

He started to laugh, and the sound increased her humiliation. "Lady, I hope you never learn the true meaning of the word." For a moment he was silent.

"You will certainly walk again," he told her acidly. "I say it again: you have yet to know true cruelty—or the meaning of real atrocity. And though you did not perhaps leap into my arms, you did, my lady, do quite well—for a start—in the fulfillment of your promise."

"No . . ." she protested feebly. "I hate you!"

"Hmm. Well, dear Concubine, hate away. I'd say that we've begun." He ran a finger along the length of her arm. She tried to shake him away.

"Don't! You've done your damage! Leave me alone!"

Again his laughter filled the night, and now there was honest amusement in it, warm and lulling. She could not protest him when he forced her around to face him.

"Nay, lady! Done my damage! Why we've just begun! I wouldn't dream of denying you a true chance to prove your worth, and discover deeper delights!"

"Delights! I scorn your touch—"

"Always the liar, aren't you, Genevieve? But we'll see if we can't cure you of that!"

She instinctively lifted a hand to strike him; he caught it, still chuckling. And when he lowered his head to kiss her, dulcet tremors raked her spine; her flesh, attuned now to his, burned and trembled with anticipation.

But he broke away from her, still amused. "A pity I'm in desperate need of sleep," he told her, rising and reaching for his shirt. "But don't despair—I'll see that you're not neglected."

Genevieve made a mad scramble for the covers, pulling them about herself and watching him with wary surprise. He had said that he needed sleep, yet he was dressing. Thank God! she assured herself quickly, yet she didn't understand or trust his departure.

"You're—going to leave me alone?" she asked, lowering her head quickly at the hopeful tone of her words.

"I told you—I need to sleep," he said curtly, stepping into his breeches. "And lady, I'd never turn my back on you."

Carrying his boots, he headed for the door. Genevieve called out to him.

"You—you mean that I may keep my own chamber? Alone?"

He smiled. "Alone except for those times when I choose to occupy it." He shrugged. "Aye, you may keep it. Unless, of course, I tire of torturing you. Then you may be ousted to a dungeon. I haven't quite decided yet."

"Dear God," Genevieve said slowly, her voice lowering to a growl as she began to understand her role in his life. "You are the most vile, most loathsome, most—"

"Good-night, Genevieve," he told her coolly, and left.

She stared at the closed door for a long moment, then flew from the bed heedless of her nakedness.

She hurled herself against the door; as she had expected, it was barred from the outside. Shaking suddenly from the cold, she slowly sank against it, folding her arms over her tender breasts. She became suddenly aware of the feel of him still about her body.

Genevieve burst into a ragged fury of tears.

Chapter
Eleven

GENEVIEVE WOKE SLOWLY, with a sense of discomfort. The fire had gone out in the hearth, and she was cold. But it was morning, and the sun streamed through the archers' windows.

Tears sprang to her eyes again as she remembered last night. She hugged her pillow to her breast and sank further into the warm nest of the bed covering, wishing fervently that she could sleep again—and dream that Tristan de la Tere had never entered her life. Thinking of him brought a burning to her body, the deepest sense of shame she had ever known.

Briefly she cried—but most of her tears were spent, for she had cried violently through so much of the night. Once he left, she had given herself over to sobbing—something that could only be done when she was alone. Never before him. She would never break before him . . .

Yet she had broken—last night.

She closed her eyes and bit her lower lip, and vowed again not to fall. The battle had been lost last night; but not the war. She could not counter his brawn. But there were other ways to surrender. Perhaps he could force her to submit, but he couldn't force her to care for him or even accept him. What was the body but a shell? she thought scornfully.

But even in her current miserable state Genevieve could not persuade herself that she had merely submitted.

She certainly wasn't going to label what she had done.

She didn't want to wallow in self-pity; and as the sun steadily brightened the room, Genevieve cast off her despondency and decided to rise. Upon that point she paused again, for she felt sore and strange and somehow unable to function properly.

"Stinking Lancastrian bastard!" she swore with soft fury. She knew she was in danger of sinking into tears again—which was exactly what she had determined not to do. She would never, never give him the pleasure of seeing her so broken. No matter what he threatened or did.

She inhaled sharply, hugging her knees to her, and she knew that that wasn't really true. She had told him that he could slay her, that he should send her to the Tower, to the block, to the hangman. That wasn't true at all, and it was one lesson that came home to her painfully that morning. She didn't want to die. She hated him, she despised him, for what he had done . . .

And for what he had forced her to feel . . .

But it was better than death. Better than feigning bravery while waiting the headsman's blade.

She stood and hurried across the cold floor to reach a trunk. She opened it quickly—half expecting to find that her things had been stolen and plundered. But they were not, and she found a soft robe to wrap about herself, and when she had done that she frowned.

It was late. Obviously very late, and no one had come to her. A little breath of hope swept to her lungs and she raced eagerly to the door, wondering if it had been unbolted with the morning.

It had not.

She stepped away from the door, squaring her shoulders. She swallowed back the bitter memory that she was his prisoner in her own home. She found new resolve and swore aloud that she would escape him. The Crown of England was such a shaky thing. There were still men on the Yorkist side with claims more credible than that of Henry Tudor! They would rise against him, just as he had risen against Richard.

And the fratricidal war would go on—as it had been, she thought wearily. More noble heads would roll.

She paused for a minute, inhaling deeply. For England, it would be best if the wars stopped here, if Henry Tudor proved himself a strong King and an effective ruler of the warring nobles. It would be best if the whole nation were to bind together and concentrate on the well-being of England's people.

A bitter smile crossed Genevieve's lips. Peace would be such a good thing, but it was hard to wish for it with her whole heart and soul when she had lost everything in the last insurrection—when she was here in her own castle as his prisoner. Last night was still so close that she could inhale and breathe his aroma upon her own flesh; she recalled it all, painful moment by painful moment. I will not remain his prisoner, she thought. I will not, I will not . . .

Genevieve had no plan, just enormous conviction. The words were all that she had, but she clung to them desperately. She had to remember who she was, that a cloak of pride and honor was all that remained that she could truly call her own.

Genevieve went to the door and banged on it. She desperately wanted a bath. She couldn't bear to feel herself, to feel him . . .

No one came when she banged on the door, although she was certain that anyone in the hall below must have heard her. She turned around with a frown.

Then her glance fell on her beautiful bed, with the draperies destroyed and the sheets . . .

A foul oath escaped her and she lost her newly regained determination for a cool pride. In a whirl of fury she wrenched the covers from the bed, swearing, and stomping them beneath her feet.

Finally her fury wore her out and she stopped, dangerously close to tears once again. She clenched her teeth, commanding herself to hold on to her anger: anger could give her the will to remain calm and patient until she found a chance to escape. If she could only convince him that she was totally untouched, really untouched, on the inside.

She shivered. Who would help her if she defied him now? He had offered a certain mercy—conqueror's mercy! she thought disdainfully—and been betrayed. Once a man had seen the deadly depths of his dark eyes and the strength of his vengeance, it seemed doubtful that he would go against the victor again . . .

Genevieve spun suddenly, aware of footsteps and laughter in the hall. She ran to the door again and banged on it, demanding that it be opened. The footsteps faded. Whoever had been there was going away again.

Puzzled, Genevieve stepped back. This was her castle! They were her servants! The men who were freemen had become so by her father's good grace. Her eyes blazed and narrowed. She understood exactly what Tristan wanted her to understand—that she was an insignificant prisoner.

Genevieve kicked the bed and was then silently sorry because her toe hurt horribly.

He probably knew how desperately she wanted a bath! But he would let her suffer and agonize and wonder.

She mulled over the prospect. Then she walked over to the door and let out a long, high-pitched scream, allowing it to fade only a second before shouting, "Fire!"

The door opened so quickly that she surmised that a guard had been before it all the while. She reacted quickly, though. While he rushed into the room, she sailed serenely out.

She was down the stairs before he missed her.

The great hall was empty; she could hear voices coming from the counting room, but she ignored them and went straight to the bell pull. As dear old Griswald appeared from the kitchen, Genevieve gave out a glad little cry and gave him a hug, which he returned. Then the gruff old man stepped away, embarrassed at overstepping his class and his bounds. "Lady, you are well! And you stand before me! I had heard—"

Griswald got no farther, for the guard had come rushing back down the stairs. Tristan and Jon emerged from the counting room, and the guard stopped short, turning a furious red beneath Tristan's hard, condemning stare.

Griswald—who loved her, Genevieve was certain!—turned around with amazing haste for his years and fled back toward the kitchen. Tristan spoke to the young guard.

"What is the meaning of this?" he asked quietly. Genevieve was amazed and annoyed to feel like a piece of furniture, being discussed as if she were not there, or worse, as if she couldn't understand the language.

Or if it didn't even matter.

"The—uh—lady screamed, milord Tristan. High and terrible, and then I heard a shout of 'fire' and I rushed in to see to it and next thing I knew . . ."

Tristan gazed at her, darkly, obscurely.

"Should you hear such a scream again, Peter, you must allow the lady to burn." With no expression he moved his eyes from Genevieve to the guard. "Is that understood?"

Peter lowered his eyes, and Genevieve felt a molten fury spread throughout her. She realized dimly that she just could not accept the truth—that nothing moved him, nothing touched him, nothing swayed him. He meant not just to keep her in Edenby against her will—he meant for her chamber, that one small place, to be her prison.

His eyes were on her again. He bowed slightly, in mockery, and actually offered an arm to her—to escort her back to her prison!

She ignored him, her heart thudding furiously. She could not admit even to herself how desperately she wanted to feel the open air against her cheeks.

She walked to the hearth; a cheery fire burned brightly here. She turned her back to him. She had to find courage. To show it, at the least. She rubbed her hands together, warming them, and spoke coolly over her shoulder.

"I am sorry to disturb the victor grabbing at his spoils, my Lord Tristan, but I experienced a horrid thirst—and a near maddening desire for a bath."

"Genevieve."

It was a dry command. She was supposed to turn around. Her heart began to flutter. If only she could reach the door. If only she could fly. Like an eagle, like a hawk. Soar, far above them all in the sky, fly to freedom.

She didn't turn around. He repeated her name irritably and still she didn't move. An oath suddenly exploded from him, and it was not without a certain kindling of fear that she heard his footsteps strike against stone as he approached her.

"Tristan—!"

It was Jon who spoke then. And in his voice Genevieve heard welcome tones of empathy.

But Tristan was not to be stopped. He kept coming—and at the last moment of his approach, Genevieve lost her nerve and swung around.

He put hands on her shoulders, and she fought back a gasp that rose to her lips. She lifted her chin and allowed scorn to burn from her eyes—but he returned that stare with eyes black as night. With his touch and his merciless gaze upon her, she quailed inwardly, terribly aware of his strength and his masculinity.

"Will you come of your own accord . . . ?"

He did not bother to state the alternative, but it was there, louder in its lack of utterance than a spoken challenge. Genevieve felt courage flood back into her.

"You've lackeys by the score to follow your commands, Lord Tristan. I shall never be one of them. You've your power and you've your might and you're on the winning side—for the moment. But I shall never bow down before you. You may take your vengeance as slowly as you like. I shall fight you every inch of the way."

He watched her for a long moment, and a spark touched his eyes. Whether it was respect, amusement, or the slow kindling of his temper, Genevieve did not know. For the duration of one heartbeat, she thought that he would give up his plans altogether—that the prospect of forgiving was tiresome. But no.

"So be it," he agreed softly, and stooped swiftly, grappling her slim form with little courtesy or care, and tossing her over his shoulder.

Her reaction was far from ladylike. Incensed and despairing, she railed against him, spitting out the most heinous oaths, kicking, raging, and beating against him. With equal determination, he remained calm and stoic, merely turning and starting for the stairway. He raised his voice just slightly to be heard above her as he spoke to Jon.

"Excuse me, Jon, will you? I shall be back presently. Nay, wait. Let's just convene again in say . . . an hour's time?"

Genevieve had no idea if Jon replied or not; panic seized her, and she instantly began to wonder if fighting this thing out at every turn was such a good idea. Aye, she could be a tremendous thorn in his side, but at what price to herself?

"Nay!" she cried, suddenly stiffening, leaving off her pitched battle and her oaths to plant her hands against his shoulders and try to strain against his form. "Nay, brave victor!" she cried, trying not to falter. "Don't let your prisoner distract you from the running of your stolen estates!"

She saw then that the wicked, gleaming spark in those night-dark eyes of his was amusement—and deadly challenge.

"Oh, I believe that my stolen estates will withstand a minor interruption," Tristan said. He curled his lip—and his smile assured her that if she meant to create trouble, he would gladly finish it with her.

"I will walk!" The words nearly choked her. To her horror, Genevieve realized that the hall was beginning to fill—with Tristan's men, with the servants, and even her own kindred. Edwyna was there, standing upon the stairway, stricken, her hand at her throat, her face ashen. And Tamkin, dear Tamkin, behind her on the stairs.

They were clearly distraught, but they didn't dare interfere. And here she was, fighting a losing battle, drawing them into it. Oh, God! She didn't want them to suffer on her behalf.

"I will walk!" she repeated in a frantic whisper.

But it was too late. He ignored the audience that assembled in silence and strode up the stairs. He excused himself with an odd and distant courtesy when they started to pass Edwyna and Tamkin.

"Please!"

It was Edwyna. At first Tristan did not stop when she put her hand upon his arm; it was as if he did not even notice her touch. But she plucked at the fabric of his shirt and he halted, waiting politely for her to speak.

"Tristan, I beg you, give me leave to see her, speak to her!"

The anguish in her tone would surely reach even a heart of the hardest stone.

But not Tristan's. He spoke kindly to Edwyna but denied her request. "Edwyna, no. In time, perhaps."

"Tristan, even the prisoners in the Tower of London are granted some concessions!" Edwyna pleaded. And Genevieve, slung over Tristan's back, was startled by her aunt's tone and her familiarity. Edwyna had accepted the Lancastrian conquerors.

Tristan sighed softly. "Nay, lady, lest this wild kin of yours destroy the peace you've found yourself. She will embroil you in her never-ending plotting, and I'd not see that. In time, perhaps."

"Please, Tristan—"

Edwyna was close to tears. Miserably Genevieve cried out to her. "For God's sake, Edwyna! Don't beg! Never plead so pathetically to one who has murdered and pillaged to steal his place above you!"

She struggled against his hold, longing to meet Edwyna's eyes. His arms tightened, a little convulsively, and she knew that she had touched a sure chord of anger in him. Still he remained courteous to Edwyna, and Genevieve—for all that she earnestly desired mercy for her aunt—bitterly resented the ease with which Edwyna had accepted her fate.

"Milady, if I may pass . . . ?"

Edwyna was left with no alternative. Genevieve managed to raise her head as Tristan's long strides set them in motion again. She was still so pale, and pain lay written across her features. Her eyes were desperately beseeching as they met Genevieve's. Give in! Those eyes pleaded. And yet Genevieve knew that she could not.

Tristan made a sudden turn, opening the door to her chamber with a sturdy kick. A second later she was set down hard upon the bed. She scrambled quickly up on her elbows, prepared again to move if she found herself under attack.

She was not, however, under attack. He stood with his feet slightly apart, hands on his hips, staring down at her. "I'd take care in the future, lady, about false alarms. Have you never read Aesop's fables? If ever this chamber should catch fire, you might well perish within it, for no man will be fooled by your cry again.''

"If you told your men to answer my summons," Genevieve stormed in return, "I would not have found such subterfuge to be necessary."

"Madam, you would have been answered in time. I was engaged, else I would have come."

"I did not want you. I wanted one of my own servants!"

"You would not have starved," Tristan answered blandly.

Genevieve rolled quickly from the bed and faced him across it. "Edwyna spoke the truth, oh noble lord," she said, with all the contempt she could muster. "Even in the Tower, one is fed—and granted visitors!"

"But you're not in the Tower, are you Genevieve?"

"I would rather be there! I've the right—"

"You've no rights. None at all, lady. You gave them up the night you tried to kill me."

Genevieve felt as if the chamber, large and airy, were closing in on her. He had that effect. When he was present, he filled the space with the sheer power of his will.

"I am at a loss to understand," she said, "why you would deny me such simple things as bathing water and sustenance—"

"You're not being denied anything," he told her. "You are simply not the grand mademoiselle here any longer; the servants are mine, not yours. When I decide—"

Genevieve simply never had learned prudence. Never. She interrupted his speech by snatching a pillow from the bed and hurtling it across at him, swearing hoarsely and unintelligibly.

He paused, obviously straining for patience, as he caught the pillow. He arched a dark brow at her to indicate the vast stupidity of her action. Genevieve could not retract it, though, and so she stared at him, uneasily aware that she was growing more and more alarmed. Her breasts rose and fell with each breath.

He looked down suddenly, finally aware that he stood on the linens Genevieve had wrenched from the bed. He looked from the bedding to her face with a hard and curious smile forming on his lips, a smile that deepened with the acute embarrassment she betrayed, a tell-tale emotion far beyond her control.

"You do have a temper, Lady Genevieve," he commented softly.

She turned away from him, quickly then, feeling defeated and frantic. She just wanted him to leave.

"I won't attempt to elude your guard again," she said. She wanted the words to be firm. They were not. They came out like a whisper, and worse, that whisper broke and faltered. "You—you can leave. Run the—your—estates."

He laughed, hollowly. "My stolen estates?"

"You cannot deny they are stolen!" she cried, and then she wondered why in God's name she had answered him. She could feel his eyes upon her back. Her knees grew weak even as she tried to stand strong.

"You needn't worry, Genevieve. You saw fit to—disturb things, and so you have done. I am disturbed. You are neglected and lacking things that you desire. I am here now. We shall remedy your grievances."

He moved to the door and called to the guard to see that food was sent to the Lady Genevieve. Then she felt his eyes on her back again. "And water, wasn't it, my lady? A tub and hot water?"

She shook her head vehemently. She didn't want it anymore—not while he was in the room.

"Oh, but you did request water! Actually, I believe it was a demand. You did ask for it . . . ? Peter, please see that the kitchen lads bring a new tub of hot water immediately."

He closed the door and leaned against it. Without turning around, she knew what he was doing, she knew how he would look; cold, ruthless.

A warm trembling took hold of her. Cold? Nay, not when he held her. Then he was fire. Yet the fire was a shell. The body, as she had assured herself, was nothing but a shell. And just as she swore that he would never really touch her, she realized that she had touched even less in him.

"Ah! Here we are!" He moved, opening the door at the sound of a soft tapping. Genevieve didn't turn. She stood still as she heard the boys grunting to bring in the tub, panting slightly to carry in the heavy pails of water and remove the tub with yesterday's bathwater. A woman spoke softly to Tristan—Addie, from the kitchen, Genevieve thought vaguely. The footsteps retreated.

The heavy door closed, the bolt fell. Was he inside with her? Or had he gone?

She spun around hopefully at last, but her hopes were dashed against the implacability of his rock-hard countenance.

His booted foot was upon a trunk and he leaned casually on an elbow, watching her. He waved an arm out to her dressing table, where a tray of food was set and then to the tub before the newly lighted hearth, sending gusts of steaming mist into the air.

"You did require a bath, milady."

He was laughing at her, enjoying her discomfort tremendously. She managed to smile sweetly and speak with sarcastic insinuation.

"Aye. I did require it. I have never felt so polluted in my life."

Her eyes lowered, long dusky lashes falling like mysterious shadows over her cheeks. Genevieve flinched slightly, wondering at her own madness to further aggravate him when she knew him to be unyielding.

He gazed at her, shaking his head as if in sympathy.

"Polluted?"

"Horrendously."

"Then by God, lady, I did you a most serious disservice! One that we shall set to rectify immediately, with all apology!"

Genevieve's eyes widened with alarm as she saw him move to her dressing table and look through the vials and bottles there. He quickly grasped one and turned to her with exuberance which, though feigned, restored all the dashing youth to his features.

"Roses! Attar of roses, yes, I think that quite appropriate, don't you?"

Genevieve could not respond. She braced herself against the wall, watching him as he strode to the tub, pouring out a measure of the liquid, inhaling as he breathed in the scent of the flower.

"Hmm!" He turned to her. "I wonder, lady, if the vial contains the fragrance of the red rose or the white. Or if it even matters, once the rose is stripped down to the basics."

Genevieve did not move or reply. She kept her eyes most warily upon him. His smile deepened, and she swallowed uneasily, for it suddenly seemed there was no maliciousness about him—just a streak of wicked mischief that was more frightening than his portent of anger and true violence.

"Can't you go back to the counting room?" she breathed out, backing away from him. "Jon! Surely it is near the time that you promised to meet with him again!"

"Nay, lady, that remains long, long minutes away. You have chastised me so severely upon my treatment of my prisoner! Now I find that prisoner just wallowing in mud and dirt and in true distress. What kind of captor would I be, to leave her so?"

He reached for her. As his strong bronzed hands closed around her, she wished with all her heart that she had waited patiently for someone to come to her.

His grip was strong, very strong, and it was as if there was a fever about his body. A tension, crackling like thunder and lightning, as explosive as gunpowder. She stared into his flashing eyes and realized with true alarm that he was not seeing the prisoner who had vowed to fight him—but the prisoner who had proved to be a more than submissive toy.

"Nay! I'll scream! Loudly, horribly! Everyone on the estate will know exactly what the new lord—"

His laughter interrupted her. "Aye, they will, won't they, madam? And if those screams continue, they will know exactly what *you* are doing . . . and those screams and cries have a certain cadence, have you noticed? Not yet, well, you will . . ."

"Oh! I hate you! Let me be!" Genevieve watched as the mischief and the laughing, reckless desire left his features. She saw the stark planes again, caught in harshness, caught in anger, and her breath wavered. How could you hate with such vehemence, and yet know such . . .

Desire. She felt it unmistakably then: Heat and excitement and a shaking in the limbs and a weakness that was also a strength . . .

No!

She cried out softly and wrenched from his hold in absolute confusion. She couldn't escape him. She knew that. She just wanted to buy some time and convince herself that she despised his touch. That this new discovery of herself in his arms had been nothing but absurd and protective instinct—and was not a strange new wonder to be coveted . . .

He caught her arm and swung her around with grim purpose on his face. Then caught her more securely about herself, but the fabric gave way under the force of his tug.

"Don't—"

She choked out the word, but he had lifted her, lifted her naked against him, and his long strides were bringing her to the steaming heat of the tub.

"Please, don't . . ."

The water, hot and aromatic, met her. He leaned over her, securing her hair over the rim of the tub. Dear God, he could move swiftly. Swiftly divest himself of boots and hose and tunic and breeches and stand, magnificent, before her.

Magnificent beast . . . she thought fleetingly. Beautifully young and rugged, muscled like steel, a power like a storm, sweeping everything in its path.

He paused for the sponge, for the soap, and then joined her. Genevieve watched with the greatest alarm as water sloshed over the tub, panic driving her heart to a staccato beat. Dearest God, it was awful, it was like a spell, it was like some terrible thing that she didn't want to see, and yet it was there. His knees drew up to hers; the tub was too small for the two of them and she felt him keenly, everywhere, and she felt again all the things that she did not want to feel . . .

Roses . . . red or white . . . it didn't matter once you got down to the basics.

That the very masculinity that gave him his power was a potent drug like no other. His hands were magic, his body hard and strong and fascinating against hers. The deep, sweeping caress of his kiss was a breathtaking spell that whirled her into a dark and hypnotic realm where she had no choice, but to gasp and call his name and surrender, not to the man, but to the sensations, to the ancient throbbing of an inner fire and a primeval rhythm . . .

He faced her. The devil's own taunt in his eyes, the mischief returned. Youth and laughter all about him, in his crooked, mocking grin. "Ah, lady! That I neglected this duty! To aid you in the cleansing of the horrible filth!"

She tried to break the spell, to stand up, but her feet and legs were entwined with his. He laughed and gripped her hands and pulled her slowly back, bringing her body, wet and sleek, to rub with his, her breasts to crush against the hard wall of his chest, vulnerable softness against hair-roughened strength.

Their eyes met. She did not blink. She was mesmerized and barely registered what she saw in the intensity of his gaze.

It was gone. The hardness, the coldness. For that timeless eon, she felt warmth, and then she saw nothing, for his eyes closed and his arms clamped around her; and his kiss, as hot and wet as the steam that swam around them, invaded her body with the flood of desire. His hands touched her, creating exquisite fire.

At some point he stood. His arms locked around her, and his eyes locked with hers one more time. Water sluiced and fell from them both, and they were heedless of it.

He stepped from the tub and bore her to the naked mattress.

There was no further play, no taunt. Nor was there pain. Just a burst of passion, like a storm, striking deep, intense. A whirlwind in which she was vaguely aware of his movements. She dug her fingers into his shoulders, and cried out at the final touch of shimmering steel.

Passion, risen swiftly, spent in thunder, spilled upon her.

He lay against her, his hands still upon her.

And now their passion cooled.

"Oh!" Genevieve cried out in a choking fury. She wrenched herself out from beneath him, leaping away in horror to snatch the remnants of her robe from the floor to throw about herself. She uttered a cry of dismay as she caught his eyes, watching her from the bed. He would laugh, she thought, because he could so easily make an awed fool of her!

But he didn't laugh, he only gazed at her thoughtfully until she tore her eyes from his, striding to the hearth to fall before it in misery, her back to him. She wouldn't cry. She wouldn't. Even after he left. And he would leave now. Don his clothing and go back to Jon and forget her in a matter of seconds while she . . .

He did. He stood. She panicked for a moment, thinking that he was coming to her, but he did not; he returned to the water. She heard him splash it over his face and wash.

She felt him watching her, felt his movement as he grabbed a towel and watched her trembling back and tangle of hair as he dried his face.

She closed her eyes. In the silence that reigned between them, it was easy to pick out his every movement. His shirt, slipping over his head, his hose, his breeches, his tunic . . . his boots.

"Don't forget, milady, that your sustenance rests here on a tray," he reminded her. "You should eat before your dinner grows cold and unpalatable."

"Get out of here!"

He did laugh then. Softly—curiously bitter.

"Ah, yes! You're absolutely filthy all over again now. Do forgive me, milady! But then I must say, you do come closer and closer to fulfilling that promise you swore to me."

His voice was angry. She braced herself, but all she heard was a loud bang as the door slammed shut, with such strength that it seemed to groan in protest.

Chapter Twelve

" 'TIS A BEAUTIFUL day," Jon commented to Tristan, as they rode out of Edenby.

Indeed it was beautiful. A fall day, of which the poets might write in ecstasy. The sun was overhead, high and brilliant, and a soft breeze stirred over the hills and meadows and fields. Leaves offered a rainbow of colors, yellows and oranges and reds and magnificent magentas. It was the season of harvest and plenty. The horses knew it, the cows and sheep in the fields knew it, even the bees and birds flying about them knew it.

Tristan merely grunted.

Jon watched his friend. Tristan's features were set and dark, as if a thundercloud had created the scowl that hardened his face.

"Remember, friend," Jon said to him softly, "that we are on a mission of good will. That frown you wear like a tyrant's mask does not speak much of peace and harmony."

Tristan gave himself a shake, as if to rouse himself, and regarded Jon.

"Aye, Jon. It is a beautiful day. Autumn in all its glory. All about us speaks of nature's splendor and God's blessings to man. The land does not seem to know what momentous things befell it. That Richard was slain and Henry made King.''

There was still a trace of bitterness in Tristan's voice. Jon did not reply immediately, but spurred his mount again and rode along beside his friend and lord.

"Now you are the one who frowns," Tristan commented.

Jon shrugged, and eyed Tristan curiously. "I have seen you in many moods, Tristan. I have seen you in rage and in the gravest pain. I have known your wise judgment and seen your kindness and mercy in their best action. I've watched you stare death in the face without fear, and I have seen you harden like rock, merciless and cold."

Tristan's face grew rocklike then, and the darkness of a storm seemed to settle about his countenance as he stared at Jon, wary of the words yet to come.

"Yet I have never seen you like this—restless, angry, ever morose."

"There is a great deal on my mind since Henry has taken the throne. The country must find peace."

"Oh, aye. And so must you."

"A man's peace comes only in death," Tristan retorted with a snarl. "We turn ahead—see, where the cottage sits amidst the flock of geese."

Tristan urged his mount to a canter. Jon sighed and followed suit.

They came to the cottage, the same type structure of mud and thatch and daub that they had ridden to so many times already this morning. The tenant farmer, a graying man and his three great lads, awkward and big like mastiff pups, came rushing out to meet them. He bowed to Tristan again and again, and Tristan's countenance improved while he spoke, telling the farmer gently that Henry Tudor, Henry VII, now governed from London. Nothing would change, though he, Tristan de la Tere, was now the duke, the overlord, of his lands. Rents would not increase; they would work together for the good of the land and the people.

The farmer seemed awed; the lads likewise. They stared at Tristan, but had little to say. One of the boys found his tongue at last to assure Tristan that their rents would be paid, that their land was good, that they were willing to work hard.

"Richard, Henry, Tom, 'er Pete," muttered the youngest boy. And he had the cheek to grin at the two mighty knights mounted on their great steeds before him. "Makes little difference to us toiling the fields!"

To Jon's surprise, Tristan laughed, and the tension seemed to ease away from him. The old farmer gazed at his new lord, and his mistrust, too, seemed to melt away. Jon inhaled and exhaled with a strange relief. Tristan would have never hurt the lad, but Jon was grateful that he was amused by him, and not angered by his words.

But then Tristan sobered suddenly. "Would that Edgar Llewellyn had seen it that way," he murmured.

A woman poked her head out from the cottage door, then hurried out to greet them. She had an ample bosom and tremendously rosy cheeks. Her hands, Jon saw, appeared old and gnarled, far older than her face, so pretty with its blush, despite her graying hair.

She curtseyed with a further blush to Tristan and Jon, acknowledging Tristan the lord of the lands. She called herself Meg and said that her husband was Seth, and asked if they had been riding long, if they wouldn't like to wet their throats with her ale, and perhaps warm themselves with her stew.

"I offer so little, yet I offer it with my heart, good sires."

"Ma'm is a fine cook, milords!" the lad said.

Tristan looked at Jon, whose face betrayed his hunger and interest. "Thank you kindly," said Tristan, "your offer is cheerfully accepted." He grinned at Jon, and they dismounted.

"Sire! Trust me with these beauties, I pray thee!" the boy implored Tristan.

"That I do, boy," Tristan said. "What do they call you?"

"He's named for the good Saint Matthew, he is," the woman, Meg, said.

"Matthew, then, take the mounts. I see you are fond of horses."

"I am."

Meg blushed an even rosier hue at the new lord's interest in her offspring. She cleared her throat nervously and apologized for her humble abode. Tristan waved away her awkward words, ducking to enter the little cottage. From his fine magenta cloak and shining leather boots to the hard but beautiful precision of his features, Tristan seemed grander than his surroundings. Nonetheless, he was quite at home, and quick to make the woman easy. Jon was puzzled but pleased because here, at last, Tristan seemed young again. Able to laugh, to sit, to relax, as he had not done since they first came to Edenby.

They were served ale and stew at the rough hewn table before the hearth. The boys remained outside, the farmer stood, and Meg rushed about to serve them, chattering. She spoke about the spring planting, about the people, and then, nervously and accidently, she murmured, "The pity is our dear Lord Edgar, he were so fine a man! Slain in battle, as it were . . ."

Her husband spoke sharply in panic; Meg cleared her throat in horror—and spilled ale upon the table.

Tristan caught her wrist and spoke gently. "A brave man's death in battle must always be lamented, mistress. And your Lord Edgar was most certainly brave."

"I beg—" Meg began.

"You need beg nothing. Your words were not ill-taken."

Meg glanced at her husband; she sighed with relief. She quickly brought a cloth to sop up the ale, then returned to the hearth, to the great black kettle of stew, offering them more. As she dished up the stew she glanced at Tristan uneasily, but then it seemed that her curiosity was stronger than her fear and she asked tentatively, "The Lady Genevieve . . . his lass. She fares well?"

Tristan stiffened, and Jon tensed, worried that Tristan might grow suddenly violent. But nothing happened. Tristan lowered his head over his bowl. "She fares well," he said simply.

The ease, however, was gone. They finished quickly, and stood to depart. Tristan thanked Meg in mild tones.

When they came out, young Matt was still marveling over the horses. Tristan paused, then told the boy that if he was interested, he must come to the castle and hire on as a groom. Matthew's face lit up like a bright spring sky.

"I'll come, milord, I'll come!"

"Seth, did you hear!" Meg whispered with awe.

"I did," Seth said, walking over to Tristan, who had just mounted his horse.

"Bless you, milord. For the boy, we bless you."

Tristan shook his head, startled by the gratitude, thinking it too much. "He's good with animals. He'll do his work well."

Tristan waved a gauntleted hand and nudged his mount into a brisk canter. Laughing, Jon followed suit. Far out into the fields, he caught up with Tristan.

"You uplifted that poor lad! You took him from the fields, from hardship, from—"

"Jon," Tristan groaned, "they were living in no hardship! They are proud tenant farmers making a good living from the land. Now will you leave me be!"

Jon bowed, mockingly humble. "You've stumbled upon the greatest loyalty, Tristan." He suddenly became serious. "Truly, Tristan. Yesterday, you took that young lass from that poor widow's place and gave her work as a lady's maid. Today, the boy—as groom."

"Any estate must have workers, Jon."

"Aye, but you've done them well."

"Nay. Think on it, Jon. Old Edgar's household servants were caught up in the midst of battle. 'Tis not always a good thing, to be close to greatness."

He broke off suddenly, and they fell silent. The autumn day lost its beauty, for they were both remembering the murders at Bedford Heath.

Tristan had paid dearly for being close to Richard—for insisting, in all honor, on a fair accounting of the disappearance of the Princes.

He had paid with everything, and nothing could ever make up for it, Jon thought. The cool breeze seemed to turn suddenly and violently cold, and Jon shivered. The Lady Genevieve, having struck a blow upon a man already in pain, would not be allowed to forget, either.

"Never mind," Tristan muttered darkly, spurring his great piebald mount and taking off with speed again. Jon followed him, greatly worried, wondering whether to attempt to speak with Tristan once more or to wait. They had not been here long. Maybe Tristan would learn new temperance as the days passed.

He hoped so: this should be a time for healing. Richard III was dead, Henry had taken the Crown of England. Edenby had been taken, too, and even the Lady of Edenby. All of Tristan's grievances had been brought to a certain justice. It should have been a time for him to come to know laughter again. Instead it was worse. Even in the times of greatest pain, Tristan had never been so moody and grim.

Tristan reined up as they came upon a cliff that over-looked the walls and the castle from the west. Jon halted beside him.

The walls were slowly being repaired; the metalsmiths were at work again, and farmers sold their crops. Edenby itself was healing. Now, Jon thought, if the new lord could only do so himself . . .

"Thirty-eight, thirty-nine, forty."

Forty. It took Genevieve exactly forty paces to walk from the door of her chamber to the wall. How many times had she counted out those steps? How many times could she do so again before she lost her mind completely?

She walked back to the mantel and held her cold hands out to the fire. The chamber was chilly. Outside the sun was shining so that one might be warm, but here, in this stone prison, the warmth of the sun did not penetrate.

Genevieve reached out to grasp the stone, praying that some of its cold and strength would seep into her. She was insane already, she decided, because she was so desperate to see someone—anyone!—that she would even welcome a visit from Tristan.

But he hadn't been near her in three days. Nor had anyone else, really. Once, early each morning, a different servant had come to clean the room, bring water and food, and then go away. And once, each evening, one of Tristan's Lancastrians had knocked upon the door to deliver another tray of food. Now, in three full days, she had not had an hour's worth of company other than her own.

There was noise from the courtyard, far below. With pathetic eagerness Genevieve raced to the archers' slit.

Her soft silk skirt rustled as she climbed upon the chair. As she looked out she stiffened. The noise was that of Jon and Tristan returning from somewhere. Tristan was riding that mammoth piebald stallion of his. There were shouts at their arrival; a groom came running out to take the horses as the two bareheaded men dismounted, their mantles sweeping around them in the soft of the autumn breeze.

Genevieve started to step backward, almost forgetting that she stood upon a chair—for Tristan was staring up at her windows. He couldn't see her, she knew. The slit was too narrow. But she could see the dark expression, the brooding emotion of his face.

It was frightening. Her hand flew to her throat, for she saw that he had not forgotten her. Nor had he softened in the least.

She shook her head slightly. Against her will, she recognized that he was probably the most striking man she had ever seen—the tallest, the strongest, the most handsome and intriguing of face and feature. He was the very picture of the noble. He might have been a hero of legend, a dashing young prince sent to rescue a princess.

"Nay, he is the dragon!" she breathed out. For if he was the most striking man she had ever seen, he was equally the most ruthless.

"Jon! Tis-tan!"

Genevieve started at the sound of the childish voice. It was Anne!

Anne! Oh, Annie, go back, Genevieve thought, as her little cousin came running out the door, braided plaits flying behind her. Jon caught her up in his arms, laughing, and to Genevieve's amazement, she saw that Anne said something to Tristan, and that Tristan laughed, and then took Anne from Jon to set her upon his shoulders, where she could pat the great piebald horse on his smooth nose. Anne laughed with delight, perfectly happy to be perched upon Tristan's broad shoulders.

"Oooh, Annie! Even you're a traitor!" Genevieve murmured, then she caught herself. She should be glad: Anne was living like a little lady, as she had been before.

Genevieve stepped down from her chair, suddenly cold again.

But what happened when it was all over? When Jon tired of Edwyna, when Tristan grew bored of his vengeance. When they were all thrown from "his" property?

She spun around, hearing the bolt lift on her door. Her heart began to pound ferociously, then she realized that it could not be Tristan. He was probably still in the courtyard and not even he could have come into the keep and up the steps so quickly.

There was a tapping.

Tristan did not tap. He entered when he so chose.

"Come in," she said.

A young girl came in. A young girl with huge brown eyes like velvet, an enormous bosom, and full, swaying hips to match. She stared at Genevieve dreamily, then, as if suddenly remembering her manners, she dropped a little curtsy.

"Milady. I'm Tess. I'm to be your maid. I'm to clean the room and bring what you might require."

"Tess. How . . . nice."

The girl seemed to think so. Genevieve did not. Where was Mary? Dear Mary, she missed her so keenly! This girl . . .

Genevieve wished that she had something to do. A piece of tapestry, a book to read. Something to pretend that she had an interest in!

She had nothing. She moved over to the fire, and merely sat before it as Tess walked about the room, straightening this, folding that—and sighing continually.

Curious at last, Genevieve turned around. Tess was at her bed, smoothing the covers with a rapturous look on her pretty face.

She seemed to feel Genevieve's gaze, and she looked at her, smiling. A slightly sly smile—as if she were indeed glad to be a lady's maid, but aware, too, of the curious position of her lady.

"This . . ." she murmured, "this is where he lies!"

"What?" Genevieve said.

"The Lord Tristan. His head rests . . . here. His body . . . stretches out so. Shoulders, chest, legs . . ."

Genevieve felt a wracking pain thunder against her temple. She forced herself to smile. Oh, God. This was all that she needed—absolutely all that she needed to truly go over the brink. This sweet slut of a farm girl to come mooning about her chamber over Tristan de la Tere! Where had she come from!

From Tristan . . .

Was that where he had been these days? Leaving her in peace, and finding better occupation elsewhere?

She didn't realize that she had curled her fingers into fists until she felt her nails digging into her palms. Somehow she kept on smiling.

"Tess, I believe the room is fine now."

"Oh, but I am to serve you—"

"I want my privacy, Tess."

Unhappily, the girl drew her work-roughened hands from the sheets and turned to depart. "I'd have thought," Tess muttered beneath her breath, "that she'd have been glad of me!"

The door closed with a little bang. Genevieve felt the most absurd temptation to throw something at it. A meal, untouched, awaited her on the dressing table. She approached it with vengeance, thinking to take the tray and hurl it across the room. But she paused, her hand in the air, and noted the full bottle of Bordeaux upon it. Wine to ease the spirit.

She ignored the food, poured wine, and drank it—quickly. Ah, it went down so easily! Again she poured, and again she drank, and the edges of pain blurred.

She walked and walked and walked . . . swearing, vowing that she would get away. If she were just careful, patient. If she could just wait until their guard was down. There were places to go, surely, things that could be done. There was a convent just beyond the mountain pass. If she could reach the sisters there, she would find sanctuary, and not even the King would dare to defy that sanctuary.

Eventually, she promised herself, she could get to France—or Brittany, where her uncle lived. She would do it! She had to.

Exhaustion overtook her. Exhaustion—and the half bottle of Bordeaux she had managed to consume. She fell first to her knees before the hearth, and then stretched out, laying her hot cheek against her arm. Why, oh, why did she feel this tempest inside of her? She despised him, and what he felt for her was even darker, more intense. She didn't want him touching her. She could swear up and down that she did not want him to touch her again, but . . .

When he did, he was magic.

It was shameful!

It was the heat she had known from the first, the rippling sweet liquid that filled her body, that spilled from it. As if an alchemist had found them, and created for them a simmering fire that smoked and burned and erupted.

"I've got to get out!" she whispered aloud to herself, feeling more desperate than she had ever felt before.

Tristan did not come to dinner.

Jon, Edwyna, Tibald, and Father Thomas were all at the long banqueting table. It might have been a strange gathering, Jon thought with humor, except that the priest did not seem to condemn him too keenly, and he wondered suddenly, with a little beat of his heart, if that shrewd man knew what was on his mind.

He was in love with Edwyna. With the softness in her eyes. God—had anything on earth ever been so blue? He was in love with her whispers, with her smile when she opened her arms wide to embrace him at night. She was a little older than he, and a widow. And a damned Yorkist at that.

But he was in love with her. And Father Thomas seemed to know it, so all was cordial at the table. There was light conversation, there was laughter, there was ease.

But of course Tristan was not at the table. And Father Thomas' eyes, as well as Edwyna's, often strayed to the closed door of the counting room, where they all knew that Tristan worked.

Father Thomas, Jon decided, was no coward, for he had never shrunk from letting Tristan know that he considered his treatment of his prisoner much less than Christian. Tristan had let him know that if he could not abide the situation, then he must desert his flock and find his living elsewhere. Father Thomas had merely closed his mouth, and now contained his opinion—and condemned with his eyes.

When the meal ended Father Thomas said that he must see to the care of a newborn child, for the mother was not faring well. Edwyna smiled beautifully at him and murmured that she was going to kiss Anne good-night. Tibald had to go out and see to the castle guard and the prisoners.

Jon sat and drank his ale. He stared at the door to the counting room and hesitated, then stood. God's blood! He'd known Tristan all his life. Surely that counted for something! And he could not bear his friend's agony.

He strode quickly to the door and knocked upon it. Tristan bade him enter with a grunt, and Jon came in.

Tristan did not look up. He frowned over a ledger, yet Jon wondered if he were really reading it.

Tristan looked up at last, dark brows arched in a question. Jon smiled a little sheepishly and slid into the chair before the desk. "You didn't come to the table," he said.

"I have been studying these. See here—" Tristan shoved the book toward Jon. "There are farms a day's ride from here that belong to Edenby."

Jon studied the figures and the listing of acres and land. He nodded. "I wonder what those people know of recent events."

Tristan sighed and pushed away from the desk to stretch his legs upon it. "I'll ride out on the morrow and see these people. There are at least a hundred in these far-stretching lands."

Jon frowned uneasily. "I'd best come with you. And a small contingent of men. There could still be rebellion in these parts."

"I'll take Tibald—I need you here. I won't be gone long. A day or two at most."

"Come back quickly." Jon said. He hesitated again. "What Edenby needs is a new consistency, a return to normal living."

"A firm, guiding hand," Tristan murmured. He thumped his legs back to the floor and filled a pewter goblet with wine from the flask at the edge of the desk. "Ah, yes! A return to day-to-day living! It's all that a man asks, isn't it, Jon, from the lowliest peasant to the highest king! Life! Health— happiness!" He raised his goblet.

"I'm gravely worried about you!" Jon blurted out.

"What?" Tristan retorted, surprised by the words.

"Before God, Tristan! It is over! It has gone your way! Richard lies with the worms! Lisette, your family—they have been avenged. You hold Edenby. You've punished those who betrayed you! What haunts you now?"

Tristan grew so angry that Jon expected a blow. Tristan exhaled slowly, watched Jon, then drained his goblet of wine.

"I don't know," he said.

"Tristan, you even hold—her."

He smiled slowly, very slowly, settling back once again.

"Aye, I hold her."

"And have not been near her these three days!"

Tristan arched a brow. "You watch me so closely?"

"I know you," Jon said stubbornly.

Tristan stared at him for a minute. Then he leaned toward him, and his smile was bitter.

"I thought I should end it, Jon. To know vengeance, and then peace. Not to slay her, but to take from her, as she meant to take from me. Yet . . . it doesn't end. I thought to quench a fever, yet the fever grows. I cannot release her. I cannot go to her."

Jon shook his head. He sought for an answer.

"But she . . . she is yours," he said softly. "If that is what causes the brooding, go to her. Have her, love her—"

"Nay, never love, friend."

"Then . . ." Jon was confused, but he managed a laugh. "Then, Tristan, it need not be love." He leaned closer over the desk and helped himself to the wine. "Whatever it be, milord, have it! Before God—spare us who serve you well and have that lass!"

Tristan stood abruptly.

"What—" Jon began.

Tristan grinned. "You said, my friend, 'have that lass.' I'm leaving tomorrow, so it had best be tonight."

He swirled, and Jon watched him go. He was still for a minute, then he helped himself to Tristan's wine, and smiled. It really hadn't been a bad night's work.

Tristan wondered at himself as he mounted the stairs. Wondered at the sudden beating of his heart, at the ragged way that his breath rushed from his lungs, and back to them again. His pulse throbbed. This longing, lust, was a fever that never subsided, a hunger that was never satisfied.

He'd stayed away because he hadn't understood it, and he was nearly afraid of this driving thing. He could not let her go. He had taken what he thought he had wanted, and still he wanted more.

He shook his head. And outside the door he nodded to the guard and slipped the bolt, and then he stood still, smiling suddenly. Tonight he did not care to seek answers. He only sought her.

The door closed behind him. The room was dark and dim. No candles were lit, and the embers were low in the hearth. At first he did not see her. And then his body seemed to freeze, and his heart caught in his throat.

Oh, God in heaven. She was there . . . stretched out on the floor, her head over an arm, her fingers, elegant, long, white as death in the surreal dimness, dangling fragile before her.

Her hair cloaked her. Gold and long and all about her like angel's hair. In the way she lay, the way she stretched out, it was just like . . .

Like Lisette.

He closed his eyes, suddenly feeling weak. Tremors of dark and deadly fear streaked through him. She was dead. The way that she lay, she was dead, she had taken her own life . . .

Strength came to him, strength and a little madness. He strode across the distance in seconds, falling to his knees

beside her, sweeping his arms about her to drag her into his
arms.

Her head fell back. There was no blood upon her throat.
His hands were clean of it.

Her eyes opened slowly and something beat inside of him.
A pulse of relief, of shocking ecstasy. He wanted to laugh at
himself and yet he could not. She had slept. She had come to
the fire and slept, and even now that exhaustion stayed with
her because her eyes opened so slowly and so softly and fell
upon him like gentle violets, misted with confusion.

"Tristan?" The puzzled whisper of his name touched a
spark that sizzled down the length of his spine and he laughed
softly, with just a touch of ragged harshness to the sound.

"Who else, milady?"

He stood with her. Instinctively, her arms tightened around
his neck. He carried her to the bed and laid her there, and her
eyes were closed again, her breathing came easily, and he
thought that he had barely interrupted her sleep.

He stripped silently in the darkness, then stretched beside
her. He pulled at the silken bodice of her gown and when it
parted he slipped his hands upon her flesh, tenderly, evoca-
tively, and rose over her to take her lips in a kiss. Soft . . .
gentle . . .

She tasted sweet, as sweet as wine. He tasted her again,
and smiled to himself, for indeed she tasted of fine, fine
wine.

Bordeaux.

And perhaps even then she slept for she responded drows-
ily. Perhaps she dreamed of a different man, a different lord,
coming to her in love, coming in the dark of night.

She moaned, gently slipped her arms around him again,
arched to press against him; his hands cupped and weighed her
breasts. He freed her then of the constraint of clothes, held
her, loved her, revered the perfection of her form, full breasts,
exotic nipples, slim waist, flaring hips, and all so soft, so soft
and warm, and like silk to his fingers . . .

For eons he heard nothing, knew nothing, but that softness.
The pulse of heartbeats rising. The whisper of her breath,

growing ragged, the sounds that caught in her throat, gasps that found no true voice, deeper, sudden, sharp and sweet.

And fever rose. Softness to tempest, tempest to splendor, eons passing . . . locked together. Knowing the release he had needed so desperately.

Moments of peace when tension exploded in climax and brooding anger seeped into her along with the flood of his seed.

Peace . . . so complete in the darkness that he breathed long, and then . . . held her against him. His hand, just beneath her breast, bringing her back against his chest, her hip curled to his, their legs entwined, her hair, that glorious cloak, swathed all about them both.

Peace so great that he slept.

Tristan awoke at dawn in horror, for he had sworn to himself he would never sleep beside her. Just outside, light was beginning to streak through the remnants of night. Beautiful light. Shafts of crimson and gold.

He bolted from the bed and dressed quickly. He tried to keep his gaze from her, but he could not. He stared down upon her.

She was still curled on her side, naked and innocent in the morning light. In spite of himself, he dwelt on her beauty. Her skin was so fair, her breasts so perfectly shaped, firm, and crested in dusky crimson, hidden now, like shy maidens, peeping out from strands of that golden hair.

Golden hair . . . skeins that fell over her, her shoulders, the curve of her hip, the roundness of her sleek, smooth bottom. Glowing tendrils of sunshine and splendor that fell rich and thick over the bed, where he himself had lain. Wisping over her delicate features, the soft rose of her cheeks.

She smiled in her sleep. Just the smallest curve of lips that were parted but a breath. A mouth still soft and damp and sensually alluring.

He wanted to crawl back in beside her, and wake her—be it rudely, be it roughly. If he waited much longer, staring at her so, he realized with a harsh scowl, he would do just that. With a guttural oath he turned and dressed.

He shook himself as he exited her chamber, nodding curtly to the guard, squaring his shoulders. Why was it that each time he availed himself of her passion he knew a greater tempest inside? A greater need. Why could he not feel himself shriven—free?

In the hall he started shouting orders. Few were up yet—they would arise damn quickly. Tristan was anxious to be gone.

Tibald appeared and quickly readied himself; the horses were assembled in the courtyard. Jon, hair tousled and apparently still half asleep, came to see him off, Edwyna at his side.

She rushed to Tristan when he had mounted his horse.

"Please, Tristan, may I see her? Just to bring her some books?"

He hesitated, clenching his teeth together tightly. He looked over Edwyna's head to Jon. "Bring Genevieve out for an hour each morning that I am gone. Let her walk, let her be with Edwyna." He looked quickly back to Jon's blue-eyed love; Edwyna kissed his hand and Tristan scowled, embarrassed by her gratitude.

"Edwyna! Please, for the love of God—"

"Thank you, Tristan." There were tears in her eyes.

"Just watch that niece of yours, Edwyna. She is sly."

"I'll watch her!" Edwyna promised joyfully.

Tristan was suddenly irritated. He'd given in because of Edwyna, wide eyed, so pure, so sweetly innocent of malice. And so damned grateful for such a small favor. And because Jon delighted so in her company. Yet he wasn't sure that Genevieve deserved the concession. He remembered the night, the sweetness of the night, life itself, bittersweet.

Before he rode out he paused. He was angry with himself, but determined not to show it.

"Ah, Jon! I've a request!" he said, holding back the piebald when the stallion was as anxious as he to be gone.

"Name it," Jon said.

"See that Lady Genevieve is delivered a case of our best Bordeaux, will you?"

"A case, Tristan?" Jon frowned.

"Aye."

Jon shrugged. "As you say."

Tristan smiled as Edwyna handed up the stirrup cup. He drank deeply, cheerfully bade them farewell, and rode out, with Tibald and his contingent close on his heels.

Chapter
Thirteen

GENEVIEVE FELT ABSURDLY sheltered. She'd been dreaming, and the dream had been good. Soft and gentle and full of whispers. As if she had been cocooned in tenderness.

Genevieve heard the commotion in the courtyard, but heard it dimly. It seemed that she had to fight past walls of cobwebs to wake up. Her head felt heavy, like lead. When she opened her eyes, the sun hurt them. For long moments she didn't try to move. She accused herself of being a total fool for drinking so much red wine. Anyone—even Annie!—knew that gulping red wine would either make you sick or give you a horrendous headache.

She sat up, clenching her temples between her palms, groaning, giving up, and crashing back to the mattress.

Something was going on in the courtyard, she told herself dully. She couldn't seem to rouse herself enough to care.

She closed her eyes and wondered curiously at the sense of well-being that she had felt. Her fingers plucked at the coverings, and then she bolted up suddenly, staring across to the hearth, now cold and barren.

She was naked and in her bed and she hadn't been dreaming. She'd had the company she'd craved during the night.

"Oh . . ."

She moaned aloud at the shooting pain that ripped through her head again. How could he! Damn him a thousand times over! Ignore her for days and then just happen to walk in when she was in a stupor. Of all the damnable, bloody nerve. The situation was intolerable.

She heard a sound, loud and grating. The bolt was slipped. Genevieve made a dash to crawl deep and far beneath the covers and pull them to her chin. If it were he . . . if he were back, she swore—swore before God the Almighty!—she'd not so humiliate herself again. She'd scratched his devil's eyes out, she'd—

Someone knocked, and it sounded to Genevieve as if the walls themselves were tumbling down. It wasn't Tristan. Tristan did not knock.

Ah . . . the greatest insult to the greatest injury. The sunshiny, red-cheeked, cow-breasted sweet young thing called Tess was back. She bounced in, cheerful, and atrociously loud.

"Good-morning, milady! I've brought you food—" She nodded her head, indicating the tray she carried. "—and I thought I'd ask you quickly if you'd like a bath. Perhaps you'd care to wash your hair, since the sun will dry it—"

Genevieve forgot her rancor with the girl at those words. "The sun?" she interrupted eagerly.

"Aye, milady, while you're walking—"

"Walking?" She almost bounded from the bed before remembering that she wasn't dressed. "Tess, where am I walking to?"

Her heart started to skitter and leap. Walking . . . was he letting her go then? Was he going to release her, send her somewhere?

"Walking, milady. The Lady Edwyna said that you might be with her for an hour, and that she was sure you missed the sunlight and the fresh air sorely. Here—"

Tess moved on into the room to set the tray down. Genevieve frowned, curious and suspicious as to what had brought on this freedom and strange generosity.

Tess turned to her. "Shall I call the boys with water?"

Genevieve stared at her blankly for a moment. She started to reply, but then another rapping fell upon the door, and she was made viciously aware of her headache.

What now? she thought. Her little domain had been as silent as the grave for day upon miserable day, and now it suddenly felt like the grand crossroads in London.

"Yes?" she demanded sharply. The door opened, and in came young Roger de Treyne, the handsome Lancastrian who had shown her such sympathy on the long ride to Edenby. Several of Tristan's men were behind him in the hallway. They had been laughing and talking, and suddenly went dead silent, staring at Genevieve, who was still lying in bed.

Brilliant color flooded over her. Roger didn't even speak; he just stared, transfixed.

"What goes on here?" came a sharp voice.

The speaker that sent the men stumbling away was Jon of Pleasance. Genevieve knew his voice. Then he, too, was at the door, frowning at Genevieve bundled in her tight wad of covers.

He cleared his throat and tapped Roger on the shoulder. "Put it down, man, put the damn thing down!"

Only then did Genevieve realize that Roger was carrying a large crate. She looked at Jon.

"What is it?"

"It's from Tristan," he said simply. "Roger! In the corner! Put the damn thing down now, and go on!"

Roger did. He stepped into the chamber, set the crate in the corner, then turned and gave Genevieve a deep and appreciative bow. "Milady, it is wondrous joy to see you," he said.

"Good morrow to you, Roger," she murmured.

Jon cleared his throat. "Roger, Tristan does return."

"What? Oh!" Roger straightened quickly. "Milady," he murmured to Genevieve, and he quickly took his leave. Genevieve watched him, angry in his behalf. Was Tristan such an ogre then that even his own men needed to fear him?

Jon was still there, in the doorway. Genevieve turned her gaze to him. "What is going on? What is it? Tess said that—"

"The crate is a gift from Tristan." He hesitated. "A true

gift—the contents came with us, milady, and not from Edenby. And aye, yes, I'll be back with Edwyna for you in an hour—for an hour only, Genevieve. Is that time sufficient for you?''

She smiled at him. "To leave this room?" She laughed. "Jon, give me but five minutes, and I shall be ready!"

"An hour, milady," he grinned. He closed the door.

Tess let out a sigh. "Oh, milady! He sends you gifts!"

Genevieve looked at the girl and frowned. She gathered the covers about herself and climbed curiously from the bed. She hurried over to the crate and found the lid easy to open.

It took her several seconds of staring to realize what the crate contained. Then she plucked out a bottle and stared at it, dead silent as color flooded through her again—far more brilliant than her earlier blush, her shame was mixed with blind fury this time.

"Oh!" she screamed wrathfully, heedless of Tess, heedless of anything or anyone. She definitely had not dreamt the night, she hadn't imagined any of her own part in it. And leave it to Tristan to mock her, to send a whole case of the deadly stuff that had done her in!

"Milady!" Tess cried.

The bottle had crashed against the wall. Crashed and shattered, and wine ran down the whitewash. "I will kill him!" Genevieve swore. "I swear it!" She stalked the room, with the bed coverings flowing behind her. "Damn him! Oh, God, damn him! To eons in hell! To fire and pitchforks and may he rot and—"

"Milady, please!" Nearly in tears, Tess stood before her, as if she wanted to run but knew not where. As if she had been ordered to serve a demented witch.

Genevieve stopped dead still and approached the girl.

"Get him up here," she said.

"I can't—"

Genevieve gripped her by the shoulders.

"You must! Tell him to come—now!"

"Milady, I cannot! I—"

"Do it!"

Tess gave out a little scream and began to pound loudly on the door. It flew open; Jon was standing there.

"What goes on here?" he demanded.

Tess started to talk, but she was so incoherent that Jon pushed her on out and looked at Genevieve for some clarification. Genevieve came at him, all bundled up in linen and fur, her hair streaming behind her like some mighty, golden banner. She was flushed and her eyes glittered, a deep entrancing silver. Jon was too fascinated for a moment to realize that she was near hysteria.

"Genevieve! What—"

"Tell Tristan that I want to see him!"

"Genevieve, I cannot. Tristan is gone."

She stopped still. She stared at him suspiciously, warily.

"Gone? For . . . good?"

He ducked his head, for a smile came to his lips at the hopeful sound of her voice.

"Nay, lady, not for good. He has gone to the outlands, and will be away two days or so."

"Oh." She grew calm, and smiled at him—a beautiful bewitching smile. "Gone . . . for two days," she said politely. "Then, this kindness, this outing, is something for which I must dearly thank you, Jon."

"Nay, Genevieve, Tristan gave that order."

The gentle smile slipped away, and her eyes grew icy.

"Ah. As he ordered the Bordeaux?"

"Not to your liking, as I see," Jon commented.

Genevieve waved a hand in the air, sweet once more. She crossed the room and knelt before him, kissing his hand quickly. "Thank you, Jon, I shall be ready in an hour."

Jon cleared his throat. "One hour, aye, milady. Shall I, uh, send Tess back to you? Do you wish water?"

"Oh, aye, if you please, Jon."

When the door closed Genevieve was hard pressed to contain her joy. Tristan was gone! And she was going out with Jon and Edwyna—who would be so easy to dupe!

She bit her lip, feeling suddenly guilty. Jon and Edwyna were the only people willing to fight for her these days; they didn't deserve Tristan's wrath. She closed her eyes, swallowing back her worries. Tristan could not really blame Edwyna, and Jon he would forgive. Besides, she couldn't think about them now. She had to plan.

Tess came back to the room, still ill at ease. Genevieve smiled sweetly, chatted while she bathed, and even allowed Tess to brush out her hair when it had been washed. Genevieve was entirely sweet and convivial.

Genevieve was careful to wear her hardiest hose and her most comfortable gown, and she took her warmest hooded cloak. While Tess was busy straightening the bed, Genevieve dug deeply into her wardrobe for her small jewelled hunting dagger.

When Jon and Edwyna came for her, she was ready. Guilt seized her anew as Edwyna rushed in and hugged her with fierce joy; Genevieve felt doubly her betrayal. She'll have to understand, please God, make her understand! Genevieve thought.

"I brought a picnic," Edwyna said breathlessly, looking at Jon with pleasure.

"Oh, lovely! Oh, I do thank you!" she said to Jon. She lowered her eyes and asked humbly. "Could we possibly have our picnic in the meadow to the west?"

"I hadn't thought to go beyond the castle walls—" Jon began.

"Jon!" Edwyna whispered to him, but Genevieve could hear the words. "Really! She is but a slip of a young girl and you are a full-grown knight! Surely you will be master of the situation."

His pride thus appealed to, Jon wasn't left much choice.

"All right," he said. "Shall we go?"

"Aye!" Genevieve said. "Oh, but Jon, one more thing? This—this gift of Tristan's. It is truly mine?"

"It is."

"Good."

Genevieve's voice grew cold. She turned back to Tess, now straightening out her dressing table. "Tess?"

"Milady?"

"The wine, I'd like you to have it. As you might have noted, I really don't care much for Bordeaux."

"I couldn't—"

"Please, please, do!" Smiling serenely, Genevieve closed the door behind her.

There! He apparently liked Tess, and sodden women appealed to him. Well, he could have his over-endowed little farm girl—just as sodden as he liked!

It could have been a wonderful picnic. The autumn leaves were glorious, and the sun shone brilliantly overhead. They brought a hamper of fresh-baked bread, new dairy cheese, and little kidney pies, all prepared with special tenderness by dear old Griswald. Jon had shrewdly brought a small cask of ale.

Genevieve realized as she ate that she really did like Jon. He laughed easily, he had a quick wit—and he was in love with Edwyna. It showed in his eyes, in his voice, in every little nuance of tenderness and care that he showed her. Watching them, she sighed, and it occurred to her suddenly that they shared something she had always craved. It was love, wondrous love—the love that stirred poets to write and balladeers to sing.

He was short with Edwyna only once—when Genevieve asked about Tristan's previous home and his past. Edwyna gazed at him with anxious eyes and started to reply, but Jon jumped in.

"Edwyna! Remember his words!"

Edwyna lowered her eyes and said simply, "Jon and Tristan are both from the north. A day's ride out of London."

Genevieve narrowed her eyes. So! Edwyna couldn't even talk because of "his" words! His—Tristan's!

She asked Jon for more ale, careful not to let him see her expression. She must make her escape soon. Tristan! Soon, she assured herself to give courage to her plan, she wouldn't have to care any more. She wouldn't feel the horrible, aching conflicts! She would no longer succumb to the power of his touch. Nor would it matter that, for him, it was all a taunting game.

He had told her that his chivalry was buried somewhere; so, it seemed, was his heart. And the "pleasures" that he enjoyed with her he enjoyed elsewhere, she reminded herself, thinking of Tess. Yet why this should be a bitter blow, she knew not.

Relaxed, comfortable, Edwyna lay back on the oxhide blanket, laughing at something Jon had said. He leaned over her, whispering. They were completely caught up in themselves.

They were in the midst of a huge field; to the west were hills, blanketed by forest. Genevieve stood.

Jon was not so enamored as to forget her. He was on his feet in a moment. "Genevieve?"

"I'd like some of the fallen leaves, Jon. I could fashion bows in all those hours that I'm locked away."

He looked at her uneasily. He gazed down to Edwyna. Edwyna looked at Genevieve suspiciously.

Genevieve gazed from one to the other—as innocently and as sweetly as she could manage. Guilt riddled her spine.

"Stay close!" Jon warned her.

"I will," she promised meekly.

And she did at first. She stayed closer than she meant to be, and her ears burned. Jon did love Edwyna. He was telling her so. And she was whispering in return, in awe and in tenderness.

Genevieve stooped and collected, stooped and collected—and came closer and closer to the border of the trees. She slipped into them and chanced one backward glance.

Tears stung her eyes at the sight of them—so in love with one another, and so beautiful together.

And for the most absurd moment, Genevieve had second thoughts. She had a vision of Tristan bending over her thus, not in the fire of raw passion, but with tenderness. Tristan, no longer the magnificent beast, but her knight, loving and gentle . . .

She shook her head, dispelling the mood. Good God, had she gone mad? Tristan hated her, he used her. She must escape him for the salvation of her soul! She was not strong enough to resist him—some alchemy had made them explosive together. No matter that she denied him; she was molten at his touch.

She straightened, turned and ran.

"Marry me," Jon was saying.

Edwyna stared at him, blue eyes growing as wide as the sky.

"Marry me."

"But—"

"You said that you loved me."

"I do. Oh, God, Jon! You know that I do! But you're . . . and I'm . . ."

"I'm a man, and you're a woman," he teased. "We're definitely the right two sexes."

She started to laugh, but the pain tripped her up. "Jon! I am one of the vanquished enemy, remember!"

"You are the greatest beauty to ever touch my life."

"No, you're the greatest wonder I've never known, I've never felt—oh, Jon! Can this be possible? I'm a widow, I'm not young, I have a daughter—"

"And I swear to you, I'll love her as my own."

"Oh. Jon . . ."

"Then you'll marry me?"

She started to cry.

"Damn, Edwyna—"

She threw her arms around him and kissed him, and kissed him—and kissed him. And still she was crying. "I shall marry you! Oh, my God, yes, Jon, yes!"

He lost himself then. Lost himself in her eyes, in her kiss, in the arms around him. Suddenly Edwyna went rigid with panic. "Jon!"

"What?"

"Where's Genevieve?"

"Damn!" said Jon, springing up. "Damn her!"

Quickly scanning the fields, Jon burst into a sprint. He raced to the edge of one field, but the forest was thick, and he would never spot her on his own. Damn her! He'd been warned not to trust her.

Jon returned to Edwyna, who was glumly packing away the picnic. He was enraged. "You planned it!" he accused Edwyna. "It must have been amusing. 'Oh, Jon? I can handle Jon! I'll seduce him, and you run!'"

"What?" Edwyna gasped.

"This morning, madam! Remember your assurances? 'She is but a slip of a girl, and you're a full-grown knight.' Edwyna—you—bitch!''

"You're wrong."

Jon refused to look at her.

"Jon, you must believe me! I swear, I didn't—"

Fury possessed him. He slapped Edwyna with such force that she crumpled before him, sobbing. He didn't care—he just hurried away, shouting for the guard.

Genevieve could only run a short distance at this speed before she doubled over with pain. Gasping, she straightened, wondering how long it would be before they came after her. She had to go farther—they would have horses. She started off again. Running, slowing, running again. Thank God that she was young, that she was fleet of foot. And yet it might not be enough. She was near exhaustion when she heard the sounds of pursuit. Horses' hooves crashing over the bracken, shouts rising, even a trumpet flaring.

Jon had called out half of the castle! Genevieve thought with dismay. She'd never elude that many men. She prayed that they had not brought the hounds.

Tiring again, Genevieve looked up. She had but one chance—to climb a tree. Wait until they passed her by.

She hesitated. The sound of shouting, of horses crashing through the brush, came closer and closer. Genevieve climbed.

The search party was directly beneath her. Through the leaves she could see Jon and young Roger, who had stopped for a consultation. Genevieve winced, barely daring to breathe.

"Farther!" Jon said furiously. "We hunt until we find her."

Roger said something to Jon, who laughed bitterly. For a moment he sounded like Tristan.

"I deserve his wrath! I fell for everything that woman said to me! But, you see, he warned me about Genevieve, and not Edwyna!"

They spurred their horses and went on. Genevieve bit her

lip to keep from crying out. Oh, you fool! She wanted to tell Jon. She did nothing to you but love you!

What had she done? She had ruined any chance of happiness for the aunt who had loved her and fought for her! Genevieve felt ill.

But she couldn't possibly go back. She could only pray for Edwyna—and hope that God would choose to show mercy.

Genevieve was miserable. Her arms and legs ached terribly, but she dared not climb down—daren't even move, until they had ridden far past. She waited in loneliness and guilt, until night fell.

Things had gone well, Tristan thought, very well indeed. He was returning with all manner of gifts from his tenants— many of whom had never seen Edgar and therefore could not mourn his passing. Tristan had spoken with farmers about the new system of rotating crops. He had talked with the shepherds about prices for wool.

He was even feeling somewhat sorry for what he had done to Genevieve. The people might not have seen old Edgar, but they did know his daughter. "She come to us in the fever, ye ken?" an old woman had told him. So she hadn't always set herself upon a pedestal, he told himself. She had chanced illness and death to bring succor to those afflicted.

Home. He stared up at the castle once he had ridden past the gatehouse. Home. By God, it was becoming home.

He swallowed. He felt glad—and anxious. Already, he felt trembling inside of him, and rising heat. After a meal and a long drink of ale, he would go to her. She could rail against him or ignore him as she chose; he would hold her until she admitted that she had to come to him. He would make love to her because he had to; and he would sleep beside her tonight because he wanted to.

He called out to Tibald and the men to take their rest. Young Matthew, smiling and shy and handsome in his new livery, came running out to take the piebald. And Tristan started for the great hall.

He knew before he reached the doors that something had gone wrong. Jon opened them; Jon stood before him, grave, proud, and penitent, all in one. His saddle pouches were slung over his shoulder, as if he only awaited for Tristan's return before undertaking a journey. Jon bowed before him. "She escaped me," he whispered. "She—she tricked me. Against all your warnings. I swear, though, I shall find her. I have betrayed your faith. I—"

"Jon, Jon—cease!" Tristan said wearily. Curiously, he felt no anger toward Jon; he just felt cold. He walked past Jon and up the steps. Griswald was there, hovering nervously, anxious to see to his needs.

Jon followed him. "Tristan, I—"

Tristan took a goblet from the tray Griswald offered. He swallowed deeply.

"Jon, tell Matthew for me please to feed the piebald lightly, and leave his saddle upon his back. I shall go for her myself."

"Tristan, damn you, I failed you!"

"Nay, Jon." He actually smiled. "I gave her the freedom; it shouldn't have been done until I returned. I need you here. If you owe me anything, you owe me your service. Here. Griswald, bring me something to eat, in the counting room. And pack some food for me, too, please. And ale."

Jon stared at him in disbelief. "I'll just change my things," Tristan murmured.

He walked up the stairway, heading for the master chamber, but paused at Genevieve's open door. He stepped inside and he saw the wine stain against the white wall.

He left the room hurriedly and changed his clothing, wishing he had time to bathe. His good mantle he exchanged for heavy wool, his dress boots for a heartier pair with thick soles, and he started back down the stairs. He still felt a terrible chill. Am I angry? he wondered. Furious. So furious that I dare not let it go. And why? Because she has betrayed me again, when I needed her.

Jon was still in the great hall. Tristan slipped silently into the counting room, where he found a plate of roasted lamb and mint jelly. How smoothly this place runs, he thought idly.

He drew out his map of the area, certain that he knew

where she would run. He pinpointed the destination, then rolled the map to take with him.

He started into the lamb. Not because he was hungry, but because he knew he would need the sustenance if he was to catch her.

"Tristan!"

A voice, soft, feminine, hesitant, called out to him. He had not closed the door. He looked up to see Edwyna there, stricken as she watched him.

He sat back. "Lady Edwyna?"

She came into the room and knelt at his side, staring up at him beseechingly. "I swear, I had no part in it! I didn't know! I should have guessed, but I thought . . ."

He interrupted her, frowning as he reached down to lift her chin. A slight bruise remained on her cheek. She flushed and pulled her chin away, murmuring, "Jon thinks that I—planned it."

"Good God," Tristan breathed.

He was on his feet, racing out to the hall. "Jon, damn you! You struck her."

Jon reeled around in stunned surprise and his face, penitent until now, suddenly darkened with anger. "You, Tristan, are going to tell me how to handle my woman?"

"You struck her!"

"She caused it!"

"I don't believe that!"

Edwyna was behind him, soft tears falling from her eyes.

"Jon, I swear to you that I did not!"

"Man, what is wrong with you?" Tristan demanded hotly. Incredulously he realized that he and Jon were about to come to blows.

"Jon, please . . ." Edwyna came between them, going to Jon like a supplicant. Crying, she fell before him. "Please!" she whispered desperately.

"Have you no compassion in you?" Tristan shouted.

"Why should I? You have none!"

"I have been betrayed, and you have not!"

Tristan spun heatedly around, leaving them together. He stomped back into the counting room and collected the few things he needed and came back out. Edwyna was on her feet again, still crying, but they were close and Jon was whispering to her.

They broke apart, realizing that Tristan was back.

"I am coming with you," Jon said. "It is my fault."

"No. I am going alone. I'll find her."

"You must!" Edwyna said. "There are bears in the hills, and wolves and—" She broke off then, as if just realizing that at this point it might be better for Genevieve to meet with a wolf than with Tristan. She swallowed.

"And trappers—wild men, who acknowledge no king or authority."

"Tristan," Jon said, "fifty of us went in search of her and could not find her! Please, at least let me—"

"Jon, I will find her, because I know where she is going. I know her mind, better than you—" he paused, and smiled wryly again. "Better than Edwyna, even. She is on foot, I hope? You two didn't provide her with a horse?" The query was lightened by his smile. They both flushed and looked at one another uneasily.

"Nay. She is on foot," Jon assured him.

Tristan started out the door, then he turned back. "Edwyna, there is a small tower room, I believe."

"Aye," she replied, looking curious.

Tristan's smile was grim now. "See that Genevieve's things are taken there. And that mine are transferred into her chamber."

He left them standing there together and hurried out. The night had grown chill. He wondered vaguely if she were cold; then he hoped bitterly that she was.

But as he took the reins of the piebald from Matthew and thanked him and took his leave, he remembered the terror in his heart when he had come upon her that night, sleeping at the hearth, and he had thought her dead.

He rode out of the walls, and he looked up at the rising moon. "I pray, lady, that no harm befalls you," he whispered, and then he nudged the piebald into a fleeting gallop. Haste might make all the difference.

Chapter
Fourteen

BY THE TIME darkness fell a second day, Genevieve was feeling truly wretched.

One cramped, cold night in the open had been bearable. She had learned in that time though that she wasn't so fond of darkness as she might have imagined. She had always loved the outdoors. But now she was not quite so fond of the forest. Last night she had lain beneath the tree she had climbed, and she had slept little. It had been colder than she had expected, and she had awakened long before dawn. She had begun to imagine that a branch was a snake, and soon she was afraid of every rustle and movement. Every whisper of the breeze, every soft fall of leaves. She thought of the wolves that sometimes prowled here and the bears that occasionally foraged in the lowlands.

By morning she was thirsty, but by daylight she was on her own ground. She'd known where to find the brook, where to drink and bathe her face.

But by midday, after walking all morning, she was famished and she had moved quickly enough that she was no longer familiar with her surroundings. She found berries and congratulated herself on her prowess, but the berries had only made her hungrier. In the end she was forced to realize that she was ill-equipped to deal with simple survival.

She'd never thought much about food before. Now it was on her mind constantly. She reminded herself sharply that if she just managed another day, she would be with the Sisters of Good Hope, and they would be good hope for her indeed. She could stay with them until she felt it safe; then she could venture forth and leave the country—Henry's country—for Brittany, where her mother had been born.

Genevieve refused to think about discomfort; she had to keep walking. Darkness seemed to be falling very early. The tree branches overhead formed eerie shadows, as if they could reach down and touch her, brush her cheeks like spiders' webs. Twigs snapped all around her. In spite of herself, Genevieve was frightened.

But she kept going until she could hear the soft melody of a brook through the trees. Leaving the darkening trail, she hurried to it and drank thirstily.

This seemed as good a place as any to try to sleep and let the night pass. Not too close to the water, lest there be snakes; not too far from it, for it would be wonderful to wake beside it, to drink and bathe before she started out again.

She leaned against a tree trunk, and again thought tortuously of food. Griswald's bread, fresh and aromatic. His steak and kidney pie . . .

Stop! She warned herself. Good God, she was healthy and well padded! One more night would not hurt her. One more desperate night spent to escape a fate . . .

Worse than death? She taunted herself wryly, and she breathed deeply before she could not bear some of her own thoughts. She ached with homesickness, and of all absurdities, sometimes the very man she longed so fervently to escape merged with thoughts of things that she would miss with all her heart, forever.

From somewhere nearby, a branch snapped. Startled and wary, Genevieve pushed herself up and looked around. She almost called out, but caught herself.

How foolish! she thought, her heart thumping. It could be a

preying wolf, and if it were, the creature certainly wouldn't heed her call! It could be a man . . .

A hermit perhaps, or a huntsman. A trapper—or did it matter? She didn't dare trust a stranger in the woods. She closed her eyes, swallowing. If some filthy vagrant were ever to touch her in the way Tristan had, Genevieve might truly think her life not worth living.

She held her breath, for a long while she heard nothing else.

Then again, nearer, a branch crackled and snapped.

Panic sent her heart shooting up to her throat. Silently she scanned the ground around herself. She saw a long heavy stick and reached for it. With her free hand, she reached into the pocket of her skirt for her elegant little dagger.

If it was a wolf, she thought miserably, it was a big one. But wolves were really cowards, weren't they? Hadn't her father told her that once? They usually hunted in packs, and they preferred smaller animals . . .

Maybe a big wolf would consider her a small enough animal!

An owl suddenly let out a horrific shriek, swooping down almost on top of her head. Genevieve let out a long shriek herself and jumped to her feet, waving her arms madly above her head—and striking herself with her stick.

Well, she told herself. It could have been worse! She could have sliced herself with the damn dagger!

"Stupid owl!" she swore. And then . . .

She could have sworn she heard a soft echo of laughter. She turned and spun about, straining to see through the darkness. There was nothing. Nothing but the whisper of the wind through the leaves and the gentle tumbling of the brook over the pebbles in its path.

She sat down before the tree again and hugged her arms around her knees. She didn't sleep; she dozed fitfully, to awake in cramped misery time and time again.

Morning came at last, and with it light.

She let out a long, long sigh of relief, since along with the light came fresh courage. Genevieve stretched and arched her back and looked around. She was completely alone. She smiled up at the sun streaking through the trees. It was bringing warmth already. It was casting shimmering rays upon the brook. Genevieve dropped her stick and her dagger, shed her cloak, and hurried toward the bank.

The water was cold, but the cold felt good. She looked around herself again, oddly uncomfortable, as if the trees had eyes. But she saw no one.

She struggled and dragged her gown over her head and tossed it over on top of her cloak. She hesitated, then pulled her shift off, too—modesty suggested she keep it on, but if she wasn't cold now, she would be when she came out, and it seemed much smarter to keep the garment dry. Once she had cast it aside, she hurried into the water, gasping as the cold awoke her thoroughly. She laughed then because it felt so good against her flesh. It soothed the blisters on her poor feet. She wound her hair high to keep it dry, and kept on moving into the water—longing only for soap.

At last she rose and started to walk to the bank, feeling revived and enlivened, and ready to start out again. Soon she would be near her destination. Soon—

Genevieve stopped suddenly and let out a gasp. She was so stunned that she forgot her nakedness. For there, leaning comfortably against her tree, was Tristan, whittling away at a piece of wood. Beside him, the piebald grazed peacefully. He looked at her and smiled slowly, but his smile did not reach his eyes.

"Good morning!" he called to her. "Did you sleep well, milady? Pleasant site for a bath, I do say."

Genevieve was riddled with dismay. Her heart beat in panic, and she despaired. He could not be there! But he was.

Dropping his whittling, he bowed at her slightly. He hunched down near the ground, and in another second Genevieve saw that he had built a small fire. He even had a pan with him with which to cook.

He was very well prepared—unlike Genevieve, who just stood there, naked, staring at him!

Tristan looked at her again, and she thought that his casual greetings were the greatest lies that she had ever known: His expression assured her that he was just longing to throttle her.

God help her—she never did think quickly enough in his presence. It didn't occur to her that if she forded the stream, she would arrive on the other bank with nothing, absolutely nothing—not even a shift. It only crossed her mind that it was possible that the man could not swim. On that journey home from London, he had not swum after her—he had come in a boat. It seemed like sound logic.

She turned and raced quickly into the deeper water, and plunged heedlessly into it.

She knew moments of elation, then joy, and an astounding sense of freedom. He did not come after her! Each stroke brought her closer and closer to the opposite shore. A few more strokes, and she would be there. Oh, she could see it! The other bank, seeming to reach out to her, seeming to offer the succor she so desperately needed. Ten-feet, and she would reach it—

She gasped, and then choked, and then thought that she was drowning for sure. He pounced upon her, and then wound his fingers through her hair. Suddenly she was flying through the water—as he towed her by her hair, using massive strokes with one arm and the powerful kicks of his legs.

Mistaken again, she told herself dully—the man could swim.

He dumped her, panting and gasping and entangled in the sodden mass of her own hair, on the bank. She looked up and saw with dismay what had caused his delay in reaching her.

He, too, had chosen not to to soak his clothing. He stalked past her with long strides to retrieve his shirt, watching her as he slipped it back on, then donning his leather tunic, wool hose, boots, and leggings. All that, and she had not yet managed to move.

He came back silently to her, dropping her shift upon her back. "You are in my favorite state, milady," he said, and surely the water was no colder than his voice. "But if I ever decide to kill you, I'd not have the means be pneumonia. Get dressed."

Shivering and miserable, Genevieve stood and turned her back to slip into the shift. She realized then that he was at her back. She started, but realized that he merely intended to help her back into her gown. When that was done, he wrapped her cloak around her. She sat, too miserable and exhausted to care about the state of her hair, and leaned against the tree. Silent.

A second later something was pressed into her hands. It was a metal cup, warm to the touch, and something steamed from it, smelling wonderful. She looked at him uneasily. He had returned to the fire; his back was to her.

"Warmed ale, nothing more. I noted that you did not seem to appreciate the wine."

"Insult to grave injury, milord."

"It was but a thank-you gift."

"For what I did not intend to give!"

"Ah, but Genevieve! You offered so much so generously."

"Rotten, scurvy-bastard!" she swore. He did not respond. She sipped at the ale, warm against the chill that had invaded her.

"How—how did you find me?" she asked him wearily.

He turned to her, then sat again himself, leaning against another tree close to his fire.

"There seemed to be but one place you could go." He waved the arm with the cup past the brook to the hill that rose above it. "You were almost there, milady. The convent lies just over that crest."

Genevieve was truly dismayed now. She was so close! If only she hadn't stopped last night. "I almost made it."

She hadn't realized that she had said the words out loud until he suddenly started laughing. She swerved her head quickly to stare at him again—and found honest laughter in his eyes. He was truly amused.

"Nay, milady, you did not! I'd have accosted you last night except that you did not seem to need me. You defended yourself nicely against that vicious owl!"

Now he laughed so hard that he had to set his cup down.

She inhaled sharply. "You were there!"

"All along!"

"You bastard!" She was on her feet, furious. She'd been scared half to death—and it had been him.

"You were afraid of wolves, I take it?" He grinned.

"No. Wolf. Singular. And I had damned good reason to be!" she yelled at him. He started laughing again.

She strode toward him, thunderous, angry—ready to douse his laughter with warm ale. But he was on his feet long before she could reach him, grasping for her wrist. "Oh, Genevieve! At this point, do you really think that would be wise?"

There was a warning behind the laughter. A real warning. She bit her lip and stepped back. "No. No, it wouldn't. I want the ale—it would be wasted upon you!"

The fire sizzled suddenly; he hunched down again and Genevieve stared at the pan, seized suddenly with a rampant, nearly desperate hunger. Two beautiful fish were sizzling away in the pan, and upon the pack set by the fire, bread and a wedge of cheese had been set out.

Genevieve was ravenous, and her hunger growled loudly within her. She turned her back, not wanting him to see her eyes, how sorely, how badly, she wanted her share of that fish. But he had heard that less-than-ladylike growl and was chuckling softly. She sank down into the soft moss at the base of her chosen tree and stared straight out before her.

To her chagrin, he seemed willing to ignore her.

"Perfect!" he proclaimed. She didn't watch him—she heard him fix a plate with fish and bread and cheese, and she waited for him to bring it to her, as he had the ale. But he merely sat back against his tree again and began to eat.

"This is better than the rabbit I caught last night."

She couldn't help it. She turned on him.

"You son of a bitch! You had a rabbit last night, while I was starving! You let me wait until morning when I was scared to death and—and—"

"It probably did your sweet soul good, my love."

"Bastard!" she went on. He didn't appear to notice. He ate his fish, licking his fingers.

"Hungry?" he asked when she paused for breath.

"No!"

"Good, I wouldn't mind the other myself."

"Fine! I'm surprised that you haven't starved me before now."

"So am I."

"You really do hate me."

"You are keenly observant!" he snapped, but then he paused, staring at her a long moment. His voice softened. "Actually, milady, I don't know what I feel. I do know what the facts are, though. And you are mine—until I choose it to be otherwise."

Something about his tone gave her a breath of hope. She rose and crossed to him quietly, then knelt down beside him, seeking out his eyes. "Tristan, you could choose to release me now. The convent is just over the hill. Please, please! Tristan, I didn't take anything with me. Just the clothing on my back—"

"And the dagger."

"Nothing! I didn't touch the jewels, I didn't—"

"I daresay that you didn't have the time to think of them," he answered her softly, his eyes fully on hers.

"Does it matter?" she cried, pleading. "Tristan, I took nothing of value, there is just me—"

He touched her then, reaching out a hand to cup her chin, his thumb halting her speech.

"But you did, you see. To me." He stroked the sopping mass of her hair and said, "This. This is grander than any jewel, Genevieve."

He drew his hand back, as if he had not intended his word. He looked at his plate, and his voice grew harsh.

"I'm sorry, Genevieve. At this moment you are of value to me." He looked up again, and she was amazed at the changes that could take place in him. His eyes looked black again—they had changed color with his mood.

He set his plate down and pushed her impatiently from him. Finding another of his flat pewter plates in the leather sack, he prepared it for her, filling it with fish and bread and cheese.

She shook her head miserably in denial, her eyes downcast.

"Eat it! And eat slowly, or you'll be sick."

She took the plate, and she began to eat, woodenly. But then she was so hungry that she began to gulp her food, forgetting all else. He stopped her, jerking the plate from her.

"I told you—slowly."

She nodded, not returning his look, and he returned the plate. He walked away, and she heard him talking softly to the piebald horse. Genevieve wondered dismally if he had ever spoken to a woman as tenderly as he did that great animal.

She finished. Unbidden, she took her plate and his to the stream and cleaned them both, drying them upon her skirt. When she returned to the trees she found him carefully stamping out the fire.

He took the plates and returned them and the mugs to his sack and tied the sack to the back of his saddle. Genevieve was close enough to the piebald for the horse to lean down its massive nose suddenly and nudge her. Taken off balance, Genevieve laughed and straightened herself and patted him on the nose that had just roughly moved her. He came closer, like a big puppy, longing for affection.

"He likes you," Tristan commented dryly.

She cast him a quick glance. "Why shouldn't he?" she retorted.

She felt Tristan's shrug. She ignored him and lightly scratched the horse's chin. "Hello, young man!" she told him softly. And then she chanced a glance at Tristan again.

"What's his name?"

"Pie."

"Pie," she repeated. "My God, he's so massive, and so tame!"

"Like a pup," Tristan said.

"And he rides into battle, against shot and powder and swords," Genevieve murmured.

"So do men, milady, and many who must face cannon are in truth the most very tame of beasts. He is well trained, Pie here. Don't ever think otherwise."

"I was not thinking along that line at all."

"Good. We're heading back. Now. And don't try to elude me again, Genevieve. There are beasts in this forest. More wolves than you might think."

"I'm surprised that you care."

"I don't like my battle rewards mauled."

She didn't reply. Pie chose that moment to snort and nuzzle her again. You liar! she thought. Pie is as gentle as any horse she had ever encountered, and her father's stables had always been full.

Tristan began to walk out of the trees, and Genevieve followed him. When they came to the path, Genevieve could see what she had not been able to discern in the darkness: The convent walls rose right above the road, not a half mile away. She was so close that she could almost touch freedom. Smell it, sense it, feel it.

She might never come this close again. Ever.

"You've blisters?" Tristan asked her.

She nodded.

"I'll walk awhile. You can ride."

She stood meekly still, lashes sweeping low over her eyes, while his hands spanned her waist and he lifted her high. She took the reins and walked the horse dutifully behind him as he started out.

Then she leaned low, and whispered softly to the creature; then she pulled the reins to the right and dug in her heels.

The horse, beautifully trained, spun cleanly about. He was incredibly agile for his size, and he took off with a jolt that nearly sent Genevieve flying from the saddle. Within moments he was at a canter, as smooth as silk.

Genevieve bent low, gripping a handful of his mane along with the reins. The cool air flew at her, sending her hair flying, stinging her eyes. But day had never seemed more beautiful; it was almost like flying to freedom.

Pie's hooves tore away the turf. They mounted the cliff together and they sailed down it. She could see the convent. The low fence before the gardens, the high walls rising behind it. She could see the Holy Sisters tending to their garden patches, like awkward birds in their full black garments and wing-like hats. She could see them, she could almost touch them. They could see her, surely—

She didn't hear the whistle—not at first.

But Pie did. He stopped dead on a hair. And then he whirled around, and this time he did unseat his rider. Genevieve came hurtling into space; Pie was so big that it was a long, long fall. She saw stars when she hit the ground.

Her head cleared just as she felt the ground beneath her thundering. For a moment she thought that she needed to roll, that the horse might trample her. Then she realized that it wasn't hooves at all, the horse was standing perfectly still.

Feet were causing the ground to seem to quiver against her ears. Gasping, she pushed herself up. Tristan was coming, running like some ancient Greek athlete. Genevieve quickly stumbled to her feet and tried to weigh the distance. The nuns could see her! They were shading their eyes and looking at her.

She started to run. The distance between her and the wall and her and Tristan seemed to be the same. Perhaps she couldn't leap the wall, but if she did reach it, surely Tristan could not drag her back. Not with this flock of sainted ladies looking on.

She could barely breathe. Her blisters burned into her feet more deeply with every step and it felt as if long needles tore into her calves. It didn't matter. She could see the disbelieving look on one young sister's face. She could almost sail over the wall . . .

Suddenly she was sailing but not over the wall. She felt a sharp impact and flew up into the air, then came down hard. She twisted and tried to rise, but a hard weight bore down on her.

She gasped for air, and stared up into Tristan's eyes. His dark, sweat-gleaming features were grim; his lips were parted.

"God in his infinite heaven!" Came a voice, and Genevieve felt a thrill of joy again, for one of the sisters was coming to the little wall, staring over at them. She almost smiled; she was glad that she didn't because Tristan's eyes were narrowing and she realized, too late, that he had a few plans of his own.

"Genevieve, my love, my life! I warned that you must take care with Pie! Dearest!" he cried.

And he leaned over and kissed her.

She fought that kiss, twisting and flailing. But his hands were flat on her hair, right next to her face, pulling it to keep her head still, and his weight was such that she could not even squirm. In seconds she wasn't thinking so much about escape as she was life—she could barely breathe.

"My goodness!" murmured one of the sisters, shocked.

Tristan moved from Genevieve then, just as she thought that she would pass out. She was desperate for air, she couldn't begin to speak. Tristan stood quickly, swept Genevieve up in his arms, and bowed to the sisters.

"Good day, ladies! Forgive me, please! God's blessings upon us all." He smiled sheepishly. "Newlyweds, you know."

Titters of delighted laughter followed his words and Genevieve quickly found her voice.

"Newlyweds, my—"

The rest was muffled; another suffocating kiss fell her way. She watched him raise a gallant hand to the sisters and wave.

To Genevieve's dismay, they waved in return; a few of the younger ones looked rapturously enchanted, but one or two of the older ladies shook their heads in disapproval.

They returned to their work.

And Tristan quickly carried her back to the piebald and set her down with a thud. She gasped, still thinking that she might cry out for help. He was ahead of her once again, clamping a less than gentle hand over her mouth.

"One word, one word, and so help me God, Genevieve, you will have blisters on your rear to match those on your feet, Holy Sisters or no, I swear it!"

Exhausted, more than certain that he would carry out his threat and less than certain that her scream could be heard, Genevieve heeded his warning. She leaned her head against Pie's great neck and continued to gasp for breath.

His sudden grip about her waist was hard and harsh and she almost landed on the other side of the horse when he lifted her. He didn't hand her the reins. He set a foot in the left side stirrup and mounted the horse behind her. Pie flicked his tail and started up at a canter.

Tristan rode hard. Genevieve stayed as straight as she could. The wind seemed to blind her, and in time she wondered that Tristan could be so hard on the horse that he was so obviously fond of.

And then they slowed. He was silent, but he was there. And upon the animal's back, they were forced far closer than Genevieve wanted to be.

She was so tired.

Tristan didn't speak. And at long last, growing cramped in the saddle, Genevieve asked, "How long—'til we reach Edenby?"

"By nightfall."

Tears rose bitterly to her eyes. It had taken her so long to walk! It had been such a hard, desperate journey.

I should have figured out a way to steal a horse! she railed silently against herself.

But she had not. And Pie could eat twice the distance she had made in less than half the time.

They stopped only once, and Tristan still had nothing to say to her. He handed her food without a word, and she ate without a word. They both drank ale from the same cup without a word, and then started out again.

This time Genevieve could not remain rigid. She was exhausted from lack of sleep and exertion. In time her eyes closed of their own accord, and her head fell back against Tristan's chest; his mouth compressed in a tight line.

Genevieve woke with a start, certain that she was falling. She was falling, but only into Tristan's arms as he lifted her from Pie.

"Where are we?" she whispered sleepily.

"Home," he told her curtly, and she instantly began to fight his hold.

"No, milady, not now!" he told her, and his arms tightened.

He shouted out an order, and someone came for the horse. Then with his long, sure strides he carried her up the steps and into the great hall. The doors opened, and all the warmth of the hall seemed to come flooding out to them.

Jon was silhouetted there, with Edwyna behind him. They stepped back for Tristan to enter with Genevieve.

"You found her!" Edwyna cried. But she didn't look at Genevieve, and Genevieve knew that she was glad of her recovery—but angry.

And why not, Genevieve thought. You used her and you used Jon and you betrayed their kindness and your trust.

"Aye, I have found her," Tristan replied shortly. He strode on past them, Genevieve struggling against him.

"Tristan, please, just let me tell them . . . Edwyna and Jon that—that I'm sorry. That—"

He didn't stop walking. He looked down at her skeptically.

"Sorry that you escaped?" he whispered the taunt.

"Nay! I must escape you, and you must realize that! I am sorry that I—"

"Betrayed them?"

"Damn you, please, just let me—"

"They really don't want to speak with you, Genevieve."

She didn't have an answer for him because she was staring at the door to her room—as they went on past. Tristan walked to the next staircase, the one leading to the tower.

"We passed my room."

"My room, milady."

"What—"

"I have discovered that I'm fond of that chamber."

"But . . ."

Her voice trailed away in disbelief. They had reached the top of the winding stairway, and with the shove of a boot he had pushed open the one door there. He stepped in, and Genevieve gasped again with startled horror.

The tower room had been opened and cleaned and especially prepared. For her.

There was a hearth here, the focal point of the room. The bed was large and soft and ample, and there were chairs and a table. Her trunks lined the walls.

There was but one window, though. One lone window that sat high, high above the ground with nothing beneath it. It wasn't that it was a terrible room or a particularly drafty room or a cold room. But it was just so isolated.

Tristan set her down upon her feet. Her legs, cramped from so much riding, would not hold her. He caught her when she started to fall and carried her to the bed.

He stepped back and Genevieve sat up quickly.

"Here? You're—" she could hardly speak the words. "You're locking me up—up here?"

"Aye," he said, looking coolly regal.

"You chased me all that distance, ran me down like a fox, to drag me back and lock me up in the tower?"

"Aye, milady, that I did."

Genevieve felt faint—but somehow, suddenly strong at the same time. She shrieked out, insane with anger, and wishing in those dark seconds that she could have killed him. She pitched herself off the bed like a snarling tigress, and she was so swift that her first blow reached him, her nails raking a pattern across his cheek, her force nearly sweeping him from his feet. He rallied quickly, though, catching her disastrous tangle of hair and jerking her head back so sharply that she cried out, giving up the fight. He released her and she sank to the floor, and yet she had never been less beaten. She stared up at him, hating him, venom turning the tears in her eyes to a crystal mercury that condemned as no words could.

"You are a monster," she told him softly. "I have never met or seen or known of a creature on this earth less merciful."

He didn't answer her right away. Then he hunched down slowly until he was on a level with her, looking deeply into her eyes.

"I have tried to be merciful, milady."

"You are cruelty itself!"

"Nay, milady. Shall I tell you what cruelty is?" He had gone very tense, and he stared at her with pitch black eyes, but suddenly Genevieve knew that he was not seeing her at all, that he didn't look at her, but beyond her.

He didn't touch her; his fingers knotted together before her, so tightly that the knuckles were white.

"Cruelty . . ."

His voice was almost a whisper, and carried some pain that she could barely touch yet seemed to invade her.

"Cruelty is a man waking to an alarm in the night, slain in his own bedroom. Cruelty is a peasant woman slain in the midst of her baking; or her husband, old and gray, butchered with his own scythe. Cruelty is rape—true, brutal rape. And it is death on top of that rape, even though she screamed, even though she surrendered, even though she begged and pleaded that they not hurt or cut or maim her but let her live just for the child that she carried . . ."

His voice trailed away.

It was as if his eyes focused on her again, and could not bear what they saw.

He stood abruptly, then stiffened. Genevieve raised her head, unaware that tears she could not understand were falling silently down her cheeks.

There was someone standing in the doorway.

Tess. Red-cheeked, bright-eyed, bobbing, and eager to please.

Tristan didn't seem to notice her. He stepped to the left to go past her.

"Milord . . . ?" Tess queried.

Tristan looked back into the room, as if rudely reminded of something.

He shrugged.

"Clean her up," he told Tess crudely.

And then he walked away, the sound of his footsteps quickly receding as he hurried down the winding stone stairs.

Chapter
Fifteen

"I'M GOING TO be married!"

Edwyna said the words with such loving reverence that Genevieve smiled despite all of her misgivings, and returned her aunt's tumultuous hug.

It was a wonderful thing—surely. Edwyna loved her Jon. Even if he had been part of disaster and desolation, part of Edgar's death, part of it all. She loved him and he loved her, and if Edwyna could forget, then everything was—well and good.

"I'm so glad for you," Genevieve murmured, and she kept any bitterness to herself. She had been stunned and then heartily glad when Edwyna had come to her this morning, since she had wondered if Tristan had intended to keep her locked away from all society except that of his bouncing little doll, Tess. And she had wondered, too, if Edwyna would forgive her, since Genevieve's actions had caused Edwyna a fair amount of heartache.

Edwyna, her eyes as bright as the stars, pulled away from Genevieve. "Tomorrow, Genevieve! Father Thomas is going to marry us tomorrow in the chapel. Oh, Genevieve, I am so very, very happy!"

Genevieve had to swallow sharply and look down at her hands. She loved Edwyna; she was happy for her. But she felt more lost and desolate herself than ever. God! What had happened here? Life was going on. Father Thomas prayed in his chapel, the peasants worked in the field, and old Griswald labored in the kitchen. It was almost as if . . .

As if nothing had ever really happened. As if apocalypse had never come. Even with Edwyna, life was going on. Beautifully. She had fallen in love with the invader.

Only Genevieve was left to pay. Pay the price of treachery. She fought her imprisonment, frightening and angering them all, but damn it they'd all been a part of it; yet she was the one now being condemned.

But then, she thought with a shudder, she was the one who had raised a hand against Tristan, and by God, she now believed that his chivalry and his heart were indeed buried forever.

She hadn't forgotten his words, nor his look, all through the night. She hadn't understood completely, but she had felt something and she had known pity—which he would not want, of course, especially from her—and an even deeper fear and desolation for her own future. There was no mercy left in the man.

She turned suddenly from her aunt, not wanting Edwyna to see the tears that burned her eyes suddenly and inexplicably. "I'll be thinking of you every moment. I'm sure it will be very beautiful."

That was it, of course. Edwyna was going to be married, bound before God, and it would be beautiful and there would be a feast and maybe even dancing and . . .

Genevieve would not be there. She would be the prisoner in the tower, tainted, forgotten.

"But you must be there!" Edwyna said. "Oh, Genevieve, you need but ask Tristan, and he will relent!"

Genevieve turned back to her, straightening so that she would not betray her disappointment. Edwyna had not seen Tristan last night when he had spoken to her. Had not seen the fury, the distance, the pain—or the barrenness that remained.

"I doubt," she murmured softly, "that he will speak with

me today, much less listen to any request. And—'' She hesitated, unable to explain to Edwyna that it was one thing to lower oneself to beg when there was a prayer of being heard, and another when there was not.

''I cannot ask him, Edwyna.''

''But Genevieve—''

''I cannot. Truly, if I sent for him, he would not come. I know it. And I really—I really cannot even send for him.''

''Perhaps I can ask him,'' Edwyna murmured. ''Or Jon.''

Genevieve shrugged and tried to smile gaily. ''Edwyna! Please, this is going to be a wonderful day for you and Jon. Your day. Don't mar it, don't cast a dark cloud upon it! Enjoy it and, please, don't worry. I will be with you in spirit, I swear it!''

Edwyna was still unhappy. She walked over to the mantel, frowning, then turned back to her niece.

''Genevieve, you simply do not handle him right.''

Genevieve threw her arms up in the air in exasperation. ''I do not handle him right! Edwyna—he has taken my inheritance! He killed my fiancé and my father—''

''Battle killed them.''

''He invaded my house, he invaded me, and you speak to me of handling him!''

Edwyna didn't look at her. She stared at the fire.

''I like him, Genevieve. I admire him. I find him just and often chivalrous, and though hard perhaps, he is fair. He has dealt well with every man and woman here.''

''You will excuse me if I do disagree!''

''Ah, Genevieve! If you had just accepted—''

''Accepted! He dragged me back, he locked me up, he—''

''He took what was originally offered, don't you see? Oh, Genevieve! That is the way of things. They won—we lost! If you would not take it all so to heart—''

''I have to take it to heart! An extremely personal affront, my God, Edwyna, please! You have fallen in love with Jon—I am glad. Glad of your future. But don't expect acceptance from me! I hate him, I find him ruthless, I . . .'' Her voice trailed away suddenly as she wondered how much of her own defense was a lie. She was silent for a minute, then said, "Edwyna—what happened to him?"

Edwyna hesitated. "He—he doesn't like his past discussed," she murmured. "He's still furious with Jon for having told me about it."

"Before God, who is here with us, Edwyna! You condemn me for fighting him, yet you won't help me understand him! I know—something. That his people were attacked, that . . ."

"There was no battle, Genevieve," Edwyna interrupted. She sighed. "They were Yorkists, then, you see. His family. Tristan was close to Richard—"

"What?" Genevieve gasped, astounded.

Edwyna nodded. "When King Edward died and the Woodvilles were scrambling for power, Tristan's father was among those who believed that Richard had to step in for the good of the country. But then the young Princes were taken to the Tower, and Tristan made an open stand against Richard, demanding that the boys be saved. He could not support Richard as King if Richard had murdered his nephews. Anyway," Edwyna murmured, "he and Jon and another rode homeward after this demand and found—total devastation. Farmhouses burned to the ground, the farmers' wives raped and slaughtered, the men killed. And it became worse. His father, his brother, his brother's wife—and his own, all slain. Jon—Jon told me that it was awful. That no dream of hell could be worse. Tristan and his wife were expecting their first child, and Tristan found the baby, miscarried in the events, beside his wife." Edwyna hesitated. "With her throat slit."

Genevieve felt suddenly and viciously ill. She sat down on the bed, cold and miserable.

"I am sorry," she said. "I would be sorry for any man. Yet—I did not do this to him. I—"

"No, you beguiled him, invited him to your chamber—and attempted to murder him with a poker."

"Edwyna, dammit! The deed was not all mine!"

"I know," Edwyna murmured softly. She looked as if she were about to cry herself. She turned around quickly. "Look— I've brought you Chaucer and Aristotle and that Italian writer you're so fond of. I've got to go before—before someone thinks that we're plotting again." She came to Genevieve and gave her a fierce hug. "Oh, Genevieve! You'll receive your freedom. Just be patient, be silent, and it will come. And—"

"What?" Genevieve whispered. Edwyna was about to leave her again. Alone. With her thoughts, her memories, her nightmares—and the emotions that she did not want to feel.

"Ask him! Ask him if you cannot be there tomorrow, for me?"

Genevieve smiled, curving her lips into a bitter smile. "All right," she promised. "If I am able, I will ask."

Edwyna was gone. Tess had come and gone, and Genevieve immediately felt the oppression of being locked in and a panic that tore at her.

Edwyna was so lucky . . .

And she couldn't understand at all. She was living in her own little paradise where love was the only answer. She couldn't comprehend the darkness in a man's soul, the twisting torment, nor did she know of the strange fire between them . . .

Or of Genevieve's very real and very simple fears.

To give in to him would be foolhardy and stupid. He would never care again—he was only capable of using now. Genevieve could not be anything to him, no more than the moment's amusement he found with any woman.

And in time . . . she would be used up. If she could always remember that she was but a shell, she could survive it. She could begin again anew, in another life, far away.

He robbed me of everything. For that alone, I must always despise him, she told herself with irrevocable logic. And it was true. Perhaps he had not become a wild animal; perhaps he had remembered mercy, so that he did not plunder and butcher wantonly.

But he had forgotten the mercy of the heart.

Genevieve opened up a page of one her favorite books by Chaucer. Strange, Geoffrey Chaucer, long dead and buried and known for his writing, had been such a close part to all that was happening now! His beloved sister-in-law had been the great love of John of Gaunt, the woman who had lived with him for years and years and borne him his Beaufort bastards and then—in the last years of their lives—become his wife at last! It was a beautiful story, sad, and full of the greatest depths of love. And the Henry who now sat on the throne was a great-grandchild of that bittersweet affair . . .

She closed the book. There were tears in her eyes. In her younger years she had often cried over the wonderful romance of Chaucer. But she didn't cry now for the words on the page.

She didn't know if she cried for herself, or for Tristan, or the fate that had made them irredeemable enemies.

By the late afternoon she felt her solitude keenly, and she paced her small enclosure in panic. Again she feared that she would go mad—she hadn't been here long at all, and if he chose he could keep her here for days, weeks, months . . .

Years.

Time passed so slowly.

She had bathed, she had spent long, patient minutes removing all the tangles from her hair. She had washed it and dried it and braided the long strands. She had sewn rents in her dresses, she had read, she had tried to draw out a pattern for a tapestry.

And still the day wore on.

She cast herself upon the bed, chin on her knuckles, and found herself rising in fury against Tristan anew, and wondering why. She expected nothing from him. But Tess-of-the-gargantuan-breasts had not made another appearance, and Genevieve could not help but agonize over the image of the two of them together. Tristan, wrath forgotten, laughing and teasing, with his eyes not dark but that fascinating indigo, his hair dark and tousled over his forehead. And Tess—gushing! So awed by everything great-guzzling down the wine that Genevieve had insisted that she take, and being the sweetest, most pliable little toy . . .

Making no demands. A farmer's daughter—who had never raised a hand against him. Causing no discomfort in his soul. Oh, what a cute little plaything she would make! Tristan could turn from her to business without a thought. He would never marry her, of course, but Tess would know that from the onset and be content with the gifts received from easy service to such a noble lord. And he wasn't even old and ugly; he was young and muscled and handsome and—

She rolled on the bed, pressing her hands to her temples in shame.

Take Tess, take her, have her, just leave me be!

He was leaving her be. She felt like laughing hysterically. She had enough pride not to beg the guard beyond her door to send for him. Maybe it wasn't pride. Maybe it was the simple knowledge that he would not come.

But she had hoped against hope that he would come to her. If he had come, she would have taken the chance and asked if she might not attend her aunt's wedding. She swallowed, promising herself that she wouldn't beg. She would ask. If he refused, she would coolly accept it. She would be regal and poised and distant, and he would know that she didn't give a tinker's damn, that she had learned to wait with patience, await the freedom that had to come . . .

He wasn't coming.

She flew to her feet again and thought of the endless days and nights ahead of her. Awakening each morning—awaiting nightfall just so that she could sleep again. The prisoner in the tower of Edenby Castle. Years could go by. Years and years. One day people would pass by and they would wonder, who was the ancient hag in the tower of Edenby . . .

There was a soft tapping at the door. Genevieve flew to it, then composed herself. It might just be Tess, all flushed and happy and . . .

She forced a calm expression and said softly, "Yes?"

The door opened. It was Jon. Genevieve flushed. She had made her peace with Edwyna, but she knew that Jon must still feel the deepest betrayal.

"Genevieve," he bowed slightly to her.

She swallowed, wondering why she felt it necessary to apologize to this invader.

"Jon . . . I'm sorry."

"Umm. I'm just sure that you are."

"Jon, really, I'm sorry that I betrayed your trust. Oh, God,

Jon, can't you understand! Think of my life! Could you bear it? Wouldn't you have done—anything?''

He grunted, yet she thought that he did understand.

"Let's go," he told her.

Her heart began to thump. "Where?"

"Tristan has asked to see you."

A shivering sensation swept through her. She had no idea of what to expect. She had wanted to see him, but now . . .

Had he thought of some other form of punishment for all the misery she had caused him with her flight and her continual efforts to elude him?

"Now, please, Genevieve."

She fought the unease and fear that swept through her and followed him out to the winding staircase. She placed her hand against the cool stone so that she would not trip as she went down. She tried to talk, to break her terrible tension.

"Jon, I'm very happy for you. For you and Edwyna."

"Are you really?" he asked coolly.

"Of course! She is my aunt and I love her."

He didn't respond and she fell silent. They reached the second floor landing and Jon gripped her arm and led her straight to the door. He opened it and pushed her inside. She heard the door close behind her.

She stood still there, barely daring to breathe.

It was dark now, but the room was bathed in soft light. Red glowing light from the fire, and a softer, white moonbeam light from the candles.

Tristan was by the mantel, his back to her. His hands were lightly clasped behind his back and one foot rested upon the stone step before the fire. He wore no mantle or tunic, just a white shirt, skin-fitting breeches, and his high leather boots.

Everything seemed gentle in the light. Gentle and soft and surreal.

But she trembled despite it. Trembled, and thought that time elapsed in slow, slow eons before he turned to see her there. The expression in his eyes, sheltered by the soft light and shadow was unfathomable, yet she saw that he surveyed her slowly from head to toe.

"Good evening," he said.

She swallowed, startled that she could not speak, and nodded in acknowledgment of his words. But he said nothing more and his steady gaze unnerved her so thoroughly that she found her tongue at last.

"Why have you sent for me?"

A smile cut across his dark features, only slightly ironic, and one dark brow arched upward.

"Surely, you know."

She flushed, there was such astounding insinuation and intimacy in his voice. And she lowered her eyes, not in horror at first, just warmed by his tone, and—to her complete self-reproach—anxious.

But then, unbidden, a picture of him with Tess rose before her eyes, and anger settled in. Did he play with one toy during the day and another at night? She couldn't bear the thought; it seemed an absolute insult. It angered her, and it—

Hurt.

It is jealousy, she warned herself, then cried out inwardly that it was just the outrage . . .

He moved from the mantel, and she looked up quickly. They had never made . . . planned love. She had never stood there and awaited him. She had always . . . fought it.

He didn't come straight to her. She saw that a meal had been set up before the hearth, small chafing dishes with silver covers awaited them, chairs drawn before each. And there were two of her mother's gold rimmed crystal glasses with the long twilled stems there, each filled with something clear and white.

He had paused at the table, picking up the glasses. And when he approached her she felt everything inside of her go weak, as if she were composed of nothing but the lightly dancing water of a stream in spring.

He was smiling still, a small crooked smile, and his eyes were their deepest blue, a fascinating indigo with centers the warmth of dazzling fire. He had never appeared younger, never more handsome.

Never more dangerous.

He handed her a glass, and mechanically she took it. She sipped at the liquid and it soothed her hot, parched throat. It was sweet and dry all in one, and delicious.

"What is this?" she murmured.

"No poison, I assure you. Knowing your keen distaste for Bordeaux, I decided upon this. Wine, white wine, a German variety."

She tensed at his reference to the Bordeaux and looking down quickly sipped more wine, then remembered with remorse the effects of doing so.

He lifted a hand, indicating that she should go to the table. Genevieve quickly sailed past him and sat. She swallowed more wine, but noted his smile and quickly set her glass down.

"Are you hungry?" he asked her.

"No, not really."

He served her anyway, small portions of steaming fowl and sweet cooked apples in pastry and autumn greens.

"Strange. I would have thought you'd still be starving," he murmured.

She had no reply and he found her eyes on him in a curious fashion he had never expected. She studied him. Not as the invader, but as the man. And suddenly he did not want to meet her gaze, mauve this night, like summer violets.

"And I wouldn't have thought that you cared," she said at last, and picked up her fork, her gaze lowering from his that she might push her food around on her plate rather than consume it.

He made an impatient sound, an angry sound, and she looked back to him, startled. She was instantly defensive and, he saw, ready to spring from her chair, for what good it might do her.

"You left me in a great deal of wrath," she said nervously. "I did not expect you to . . ." Her voice trailed away to an uneasy silence.

"So I did." he said after a moment.

Color flooded her cheeks, and he realized that she was thinking his call had little to do with temper or emotion, and everything to do with simple desire. He didn't wish to tell her he was sorry because, in truth, he was not—he had, in his estimation, been merciful beyond bounds. But yet he'd felt something . . . and this was, in his way, the best he could do in the form of an apology.

"I'd have thought you might have enjoyed the idea of wine and a leisurely dinner and—"

She interrupted him with a bitter laugh. "Aye, surely!" she cried caustically. "Here I feel far more like the courtly courtesan than the peasant whore!"

He rose impatiently, nearly knocking his chair to the floor. He paced before the fire and cast out his hands. "What do you want from me, then?"

She inhaled sharply. "Freedom."

And then she was startled, as always, that he could move so swiftly, for he was at her side, lifting her chin to bring her face upward to his. "Freedom! You fool, you'd have had your freedom, yet what you are given seems never enough, and you must strive to take more! Freedom! To run through the woods? To risk hunger and thirst and the attack of wild beasts, and aye, lady, the attack of the greatest beast, that who walks on two feet! Tell me, Genevieve, what of your freedom had you had stumbled upon one of these? Or perhaps it wouldn't have mattered to you had you done so, perhaps you would have found a woodsman a fine companion! Perhaps you would have found yourself a prisoner again, lady, in far more difficult circumstances, my fastidious little love! Or would it have mattered? Tell me, I am anxious to know!"

"You hurt me!" she cried, trying to wrench her chin away.

She was not forced into a reply and he did release her, for there was a discreet tapping then on the door. Tristan exhaled with impatience.

"What is it?"

The door opened and Tess entered, bobbing a curtsy. "The trays, milord. Shall I take them away?"

"What? Oh, aye, the trays. Take them away."

Tess came in and Genevieve felt herself growing rigid and watching the girl against her will.

Found herself wondering . . .

She lowered her eyes quickly, feeling ill. It was her room! Her chamber, her bed . . .

Tristan had turned, one foot planted upon the mantel step,

an elbow leaned against it—his back to them both. Tess smiled radiantly at Genevieve and collected their dishes. Then she bowed again and hurried out.

Tristan spun back around. "Genevieve—"

She was on her feet, furious. "Aye! A thousand times over I'd have preferred the prison of a woodsman. Be he gray haired and toothless and a hundred and ten years old! You fool! You rutting fool! What is this kindness, this mercy of yours! You offer me dinner in my own room—a dinner of my own food!"

To her astonishment, he gazed curiously at the door, then back at her. And he did not rail in turn. He laughed.

"Oh, you are insane!" Genevieve muttered.

He walked toward her, slowly, still smiling. And not with malice, nor with sarcasm. She stopped suddenly, having come to the dais and knowing that if she walked farther, she would bring herself dangerously near the bed.

He stopped before her, drawing a intriguing line from her cheek to her lip with the tender touch of his thumb.

"What is this sudden temper?"

"Sudden? There is nothing sudden about it!"

"Aye, but there is! You came here tonight in a mellow mood. And you sat with me so gently! No silver sparks of fire lit your eyes, but rather something soft and most feminine. And understanding why I had sent for you, you knew no great alarm. Yet now again it has become the outrage. Has this to do with the girl?"

"What girl?"

"Tess."

"If you bedded with Tess or a thousand such cows, it would have no import to me!"

He started to laugh again to her vast dismay and actually whirled away from her to leap upon the dais. Then he cast himself backward upon the bed and laughed again.

Genevieve spun to stare at him incredulously. He was upon his knees, leaning against the left post and laughing with still greater amusement at her stunned expression. Then he leapt downward again with the spring and agility of a youth, coming back to her and catching her shoulders.

"You do mind, milady. Terribly."

"I mind that—that—"

"Ah, yes! That you were attainted, attacked, taken! Poor, my lady! You lie through your teeth! There are things in life we both know, milady—" He paused to bow extravagantly to her, and yet it was truth he spoke with that deep edge to his voice. "Milady, Richard III is dead and Henry rules England! My allegiance has paid and yours has not, and you fought a battle and lost. Edenby is mine—as you are mine. We both know this, and in your very strange way you do accept it!"

"Never! And don't be absurd! We both know that England teems with nobility with far more right to the throne!"

"You seek another insurrection? Nay—you know that would be a long time in coming, and with less hope of success than the sun would have to rise with the night! You mind, dear Genevieve, that you believe I chose that farm lass for her—assets!"

"Oh, how absurd." Genevieve was very careful to sound bored and droll and uninterested. She slipped past him, fingers trembling, grateful that Tess had left the wine glasses. She grabbed hers quickly and nearly drained it, then started to cough, and to her annoyance, he began to laugh again.

"Genevieve."

"Aye!"

"Come here!"

She turned. He was seated upon the bed, his arms crossed over his chest. She did not move.

"Come here!"

She could resist, she could make him come to her. She was so ruffled that he would well deserve the fight . . .

Yet she was suddenly tired and weary and so very frightened that she had given herself away; nor could she forget the things that he had said to her, the horror he had known. Once long ago, he had probably been charming, quick to laugh, and to tease—and be tender. Once, his wife might have known a most gallant young knight. She might have lain with him and laughed and teased in return, and it might have been . . . beautiful.

Yet Genevieve only saw glimpses of that man. She knew

the warrior, the invader. And it was the invader commanding her now. Still tonight she found that she could not disobey that command.

She came to him. And when she stood before him, he set his hands around her waist, and suddenly hiked her up and over so that she lay beside him. He brought his palm against her cheek and he stared into her eyes; and though his smile remained, his laughter had faded.

"I brought her here, Genevieve, because her mother was widowed, because their land is nearly worthless with no man to work it, because she needed the income and was eager to work."

Genevieve swallowed. "A—pity," she murmured. "She adores you."

"Does she?"

"Tristan—"

"Tell me, how do you know?"

"Tristan, please—"

"Never, Genevieve, have I touched her. Does that please you?"

"I told you—"

"I know what you told me. But I'm telling you what is truth anyway. For the moment, my dear and thorny white rose, you supply the most incredible fascination."

It was ridiculous and yet she felt a thrill of joy at his words. Because this is my room, only, she promised herself. But when he lowered himself over her, taking her lips in a gentle kiss, she threaded her fingers into his hair, and that kiss deepened and deepened until it seized them both into the fire of longing. And when he raised his head at last she felt light and nearly like a maid with her suitor, much more aware of the empathy she felt than of the hatred. And when he manipulated her to her side to remove her gown, she felt the steady heat and caress of his fingers, and spoke softly.

"Tristan?"

"Umm."

"I . . . was frightened in the forest. I lied. I'd have died a thousand times over if I'd been taken like—like this—by some hideous creature."

His reply was a whisper against her earlobe, warm and moist, and causing her to come alive. Her clothing seemed to melt away from her. And she did not hide. She flushed and she lowered her lashes, but not so far that she lost her view of him as he disrobed. And then her eyes did close because, before God, no matter how indecent the thought might be, she was glad that he was so muscled and so toned, so sleek and bronze and healthy as he came toward her. Nature was perhaps God's truth—she could not deny her wonder with the strength of his shoulders, the taut, flat muscles of his abdomen, the . . .

She flushed again with the thought but the thought continued, as it must, for his hunger for her was strong and evident, and oh, God, she thought that magnificent, too. Pulsing, throbbing, hard . . .

"Tristan."

"Aye."

"I am . . . sorry."

He tensed, and she was indeed sorry that she had spoken. He knew of what she spoke, that which had happened long before, and mention of the past had been foolish.

"Don't speak of it." The tone was harsh and he was still, and to her astonishment, she stretched out a hand to him.

"Tristan."

His fingers entwined with hers and he was beside her, atop her, whispering, "You are not, then, so distressed to be here tonight?"

"Nay, milord, I am not distressed to be here."

She touched him that night. Laid her hands hesitantly against his chest, fascinated by the coarse feel of the hair. Dared to run her fingers teasingly over his flesh, to place her palms against his face and know his features. He already knew her so well, yet seemed to know her more intimately each time.

This was their world. A place where they could go where nothing else mattered. Passion . . . Genevieve remembered distantly that Edwyna had warned it was dangerous. That it could bring the gravest pain . . .

But it was the greatest wonder. The writhing and the

striving, and the feeling of driven, shimmering heat that rose and rose and burst upon her with such splendor. Such sweet splendor.

She knew that she cried out, that she should have been embarrassed, that no lady knew such wanton sensations. Yet how could one fight them, and how could she care, when he was with her, so a part of her, inside of her . . .

And ever magnificent still.

And so pleased with her. Gentle, tender, holding her against him. So close that she was able to touch his cheek again, look into his eyes and whisper, "I—I was not displeased by your summons this evening."

He smiled. He leaned upon an elbow and found the tie in her hair and with patience began to unravel the braid, spreading her hair out on the sheets. His hands gloried in it, he laid his face against it, and his lips fell against the flesh at her throat and tasted the salt of their first union. She shivered and moaned as his caress of teeth and tongue and lips moved to her breast, and traced ever downward, and again, with shock, she felt the astounding spread of fire, from the intimacy of that kiss a cascade of ardor; she protested it to no avail, for he held her to his whim until she would have died for him, and found herself incoherently whispering just those words . . . wrapping him with her then in near frenzy. A wanton thing, wild, and in those moments, incredibly free. How could this thing, so splendid, grow ever more so, each time . . .

She slept, in exhaustion, where she lay with him. In her own bed, in her own room, in his arms.

Genevieve was wedged deeply into the covers. She was more warm and comfortable than she could ever remember being.

She was aware of some movement, yet knew that she need not be disturbed as yet. Still in twilight sleep, she heard the door open, and knew that Roger de Treyne was there, speaking to Tristan. She knew that Tristan still lay abed, and that his hand rested lightly upon her rump, and that it was embarrassing to be here, like this, and to be seen . . . like this no matter the mound of coverings that sheltered her.

But in her twilight sleep she knew that there was nothing to be done about the matter—all knew her role in this new Tudor reign, and she was simply still too tired to fight it.

But when Roger had gone, Tristan quickly leapt from the bed, and Genevieve began to attempt to open her eyes. She heard him mutter out, "God's teeth!" as there came another rap upon the door, very hesitant. Genevieve turned in time to see him stumble quickly into his clothing and approach the door to swing it open.

This time it was Jon. Genevieve did not hear the words spoken between them, but Tristan followed him out of the room, and Genevieve remembered that this was Jon's wedding day, that he and Edwyna were to be married.

"Genevieve!"

She blinked at the soft whisper of her name. Edwyna stood hesitantly in the doorway.

"Where is Tristan?" she asked, taking a nervous step into the room.

"I don't know."

"He's—not here?"

"No."

Edwyna sailed quickly into the room, and she was flushed and totally beautiful and young as she perched at the foot of the bed.

"Did you ask him?" she demanded anxiously of her niece. "Did you ask him if you could come to the wedding?"

Genevieve shook her head. "Not yet, but . . ." She paused, biting her lip. Edwyna was so eager! Genevieve thought of Tristan sleeping beside her when he had sworn once that he would not, and of those strange moments during the night when they had both made the oddest confessions. For the bitter enemies that they were, they had come curiously close to friendship.

"Edwyna . . ." She could not help but smile and hug her pillow and say like a conspirator, "Oh, Edwyna! I think that I shall be there!"

"Oh, I told you, Genevieve! You must only give a bit to have your way with a man! Cajole and act sweet rather than hostile! You did wonderfully!"

Edwyna leapt to her feet and raced for the door, while Genevieve pondered her words. But then her aunt stopped abruptly, and Genevieve stared at her startled—then knew why.

Tristan was in the doorway, leaning back against the frame in a quite leisurely fashion, arms crossed over his chest, one foot casually angled over another. He swept a bow to Edwyna, who colored in horror—and then raced past him as he indicated that she might.

Genevieve swallowed sickly at the hard twist of his smile as he approached her and stopped before the dais.

"Were you about to ask me something?"

She didn't reply, but sat stiffly hugging the pillow to her breast, heartily glad of the wrap of covering about her.

"Ask!" he commanded sharply. "Why the silence? It is your aunt's wedding day, and most surely you wish to attend."

"Aye!"

"Aye, most surely!" he laughed, and she did not like the sound of it. "Most surely! So you would slyly barter favor. Not, milady, that I am so adverse to barter! But one is usually aware of the price and the payment well in advance!"

"I don't know what—"

'You know exactly what! 'Tristan!' " he mimicked, " 'I am . . . sorry. I am not distressed to be here.' And a touch as soft as the words! Well, Genevieve Llewelyn, I shall remember in the future that you always come with a price, and take care to know it ere I enjoy the fruits of your sweetness!"

"What!" She felt tears welling within her, behind her eyes, and she was furious for them. "Oh, you fool! I did not—"

"Spare me, my love. You may attend the ceremony."

He turned and strode from the room, the door thundering in his wake.

Edwyna was married in the chapel where she had been baptised, and for the curious mixture of guests and the circumstances of the wedding it was beautiful still. Listening to the vows given, Genevieve knew in her heart that Edwyna would live far happier than she might have had the Tudor King never come to power, for Edgar would have made her another "advantageous" match, and she would have meekly married whatever man her brother had chosen, no matter what her heart.

There was a feast and there was dancing, and Tristan, who had not been near Genevieve since that morning, took her then into his arms to move to the tune of the harp and the lute. Took her hard, with arms that were ruthless, so that the harmony of their movement became nothing but mockery.

"The marriage is over, milady. Was the sacrifice of honor worth the price?"

Genevieve inhaled sharply, nearly tripping as she missed a beat of the music.

"What honor have you left me!" she exclaimed.

"I see, milady. I created the harlot, I should accept her terms?"

"Nay, milord, you are simply a fool—"

"I played one well."

"Nay—"

"You attended your wedding. I wonder, what new favor can I devise to draw you into your giving state?"

"What favor do you need? You take what you want!"

"Ah, lady, you are wrong! No man can take what you 'gave' last night! What can I promise now? A return to your room, perhaps. Greater freedoms to be earned? I confess, this barter does appeal to me! Let's set our prices, and our payments!"

Genevieve curiously felt as if she had never been hurt as she had at that moment, wounded, ridiculed—and dishonored. She jerked from his hold, heedless of his anger or of any around them.

"You know nothing!" she choked out to him. "Take and give!" she mimicked furiously. "Well, sir, you should know that certain things cannot be sold or bartered either, that they come from—"

She broke off. The word was "heart," and it was not a word to be used with him, for he had none.

"Go to the devil, Tristan de la Tere!" she swore fervently.

"Go to the devil, sir, and I shall go to my tower, where I will stay with the greatest pleasure!"

She spun about and ran for the stairs.

"Genevieve!"

She did not heed him. She raced up the steps to the landing, then on to the curving stairway, and up each of those steps, too. She needed no warder, no jailer then, for her heart thumped with agony, and she slammed her door closed, cast her weight against it, and sank down before it.

Tristan watched her go, and paused—and then started after her.

But before he could reach the first landing, he was halted. The wedding party was halted. There was a new guest in the hallway—a messenger from the King.

Curiously Tristan came to the man, who bowed low before him.

"Your grace, King Henry sends me to summon you hastily to his Court."

"What brings this haste?"

"Insurrection, Sire! Sly plots afoot, and the King has need of you."

Tristan paused, his eyes straying up the stairway, then his entire countenance hardening.

"I'll ride with you," he told the messenger. "Now."

He paused only long enough to leave Edenby in the hands of the newly married Jon. And then he rode out for London.

Chapter
Sixteen

THERE WAS NO indication of trouble when Tristan reached Henry's Court in London.

Indeed all seemed to be going exceptionally well. In the halls of Westminster there was all manner of activity.

Harpists, trumpeters, pipers, and lutists sat about, occasionally testing their instruments, awaiting their audiences with the King. Sir Robert Gentry, an old acquaintance of Tristan's, greeted him from an open solar with one of his prime hunting hawks upon his arm, anxious to give the bird to Henry—it was well known that he enjoyed the hunt.

If anything, the Court seemed quiet and in no great fear of revolt.

One of Henry's clerics—face smudged with the ink he used to keep his records—came to tell Tristan that the King was aware of his presence and most anxious to see him alone when the time became appropriate. The man went away, mumbling as he read over his records, "To the lute player, two shillings; for the Portuguese falcons, one pound . . ."

"Interesting place, eh?" Robert said.

"Court remains much the same," Tristan said simply. Sir Robert shrugged with a grin.

"It does, but it doesn't. Already Henry is placing a very high import on the red rose and the white—romanticizing the past thirty years. I listened while he spoke with a horde of scribes and clerics. I tell you, Tristan, he is a clever man. He will hold that throne of his. Richard is barely cold in his grave, and already he has changed from a handsome, frail young man to a hunch-backed horror. At the same time, it seems, our new King will pay for a fine tomb for his predecessor." Robert shrugged. "They talk of a new age; our King is a conservative. A clever one."

Tristan nodded idly at Robert's words, as a strange pall settled over him. Looking past a young dancing maid with a tambourine and a fellow holding the leash of a bear cub he saw a man he had not expected to encounter again. He stared long, determined to be certain that he was right. His heart beat fast, and a roar began in his ears, thundering like water. His hand fell to his sword, and he was startled by Sir Robert's touch on his arm.

"Tristan, we stand in the hall amongst a melee of minstrels and dancers, and you look like the Black Death! Sir, take care!"

Tristan gave himself a little shake and stared at Robert. He clenched and unclenched his fingers and inhaled sharply to ease the tension inside of him. He nodded across the hall.

"That man. I knew him in the final days before Bosworth. His name is Sir Guy and he was attached to the old Lord of Edenby. I fought against him. What is he doing here?"

Sir Robert turned. "That young fellow—there? Why, yes, he is Sir Guy Tallyger, recently of Edenby. Aye—he was a Yorkist. But he attached himself to the Stanleys, or so I hear, at the battle. He proved himself a brilliant fighter, slaying men to the right and left of him, defying death. The King is quite taken with him."

"What?" Tristan swore in disbelief.

"I know only," Robert whispered for Tristan's ear alone, "that King Henry claims him a hero, and one should take care with the King—for were you he, de la Tere, you would surely tread warily—you would consider men either for you or against you. And if Henry claims Sir Guy loyal, then that he must be!''

"Loyal!'' he came out with a growl. ''That man was part and parcel of a pact of treachery. I'd thought him dead—killed perhaps at Richard's side—not Henry's.''

"Tristan!''

Tristan turned quickly, knowing the voice. Henry Tudor had left his solar behind to come into the hallway. Women dropped low in curtsies as he passed; men bowed—the hall went still.

"Tristan, you arrived in good time,'' said the King, throwing an arm around his old friend. ''Come, we must talk alone.''

"Of course, Your Grace.''

Henry led Tristan back to the solar. The King closed the door himself before of any of his entourage could follow.

"God's blood!'' Henry swore then. ''Already!'' He threw his hands up before him, then clasped them behind his back and began to pace. ''In the north, and in Ireland! I am no fool, Tristan. And I will have various Plantagenet offspring to deal with, I know it! But the claimants themselves, they will wait. They will need a few years to gather their forces about them!'' He strode to his desk and slammed a fist against a paper there. ''Sir Hubert Giles of Norwich! My spies have warned me that he is gathering a force—to ride on London. Sir Hubert—no one! He would put Warbeck on the throne! He is a stupid fool—''

"Henry, aye! He is a stupid fool,'' Tristan dared to interrupt the tirade. ''Where does he think that he will get? Why, Your Grace, do you let it upset you so?''

Henry sank into the massive, claw-footed chair behind the desk. ''It is a fearsome thing to take a Crown,'' he said simply. ''But, my God, Tristan! I do mean to do right by it! Will you look at the things that have gone on! Oh, aye, I do intend to twist history! God in his infinite wisdom knows that these 'Wars of the Roses' were not devastation to the land—just to a damnable Norman aristocracy! Peers! There will be eighteen in the realm for my Parliament! Before Edward's

reign they numbered somewhere in the fifties! Frenchmen—
still! All these long years after the Conquest!''

Tristan arched a brow. De la Tere was a Norman name—he,
himself, sprang from one of those Norman families—just as
the Plantagenets had, and John of Gaunt, through whom
Henry claimed his right to the throne, had been a Plantagenet.
So what point was Henry really trying to make?

The King rose suddenly. ''I am worried, Tristan. Look at
the family fueds that have been taking place, the wholesale
murder and pillage. I tell you, Tristan, it might be the wars,
and it might be the times. Look at . . . look at Bedford
Heath,'' he added softly. ''The horror of such slaughter.
Such things will not come again! I will not hurry to create
peers and nobility, I do swear it! These barons will not
become so strong that they think they can rise up against me
and murder those who are loyal to me. It will end here, I
swear it!''

Tristan tensed at the mention of his birthright, but said
nothing. Henry gazed at him, seemed suddenly weary, and
sank back to his chair.

''I'm sending you north, Tristan. I'll provide all the men-at-
arms, but you'll be in command. I've sent to Bedford Heath
for Sir Thomas to ride with you, since all is peaceful there
and I know that Jon of Pleasance keeps control at Edenby.''

Tristan felt instantly uneasy. Aye, Jon could keep control,
but Tristan did not want to spend time away. Edenby meant
everything to him. It was his purpose in his life—subduing
the place and bringing it to new peace and prosperity. He
couldn't stay away. How could an absent lord expect to hold
authority?

''Henry—''

''Tristan, I need you.''

Tristan lowered his head for a minute, clenching his fists
tightly behind his back. He understood. Henry wanted the
rebels broken in fair battle, and he knew that Tristan would
do it. And no man who expected to live well and prosper
refused his King.

''As you say.'' But he looked up abruptly, ready to challenge the King anew. "Henry, you have in the hallway a certain Sir Guy—"

"Ah, yes, Sir Guy. He will travel with you."

"What?" Tristan did not want that traitor at his back again. But neither did he want the man out of his sight. "Sire, perhaps I never fully explained the things that happened at Edenby. The Yorkists surrendered there first in an act of treachery. The castle was turned over to us, but we were drugged and many men were slain or imprisoned. Sir Guy—your noble warrior of Bosworth!—was a part of it."

Henry shook his head, eying Tristan carefully, and Tristan knew that he had heard the complete story.

"I know of it. Sir Guy came to me, Tristan, with his humble admission. He told me of the betrayal, yet swore that he had no wish for it. He was quick to battle the Yorkists on the field. I saw him, Tristan, with my own eyes. He battled my enemies fiercely, and I believe, if you allow him, he will serve you well."

Tristan did not believe it one bit, but he had no evidence to prove that the King was wrong.

"When do I go?" he asked.

"Parliament will sit, Commons and Lords. When the session is out you will ride. Meanwhile, my friend, you are my guest. No comfort that I can offer will be too great. Banquets, entertainment, perhaps a joust or a pageant . . ." The King shrugged. Henry love pageantry, in many forms. And now he was King, free to indulge.

Tristan bowed to him stiffly. He did not want to idle his time away in London, and then in battle. He wanted to return to Edenby.

"How go things in Edenby?" Henry asked suddenly.

"Well enough."

Henry nodded, watching Tristan.

"And the Lady Genevieve?"

"She fares well enough."

Henry shrugged suddenly, grinning. Business was at an end. "You were right to extract a promise from me concerning the girl. What good revenue I could have earned bartering the maid in a marriage contract! I should have become her guardian and procured a vast sum from many a man, here or abroad.''

"But you did give me a promise, Your Grace."

"Aye. But what of your plans for the future? You are not intending marriage?''

Marriage. A shooting agony streaked through Tristan. All that he could remember of marriage was death. It had somehow become a hallowed thing, and the mere mention of the word the greatest disrespect to Lisette.

Marriage? To Genevieve, of all women . . . to the golden blond witch who had tried to murder him, who had buried him, who was now, in all justice, his property. His mistress, concubine, whore—aye, even his obsession, his fascination! —but never his wife.

"Nay, Sire, I'll never marry again."

Henry sighed. "You make too much of marriage, Tristan. It is a contract between two families most often rather than between a man and a woman. You are young; you will marry again.''

Tristan smiled vaguely. "I will not marry again."

Henry shrugged. "Perhaps then, at some time in the future, you will release the girl to me."

Tristan grated his teeth together; Henry wanted her back, he knew it. But even as King—or especially as King—Henry would not go back on a promise. And Tristan would never give her up until he had . . . purged himself of her.

He exchanged a few more words with the King, then went to gather his belongings and settle into his rooms in the castle. Dusk was descending and dinner would be served soon, but Tristan had no interest in the meal.

He lay upon his bed and stared up at the ceiling. He grew tense, musing on Sir Guy. He could not fathom how the man—any man!—had allowed Genevieve to be the instrument of attempted murder. Unless Genevieve had begged the honor. Still a father would not have allowed her to barter herself, nor a brother. Or a fiancé.

But he had seen Guy watch Genevieve. Watch her in the hall that fateful night. And he had seen that Guy had blanched each time Tristan had touched Genevieve, and he knew that

Guy was in love with her. Perhaps the man was just a fool! Tristan thought—for only a fool would fall in love with her.

And with that thought he wondered about himself again, curious at the ache that welled within him. I am bewitched, he admitted. Bewitched . . . he promised himself, but never in love.

Love had been that tender emotion he bore Lisette; love had been the happiness with which she had promised him a son.

It was all so long ago. He felt a sudden pain, sharp and debilitating. Yet that pain did not stay with him now. It struck, and it faded, to be replaced by a longing for Genevieve.

"Aye, bewitched!" he said aloud, and then he swore—because he was so anxious to return to Edenby, and her.

He rolled over, restlessly, thinking that he should go to dinner, that he would be hungry in the night. He simply had no taste for Court.

At last he rose. The light was gone and he lit a candle to dress by. Edenby—and Genevieve—would be there when he returned. There was no urgency. She would be there in the tower—for the simple reason that victory had been his.

He left his apartment and paused again in the hallway as he thought of Sir Guy. Genevieve had no recourse but to await Tristan's return. But Sir Guy—who had plotted with her, used her, exposed her to dishonor—would be riding with him. It seemed the greatest irony. Tristan smiled grimly.

"Be grateful, Sir Guy, that she was not yours," he said aloud. "Adore her from afar if you like, but keep your distance, sir. For, I swear, in time I will prove you false! And if you are dreaming of some future in Edenby with Genevieve, then surely you will die, sir, for she is mine, and what is mine I do not relinquish!"

Then Tristan laughed, aware that he was talking to himself. He hurried along the darkened, empty hallway, and as he neared the great hall where dinner would be served, he began to see friends and acquaintances, men who would ride with him, men who would sit beside him in the Parliament.

He had been reserved a place along the King's dais. He found himself seated beside one of Elizabeth's Woodville cousins, who was quite pretty and charming company while he ate, Tristan relaxed somewhat. He shared his cup with her courteously, as was frequently the custom, and he drank enough to feel warmed and easy.

But his eyes were ever wary, and in time he saw Guy approaching him.

Tristan stood before the younger man could reach him. He made no comment and waited until Guy bowed deeply, and stared at him then, tall and proud—and somehow apologetic—all in one.

"Your grace, I have been commanded to serve you, as you are aware, and have therefore sought this moment to beg your pardon."

And a good moment, too, Tristan thought, weighing his enemy carefully. What guest of the King would create a disturbance in the banqueting hall?

Guy had light hazel eyes and sandy hair and the fresh appeal of anxious youth. A scar nicked his cheek—obtained at Bosworth Field, no doubt, Tristan thought. A well-trained knight; but then Tristan felt no doubts about the man's prowess in battle—it was his loyalty that was suspect.

"I have heard that you fought for Henry at Bosworth Field," Tristan said. "Tell me, sir, what brought about your sudden change of heart?"

"A goodly number of things, milord," Guy said gravely, "and I pray that upon our journey northward you will allow me to give you a full accounting of them."

"Oh, I will," Tristan promised gravely. "Indeed I will."

Guy bowed deeply to Tristan and to the young Woodville heiress, and then took his leave. Tristan watched him go.

Parliament sat, and Tristan was part of it. Henry was duly accepted and his will became known. Men argued—and the government went on.

The days passed pleasantly enough. Tristan was reunited with Thomas Tidewell, and he managed to listen, without too much pain, to Thomas' accountings of the property at Bedford Heath. Richard had attainted Tristan's property, but had been too busy to make it more than a show of words. Thomas had remained, and of course with Henry's ascension to the throne, the property had reverted back to Tristan.

There were great feasts every night and fascinating entertainment. One night there was a group of dancers, agile and fascinating, and Tristan was elated to discover that he felt a hum of desire for one of the girls, a little redhead who could leap like a deer. Yet when the King called her near he found himself thinking that her face was too round, her hips were too wide, and that her eagerness did not appeal to him.

He tossed her a coin and sent her away—and then retired quickly for the night. He wrote Jon a letter about Thomas and his report on Bedford Heath and on the curious appearance of Sir Guy. Then he stretched out on his bed, anxious for sleep—but plagued by nightmares of Lisette and the baby floating in pools of blood. When he awoke he longed to be at Edenby, with Genevieve. His passion for her provided such a tempest of physical appeasement that he could forget the past.

Parliament ended and Tristan at last was able to leave with Henry's troops for the north. Thomas rode at his side and Sir Guy was never far behind him.

When they reached the rebels' castle, they were forced to lay siege. Tristan was wary, but this place was no Edenby.

Tristan was patient and cunning. They did not lose a man. The residents and soldiers came out after eight days, laying down their arms, begging for mercy, swearing they would all give their oaths of loyalty to the King.

Tristan thought that Henry would feel magnanimous, since, though he had a few wounded, he had not lost a man. He ordered that only the ringleaders be taken to London for trial, and sat with a jury of twelve of his own men to accept the surrender of the others, hear their oaths, and grant them pardon.

Sir Guy sat with that jury. And unobstrusively, as he had for all the time that they had been together, Tristan watched the younger man.

Guy had battled well. He had stormed the gates; he had shown no fear. His personal valor during the suppression of this rebellion had been faultless. He had consistently shown a respectful demeanor toward Tristan.

But Tristan recalled waking in his burial bed of rock and stone, and he knew that he would never give up. There was a fault with Guy, and so help him, he would find it.

Guy did not mention Edenby or Genevieve until they neared London with their contingent of five hundred men. Only then did he ride quickly to catch up with Tristan, at the head of the column stretching like a great, breathing snake through the outlying towns.

Tristan knew that he was there. He sat calmly on the piebald, staring straight ahead, making no acknowledgment, forcing Sir Guy to at least clear his throat.

"Milord?"

"Sir Guy . . . ?"

"Forgive me, I have to ask. Edenby was—my home. I had a manor just outside the walls, toward the forest. How fare the people? Old Griswald in the kitchen, and Meg! Older still. And—"

"The Lady Genevieve?"

Tristan was surprised that he could make the suggestion so coolly. Sir Guy lowered his head.

"Aye," he said softly. "How is my lady?"

"Well," Tristan said curtly. "Edwyna has recently married."

"She has! Who—I mean, may I inquire—"

"She married Jon of Pleasance. I believe you met him. He was there the night that Genevieve, er, killed me. You remember?"

Guy did not look up.

"She married—one of your men?"

"Aye."

Guy swallowed and licked his lips. "And the Lady Genevieve—?"

"She has married no one, if that is what you're asking."

Guy thanked Tristan quietly and turned his horse around, riding back to the rear guard.

Tristan did not think long on this interview. He was almost quit of the man. He could see the spire of Westminster and he knew he was almost home.

*   *   *

Tristan spent one day in London, but even the one day seemed too long. December was already upon them. Then Henry released him, and he was able to ride for home. A fever burned within him, and he rode hard and fast, resting, when he did, more for the piebald than for himself. For one night he stayed at an abbey of Franciscan brothers. The next he rested but for a few hours, unable to sleep, brooding as he stared up at the moon.

Almost there, almost there, almost there . . .

He did sleep, against the hard back of his saddle. But as dawn came he woke with a start, realizing with horror that his own scream had wakened him and that he was staring at his hands, trying to wipe some invisible blood from his hands. Lisette's blood, the babe's blood, all that blood. He would never forget; he could only search out a semblance of peace.

He whistled for Pie, and together they found the nearest stream and drank. Tristan bathed his face and hands in the icy water, glad of its bite against his skin.

By midmorning he could see Edenby, rising from the cliffs. His heart gladdened and he quickened his speed, galloping the last few miles. At the gatehouse he slowed until his men recognized him and shouted out a welcome. In the yard Matthew was waiting to take Pie, and at the doors Jon stood with Edwyna, clasping him as he entered.

He was home. Edwyna kissed his cheek and drew him to the fire. Griswald brought warm mead, sweet with cinnamon. And Tristan sat, sipping the mead, filling Jon in on events in London, on Thomas' appearance, on the battle fought in Norwich. Yet even as he spoke he was aware of a fever of urgency. Finally he looked at Jon directly and asked, "How goes it here? With Genevieve?" He glanced at Edwyna, hard, quick. "No escapes, no breaks?" His voice was oddly harsh and cold, in contrast to the rampant fire within his body.

Edwyna flushed unhappily and looked to Jon, and Jon, bless him, looked angry suddenly.

"Oh, nay, Tristan. No breaks."

"Where is she?"

"In the tower, as you ordered, of course."

"She—" Edwyna began, breaking off as Jon threw her a

warning glance. "Well, I have spent an hour with her daily, and we—we have brought her out each day. For—exercise. Oh, dear God, I sound as if I am speaking of a prized beast!"

"Edwyna!" Jon said sharply.

"Her health!" Edwyna defended herself, staring at her husband reproachfully. "We had to bring her out; she'd have been mad. And she—"

"And she what?" Tristan roared. Tension crackled all around him. What were they getting at?

They both stared at him uneasily. Tristan returned that stare as if they had both gone mad. Then he threw up his hands in disgust. It didn't matter. He was here now. And it had been stupid to sit there so, pretending that the first thing on his mind was not to race to the tower and wrench his prisoner down into his bed. And be damned with the fact that it was broad daylight, morning still.

"Never mind. God alone knows what has gotten into the two of you!"

Tristan was up, and quickly heading for the stairway with long strides. Edwyna glanced at Jon. Jon shook his head sternly to her, and she bit her lip, remaining still.

At the second floor Tristan paused, startled by the trembling that came to him. Ah! He taunted himself, but you have admitted to obsession and fascination. You know her to be a witch, a creature either of Satan or of the angels. Beautiful beyond the earth and more tempting than ever the ripest fruit . . .

He hurried up the winding stone stairs to the tower and paused once again. He nodded to the young guard there to leave, and slid aside the bolt.

She was lying still upon the bed. All dressed in white, soft white that flowed and fell about her. Her hair was untied and loose, and heat flowed into his loins at the memory of that gold and silk entangling him, covering them both, falling over her hips and his own . . .

She turned to him, rolling with startled fear, instinctively bringing her pillow with her and hugging it to her breasts. Her eyes came to him . . . silver, growing wide, and then narrowing.

She knew it was me, he thought. She knew it was me when the door opened, yet she is startled, for none knew when I would return. And is she glad, or is she not?

Neither of them spoke. He came to her at the bed, and he caught her chin in his hand, staring warily into her face, and suddenly curious.

She was as beautiful as ever, if not more so. Silver and gold and cream and rose . . . her lips were rose, aye, yes! Like the flower, like the red rose . . .

But she was paler. Her face was thin and ashen.

"Are you ill?" he demanded, and he was startled at the hoarse rasp of his own voice.

She tried to free herself from his grasp. He let her go and she took her pillow defensively, backing up to curl against the headboard, as if he were an unknown enemy again.

"I asked you. Are you ill?"

She shook her head. He felt at a loss, and because of it continued harshly.

"Come here!"

She trembled then, but her chin rose and those magnificent silver eyes of hers sparkled out a fresh fire.

"Who do you think that you are, milord de la Tere! Gone for months, and then you return, and—"

"My whereabouts, milady, are none of your concern. Rest assured only that I am here now." He stretched out a hand to her, and when she did not take it he caught her arm and pulled her to him. She swore, lashing out at him, but he laughed, determined to have none of it, and he kissed her with such need and such passion that she had no breath to fight him. When he drew back his head from hers at last and gazed down at her she was hypnotically splendid, with that brilliant fire in her eyes and her lips parted and damp and her breasts heaving beneath that white linen.

"Let me go!"

"I cannot."

"It is morning—"

"I have missed you."

"Oh, I'm quite certain. You have been off to Henry's

Court, going forth in battle again, fighting, burning, pillaging, plundering, raping, ravishing—''

"Ah. You are jealous. You're wondering whom I 'raped and ravished.' " He laughed. "Milady, this might quite well shock you. Most of your sex might well be eager and anxious to rape and ravish me."

"You conceited oaf! Bastard! I do not care in the least, I assure you! Go back to them then, just let me—"

She broke off, catching her hand to her mouth, swallowing fiercely. Her eyes were suddenly huge with misery and alarm.

"What is the matter?" he demanded of her, so startled that he eased his hold, and she, scrambling like a nimble deer, leapt from his hold to the ground, barefoot, shaking her head, and trembling.

"Damn, Genevieve, you'll not—"

"Please! Please, can't you leave me for a minute!"

He stood up curiously. She looked fragile and tremulous and more ashen. Beautiful and delicate . . .

It dawned upon him slowly, very slowly. He came to her, as if in a dream, and though she exclaimed something and tried to elude him, she had nowhere to go. He caught her and with no passion tore open the night dress, encircling her breast with his hand, and knowing the weight to be great, the tiny blue lines of the veins to be more prominent, the nipples wider and darker . . .

And his hand came quickly with no tenderness low to her belly, and she shook like a wild mare captured, straining with that wildness against the manacled vise his fingers held upon her wrist.

"Damn you!" she swore. "Will you leave me be! I am sick—"

Something horrible and cold swept over him; he felt as if an icy blade pierced his heart. Visions spun before his eyes, visions of blood and of death . . .

"My God, I could wring your lovely neck!"

She had never, through everything, heard him speak with such quivering fury, and it astounded her. Deeply. So deeply. For she was the wounded party here, she the wretched one, with illness claiming her each morning, and the knowledge that life could never be the same, that society would ban her, that her dreams of any future were dead.

"God damn you!" she said, her voice low. "It is hardly my fault!"

He just stared at her. So rigid, so cold. She had not known what reaction to expect, but never this! She had thought that he might be amused, that he would laugh. But he was furious.

His eyes were cold as death and so shockingly full of hatred that she railed against him in panic again.

"Don't worry—it is none of your concern!"

He just kept staring at her. Helplessly she said whatever came to mind.

"I can be gone! It—it can be gone! There are ways, there are things to do—"

He slapped her, hard.

She fell to her knees with the force, and screamed when he wrenched her by the shoulders.

"Don't you ever, ever say such things again. Ever. You understand that there is nothing to be done! By the saints, I swear, you do anything about this and I will teach you that the world can be merciless. I will flay you alive."

As abruptly as he had come, as he had touched her, he dropped her, his eyes blacker than any pit of hell, and he left her.

Chapter
Seventeen

THERE WAS SOMETHING awful inside of him, a pain that threatened to rend his head asunder, as if a sword had split his skull.

Outside the tower room, Tristan staggered to the stairs, holding his head between his palms. He was only dimly aware of the things that he had said, and he knew that he had struck her, that some simmering emotion churned and roiled deep in his gut, that he was appalled by his own behavior. Yet he wasn't really a part of it, not that he could touch or reach, because he could only feel the pain.

His footsteps clattered hard down the winding stairs. At the landing he braced himself against the stone, then ran down the second stairway to the hall below. Jon and Edwyna were still there, in chairs before the great hearth in the hall. They stared at him sharply; he did not see them. He went out to the yard, heedless of Jon's voice calling to him.

He knew where he was going—to the sea. To the wind, to the beach where winter's breeze would be colder than his heart, where he could hope to purge the curious rage and agony that had so suddenly seemed to rip him apart. He could barely remember his own actions or his own words, but he

could remember hers. There were things to be done, she had
told him, there were ways . . .

Edenby was alive with the day. Within her walls metalsmiths worked and peasants traded their wares. The guards
and various men on duty saluted Tristan, yet their greetings
died upon their lips, for he did not hear them or acknowledge
them. He was anxious only to reach the sea wall and the
parapets—and a place against the rock and the sand where he
could be alone.

At last he reached his destination: a place on the beach
where rock just joined sand, where he could sit upon stone
and stare out at the waves, gray today, crashing hard against
the land. The water swirled and thundered treacherously;
whitecaps rose and slammed themselves into oblivion, and
the back wash bore them away again. The air was wet and
cold and tasted of salt. Tristan dragged it raggedly into his
lungs, pressing his temples inward now, closing his eyes to
breathe, and struggle for control, struggle for understanding.

God, how he hated her at times! With what longing he had
ached to see her, and yet how he had recoiled in touching her.
And before all the saints, he could not, now, with logic
returning, begin to understand why! Any man knew the natural conclusion to the mating ritual! Only a blind fool would
not have expected to sire a child upon a woman he had taken
again and again . . .

He looked up at the sky, where the sun fought a valiant
battle against the winter gray of the horizon. He stretched his
hands out before him and stared at his fingers, and in time
their trembling ceased. He knew that he had acted like a
madman.

He groaned out loud and stood, and walked closer to the
surf, hearing the crunch of his boots against the sand.

It was the past that haunted him, he knew. It was that
murderous scene at Bedford Heath.

He swore again, clenching his teeth and throwing back his
head with his eyes closed, inhaling the salt air sharply.

There were things that could be done, she had told him.

Yet she spoke of mercy. Had she none herself?

His lips compressed tightly as he stared on unseeingly to the roil of the water. Could she really hate him so much?

He closed his eyes again, and at last he felt the sharpness of the cold. She was always so beautiful. And so defiant. Ever ready to fight him, to do battle.

But not over this.

"Tristan!"

Startled, he swung around at the sound of the call. Jon was there, standing high upon the rock. He waved, and picked his way slowly and carefully down to Tristan. They stood apart from one another, and Tristan was further startled when Jon suddenly threw his arms up in disgust.

"By God, Tristan! She's pregnant with your child!"

"You should have warned me."

"A man does not treat his enemy so poorly on a battlefield!"

"I!"

"You came after me once, for the way I dared to treat Edwyna! Yet I loved her, I married her! While you—"

"Damn you, Jon, if you'd warned me—"

"Warned you? Come, come—your grace! You're older than I and well aware of the way of the world! Were you not expecting such a thing to occur? Where one tarries, as we all know—"

"Jon, damn you—"

"Nay, Tristan, damn you! Much can be laid at her feet, aye! But this?"

"Jon!" It was deadly harsh, but Jon ignored the tone.

He spoke more softly. "By God, Tristan, if any man can understand, it is I. Yet how you can find such cruelty in your heart to rail against her?"

"Nay, Jon!" Tristan cried out. "You do not understand!" Bitterly, he continued. "Always, always, she cries out that she is denied mercy! Yet what she wants to do—" He broke off, choking at the bile that seemed to fill him, and Jon stared at him incredulously.

"What are you talking about?"

"She wants to devise a way to rid herself—"

"You are mad!"

"I am not! I was with her, I heard her! You know that she despises me. Why not the seed that grows within her?"

Jon shook his head, staring at Tristan. "Perhaps her heart does not abound with love—why should it? But I promise you that she is not horrified. Nor was she surprised. The lady, it seems, lacked your naivete on certain natural inevitabilities!"

"Jon, I tell you—"

"Nay! Let me ask you a question, Tristan. Duke of Edenby, Earl of Bedford Heath—and whoever else you may be after your last adventure on the King's behalf! How did you take the news, sir? How did you greet your lady prisoner? With a grim countenance, with remonstrance? What then would you expect her reaction to be?"

Tristan stared at Jon blankly; Jon returned the stare. The wind rose between them, sharp and keening, but suddenly Tristan felt warmer, and he smiled very slowly. Jon smiled, too, and they began to laugh, and embraced, still laughing.

"I promise you this, friend. She pines for escape, aye—but she plans no harm against herself—or the babe," Jon said.

"She still plans escape?" Tristan queried. "For what? What does she think that she will do?"

"Reach the Continent eventually, I believe."

Tristan stared down at the sand, digging a heel into it. "Then she is a fool," he said gruffly. "I shall never marry, and her child might well stand to inherit."

"There are laws against bastards inheriting."

"Not when there are no legal heirs." He gazed back up at Jon. "Strange," he murmured. "One would imagine that she would hope to stay. That she would at last become meek and sweet, in the hope that I would marry her and make the child a legal heir."

"Oh, she'd never marry you, Tristan," Jon said cheerfully.

"And why not?"

Jon laughed. "Tristan, have you lost your senses entirely? You battled against Edenby, you took everything that was hers, and you—" He broke off, shaking his head. "She simply will never surrender, friend, and that is that."

"Then that is well," Tristan said softly. "But she will not escape. Not now."

"You cannot mean to keep her in the tower—"

"Nay, I do not."

"Then?"

Tristan blinked. "With me, Jon. For—now."

"Perhaps—"

Jon broke off and they both stared upward at the sudden commotion high atop the rock and parapets.

Genevieve . . .

For a moment she was framed there, against the gray of the winter's sky, and she was like a ray of sun. Hair unbound and streaming like banners of gold, tall and proud, her shoulders cloaked in white velvet that seemed to float about her. Slim and graceful, she seemed like some mythical maiden sent to dance upon the rock in enchanted splendor . . .

But the agile grace was no dance at all, Tristan thought, and neither was she myth, nor in truth anymore a maid. He remembered that he had left her door unbolted and the guard dismissed. Bless her, shrewd lass, if she had not taken the opportunity to elude them all.

She, too, had reached out to the sea for peace. The surging whitecaps and the blustering gray sky were a soft balm to her soul. Freedom had been her goal, and she had come this way, a nimble goddess, scampering over rock and shale, wall and parapet, as wild as the eternal tempest of the sea.

Tristan's grin deepened suddenly; seeking escape she had come here—straight into his arms. Her startled discovery of him and Jon below had brought forth a cry; when she had spun to retreat she had but looked into the faces of his men-at-arms, stationed on the wall. Neither up nor down—she had no way to go.

"Genevieve!" Jon called out her name with alarm, and Tristan quickly saw that her light slippers were no good against the rocks, dampened and icy as they were. She was a child of this place, as fleet-footed as a deer, yet she scampered dangerously along, seeking now to elude them by veering northward.

"She'll stop, surely," Tristan murmured.

But she did not. She did not attempt to take the path downward; she leapt from rock to rock, seeking greater speed, the wind carrying her hair behind her like shimmering sun rays, the white velvet of her cloak a cloud of light against the gray.

"Genevieve! Stop!" Tristan commanded. She did not hear him—or she chose to ignore him. Her beautiful features were knit with care as she perused each step she might choose to take.

"Damn her!" Tristan swore.

He started to run along the beach, anxious to reach her. He caught up easily, since he could run on sand, and at first she was so intent in her preoccupation with her movement that she did not see him, so close. Clutching the ragged edge of one of the great boulders, Tristan sprang upon it and began to ascend toward her.

She looked up then and saw him, and her eyes grew wide as saucers, silver-blue in alarm.

"Genevieve, stand still!"

"Nay!" she cried.

"I'll not hurt you."

She did not believe him, he saw quickly as she measured the distance from level footfall to level footfall and leapt down and away from him toward the beach. But she miscalculated the distance of one step, and she landed hard upon her hands and knees, giving a little cry. Tristan's heart stood still with alarm as he watched her just barely make the jump; he pictured her falling, tumbling down the rough and jagged edges, landing upon the sand with the white of her cloak and the gold of her hair ever marred in a pool of blood.

"Genevieve, damn you, stop! Where do you think you are going? Stand there, stay. I'll come to you—"

"I cannot—I—"

He jumped to another stone, closer, keeping his eyes locked with hers. "Genevieve, what do you think you're doing?"

Her eyes sparkled like diamonds, and he wondered if the glitter might not be tears as she lashed out at him in turn. "I was merely attempting to—leave. I wasn't trying to harm myself or . . ."

"Stay, there's nowhere—"

Her laughter interrupted him and for a moment she looked splendidly triumphant.

"Ah, but there is my lord! You simply do not know Edenby well enough!"

She turned then, and leapt again and again. Swearing, Tristan took flight in her wake, glad of his boots and worried about her slippers sliding against the rock.

But she was as agile as any wild creature as she went from rock to rock . . . until she could leap to the sand. Jon, down the beach, shouted, and started racing toward her. Genevieve was headed toward the north, toward rock; but even as he stared incredulously, he saw a crevice in that rock and knew that she meant to make good her escape there.

"God's . . . blood!" he swore, and he leapt back across the boulders, trying to reach a point above her again; his only hope of stopping her was to leap upon her.

Panting, gasping, Tristan made that flying leap, sweeping her down hard upon the sand, landing atop her, and rolling with her.

"Oh!" she sobbed out in a gasp, and she was flailing away at him, tears streaming down her cheeks, fighting him as she had not since . . . the beginning.

"Genevieve!"

He caught her flailing wrists, dragging them high above her head, straddling over her in the sand and gasping for breath.

He stared into her woebegone face, saw the sparkling brilliance of her eyes and the state into which they had both fallen, soaked and sandy and gasping and desperate. And suddenly he started to laugh, and again her tears fell and he found himself leaning forward, not angry at all, just determined. He kissed her lips lightly, tenderly, heedless of the sand, of the sea, of Jon thudding along the beach toward them. He tasted her tears and he tasted the grit and he kept laughing once they parted, and she stared at him then in silence, convinced, he was certain, of his madness. He released her and she scrambled quickly and desperately to her feet, backing away from him, her hands behind her to feel for the rock since she kept her eyes carefully locked with his.

"Genevieve—"

"Keep away from me, Tristan!"

He stretched out an arm to her, smiling, and said softly, "Genevieve, take my hand."

"Tristan, you are mad!"

"Nay, milady, not mad. Merely—sorry."

"What?" She gazed at him, startled and still. He took a step toward her and it looked again as if she had determined to fly, but he caught her hand and drew her against him, slipping his arms around her.

Her head fell back and she stared at him, her eyes glazed with tears, exhausted and despairing and wary.

"Tristan, you needn't hate me or—or strike me or—"

"I am sorry, Genevieve. Please, I pray you, forgive me."

Her eyes grew wide, but she was still tense, ready for some trick. And why not, he thought bitterly—for she hardly knew him. Damned if he'd leave again, even at the King's bidding!

"If you but let me slip through the rock—"

"I cannot and you know that."

"By God, Tristan, you are so angry, and it is not my—I did not—I mean—"

"Shush, Genevieve."

Tears sprang to her eyes once again and in confusion she tried to speak. "I swear, Tristan, I did not mean to kill—"

"I know, Genevieve."

Tristan suddenly became aware of Jon, who had caught up and stood panting behind them. They were all silent beneath the gray sky. Genevieve continued to stare at him warily.

Jon said, "It grows cold out here, Tristan. Fiercely cold."

Tristan nodded without turning around, his eyes still upon Genevieve's. He dipped to pick her up, and her arms encircled his neck. Still their eyes held each other's until Tristan started back up the path.

"I can never cease to wish for freedom," she whispered as they came back to the parapet.

He did not reply to her, and she spoke again.

"What—" She paused, swallowing painfully. "Where do we go from here? Our battle has no end."

She seemed so young then. So very young, and so very

lost. And tender, with her arms soft around him, her eyes wide, and the lashes still dampened with her tears.

"Perhaps a truce then," he suggested.

She did not look right or left as he came to the courtyard and across it and to the doors of the keep. They entered, and Edwyna let out a little gasp, rushing toward them. Tristan kept moving up the stairs to her chamber; he opened the door with a shove.

The master had returned. In the hearth a fire burned brightly. Cradling her against him still, he sat down before it, aware of how she trembled.

And he just held her. Against his body, against his warmth. Feeling her shake and shiver and inhale in jagged gasps that were the remainder of her sobs.

"Tristan—"

"Shhush, be easy. I'll not hurt you again, I swear it."

Slowly the tension eased. She rested soft against him, in the cocoon of his arms, and he knew that she slept. He set his cheek against the top of her hair, felt its angel silkiness against his flesh, and closed his eyes. He had wanted her so badly. Now he felt nothing but tenderness.

In time he stood and laid her carefully upon the bed, loosening her cloak, then bringing the covers warmly over her. He smiled crookedly, ran his fingers over her cheek, and left her to sleep. He did not bolt the door.

Tess was coming up the stairs. She greeted him with a bob and a profuse show of welcome. Tristan responded not unkindly, and told the girl to leave the Lady Genevieve to rest for the afternoon, and to see that she was brought a warm bath before the evening meal.

"She will dine in the chamber?" Tess asked.

"She will dine with us below, if she so desires."

Tristan hurried on down the stairs. Jon and Edwyna were before the hearth, staring at him, wary and trying to pretend that they were not.

Tristan warmed his hands before the fire, looked at Jon, and smiled.

"Well I'm quite certain that you've a long accounting for

me on the events taking place in my absence. Shall we,
Jon?''

He politely indicated the counting room.

Tristan grinned and called to Griswald for some ale in the
counting room and whistled as he preceded Jon to their work.

Genevieve awoke with a start. She thought at first, with
some confusion, that Tristan had returned only in a dream,
but then she felt the grit and sand upon her, and she knew for
certain that he had indeed returned.

Returned . . .

She bolted up, curious at her surroundings, having to look
around to assure herself that she was no longer within the
tower room. She was not; she lay within her own chamber,
and she had slept more peacefully here today than she had in
many weeks.

She hugged her knees to her chest, shivering as she thought
of his initial reaction, and wondering with some awe at the
vast change that had come over him at the cliffs. Good God,
she did not know what to feel. Her shivering ceased, and a
curious warmth swept through her as she thought of his
soothing words, of the fact that he, Tristan de la Tere,
relentless as steel, had sworn out an apology to her and
offered with a strange tenderness the olive branch of peace.

She felt suddenly giddy and hot, and pressed her cool
palms to her flushed cheeks. She had been tired, sick, and
wretched for so long. She had lain awake nights wondering
where he was and what he was doing.

And now she was glad of his return. She was more than
glad, she thought with a certain shame; she was nearly giddy
with the pleasure of it. Elated now, oh, aye! Elated with his
return. She was so glad of his return—and his determination
that they find some small oasis of truce.

She warmed further, remembering his arms about her,
remembering the blue of his eyes when he had looked into
hers, smiling out his strange tenderness, giving her his gentle
promise that he'd not hurt her again.

She swallowed suddenly, sharply, thinking that to be a
promise that he could not keep. She was hurt; neither of them

could change that. She was afraid to think of the future, no matter how blithely she spoke of it to Jon and Edwyna. She hadn't dared think yet that the miserable sickness that tore at her each morning was the beginning of life. And when she did she found herself feeling weak, and being ridiculously assured that she would have a strong and noble child, striking if it resembled its father . . . noble bastard though it might be. There was really little else to think. Except to wonder what would happen when he tired of her, of lust and revenge . . . When he returned one day with a bride sanctioned by the King, a woman to increase his position and wealth through her title or possessions.

Genevieve determined in a sudden fever not to dwell upon her fascination with the man who was the cause of all of her misery. She sprang from the bed, shaking her hair, wishing that she might wash it and cleanse away the gritty feeling of the sand. As she stood upon the dais she gazed curiously at the door, and with a sudden flurry of hope she raced toward it.

To her amazement, it opened. She closed it again and stood there trembling. He had said that there would be a truce.

She could run, she thought.

Run . . . and risk being dragged back—once more.

Or she could accept this matter of truce as it had been given and fulfill her part of it. And she was so tired! So weary of the fruitless attempts. He had proven time and time again that she could not escape him.

She started back into the room, biting hard upon her thumbnail.

"Milady!"

The soft call and a rap upon the door interrupted her thoughts. The door opened and young Tess stood there—cheery as ever.

"Did I waken you, milady?"

Genevieve shook her head.

"Nay, Tess."

"Ah, good, for I was told not to do so, yet the time grows late. I've told the kitchen boys to bring the tub and the water, as I knew you'd want to dress for dinner."

"Dinner?" Her heart thumped hard against her chest.

"Aye, milady!" Tess gave her a smile as big as sunshine, and Genevieve thought regretfully of all the rancor she had so often felt for the girl. Tess seemed as pleased as she for the freedom suddenly granted her charge.

"Downstairs, milady, in the great hall. You're to take your rightly place at that table. Oh, milady . . . !"

Genevieve laughed and she actually hugged Tess and Tess hugged her back, as happy as a pup.

Then Tess left her and called for the boys, and Genevieve stepped back upon the dais, awaiting the water and the bath that she had craved. She told herself primly that it was pathetic to find such pleasure in things that had been her birthright.

But she could not listen to that voice; she could only be happy. The future still loomed dismally before her, but tomorrow would come whether she found happiness in the moment or not. For the moment she wanted peace. And whether one admitted it or not, she wanted Tristan.

Tristan came into the hall at dusk, having ridden the distance of the wall with Jon.

He wondered how he would find her—defiant and cool or simply proud? Or perhaps she would have ignored the chance to be in the hall entirely, preferring to stay away. He strode in, and was suddenly still.

Genevieve stood by the fire, staring into it with pensive eyes. She was dressed in royal blue, with golden trim and an edge of fur about her wrists and hem and breast. Edwyna sat by the hearth, serene as ever, with her tapestry before her.

Both women turned. Tristan saw only one.

He sought her eyes, and they seemed neither silver or mauve but a color to match that of her gown. The firelight played upon her and caught all the highlights in her hair, making it dazzle with greater glory than the blaze itself.

And she smiled. Hesitantly, tremulously.

For the life of him, he could not move. He could not bring one foot before the other to reach the hearth.

Tristan found motion at last. He lowered his eyes from

Genevieve's and hurried toward the fire, drawing off his gauntlets to stretch out his hands to the warmth of the flame.

"There are all manner of wares being bartered and sold," he said. "Winter brings the peddlers here for warmth."

"Ah, yes! But surely not such a selection of goods as you've recently seen in London!" Edwyna proclaimed.

And Tristan laughed and said aye, London was brimming with goods—trade was already increasing again, and there was a new manner of gown being worn, having just crossed the Channel from France.

Edwyna pounced upon Tristan with questions about the City. He suggested that they sit down to dinner, where he would answer all that he could for her. Griswald appeared to announce happily that everything awaited Tristan's leisure; he smiled almost shyly at Genevieve, announcing that he'd prepared all "milady's favorites." Genevieve blushed slightly and gazed at Tristan.

He offered her his arm and she took it. And at the table he took the place reserved for the lord of the castle, and sat her in the seat reserved for the rightful lady.

Tristan knew that the delicacies served that night were none compared with those at Henry's Court; yet they tasted far better to his lips. The wine was sweeter than any he had known in ages, and the conversation flowed smoothly.

Genevieve was quiet but responsive. Tristan did most of the talking, telling Edwyna about fashions and Jon about the meeting of Lords in Parliament, the battle in Norwich, and the state of things about the City. They talked about Sir Thomas Tidewell, and Jon eagerly asked about his old friend.

And then Tristan looked at Genevieve.

"I saw an old friend of yours, too, milady."

"Sir Humphrey?" she queried softly.

"Nay, I did not see him, though I heard that he is well. The friend I speak of is Sir Guy."

Her hand lowered nervously to her wine glass. "Sir Guy? He was in—London?"

"Aye."

"In the—Tower?" she asked painfully.

"Oh, nay—he, too, fares very well. He changed sides, so it seemed, at the last minute and battled bravely for Henry."

"He—what?" Genevieve gasped out.

Tristan leaned back, watching her. A startling jealousy raced through him, keen and sharp.

"He fought for the King—King Henry, that is."

"That's not possible!"

"But he did."

Her eyes lowered, and he wondered what she thought. Edwyna anxiously changed the subject, and though Genevieve's reactions stayed with Tristan a long time, he eventually ceased musing over them, since they could not matter much now.

They stayed a long time at the table that night, all aware perhaps that they had reached a peculiar milestone. None of them mentioned Genevieve's condition, nor Tristan's reaction, not any of the events of the day. They seemed like any two young couples, enjoying each other's company.

Somewhere through that conversation Tristan looked across at Genevieve through the soft haze of the candlelight. Her eyes were on his then, curious, and though she quickly looked downward at his gaze, he had seen the seductive beauty in them, and everything about him quickened. He waited for what seemed like a proper amount of time, then rose, stretching out a hand to her, apologizing to Jon and Edwyna with a mention that he was tired from his journey.

And he tensed then, wondering if she would refuse his hand, wearily hoping that they needn't endure another battle this night.

She did not fight him. She accepted his hand, and he felt her fingers trembling as they walked up the stairs and into the room.

Genevieve stood by the closed door as Tristan crossed to the fire which burned brightly in anticipation of their arrival. He sat and pulled off his boots and watched the fire. Then he was staring at her and her heart quickened because he was so very handsome, because she could not help the loneliness she felt, the ache inside at missing him, and the hungers he had awakened within her.

He stood again and came to her. And he did not speak, but touched her hair, then drew her to him, and took her lips with the lightest touch. Then his hands were upon her gown, drawing the strings from her bodice, and with that touch she began to quiver because the excitement rose in a liquid rush, spreading heat throughout her. She did not demur as he slid the gown from her shoulders.

As his lips touched her shoulders.

As he knelt, drawing his hands so lightly over her breast, then taking her nipple into his mouth, and tugging at it gently.

She threw her head back, swallowing at the cascade of sensation that swept through her, bracing herself against his shoulders. She realized suddenly that he was looking at her face.

"Does that hurt you?"

And she shook her head, flushing. "Nay," she said softly. She shook her head again. "Nay!"

And in sudden shame and emotion, she slipped her arms around his neck, burying her head against his shoulder. He inhaled, sharply, raggedly, and was on his feet, staring down at her.

"Thank God, lady, for I could die with the wanting of you tonight!"

He carried her to the bed, and made love to her with such tenderness and passion that in the end Genevieve was certain that it had been just a little bit like dying . . . and finding Paradise.

Chapter
Eighteen

"OH, AND WE must see that Mildred—Tess's mother—is brought here as soon as possible. She is quite alone now, and from what Tess tells me she will not survive the winter if something is not done," Genevieve told Tamkin.

He scribbled another line onto the roster he wrote, nodding, then he looked to Genevieve. "Shall she work in the kitchen?"

Genevieve walked the small side hall above the chapel, tapping her steepled fingers to her chin. "Nay, I think not. Her health is fragile. But she spins the most wonderful thread—so Tess assures me. She can have a small room in the eastern wing and work in the solar, where she will have what light there is to help her."

Tamkin scribbled on the paper again and Genevieve wandered over to the mullioned windows, looking outside into the courtyard.

The winter's first snow had fallen that morning, and everything was beautiful. As glorious as a fairy tale of ice palaces and kingdoms in spun-sugar clouds. The ground was soft white, and horses passed by with their harnesses jingling, tossing their manes and tails in glorious delight. The stable boys and grooms passed beneath her now and then, their woolen cloaks and mantles bathed in a sudden spray of white. Winter's first snow . . .

She sighed suddenly, feeling her confinement deeply. Just an hour or so ago the men had ridden out, Jon and Tristan and young Roger de Treyne and Father Thomas and two of the falconers, to hunt the huge bucks moving closer to the coast for food. Genevieve had watched them from this window, wistfully, longing to go.

But she had not asked.

She'd gained a certain freedom, and she no longer felt so wretchedly idle. The castle was hers to roam, yet she knew that she was not fully trusted; guards were stationed at strategic places. She knew, without asking, that Tristan would not trust her upon a horse. When he had mentioned their outing this morning, she had watched him with her unspoken plea in her eyes; but, she had known his answer without his words.

The Sisters of Good Hope were too close, should she manage to elude him on horseback.

Genevieve sighed suddenly, leaning against the stone and holding back the drapery to stare into the snow, which she so longed to touch. Life was easier now, in the days since his return. She did cherish the change! Things had fallen into a pattern by silent agreement. Tamkin—still a prisoner like herself but invaluable in the running of the estates—worked with her frequently; in winter they saw to the welfare of the tenants and the farmers that the lords of the castle were bound to consider.

So much unsaid . . . Genevieve brooded. It seemed such a strange period of time, as if everything waited. And life was indeed, she thought, strange. Not unpleasant. Mornings she spent as she had for years, daily supervising more and more of the domestic activities within the walls. Afternoons she spent with Edwyna and Anne, sewing, talking, laughing, playing, reading, or practicing upon her harp now that she was allowed to the music chamber once again. And when dusk came Annie was put to bed, Tristan and Jon returned from their business, and they took the evening meal together, often with Father Thomas and Tibald joining them, too.

And then . . .

Then, of course, she and Tristan were alone, and the nights were often like mercury dreams. They never spoke of the future, and he never mentioned the child, and therefore she was careful to keep silent herself. What plans she might have were not for him, and what he thought or felt now he gave her no clue. She knew that she grew passionately involved, yet she dared not scrutinize the feeling that grew within her, for she could not change the truth. He was the enemy; she was the conquered prize. She could never be more; she was simply a captive kept now in her own residence, and useful there—for the time.

But she was not unhappy! So for now, until this winter's lethargy left her and she could fight the spell of the man as well as his power, she would bide her time as a part of it all. She seldom even blushed now when her servants looked at her curiously or when Father Thomas' sorrowful gaze fell upon her. Only those closest to her knew about the child, for she carried it well. But everyone knew where she slept, for Tristan had never made a secret of it or of her dishonorable position here. Perhaps it was easy not to see much in the way of the things; nothing much in appearance had changed. No one had ever rifled her coffers or her trunks. She wore her own clothing and furs and jewels and surely appeared much as she ever had.

She simply did not leave the confines of the castle.

"Milady?"

Taken from her thoughts, Genevieve moved her cheek from the cool stone to glance quickly at Tamkin. He was on his feet, holding his quill tensely as he stared at her. He had been speaking to her, and she hadn't heard a word.

"You've not been listening," he said.

She smiled apologetically at the great bear of a man who had always been such a part of her life.

"Forgive me, Tamkin. What were you saying?"

He cleared his throat. "I asked that you—give a plea for me, milady, to—Lord de la Tere." He shuffled from foot to foot, then murmured, "I stand unforgiven for my part in the events here. Others come and go now, while I—" He shrugged.

"I am forgotten. I am returned to lock and key each night. Ah, milady! I was loyal to your father, and to his cause, yet now—I cannot change the course of events, bring King Richard back to life, or set a Yorkist king upon the throne! I would bow before the winds of history and give Henry his due—Henry and his nobility. I would swear my oath to Tristan de la Tere.''

Genevieve stared at him blankly for a moment and he continued, "Milady, please, if you would just speak on my behalf . . . ?''

"Tamkin,'' she murmured uneasily, "I, too, am a prisoner here.''

"But a—cherished one, milady.''

She turned back to the window, blushing. Then she forgot Tamkin's words because there was a sudden flurry of activity below. Grooms were rushing about, and the great gates were opening while a guard formed at them. Straining to see, Genevieve gasped, for there was a contingent of a dozen or so men on horseback with banners waving bearing down on the castle.

"Tamkin—!''

He rushed to her side and together they looked out.

"They carry the dragon! The dragon emblem, Cadwallader of Wales. My Lady—they come from the King!''

They did indeed, Genevieve saw, as the men rode through the gates. She could hear trumpets blowing then, and as Tamkin had said, she could clearly see the Welsh dragon on the banners, as well as the leopard and lilies of England.

"My God!'' Tamkin said suddenly.

"What is it?''

"There! It is Sir Guy! Is the man a fool—or a miracle? He returns here—''

"He changed sides,'' Genevieve murmured, and her heart beat recklessly as she saw her old friend dismounting in the courtyard, tossing the reins to a groom. He looked upward, and though Genevieve was certain he could not see her behind the frames of the window, she could see him clearly—sandy-haired bright-eyed. It was good to see a friend, yet she was suddenly afraid of him, remembering the way that Tristan

had mentioned his name. Nor was she certain that she wanted
him here. Those who had remained behind had taken their
punishments and learned to move into the new life. Guy was
not a part of that now. He was indeed a part of the new
order—the order that had taken over.

"Changed sides!" Tamkin snorted. "The traitor!"

Genevieve shrugged wearily. Traitor—or the only intelligent one among them? Guy was outside, free and well and
apparently prospering. They were inside, prisoners, subject to
the whim of Tristan de la Tere.

"The noble Sir Guy!" Tamkin sore sarcastically. "He who
created the seeds of treachery comes to us with a smile upon
his face, while you and I pay the price!"

"Tamkin, don't be so certain that he plays the traitor—to
us, at any rate. I understand that he rode with the Stanleys at
the Battle of Bosworth Field—and the Stanleys quite suddenly chose for Henry. Perhaps Guy has come here to see
what he can salvage for the rest of us. Please, Tamkin, don't
speak on it again—"

"Oh, I'll not speak again. But be certain that I shall brood
in my heart! Shouldn't you be there, milady? 'Tis most
certainly an envoy from the King—and no one to greet them."

Genevieve stared at him, startled, and uncertain. "I—I'm
not sure that it is my place—"

"Then whose?"

Genevieve stiffened, suddenly wishing that she were locked
back in her tower room, and not faced with this dilemma.
"I—don't know. Tristan's, I suppose. In his absence, Jon's."

"And neither are here."

"Edwyna—"

"Is ever gentle, ever shy, milady. Don't leave them to be
met and greeted by old Griswald."

Genevieve stared through the glass and saw that the men
would soon be at the doors.

And that Guy still stared upward anxiously. Suddenly she
was equally anxious to see him, to assure him that she was
well, that Edenby had survived far better than any of them
might have expected. A wistful tear stung her eyes as she
remembered the last day she had seen him, when he had

ridden away to battle with such exuberance—coming to her first to profess his love.

A love she had spurned, she reminded herself. But back then she had still felt powerful and confident, and she had assured herself that she would be no man's tool.

Nay, just his concubine . . . she ridiculed herself. And yet she felt that she could never, with Guy, have known the world that Tristan had shown her; Guy was simply not the man, not the power, that was Tristan. Well—perhaps she'd have never married dear Guy; but he was still a good friend.

"I—I'll go," she murmured to Tamkin. She gave him a quick, uneasy smile and fled to the landing, nodding absently to the guard there, then pausing.

"It seems we are visited by an envoy from the King. Perhaps you would be so good as to go to the kitchen and see that we are prepared to greet the party."

The man looked startled, then he nodded in return. Genevieve hurried down the stairs. Edwyna was standing by the hearth with one hand to her throat, one atop Anne's shoulders.

"Genevieve! Thank goodness! There you are. What shall we do?"

"Open the door," Genevieve grinned. "Come, quickly, with me. Annie, darling, give me your hand."

Genevieve opened the doors ere the man at the fore could reach it. She stood back, serenely, and the first of the men introduced himself as Jack Gifford, Earl of Pemlington, servant of His Majesty, King Henry VII, come here with winter's greeting for the Duke of Edenby and Earl of Bedford Heath.

Genevieve stepped aside, inviting him in, trying not to look over his shoulder for Guy. Jack Gifford called to a group of the party to await him in the courtyard until arrangements were made, then he entered through the doors with four men behind him.

One was Guy.

"Genevieve! Edwyna!"

Lord Gifford smiled and removed his gauntlets, content to watch as Sir Guy gave both the women and then the child fervent hugs.

Genevieve hugged Guy back, but then looked nervously to Jack Gifford, wondering at his reaction. He but smiled and lifted one of his gauntlets. "I understand that you know Sir Guy," he said dryly, then bowing himself, "and you, miladies, are the daughter of Edgar Llewellyn, his sister, and his niece. I give you Father Geoffrey Lang, and Sirs Thomas Tidewell and Brian Leith."

Genevieve greeted the new arrivals with a bowed head and a murmur and drew them nearer the comfort of the hearth, explaining that Tristan was out in the forest on the hunt. To her vast relief, Griswald appeared quickly with wine for their refreshment and assured her in a whisper that he had a large haunch of venison and several fine pheasants and pigeons to prepare for a meal. Genevieve bade the guests sit, and they did, and though she longed to ask Guy a million questions, she nervously kept her distance from him. She was clearly under scrutiny from the lot of them, though it seemed that Jack Gifford was a kindly enough man, watching her with gentle blue eyes while he spoke casually of the coming winter, and she and Edwyna spoke casually enough of the weather in return.

When the wine glasses were empty Genevieve hurried toward the kitchen. As she passed beneath the arch in the walls outside the kitchen, she was suddenly stopped, hailed from behind, and tenderly spun around. Guy stood before her, his hands on her shoulders and his body pressed tensely to her.

"Ah, Genevieve! Fret not, fear not! I've come for you!"

She stared at him in panic, then quickly whispered in return. "Oh, Guy, I am so glad to see you well! But you must let me go, quickly, please!"

He did not let her go. He pressed his lips fervently against hers and did not notice that she did not return his ardor. "Genevieve! This game we'll play but a bit longer! Oh, my love! Has he treated you well?" He gazed at her anxiously then, and she suddenly felt a bit like a prized mare as he stepped back, holding her hands, looking her up and down.

"I am fine!" Genevieve hissed nervously, and then the blood drained from her face as she heard the great doors

opening again and then Tristan's voice as he greeted one of
the newcomers with surprise and pleasure.

"Guy! Go quickly, please!"

He looked grim and not so self-assured, but he touched her
cheek quickly. "Genevieve, we will be together soon. I tell
you, I have plans!"

He moved back toward the hall and Genevieve gave out a
vast sigh of relief before scampering quickly into the kitchen.
Both Griswald and Meg were there, balancing more wine
upon a tray, and Genevieve warned them that the others had
returned from the hunt. Griswald nodded and added more
pewter chalices to the tray. Uneasy and short of breath,
Genevieve was glad to be able to follow Griswald back out.

Tristan and Jon were both speaking to the young man, Sir
Thomas Tidewell, when Genevieve appeared in demure silence, her head bowed low. But when she dared to raise her
eyes they came into direct contact with Tristan's, and she
almost stepped back with a cry they were so dark and curiously speculative upon her. Jack Gifford chose that moment
to speak, telling Tristan how well and hospitably they had
been greeted to his home.

"Ah, yes," Tristan murmured, raising his chalice to Gene-
vieve, his eyes upon her once again, his tone most casual.
"The Lady Genevieve is to the manor born—but then surely,
Sir Guy has informed you of Edenby. It was his home, too.
But London must offer far more of interest these days, does it
not, Sir Guy?"

"London is a fascinating city," Guy said evenly, and
Tristan gave him an idle smile before turning his attention
back to Jack Gifford. "Milord—you had business to discuss?"

"Gifts first, Tristan. From His Royal Majesty, Henry VII!
Come outside, Tristan, and see!"

Tristan shrugged curiously; the men followed him and Jack
backed out, and Genevieve discovered that her knees would
no longer hold her; she sank back into one of the chairs.

"Oh, my God!" Edwyna wailed. "There will be trouble."

"Mama?" Annie queried her, close to tears.

"I'll take her up," Edwyna murmured.

"Aunt Gen-veve?"

"Nothing for you to worry about, poppet!" Genevieve promised Anne, kissing her on top of the head. "I'll bring her up!" she told Edwyna.

"Guy—here. Now. Oh, Genevieve—"

"Things will be all right," Genevieve said.

"Tristan is furious."

"He is perfectly mannerly."

"He must know that Guy—"

"He knows only that Guy was here! He does not know that the plan to betray him that day came initially from Guy. And they have made their peace somehow, else Guy would not dare to be here!" She shushed quickly, grabbing Annie's hand and standing when she heard the men entering again. Tristan was commenting that the "animal" was a splendid beast and that he was anxious to thank the King in person. Genevieve started to move quickly with Anne, but suddenly Tristan was blocking their way and she did not dare attempt to barge past him.

"Milady, where are you going?"

"Only to bring Anne up to bed."

His brow was arched high and his eyes were cold. "Only?" he murmured. Then he looked past her and called, "Meg! will you take the little Lady Anne up to bed, please? I'm sure that my lady is quite anxious to talk with old friends."

Genevieve could not say anything. Meg came rushing up from behind and held out her arms to the child. "Come with auld Meg, now, Annie."

Anne tugged at Genevieve's hand, pulling her down to plant a wet kiss on her cheek while Tristan stared at her. Tristan stepped aside, and Anne, happily esconced in Meg's arms, was taken up the stairs. Genevieve felt as if a chill wind blew within the hall, as if winter had truly taken root despite the warmth of the hearth.

"Tristan." Jack Gifford cleared his throat. "If I may . . . ?"

"Oh, aye." Still watching Genevieve, Tristan spoke to his guest, stepping farther away that Jack could come to her with a huge bundle packed in rough leather.

Genevieve looked at Jack blankly.

"It's for you, milady," Jack explained.

"For me? It really can't be—"

"But it is. Quite expressly, from the King. May I open it for you?"

"Ah . . . please."

With practiced ease the man tossed out the bundle and displayed a coat of exquisite fur, not brown and not pale, but a color quite close to gold.

"Oh!" Genevieve murmured, unable to resist the urge to touch it. The fur was soft, as luxurious as silk, and she had never seen such a color. She looked at Lord Gifford in confusion murmuring, "What is it? I don't understand . . . I—"

"It is, milady, a fine and rare sable, brought to His Majesty by the Swedish ambassador."

"But—"

"He wished you to have it, milady, and to wear it in good health. He said that having seen you, he could imagine no one but you in the cloak. That it seemed fashioned for your coloring alone."

Uncertainly, Genevieve stared past Gifford to Tristan. He came over to her, taking the cloak to set it around her shoulders.

"Tristan . . . ?"

"It is a Christmas gift from His Majesty. You must accept it."

She lowered her eyes suddenly, amazed that Henry had remembered her, much less that he should send her this cloak.

He had, after all, attainted all of her property to hand over to Tristan.

"Well, now, Tristan, if we may . . . ?" Lord Gifford said, and Tristan excused himself to the others, going off with Gifford for the counting room.

Genevieve stared blankly after them; Jon lifted the cloak from her shoulders, telling her he would call Tess to bring it to her room.

She turned around and found Guy staring at her, his heart was so openly in his eyes. He started toward her, but young Thomas Tidewell interrupted.

"Milady, we've heard tell that you've a wondrous chapel here, and Father Lang has told me he would dearly love to see it—and perhaps meet your local priest?"

Genevieve quickly acquiesced. She did not know where to find Father Thomas, but would gladly show them the chapel.

Dinner that evening was acutely uncomfortable for Genevieve. The conversation flowed smoothly enough, and the company was kind. Lord Gifford was a fine ambassador for the King and a charming man. He spoke easily with Tristan about the fine horse Henry had sent him, and equally as easily to Genevieve about the gowns being worn by the future queen. Genevieve discovered him to be an ardent admirer of Chaucer as she was herself. All in all she should have enjoyed the conversation.

But Guy's stare never left her.

And when the meal ended Tristan suggested that they should retire to the music room, and she and Edwyna were called upon to entertain, Genevieve upon her harp, Edwyna with the lute. Yet even that was difficult.

When the strains of song died away, Tristan came to her, placing his hands upon her shoulders with a proprietary air, and asking softly against her earlobe if she had seen to the sleeping arrangements for their guests. Reddening, she told him that the chambers all along the western corridor had been aired and freshened and that servants had brought their things in.

And Tristan took her hand in his, drawing her tight against him, smiling at the company in a most pleasant manner.

" 'Tis time then, my love, for us to retire. Milords, you will excuse us. Genevieve tires so easily these days."

She gazed up at him sharply, but he ignored her look, standing with his arms about her and a pleasant expression on his face. She felt a fury rising in her that he should so embarrass her before these men.

She did not fight him, however, knowing that any squirming on her part would but draw out the fighter in him—it was obvious he was making some point.

"The child she carries, milords," he explained, "does seem to exhaust her."

There were murmurs of surprise and concern; Genevieve didn't really hear them, for she was longing to claw at Tristan's eyes, fully aware that his words had been a taunt to Guy.

She felt ashamed; wanted to crawl beneath the stairway. She could not raise her eyes to her old friend, and indeed when Tristan caught her hand again to lead her to their chamber, she could barely see for the fury that seized her.

When the door closed upon them for the night she wrenched from his hold, spinning with that ire to accost him.

"You did that on purpose! It was cruel—and totally unnecessary! You had no cause, you had no right!"

Tristan leaned against the door for a moment, watching her with no comment. Then he strode across the room, shedding his clothing as he moved. Genevieve stared after him with her anger rising like a fire storm—he would not even give her the courtesy of an answer.

He sat and tossed off his boots and stripped away his hose, then rose, stretching. Naked muscle flexed and Genevieve tore her eyes from him to thump across to the chairs before the hearth, sitting there, her back to him.

She heard him crawl into the bed. And she felt the tension crack between them like the blaze that snapped the logs in the hearth.

At last he spoke to her, harshly.

"Come to bed, Genevieve."

"Ah, yes! Where everyone assumes I will be!"

He was silent for a moment, then asked sardonically, "And isn't it where you do customarily lie?"

Tears pricked her eyes and she knotted her fingers into the clawed armrests of the chair. Why did it suddenly hurt so? Perhaps because she had felt like the lady of the manor again this night, like a noblewoman gently born and gently bred.

Aye, she had felt like a lady. Not like Tristan de la Tere's whore.

"Genevieve!"

She wanted to tell him to go to hell and to burn there slowly for all eternity. But she was dangerously close to tears and feared that she would shed them if she spoke too long, with too much emotion. She sighed out her anger in a long breath and said only, "Leave me be, Tristan, I beg of you. Just this night."

His sudden, violent reaction was not at all what she expected. Her words had been but a whisper, and broken at that. He was upon his feet, like a panther, naked and wiry and powerful in his movement, reaching her while she leapt from the chair, gasping in alarm. He caught her arm, and she tried to wrench from him to little avail; he swirled her to him, lifting her from her feet, high against him, head tossed back and his eyes black.

"Tonight, milady? Leave you be—tonight? That you might dream in peace?"

"Tristan! I do not know what is wrong with you! Damn you, is it too much to ask—"

She broke off, breathless, as she was slammed against the bed. She called him every manner of name in her vocabulary and kicked at him viciously when he came over her, finding a good mark in his nakedness. He grunted in pained surprise and then was furious. She tried to escape, but he held her firmly by the hair, and his fingers tore her gown.

"Tristan—"

His name was a growl and she clawed for his face. Silently, with a grim look, he secured her wrists.

"Tristan!"

It was a plea—for he frightened her, and yet she could not believe that he would really hurt her. He drew her arms high above her head, lowering himself carefully over her, dire in his wrath still but offering her no harm.

"Tristan! Please! I but asked that you leave me be this night! I began no fight—"

"You began everything, my love, but I shall finish it all for you!" he told her heatedly. "Tonight, of all nights, you will lie here with me. You will not dream of days gone past, of yesterday's love, or dream of that boy's hands. You—"

"You mad Lancastrian bastard!" Genevieve hissed. She struggled fiercely against his hold and felt only his thighs tightening about her, his fingers grown more rigid on her wrists. "I was to marry his best friend—a boy that lies dead and buried in the chapel below! I never felt anything for Guy but friendship! It is not to dream of another's touch that I would be left alone—it would be to dream of the beauties of a nunnery!"

He started to laugh suddenly, and the sound was crude.

"My love, I do not see you in a nunnery."

"Tristan—"

"Nay, Genevieve, you fool! He feasts upon you with his eyes—"

"He watches me in distress! This is less than honorable, to my eyes, and in the sight of those who loved me! And perhaps it might not have been so bad! You did not need to maul me before him, like property, like a mare, like a pup. And, dear God, you did not have to announce that I—"

"That you are quite pregnant?" he interrupted bluntly.

"It was cruel!"

"It is the truth."

"And it is the truth, too, that you care less whether I am exhausted or nay! That you did it just to be cruel—"

"Nay, Genevieve," he said, abruptly weary. "It was not with cruelty that I spoke but with kindness. Sir Guy means trouble, lady. It is best for him to know beyond a doubt that you are mine. Perhaps, knowing that you are pregnant, he will not think to rescue you from this plight. Kindness again— for if he touches you, my love, he is dead."

She inhaled sharply, staring at him, for he had spoken no more in anger or in malice but in simple truth.

Confused, she shook her head. "You are wrong! I do not dream of him, nor he of me. It is the ignominy, it is his horror at my situation—"

"Now that, my love, is most amusing. Your situation is merely that which you offered yourself while the gallant Sir Guy was still in residence here. In fact, we sat together at the table that distant night, all three of us. And Sir Guy watched us walk the stairs together to this chamber and close the door.''

''Tristan, you do not understand—''

''Aye, but I do, Genevieve! I see that what was planned that night was not illicit but immoral, it was murder rather than seduction. Was it, perchance, young Guy—the gallant and horrified—who planned that attempt at murder?''

''No!'' Genevieve gasped, and she closed her eyes suddenly, going very rigid. ''Tristan, really, all that I asked was that we not fight this war tonight, that—''

''And all I asked was that you come to bed. Where you are now, milady.''

He settled against her and in the flickering light of candles and fire, his face was a demon's mask, his grin was a leer with his features shadowed and dangerously handsome, his teeth shockingly white against that darkness. And even as she stared at that grin of his she felt its cause, for her struggles had brought her bare flesh against his, and her rent gown gave way further with each breath that she took.

''Tristan—''

''Not tonight, milady? Aye, tonight, madam, more so than any other night. For sometime tomorrow he will try to come near you. And he will ask you if I made love to you during the darkness. You are dying to look him in the eye and deny it in all innocence, and that I will not allow you to do. Nay, milady, when he asked you, you will flush that beautiful shade of red that creeps over you now—because I have read every thought in your heart.''

''You've not read a thing!'' Genevieve protested, and yet she prayed suddenly that he could not read more, and she marveled again at whatever it was that flared between them. For no matter how angry she became, frustrated, furious or determined, she could also, all too easily, long for him—for the feel of his skin against hers, the pulse at his throat, and that harder pulse of his, strong against her bare thigh, insistent and insinuative and creating a quickening inside of her.

His smile deepened as if he still read her thoughts. She

went very still but failed to deter any of his motions. He stroked her cheek in a slow, tantalizing motion.

"Ah, Genevieve, trust me! I do know much about you, for I seek to know it. Would that you were a book, ah, what eloquent words there would be to read, scripted in elegance, letters that curled and curved. I'd hunger for each sentence, I'd devour all the language that lay within. I'd seek out the heart and the soul, they that ever do lie within the gold-gilded pages and the velvet binding. Not that I would scorn the cover, ah, never, love, would I do that!"

His hands upon her parted her gaping bodice, his palms, rough and urgent and tender, smoothed along her flesh, grazing her breasts and covering her midriff and waist, moving ever lower and rending fabric with a strange music until there was nothing between them but a whisper of air.

"Dream, would you, my love? For what?"

Genevieve gasped out a startled sound as he moved suddenly, studying her form as one might indeed peruse some work of art.

"Silk and velvet, my love. Did I say gilding? Nay, but gold here, solid and true, the most beauteous work, oh, this cover! So hypnotic, milady, that a man must read further whether he desired to or nay. He cannot escape the fascination of all that lies there. So I say, my lady, my love, that neither he nor any other could fill your dream as I am determined to fill your life. I adore this binding and this spine, and already the words composed within carry a story that is partly my own . . ." His voice trailed away, the reverence of his caress did not. His hands indeed adored her flesh, in a tender manner that traced the slight swelling of her abdomen and that greater, seductive swelling of her breasts. And she stared at him, trembling, aching, and whispered with amazement, "Truly—you are mad!"

"Mad! Mad you accuse me! Ah, lady, mayhap this is true! Maddened with desire that knows no end, maddened with the need to burrow ever deeper into this book, learn the pages, test the matter well within!"

"Tristan—"

She tried to rise, and he but laced his arms around her,

crushing her full and heavy breasts to his chest, her hips flush with his. He kissed her long and hard and when he was done she was falling, falling beneath him, palms hard against him to discover him, to seek to discover him, too.

Read the man, that which she could, by sight and taste and touch; all that she could touch of the elusive dream. She found herself upon her stomach, feeling his kiss along her spine, from nape to the rounded flare of her hips. He taunted and teased again, telling her what was binding and what was the finest paper, where lay the sweetest phrases and the erotic words.

She laughed . . . and laughed until her quest for breath left no room for laughter, until she stared into his eyes with her arms about his neck and sucked in a great gasp of air with shuddering wonder, as they told one splendid tale together. Laughter faded to cries and whispers, tremors of need became shudders of fulfillment, and even then they were bound together, for he held her close, chin upon her head, deep in thought, an arm locked about her waist and his fingers drawing gentle circles in that slight swell, where their child lay and grew.

Genevieve did not sleep, but wondered that all could be disaster, and still he could not only make her writhe and arch and twist with aching need to his rhythm, but also . . .

Make her laugh.

Morning came, and she woke with bright sunlight; The hall was alive, their guests had risen.

She started to rise, the covers falling from her, and saw Tristan's eyes were upon her. He gazed with a brilliant light upon the tousled tangle of her hair, where it lay over the rise of her breasts.

In mild panic she strove to toss away the covers and rise, but his arm snaked out ere she could do so.

"Tristan, nay—" she warned in alarm, but he was atop her and she was protesting that she could hear their company, that they must be up and—dressed!—and about.

He shook his head most wickedly. "Nay, I'd have my mark well upon you. In kindness, you know—for the lad."

"You're 'mark' is upon me!" she retorted, but that wicked grin increased and he whispered, "Ah, milady, there is something radiant and telling about a fresh bedded maid—I'd not have him miss the signs!"

"Tristan . . ."

It was as far as she got.

And when she was finally up and washed and dressed and trying to come down the stairs with him in some semblance of pride and dignity, she wanted to kick him in the absolute worst way.

Because his words kept returning to her. And so naturally she blushed, wondering if the others could really tell or not. And thanks to that simple game he had played on her mind, it was probably painfully evident because all she could seem to do was blush.

"Ah, yes, a radiant, radiant rose . . ." Tristan whispered when they gained the hall.

And she did kick him. Discreetly, of course.

"A red rose," he warned her with a mocking smile. "A slightly thorny but wonderfully red, red rose."

Chapter
Nineteen

IF IT HAD not been for Guy, Genevieve would have enjoyed the stay of their guests immensely.

Christmas was upon them, soft white snow continued to fall, and even under their clouded circumstances there was a great deal of merriment. Each night it seemed that Griswald prepared a finer feast, mummers and carolers came to the doors and musicians came to play in the halls.

Lord Gifford and his party were to stay through Christmas Day. Genevieve was not sure of what passed between this particular guest and Tristan, but she became aware from things said here and there that Tristan was being summoned back to Court. Why, or when, she was not sure. And while the King's men remained with them she did not ask, for certain questions brought out a cold and dry response from him. They were seldom alone together except for the nights, and the nights were something she had long since given up decrying.

She enjoyed watching Tristan and Jon with Thomas Tidewell. They were all ready to tell some tale of one another as awkward youths, exposing one foible or another. The years melted away when they laughed, accusing one another of some reckless stunt.

One such time came on Christmas Eve. It had been a grand day, with the hall opened to welcome people, the farmers and the merchants and craftsmen, their wives and their daughters. In memory of Christ's giving, Tristan and the members of the household had bathed and dried the feet of the feeble and poor and needy, and handed out coins; and when that ritual had ended, with Father Thomas and Father Lang giving out blessings to the poor and rich alike, there had been dancing. Tess, barefoot and ecstatic, had danced about the room on Tristan's arm, only to be swept from him by a bold and bellowing Tibald. Guy had thought to claim Genevieve, but Lord Gifford had rescued her from those too tight and passionate arms before Tristan could be aware of the event.

She and Edwyna danced with many a farmer and shepherd, while Tristan and the King's men held many a milkmaid. It was the custom of Edenby for the people to come together on this night. Punch was served in a giant wassail bowl, and it was a night when all men might eat, drink, and be merry.

It seemed an especially fine night to Genevieve. She was weary yet awake with the excitement. Fathers Lang and Thomas had retired to the former's rooms by the kitchen ell to discuss some theology, and the guests had trudged away home. Edwyna had retired with an exhausted little Anne. Genevieve hadn't seen Guy in quite a while. In the great hall, before the hearth, were Jon, Thomas Tidewell, Tristan, and herself. She had thought to leave them alone, but when she began an awkward excuse Tristan caught her hand and drew her to him, and she somehow wound up resting between his knees, his hands playing idly upon her hair, while they all sat back, tired, and at ease.

And in those moments Genevieve felt a strange tug at her heart, and she wished ardently that she might have known Tristan in a different life, years ago. Before that heinous crime had been done against him.

"Ah, but you should have seen his face!" Thomas Tidewell was saying, grinning at Tristan. "But that was Tristan—ever determined to prove himself to his father. He just had to ride that great black stallion, and the animal did see fit to deposit him straight way in the trough!''

Genevieve gazed up him as he stroked her cheek. ''I was all of nine years old!'' he protested. ''And the younger son. It seemed like a good idea at the time.''

''Your brother was quite amused,'' Jon remembered.

''Aye—as was the Earl. The switching he gave you was heard halfway down to London.''

''Now *that* I'd have enjoyed!'' Genevieve teased, and he arched a brow to her.

''I can just imagine, milady!''

''It was well, though, for you did learn to train that horse,'' Jon murmured.

''Aye, and Pie is another like him.''

''Genevieve knows all about Pie's manners,'' Tristan said, smiling.

She lowered her eyes, amazed at the softness of the smile that crept to her lips, too; it did not seem possible that they could share amusement now over such things between them. She was so contented, like a kitten curled at his feet; soon she was drifting to sleep.

She could not quite stifle a yawn when she said good-night to the others, and she leaned heavily upon Tristan's arm until they reached the room. She barely made it to the bed, and she lay back exhaustedly, her eyes closing immediately.

''Genevieve, you cannot sleep with your shoes on.''

She heard his voice but dimly, yet heard within soft strains of tender amusement.

''I cannot move,'' she groaned.

And he sat to take her shoes from her, rubbing her tired feet, the soles, toes, and heel, with such gentle dexterity that she smiled wistfully, her eyes still closed, and sighed with the sweetest refrain. She knew little else but that manipulation, and vaguely still that later he helped her from her gown and shift, and drew her against his warmth and comfort to sleep.

She woke to sunshine—and Tess in the room, Tristan already up and dressed, and the wonderful smell of chocolate wafting on the air from a silver server set upon the table before the hearth.

Genevieve pulled her hair from her eyes as she heard
Tristan laughing to Tess and wishing her a fine Christmas.
Genevieve almost climbed out of bed, but although she had
been naked before Tess and naked before Tristan, she'd never
appeared before both at once in such a state; so she curled
more deeply into the covers. Tess left and the door closed,
and when Tristan turned she smiled almost shyly and wished
him God's blessings for Christmas.

He smiled in turn and did not come straight to her but
paused by the table to pour a mug of chocolate. When he
reached her it was to chide her to move her rump so that he
might sit beside her, and when she laughed and did so he slid
next to her, his one hand about her as he offered her the
chocolate with the other.

She sipped it and felt a great rush of warmth and comfort
both from the potion and his arm and casual ease beside her.
And yet for all that, a feeling of the greatest shyness swept
over her and she kept her eyes lowered murmuring, "I should
rise quickly. Surely it is near time for Christmas Mass."

"Not so near," he murmured, and taking the chocolate
from her he lifted her chin with his thumb and forefinger. His
eyes were on her as light as a summer's sky, his hair was ever
slightly tousled about his forehead, and a slow, lazy smile
played about his lips. Never had he looked so handsome and
tender.

"We've some time," he said lightly, and his smile played
more fully across his features with amusement and ruefulness.
"I'd not be outdone by the King, you see."

"Your pardon?" Genevieve murmured with some confusion.

He left her once again and went to where his cloak lay
upon the back of a chair. He came back to her with a small
package wrapped in blue velvet, placing it into her hands.

She did not open it but stared at him, her eyes grown wide.
Again he sat by her side, opening the package of velvet when
she could not, setting the clasp aside to reveal a menage of
delicate gold filigree and sparkling gems. He drew them from
their nest, straightening the piece, and she saw that it was a
cap for the hair, intricate, glorious.

"The gems," he explained, "reminded me of your eyes—in

all their moods and hues. Amethysts in mauve and sapphires in blue and diamonds for their glittering fire in passion and in anger.''

Genevieve stared, her heart thundering. She could not speak, and did not know what to feel. Gladness? That he could think of her and such a beautiful thing all in one. Or shame . . . that she had proved herself so entertaining that he would think to reward her with material gain? Were it not that he had taken Edenby! That they had met as friends to become lovers! Were it not the first Christmas where her father lay rotting in his tomb alongside the man who would have made her his wife.

''Genevieve?''

She could not touch it. She kept her eyes low.

''It is—beautiful.''

He leaned across her feet suddenly, studying her, and though her eyes were low he might see them. Primly she smoothed the covers over her breasts.

''Truly, Tristan. The gift is beautiful. But I—cannot accept it. I have nothing for you.''

''Genevieve.''

He touched her chin again, lifting it. She could not read what thoughts played through his mind then, but it seemed again that he had read hers.

''I bought it in London, Genevieve. With rents collected from my estates in the north. I did not buy it to appease your anger, nor to pay for pleasure. I purchased it as a Christmas gift for a woman whose beauty it does so nicely complement. And that is all.''

Tears stung her eyes with his words, and she blinked quickly to hide them from his gaze. He took the jeweled snood from her and knelt, stradled above her, to set it upon her head, and she laughed, telling him that her hair was too wild to do the piece justice.

''Nay, I tend to like this mane of yours wild and disheveled,'' he told her, sitting back back to survey it. The gentle look of tenderness did not fade from his face, and suddenly Genevieve was glad again, and touched and warmed as if by fire.

She looked quickly downward, her fingers nervously folding over the blue velvet packaging. "But I have nothing for you," she whispered.

To her surprise, he was suddenly standing. He strode to the hearth, fingers laced tautly behind his back. Genevieve watched after him with some surprise, for he was, in a way, abruptly gone from her, and she could not read him so easily as he discerned her heart from the shades of her eyes.

"Tristan, I did not seek to offend you—"

He turned quite suddenly, yet he was still distant from her, but not angry, merely living in another age, another place, in the darker resources of his mind, and struggling perhaps to speak lightly to her.

"You have a gift now, madam."

"But I do not—"

He inclined his head, nodding toward the growing slope of her belly beneath the sheeted swell of her breasts. And though his voice went suddenly harsh, she felt that he still meant no anger against her.

"Would you give me a gift this Christmas, then milady? One that I would cherish, one that would allow me to sleep well in the night? If you would, Genevieve, swear to me only that you will care for yourself—and the child that we've created. Whether in your heart you call me friend—or your greatest foe. Swear to me only that you will guard your life, and your health, and that of the child."

She colored rapidly, knotting her fingers ever deeper in that velvet, for the only time they had ever really discussed the child was that first night of his return, when they had fought so bitterly and so strangely. She didn't know what he felt; she could well imagine that she must remind him painfully at times of his former happiness. She thought what a wondrous time it must have been for them, young and so in love, with no black clouds between them, man and wife cherishing the babe that would be.

Her breath caught in her throat, and she was very afraid and dizzy and glad. Perhaps they were still enemies; perhaps time could never change that. The world was a treacherous place; and the life could change again. That was her hope, was it not? That some Yorkist would present a claim to the throne?

She didn't know. It was Christmas; her father and Axel lay buried in the chapel. She should still despise this man with all her heart, yet for all that lay between them and for all that haunted his past, he asked her now, with near a touch of whimsy, that she guard herself—and their child. He did not seem to hate her for living when his wife did not.

"Genevieve?"

She looked up at him at last, and again she was struck by his appearance so that she trembled. Aye, but what a child this would be, for he was so fine and gallant! She was afraid again to speak. I do not hate you! she longed to cry. I am merely afraid that I cannot hate you anymore. Yet I must somehow cling to honor beneath it all and remain your enemy, you who came and saw and wanted and took, who caused my father to lie dead below . . .

She could not think of hating him at the moment. She shook her head slightly in confusion and whispered hoarsely.

"Milord, I do intend to keep my health. And . . . that of the child."

Then she was frightened by her admission; she did not want to tell him that she could easily love the life within her, and too easily love her enemy. So she jumped from the bed, carrying her covers along with her, laughing to cover her emotion.

"That, milord," she teased, curtsying as elegantly as she could in her gown of linens, "is no Christmas gift! You have given me jewels—"

"Ah," he returned, bowing to her, "but you give me jewels nightly, my love. I sleep entwined in that jewel, that golden mane. I told you once—I consider its value immense."

"Perhaps I could shear it—"

"Perish the thought, milady."

"Well then," she murmured softly, "perhaps I should just entangle it about you. Now."

With her words she dropped her sheet and stood before him, naked and proud and regally beautiful, and most sweetly uninhibited in his presence. Tristan was stunned and fascinated into silence, drawing raggedly for a breath.

"Perhaps," she murmured seductively, "I should come to you, with your gift, clad only in mine."

She walked to him, oh slowly! Seductive as a cat, hips swaying slightly, the pad of her feet so light she might have walked on air. And her hair, that crowning glory adorned in the caplet of jewels, was silk about her, floating, sailing, golden ecstacy that curled over her breasts and hips like nature's grandest cloak.

He could not move. Never before had she initiated so much as a touch, and seeing her thus enflamed his heart and his loins. Yet he could not lift a hand but only stare in amazement.

One that she surely enjoyed, for there was a subtle and lazy smile about her lips, a sensual sway to her supple movement. She seemed as practiced as Eve, and a much richer temptation. She stopped, just feet away, her hands upon her hips, a taunting tilt to her chin and the devil's own mystique in her eyes.

She pressed herself against him then, on tiptoe, winding her arms about his neck, and leaning against him in such a way that she taunted his body from head to toe, and surely felt the hardened flagstaff of his arousal. But she was mischief incarnate, then, allowing him the full feel of her breasts, then spinning away. "Perhaps I need a bodice!" she declared, draping her hair demurely then about her chest, causing an evocative display of deepest cleavage between the creamy mounds. And she spun again, and her hair with her, a golden rainfall, taunting and teasing, covering and then laying bare all that was feminine and beautiful and all that quickened his senses until they thundered.

"Perhaps—" she began in a purr, but broke off with a startled yelp because his inertia and silence were ended, he was before her, laughing like the lion triumphant, and sweeping her up and into his arms.

"Perhaps, milady? Perhaps what?"

"Oh, but, milord!" she squealed, feigning shock and horror. "You're dressed—"

"A matter easily remedied."

"I'd not have you take the trouble—"

"Ah, but I could deny you nothing. And certainly not all of myself!"

With that he made a leap that brought them both gasping and laughing and hard down upon the bed. And her eyes glittered, still a rage of excitement, as she swept out her arms, carrying rich locks of her hair with her to wrap about his shoulders and neck. He buried his face within it, and then his kisses rained so fast and furious over her naked flesh that she discovered herself taunting him no more but pleading with him, knowing not what she said, simply asking him to fill the need within her.

"You think it that simple wench? Drive a man beyond the bounds of sanity and deny him the fruit of slow temptation? Nay!"

"Tristan . . . have mercy!"

"Nay, lady, 'tis not one of my finer qualities!"

And with roving kisses and a wanderer's heady touch, he brought her again and again to a delicious precipice, only to leave her anxious and waiting and pleading . . . and begin again. It was daylight but he spared her no intimacy, staring boldly where he would, resting his head upon her thigh, bringing her near delirium with the stroke of his kiss and the whisper of his touch, then laughing when she declared that she could go no further.

Indeed she would, for most curiously, though she felt weak with the sensations he had wrought, she discovered that he would demand things of her still. When she whispered that he must disrobe, he told her that she must disrobe him; and to her great amazement she did just that, and to her greater amazement still she discovered she could truly be the wanton, covering his chest with the sultry flick of her tongue, sliding against him, lower, lower . . .

Heed his urgings, explore with fascination and ardent administration all of him. And relish, savor . . . his words of urging and passion . . . the sharp, rasping sound of his breath as desire grew. His hands, rough upon her, dragging her to him, bringing them together.

As they had never, never been before. So stunned and sated with it neither could talk, or move, but just lie . . .

But then Genevieve did move with a little gasp of alarm because there was a sharp rapping on the door, and Jon called out to Tristan.

Tristan laughed at Genevieve's panic and grasped quickly on the floor for the lost covers, pulling them over them both as he bid Jon to enter. Genevieve flushed furiously but Jon merely stood in the open doorway, his hand upon it, and wished them both good Christmas, smiling and reminding them that the hour was late, that all the guests were assembled, that, ahem, they really should dress and rise.

Tristan chuckled and held Genevieve against him despite her dismay and promised Jon that they would be right down.

Neither Tristan nor Genevieve saw the man who stood behind Jon in the hallway, looking in, noting their closeness and dishabille.

Neither of them saw him, or the murderous fury written across his features.

The door closed and Genevieve leaped from the bed, tearing into one of her trunks for clothing. Tristan rose with an amused smile and dressed with a more casual calm. But after he had helped her with her shift and the tiny buttons and hooks on her gown, his smile faded and he held her shoulders closely, staring down into her eyes.

"There's one more gift I'd have of you, milady."

Wide-eyed, startled by his tone, Genevieve stared at him in silence, her beautiful features marred by a growing frown.

"Tristan—"

"I have to leave today, Genevieve. I am to return to Court with Lord Gifford and the others."

"What!" She tried very hard not to let the surprise or dismay show in her features.

"I have to return to Court. Henry has summoned me. I do not wish to lock you in a tower room again, Genevieve. Swear to me that you'll make no attempt to escape."

She lowered her eyes quickly, wondering why it hurt so badly, why she should feel such desolation that he should leave her. The morning . . . it was this wretched morning, it had been so exquisite and they had been so close and . . .

She was seeing things that were not there, and could not be there, and dear God—where had she lost her pride and dignity along with her freedom and honor?

"Genevieve?"

"Tristan, that is not fair!"

"Genevieve, I do not want to set guards upon you day or night."

She tossed her head back, looking up at him with agony. "If I gave you my word, how could you trust it? I am still amazed that you dare sleep with me here. You swore that you would not!"

"Perhaps I am mistaken to do so."

"Perhaps you are!"

He tore from her suddenly, and she flinched. Then he spun to face her again so quickly, his unsheathed sword in his hand, the hilt outstretched.

"Take it!" he roared to her.

She could not. Dazed, alarmed, she stepped back, but he came closer once more, eyes black as pitch with emotion, tension straining the cords of his neck to tautness. He grabbed her, crushing her against him, and the smooth blade of the sword lay between them.

"Take it, milady, take it now—if you would."

"Tristan, stop this!" she cried out, near tears.

"Give me your word!" he thundered, his fingers around her wrist like steel, clamping so tightly, and she felt he was barely aware that he held her.

"Take the sword, Genevieve, or give me your word."

"You have it! Let me go, Tristan, please, this—"

"Before Almighty God, Genevieve."

"I swear it, before Almighty God, by all the saints! Just, please, Tristan, let me go, do not look at me so—"

He released her, and turned his back to her, sliding his weapon back into the scabbard. He was silent, dark head bowed. Then he turned back to her and stretched out his hand, willing her with his eyes to take it.

"Come, we are awaited."

She studied his eyes but could fathom nothing about the man. Hesitantly she gave him her hand, and they left the room together.

Even while the day wore on and Tristan remained within her reach, Genevieve felt the desolation of his leaving.

He stood by her at Mass, while Father Thomas and Father Lang gave sermons. Genevieve continually felt that both these men, her friends, stared at them with condemning eyes.

This is not my fault! she wanted to cry out. But perhaps she was beginning to feel that it was, for she was not taken against her will night after night—she had quite literally embraced the enemy to her bosom.

She lowered her head for prayer, but did not pray. Edwyna had admitted to her once that Father Thomas had gone to Tristan, appalled by the relationship he shared with Genevieve. Father Thomas, it seemed, had demanded that Tristan either wed her or release her.

And Tristan had merely reminded Father Thomas that he himself was not free of the sins of the flesh—a fact that everyone in Edenby knew, but no one discussed.

That had been that. Tristan had no thought of marriage, now or ever. Which, Genevieve proclaimed, was to her liking. She'd had no choice but become his mistress. But she could not marry him. For marriage, she would have to vow to love him, to obey him. She would have to give the vow—and giving that vow would be the greatest disloyalty. He could take her chastity from her—he could not take her loyalty. That she still owed to her father, to Axel, to those who had died in defense of Edenby.

And still she was wretched because she was frightened. Tristan had told her he would never marry anyone. She was certain that he believed her protestations and carried no delusions that she longed for marriage.

But what would the future bring? It would be one thing to run by herself, to seek sanctuary, penniless. But not with an infant. What would she do when Tristan's fancy turned and his fire for her ceased to burn? She did not want to be frightened; usually she could convince herself that she eagerly awaited that moment.

But the heart was a fickle thing, more treacherous than any man. There was not just fear, but stark terror in the idea that she longed to cry because he was leaving. God help her! She would miss the passion, and the play, and the tender moments. And she would long for them to come again.

"Genevieve, the service has ended!"

He whispered the words to her and she nodded and rose from her knees. He told her that he had to meet with Jon in the counting room and asked her with a rueful grin if she would pack his clothes.

Aye, she needed to gather his shirts and his good mended hose and join Edwyna, for the table would be heavy laden again today and the hall would be plentiful with guests before the men rode away.

But Genevieve hovered behind in the chapel, staying behind one of the pillars when Father Thomas looked about and closed the doors. Once he was gone Genevieve walked to the tomb where her father lay beside her mother, in their sepulcher of stone. She touched that stone, and the tears that had seemed so hot and heavy behind her eyelids all morning now spilled soft and silent down her cheek. "Oh, father, dear father, I love you, I do not mean to dishonor you . . ."

She touched the stone, and it was cold, and it gave her no answer to the heartache and confusion she felt. She found herself smiling ruefully through her tears and tenderly touching the face carved from marble.

"You're going to have a grandchild, though. And it will be his son. And you really might forgive him if you knew him. You might have asked him to your table, father. You'd have been glad to offer him hospitality, for he is fascinating. And what was done to him was horrible and heinous and . . ."

She broke off, knowing that he was dead; he could not release her from any vows. He could not rise up and tell her that he understood, that even Christ had said, "Love thine enemy."

She walked farther and came to the second new sepulcher, where Axel lay. She thought that the artist had done well in capturing the facial features of her fiancé. Even in marble,

Axel slept like the scholar, like the gentle thinker, more prone to a fascination with science than to warfare.

And through her tears she reflected that he might have understood; Axel was always forgiving. Ever so slow to judge others.

"I miss you, my love!" she whispered, and then she wondered why he had had to die, because she wished so fervently that she could just talk to him.

"Miss him!"

The hiss was startling loud behind her ear and Genevieve swung about in confused panic. Grasping the marble tomb behind her she stared into the furious eyes of Sir Guy.

"Guy! You frightened me—"

She broke off because his hand slashed out and he struck her full against the cheek. She cried out in amazement, clasping her wounded flesh, yet pausing when she would have struck back in simple fury and self-defense.

He really hadn't known what he had done, he was so irate, near delirious—and stabbing into her verbal barbs that were terrible . . .

Terrible, in that they dragged up every bit of shame and humiliation she had ever felt, every tug and tear of guilt upon her heart, every pain of horror and loss . . .

"—by God, Genevieve! Edgar's daughter, Axel's betrothed! Lady of Edenby, late and great. Don't come too near, don't dust her hem with a spark of love or desire. Proud, Genevieve! The ruler, the Duchess—the whore!"

"Stop it!" she shrieked, slamming her fists against his chest at last, and watching, finally, the crazed look begin to leave his eyes. "Stop it!" she whispered then, looking anxiously to the door and remembering that Tristan's wrath could be a terrible thing—and that he did not trust her with Guy.

"Why?" Guy demanded sullenly then, sweeping a stray lock of sandy hair from his eyes and watching her with pained reproach. "Your lover is busy in the counting room."

"Guy, damn you! I chose no lover! I fought to the bitter end, I fought with the weapons *you* chose for me. And when the battle was lost, I was left to pay the price, while you rode from here and became a traitor to your cause—"

"Nay, I was with the Stanleys! They rode for Henry, and I was caught into it! Richard was doomed; I fought for us, for Edenby, Genevieve! I risked my life before Henry that he might see that I was loyal—that he might give me Edenby. And you."

Genevieve stared at him miserably.

"Guy, I am attainted, and this property given to Tristan. Surely you know that—"

"And that you pay the price."

She didn't care for his tone, the deep sarcasm in it, and she started to speak but he interrupted her with a gale of laughter.

"Ah, yes! You pay the price, poor Genevieve! I've not seen him beat you! Rather I see his hand reach for yours, and those delicate fingers fit into them trustingly. I do not see him drag you up the stairs. I see your feet tread after his willingly. I see your body swell with his child, and I see your bright flashing eyes and your maidenly flush when he touches you. And I've seen you—aye, milady, I've seen you!—by his side, damp and trembling and disheveled and curled happily into his arms after his sword has thrust inside of you!"

"Guy! How—"

"Whore, Genevieve! All of London knows that you're the Lancastrian's whore! Tell me, milady, what else would you do next to dishonor your father and Axel and Michael—slain, buried!—by his hand? Marriage, milady? Do you strut and saunter and lay upon him with smiles and sighs, hoping to leave your father's spirit screaming forever as you become his wife?"

"I—"

She hated him but she understood his pain—as he could not hers. And she was ashamed.

"Excuse me," she said coolly, holding her head high. "I would pass by."

She started past him; he caught her hand and pulled her back; and when she would have screamed and railed into him, she saw the mist of tears held back in his eyes, and she could not hate him for the words he had said so cruelly to her.

"Guy—"

"Genevieve, forgive me!" He fell to his knees, holding

her hand, pressing his cheek to it. "Genevieve, I love you. I have loved you forever. I cannot bear this."

"Guy, please!" She came to her knees before him, seeking out his eyes. "Guy, please! You musn't. You musn't love me, and you musn't grieve for me. He—"

"He has to die," Guy said thickly.

"Nay, Guy! Don't be so foolish!" Genevieve cried with alarm. "Guy, were he to die Henry would—"

"I serve Henry, too!"

Genevieve shook her head impatiently. "Tristan has served Henry long and well, and they are close. Were Tristan dead Henry would but give this property to another."

"To me!" Guy proclaimed, and Genevieve shivered because there was suddenly a cunning and sly look about him.

"Guy, I don't—"

"Genevieve, Genevieve! Never have I played the fool. Don't fear, I shall rescue you soon, I swear it! And Edenby. I can be crafty and quick. Be patient, love, be patient, and wait for me."

"Guy, please, this is madness! Don't, please don't do anything! Edenby prospers and the people do well, and I cannot do anything else to endanger others again. Guy you musn't—"

His hand jerked hers suddenly, and she thought quickly enough to cease speaking. He stood, jerking her along with him, and suddenly he was touching her no longer and she was very afraid to turn and see why.

But she could hear the footsteps. A measured stride against the aisle stone, relentlessly bearing down upon them.

She was afraid to turn, but at last she had no choice. Guy stared over her head, silent and still and deathly white.

She spun, at last.

Tristan stood there, tall and regal in his heavy mantle of crimson, held at the shoulder with a brooch of the new fashion, an emblem of the white rose entwined with the red. His head was bare, his hands were upon his hips, and his expression was so dark and so severe that Genevieve trembled despite herself. She wondered desperately what he had heard of the words between them, if anything.

And she wondered if he was thinking that she had plotted and planned this rendezvous.

He smiled suddenly, bowing to the two of them. A smile that was deathly and frightening, that did not begin to touch the black pitch anger in his eyes.

He bowed. "Milady. Sir Guy."

"Tristan."

Why had she spoken? He had asked her nothing yet, and her voice seemed laden with guilt.

That cutting smile of his deepened and he nodded toward her, then gazed past her at Guy. He walked forward and touched her, and surely felt that she did not just tremble but shook like a loose leaf in a winter's storm.

"Your cheek is red, milady."

Never had she heard such a threat, such rage, kept under such taut control in his voice.

"I—fell," she lied quickly. " 'T'was Christmas, and I was anxious to visit my father's grave. I slipped trying to kiss his marble cheek."

Tristan stepped past her, viewing the statue, slipping off his gauntlets as he looked at Guy with a high arched brow. "Is that what happened, Sir Guy?"

He took a moment to answer, watching Tristan carefully, then keeping his voice level.

"Aye, milord. I came to help milady, nothing more, when I saw her fallen."

Tristan nodded then to each of them, smiling again, with a coldness that made Genevieve shiver afresh. Ah, if looks could kill, she would be fallen now, writhing in the agony of that blow!

He drew his touch idly over the marble and went on to the relief of Axel's handsome features. He touched the marble there with easy fingers and gazed at Genevieve again.

"A handsome young man. It is a pity that he had to die," he said coolly.

"Aye," she replied equally coolly. She would not tremble before Tristan, before her father's tomb!

She dared to step forward beside him and very tenderly place her fingers against the marble lips. And tears once again stung her eyes. "He had no stomach for the fight," she said honestly. "He believed that those wishing the war should be allowed to murder one another—and that we should just wait to see the outcome, as most of England was doing! But . . . he would support my father, for he was his liege lord, and Axel was very loyal. And courageous."

"Aye, as the rest of Edenby," Tristan said flatly, ignoring her speech and turning back to Guy. "Henry must be grateful, Guy, that you turned your courage and your prowess to his side."

Guy did not reply. Tristan's fingers suddenly snaked around Genevieve's wrists.

"We are leaving now, milady."

"Now!"

"Aye, milady." He inclined his head slightly toward her, and she still felt the fury in his voice such as she felt it in his touch.

"Tess packed for me. And winter's light fades quickly; we will want some daylight. Guy, you are ready to ride, I presume?"

Guy nodded stiffly. Tristan started out, his boots sharp on the stone aisle, his grip still iron about Genevieve's wrists.

The party was assembled in the courtyard. Edwyna stood with Griswald and several other servants and the boy Matthew, ready to hand up the stirrup cup to the lord of the castle and his group.

Tristan did not release his hold of Genevieve until they were outside in the courtyard. Guy followed slowly behind her, and she did not dare turn around.

Lord Gifford found her and said courteously that he would be anxious to see her again. Thomas Tidewell, Tristan's friend, gave her a brotherly hug and thanked her for her hospitality. She could only smile weakly in return. She knew that Tristan would deny that even the hospitality had been hers.

Edwyna stood there, sorry that they should go so soon. Tristan muttered darkly even to Edwyna, saying that the weather was worsening, they needed the good hours upon the road. And then he leaped upon Pie, and the great animal pranced toward Genevieve; Tristan stared down at her from that great height, straight and one with the horse, his eyes still a condemnation that burned through her. She swallowed uneasily and returned his stare. He bowed to her, courteously, coolly.

"Milady, you are at liberty no longer." He looked over her head and she turned and saw that he nodded to Tibald, who waited with arms crossed.

And her heart seemed to sink. She would not be allowed outdoors again. Tibald had his orders. He would sleep before her door now, she knew, perhaps changing places now and again with young Roger de Treyne.

She swung around to stare at Tristan again, moistening her dry lips to attempt to speak.

"Tristan, I did not—"

He bent down low to her, whispering sharply.

"Milady, take care. If I ever catch you so with him again, I will lay a whip against your flesh myself with the greatest pleasure. And I will kill him. I swear it. So be warned."

He straightened, shouted and lifted a hand, and the party of men and horses went thundering out the gates of Edenby.

Chapter
Twenty

TRISTAN SPENT THE entire journey into London trying to stay in the company of Lord Gifford—and away from Guy.

His anger was such that he lay awake at night, rigid with heat and fury, yearning to rise and drag the man from his sleep and tear into him with his bare fists.

He hadn't heard what had been said between Guy and Genevieve; but he had seen them together. And he knew, in his soul, in his blood, that Guy was plotting against him. In all sanity, however, he couldn't act—not until he had some proof against the man. If he tore into Guy out of sheer jealousy, he would beyond a doubt weaken his own case with the King. He had to steel himself to patience, to wait until Guy should show his hand. But the waiting was torture.

Jon and Thomas were both with him, though, and that was good, for their cautionary words often kept him in restraint. Jon was quick to remind Tristan that although Guy might be guilty of something, it was still possible that Genevieve was innocent.

Sometimes Jon's plea in her defense irritated Tristan—he could have sworn she had been hiding something from him when she had spoken to him in the chapel. She might well have been nervous to see him there no matter what, but he could sense a lie in her, and she *had* been defending Guy. Why? Had Guy really been Axel's good friend? Or was that a lie, too? It seemed possible to Tristan. He could not forget Guy's eyes upon Genevieve that night so long ago, when he had first come into Edenby Castle. He had expected a trick then, partially because he could not believe that a man so in love would allow his lady to welcome the victor to her bed.

Arriving in London did not much help Tristan's mood. From the time he stepped foot into Henry Tudor's chamber he realized fully that conspiracy and treachery would threaten the realm for years to come. Henry was cool but quite ready to point out things well afoot. Elizabeth's mother, the dowager queen and still Duchess of York, was already planning for her daughter's reign. Henry was not ready to act against her, but he knew that in her court she was entertaining a Yorkist faction, among them Francis, Viscount Lovell, one of Richard's closest friends, and John de la Pole, Earl of Lincoln, whom Richard might well have considered his heir after his own young son had died in 1484.

Not the least of it was the pretender, Lambert Simnel, the son of an Oxford carpenter, set up by some source to act as the ten-year-old Earl of Warwick—son of the Duke and Clarence, decendant of Edward III's son Lionel.

Henry knew damn well that Simnel was an impostor—he was holding the real Earl of Warwick in the Tower and could produce him at any time. But the trouble being stirred seemed endless. There would be a rebellion in the future, Henry was convinced. For this reason Henry had summoned Tristan. Henry knew it would take time for rebels to really gather a force against him, but there was a group of Irish lords meeting outside of Dublin, and Henry believed that he could forestall a true invasion and rebellion if that rabble could be broken.

The Yorkist kings had given Ireland home rule for some time; the Irish were naturally interested in the welfare of the Yorkist cause. However the powerful lords had yet to rise, and Henry wanted to buy some time.

Tristan didn't want to go to Ireland. His mood was so

wretched that night that Jon suggested that he might want to ask the King to send back to Edenby for Genevieve. "She could be here upon your return. With Edwyna," he added wistfully. "And Tristan, since Guy will be going to war with you again . . ."

Tristan turned a furious red. "I do not want her here!" he shouted and strode out, amazed by his own vehemence and the truth of the feeling. He found the street and freedom from all company and a cool breeze to calm him. He walked, realizing that it was true, that he was furious with her, that he was, in his heart, certain that she was plotting against him.

Sitting upon a step at last he groaned and pressed his hands against his face, and he knew that there was more broiling inside of him. It was one thing to want her, to crave her—she had captured his senses. That addiction was something he could understand. He could even tolerate the tenderness for her that he sometimes felt. He could enjoy the laughter that they shared.

But her pregnancy was advancing, and though he was anxious for a healthy child, he could not forget the nightmare, and he could not fight the pain. This was how Lisette had been, when last he had held her living form. This was the time when they had dreamed and planned. He could remember holding her so, speaking of names. His name, his father's name, her father's name, a saint's name . . . She'd promised him a boy and he'd told her that a girl with her beauty would be fine. They'd been shy together and bold together; they'd wanted the babe with such tender yearning.

Genevieve had never claimed to want his baby. She saw it only as a creation of invasion and violence . . . even carrying it, she was determined to escape, to betray him. He tried to think sanely of the factions that warred within him now. He wanted her here. He missed her fire and her warmth. Yet he hated her with almost as fierce a passion.

He sighed and rose, and headed back.

From the banqueting hall he could hear music. There would be music. Music and dancing and entertainment. It was perhaps his last night here. And God alone knew, the Irish could kill him ere he could begin to subdue them. No one had ever accused the Irish of being weak!

But he could not return to the hall. He walked quickly, with long strides away from the sounds of revelry. He might as well make an early night of it; he would need to ride hard in the morning.

Once in bed, he soon slipped into a deep slumber. And then the nightmare began. Going back, going far back, through mist and memory. He was riding again, laughing again; and Jon and Thomas were woefully merry and deep into their cups and that steady gray kept descending upon them. It should have been night, but it was not—it was smoke, and the acrid and painful . . .

It was a dream and therefore the smoke followed him like a mist, swirling around his feet, distorting pictures, taking him from one place to another. He saw the farm, trampled and razed, and the old man and then the farm wife . . . slain.

Then he was at his castle. The beautiful manor, so meticulously planned for comfort. Where wide windows, not arrow slits, let in the bright light of day.

But there was no light, just the mist. And he was running, running. Running so hard that he could hear the pulse of his heart cracking like a cannon, he could feel his sweat drop into his eyes and the pain burgeoning in his thighs. Faster, faster, and he could get nowhere through that mist.

Then suddenly, shockingly, the scene in the nursery sprang before him. Lisette, her head bowed, her hand extended, as if she reached into the cradle to stroke a child.

He knew now even before he touched her that she was dead. She was dead, dead and bloodied. But it was not Lisette he held. It was Genevieve. Golden hair matted with death and blood, mysterious eyes of myriad colors closed forever. He screamed in ragged terror.

"Tristan!"

He awoke, drenched and shaking.

"Tristan!"

It was Jon calling him. Light filtered in from the hallway, and Tristan began to feel his consciousness released from the

horror of the dream. He swallowed and blinked and somewhere recognized that it was fast approaching dawn.

"Dear God, what happened—?"

"A dream, Jon," Tristan said, but he was on his feet,
dressing with all haste.

"Wait! What are you about?" Jon dared place a hand on
his shoulder at last. His friend's shouts had reached him half
a hallway down; surely more guests would have heard and
would be wondering, and Tristan still appeared as wild as an
enraged boar.

He clasped his mantle over his shoulder with a brooch and
started past Jon.

"Tristan, wait!"

Jon followed in hot pursuit; Tristan spoke to him over his
shoulder. "You were right. I want her brought here."

"Fine. It is a fine idea, but where—"

"I am going to see the King. I go in his service. By God,
he will see this done in answer to that!"

"Tristan, it is barely dawn—"

Naturally the guards appeared as soon as Tristan strode
toward the King's door. Naturally—and a bit apologetically—
their pikes fell to bar his way, and the Master of the King's
chamber rushed out anxiously. Tristan was not to be deterred,
swearing that he had to see the King, he could not await the
dawn.

Henry himself appeared then, but smiled when he saw
Tristan. They went into his chamber.

Jon noted that Henry seemed to grow more and more
amused while Tristan spoke, sitting upon the foot of his bed,
watching his liege man with an acute gaze and a secretive
smile. Tristan paced and spoke passionately and eloquently of
all his service on Henry's behalf and how in return he desired
that Henry see to the safety and welfare of Genevieve Llewellyn;
that Henry see that she be brought to his Court to await
Tristan's return, and that the King should see to her guardianship that no ill should befall her, nor should she find herself
able to leave his hospitality should she be disposed to try.

Henry stood at last, and there was something sympathetic

about his smile; he knew why Tristan was afraid. He lifted a hand nonchalantly.

"It is done."

"What?"

"It is done. Jon will not ride with you but will return to Edenby for the lady. I'll see that she is comfortably established here, in your chambers, and provided with whatever she might need. She will be watched at all times. She will be safe, and I assure you she will not leave."

Tristan did not seem to think that it should have been so easy. He stared at Henry, hesitating.

"Is that all, My Lord of Edenby and Bedford Heath?" the King inquired imperiously.

"Aye," Tristan murmured, still confused.

"Then, let me get some sleep, milord!"

"Aye. Your Majesty, thank you."

They left Henry's chamber. Tristan sighed. "Well you are not to accompany me, Jon. I am glad. I'd have you with her."

Jon touched Tristan's shoulder. "She will be here when you return."

He accompanied Tristan back to his chamber and helped his friend put on the full armor in which he would ride from London at the head of Henry's troops.

"The King is coming to see you!"

Genevieve felt a little convulsion of nervousness rip through her. Her fingers fluttered nervously to her throat, and she jumped to her feet, allowing the soft white silk dress she sewed for the infant to float to the floor.

"When?" she asked Edwyna, who stood in her doorway looking as stricken as Genevieve felt.

She willed herself to be calm. Henry meant her no harm, she was certain. But in the six weeks or so that she had been at Court she had not seen him, and for him to make this strange appearance now—not summoning her, but coming to her—seemed very strange indeed.

And of course when one had been on the wrong side of a

dynastic war, it was always disconcerting to have the all-powerful victor make a sudden appearance.

Her heart then seemed to abruptly catch in her throat with a piercing ray of alarm.

Tristan! Oh, God, he was coming to tell her that Tristan had been killed in Ireland. That her child would come into this world not only illegitimate, but orphaned. Why else would he come to her? She was more prisoner here than guest, with guards at her door day and night. She had been "invited" to various banquets and dinners but had begged his understanding if she declined due to "indisposition"—which she was certain the King understood to mean that she was rather ill at ease appearing in her condition. She had written him a gracious thank-you letter for the cloak; he had returned the social grace. And that had been the extent of things until now. She could only presume it to mean . . .

"Genevieve!"

Concerned, Edwyna gripped her arm and lowered her back to the chair. Genevieve stared up at her aunt, her features exquisite in fear. "Edwyna? Why? Oh, my God, Tristan . . . ?"

Tristan. She missed him, and she was terribly afraid for him. When Jon had told her that he had donned armor to troop off to Ireland she had been appalled, and to her great distress she had spent that swift night before their departure in tears, most curiously praying that a man she had once tried to kill herself might survive an enemy's blow in a distant land.

It was impossible to hate a man, she had assured herself, when she felt his life inside herself. Winter had brought movement in her womb; the baby was real. Tiny feet kicked against her belly and she touched it tenderly to try to determine just what part of the child was wedged where. She was in love with her child, and therefore could not truly hate its father.

But perhaps, Genevieve had to admit, this was not the whole truth. Was the truth buried in the fears that he lay with an Irish lass even at that moment?

Fear coursed through her again; better that he lay with an Irish lass than dead upon the snow crusted land of Eire . . .

"Genevieve, nay! The King smiles as he comes! Surely, there is nothing wrong with Tristan!"

Genevieve swallowed and nodded, and then realized that she was in no state to greet the King. Her hair was unbound and undressed and she wore a simple gown of blue wool and no jewelry or ornamentation at all. Indeed her feet were bare, for she rested them upon a shaggy ox fur before the fire.

"Edwyna, I can't—"

It was too late: the King was there, a host of retainers behind him as he knocked lightly upon the door that Edwyna had left ajar, and, seeing them, stepped in. Edwyna immediately fell into a graceful curtsy, and Genevieve, coming to her senses quickly, followed suit awkwardly.

Henry bid them rise, greeting Edwyna politely, then turning his attention to Genevieve, saying not unkindly that he would speak to her alone. Edwyna's eyes widened and she was quick to bow her way out of the room.

Genevieve did not realize that she stared at Henry for long moments. She could not help remembering the last time they had met face to face—when he had turned her over to Tristan and dismissed her from his mind. She knew that already his reputation was being made throughout London. He was quiet; therefore the people considered him sly; careful, and therefore shrewd; cautious with his pennies; therefore mean. But seeing a curious kindness to him as he stood before her, regal but not pompous, Genevieve thought about the man beyond the myth. He was still young, he was not an unattractive man; though Genevieve would admit that she had found Richard more handsome. Still she thought that what was said of him on the streets was exactly what he planned should be said; he was not ungenerous, she knew. Edwyna had told her that the ladies had been whispering about the grace with which he had tossed coins to a slim and barefoot orphan dancing in the street for some small reward. His servants liked him well. Nor was he considered licentious; his loyalty to his dynastic marriage with Elizabeth seemed above any reproach. Rumor had it that he did intend to create a strong treasury for England, that he intended to break the kind of power that could lead his nobles to further civil war. He was fond of astrology and the arts and sciences, and Genevieve had never heard that his table lacked for quality or entertainment.

She flushed suddenly, lowering her eyes, realizing how bluntly she had been evaluating him.

"I am interested in your assessment, milady," Henry said lightly, and Genevieve raised her eyes to his again. He smiled, not at all aggrieved. "Do you see a monster still?"

"Your Majesty, I never saw a monster," Genevieve murmured.

"Did you not?" He came forward slightly, appearing nonchalant. Genevieve was certain that he studied her accommodations carefully; she did not know if he was satisfied with what he surveyed or not.

"Truly, I did not," Genevieve protested. She lifted her hands helplessly. "Sire, I can only say again that I but followed a sworn loyalty."

"And now?"

She shook her head, confused. "And now?"

"Do you plot rebellion?"

The thought of her plotting anything, heavy with child and forever in her rooms or in the courtyard just beyond, seemed so funny that she had to laugh despite herself. She quickly caught the sound, though, bringing a hand to her mouth with horror.

"Don't be alarmed," he murmured, idly gazing about again. "I appreciate quick reaction; it tends to tell the truth. But tell me, then, are you happy?"

"Happy?" This time she caught herself quickly, guarding any reaction to his words. "I—I do not know what you mean."

The King found the chair opposing that where she had been sitting and slid into it, indicating that she, too, should sit. Genevieve did so nervously.

"Happy, milady. It means feeling well about one's life rather than thinking ill of it."

Genevieve flushed uneasily. "I cannot say that I am really happy."

"You would just as soon leave England?"

She hesitated. "I suppose I would. In honesty, Your Maj-

esty. You must understand, I realize fully that you are the
King. My vow was to Richard; once he was dead, I meant to
truly swear my loyalty to you. But . . ." She shrugged,
smiling ruefully. "Well you are the King and you attainted
my property and gave it to Tristan. I cannot get it back.
Therefore I cannot be truly happy."

"You hate him so much still?"

The question surprised her and she answered it even more
carefully.

"Is one not supposed to despise the victor—when one has
lost everything?"

"Milady, I asked the question," Henry reminded her, with
just an edge of warning to his tone. He leaned forward. "I
asked you, Genevieve, if you still so despise Tristan de la
Tere."

She could feel a wash of color flooding over her, and
despite the command in his eyes she lowered her own and
answered vaguely, "Our relationship is obvious, I believe."

"Your relationship was obvious before it began, girl." He
spoke softly and she found herself raising her eyes to his once
again. Curiously she thought that he did not feel any rancor
toward her, and she wondered why he had been so bitterly
determined that her father and Edenby cede to him when he
had first come ashore from Brittany.

He smiled, sensing her thoughts. "Your father was a
Welshman very strongly against me. It aggravated me sorely,
and the battle was not certain you know . . ." He lifted a
hand idly; that, Genevieve knew, would be that, in way of
explanation. He stood suddenly, walking toward the window,
turning back. "You have taken care not to appear in public.
Are you so dismayed by the child? What are your intentions?"

"I—I don't have 'intentions,' Sire."

"Are you horrified?"

"No." She answered simply.

"Dismayed at a—bastard?"

She watched him, suddenly composed and poised and not
about to be cornered. "Sire, bastards have been known to go
far in life."

He laughed, enjoying the answer. "Ah, yes! You refer to

my bastard Beaufort ancestor. Well, aye, but then the Beauforts did not remain bastards. John of Gaunt married his Swineford mistress and so all was eventually well. Have you not wondered if Tristan would not eventually marry you?"

Genevieve rose, too. "Nay, Your Majesty, I have not. For I will never marry him. I cannot marry him."

"Cannot?" The King's brows rose high. "You cannot marry the man whose child you are about to bear?"

"The man brought about my father's death, Your Majesty. And he has readily proven that he can take almost anything from me. But my love and loyalty will remain mine, to give when I choose."

He watched her for a moment, then quickly lowered his eyes, and strangely she thought that he smiled with some secret amusement.

"Tell me, milady, do you give them to me?"

"Your Majesty?"

"Love and loyalty, my Lady of Edenby. Are you a loyal subject, madam?"

"Aye, Your Majesty. You are the King."

"But you would escape to Brittany if you could?"

"I would consider such a move—honorable."

"I am fond of the Duke of Brittany, you know. He was to be my keeper; he was always my friend."

Genevieve held silent. The King continued to watch her for a moment, then he asked about her comfort and she assured him that she was fine. Then she knew that he intended to take his leave, and she could not let him do so without asking as to Tristan's welfare, though she longed to feign indifference.

"Your Majesty? May I ask . . . have you heard how things go in Ireland?"

"They went very well, for the time. Eventually troops will rise, and I will battle again on England's shores. The lords currently in question have been subdued."

Her heart quickened; the baby, as if listening, too, gave a tremendous kick.

"Then . . . Tristan will be returning . . . soon?"

"Returning soon?" Henry inquired politely in repetition. "Milady, he returned last night. Good-day, then, Genevieve."

She could not reply; she was grateful that the King seemed to expect none. He strode from her room and the door closed, and she was so stunned that she sank into her chair without knowing that she had near fallen.

And then it seemed that a fuse, set to burn slowly, had come suddenly to the powder; her temper erupted like a volcano against the jagged pain that enshrouded her.

He had returned to London, he had come here . . . He was here, somewhere . . . right here! He had ordered her dragged up from Edenby and she was here at his command; and he had come back after all these months and he had not bothered to come to see her!

"What happened? What did he say?"

Genevieve was only vaguely aware that Edwyna had come back, that she was anxiously questioning her. She waved a hand in the air and then at last looked directly at Edwyna.

"Tristan is back. Did you know?"

Edwyna appeared quite honestly startled. "Nay!"

"But he would have seen Jon, surely—"

"I swear, Genevieve, Jon said nothing to me."

"That doesn't mean that he hasn't seen him," Genevieve said bitterly. Then she knew that she was about to cry, and so she bounded to her feet in anger instead. "That vile, plundering, scurvy son of horse manure! Oh! Why didn't they manage to slay him in Ireland!"

"Genevieve!" Edwyna said, shocked. Then she backed away because Genevieve was so very upset, pacing in a fury, swearing, ranting, pounding her fists against the mantel. There were tears hovering, though, and Edwyna was suddenly afraid.

"Genevieve, please!" She caught her niece's shoulders and forced her over to the bed, to sit at its foot. Genevieve fought her, trailing out a passionate string of oaths once again.

"Nay, nay! Genevieve, the babe! 'Tis not due for another two months! Would you risk his life?"

At last Genevieve grew calm. Edwyna spoke softly.

"Genevieve, please, I know that you do not want to hurt the child."

"It would be his fault!"

"It would hurt you bitterly all the same."

She seemed quiet at last. Edwyna got her to lie down, and she drew the covers over Genevieve's bare feet and distended belly.

Edwyna did not have much trouble locating Tristan; in fact had she not been with Genevieve all morning, she would have known that he was back. In the great hallways of the palace the men were talking about his brilliant tactical maneuvering against the recalcitrant Irish lords; the women were whispering about his manly appearance, with his armor and without. Edwyna but followed the titterers out to the gardens. Despite the cold March day there was a gathering about a silent fountain; a minstrel was playing his lute, and creating bawdy lyrics and a merry tune as he went along. The Countess of Hereford and a few other ladies were sitting upon a bench and laughing, and a number of men were drinking from a deep pot of steaming mead set out for their comfort.

Fools! They should all freeze in the cold, Edwyna thought indignantly, and she was further irritated to see that Jon, smiling that charming smile of his, was seated beside Tristan. The Countess—the widowed and very active Countess—was behind the two men, too close, with way too much bosom exposed for the weather.

Edwyna paused, then smiling demurely herself, sidled through a cheery group to reach her husband and Tristan. They were singing along with the minstrel, raising their cups, but Edwyna was gratified that though her husband kept singing, he also most gladly reached out an arm for her. She slipped into the slim space allowed her between Jon and Tristan. She accepted a kiss and a sip of the mead from her husband—but then turned her eyes on Tristan, who was still singing in his rich baritone, laughing, eyes dancing, and not averse to the wanton touch of the beautiful Countess behind him.

Tristan gazed at Edwyna in return and she was quite certain that he wasn't at all drunk. There was something shrewd in his gaze; he knew she had come to accost him, and coldly dared her to do so, although he greeted her warmly when the minstrel had stopped and other voices were chiming that he begin again.

"You're home, oh noble Lord of Edenby!" Edwyna said.

"Ah, sweet Edwyna! Do I detect a barb? Jon, take care! The honeyed bride yet has claws!"

"Edwyna—" Jon began.

"I am glad to see you alive and well, Tristan," Edwyna continued.

"But of course he is alive and well, Edwyna!" proclaimed the Countess, as her elegant fingers slipped down to stroke Tristan's chin. "So gallant a knight would easily beat down the bloody Irish!"

Tristan's smile slipped with some annoyance. "The 'bloody' Irish were fine men of poor conviction," he said quietly.

There seemed to be another set of fine lines about his eyes, Edwyna thought. And a slash across his hand was turning to a white scar. It was strange, she decided sadly, that a man so proficient in battle should hate it so.

He was handsome, and he was hard—and he was the knight just returned from fierce warfare, yet she was also suddenly convinced that this blasé attitude of his was false; that he really had no taste for this merriment, that instead he brooded. Like a man . . . haunted.

She lowered her voice slightly, but otherwise ignored those around her.

"You have not seen Genevieve."

"Yes, I thought I'd do her that favor."

So darkly! So bitterly he spoke! For a moment Edwyna was at a loss, but the Countess' elegant little fingers were dangling over his shoulder then. She knew that it meant nothing to Tristan. But she was suddenly so infuriated for Genevieve that she wanted to hurt him anyway—and she knew just where to strike.

"I had merely thought you might be concerned," she said lightly. "A child born at this point would surely die."

She reached him—oh, definitely!

"Edwyna!" Jon admonished her harshly, but Tristan drew her attention, snatching her hands in a grip that could crush.

"What has she done?"

"Why, nothing, milord, but she knows that you are back."

He was on his feet, striding away, with shoulders squared. Someone called after him; he did not turn.

"Edwyna, by God—" Jon threatened her.

She turned on her husband and dropped her voice to an urgent whisper against his reproach for her. "Jon, it could be true if he does not see her. She was . . . wild!"

He stared at her and she thought again how handsome he was and how lucky she was. And then his lips touched hers, and she knew that they were all right. If only she did not have to worry so about Genevieve.

Genevieve must have slept. When she opened her eyes again she felt a dull pain throbbing against her temples and then a fiercer pain that stabbed no real part of her body but seemed to tear against her heart. She had known, she had known she was nothing to him but a foe, to be broken and used—but somehow she had allowed herself to care anyway. And she couldn't stop it now; couldn't stop the pain or the feeling, nor could she cease to torment herself. Here she was, so swollen with his child that she could not face company, and there he was, out with others, not even bothering to tell her that he lived.

She closed her eyes again, then opened them wide, not at all sure how she was aware that she was not alone, but looking instinctively to the doorway.

He was there, just inside the door, with one foot upon a trunk, his elbow casually upon his knee, watching her. He was aware that she had wakened, yet he had not bothered to announce his appearance. At first she just returned that stare, dismayed by the assessment. His eyes were very dark and guarded. His shoulders seemed to strain against his royal blue tunic, and the masculine allure of the man seemed to command the very air around him. Dark hair fell across his forehead, and he looked both young and severe at once.

And here she lay, after all these months, with no dignity about her. Hair free and tangled and tousled with sleep, the wool loose and ugly about her—her feet still bare. She felt grossly misshapen, and terribly at a disadvantage.

Genevieve sat up abruptly, drawing her back to the bedpost and bracing her palms against the mattress.

Oddly enough, it was at that very moment that she came to know how very much she loved him, how painfully and deeply she did care. Wrongly—without honor, it was true. And it hurt so badly because she had never felt so lost and alone, so perfectly aware that she was not loved in return. He had not even bothered to come to her—for he had surely found other interests, other women.

"So. You are back."

Oh, she had not known that she could sound so bitterly cold herself! She saw him stiffen at the tone of her voice, and she thought, my God, I sound like a shrew—and I cannot help it.

He didn't reply. He walked over to the bed and she didn't know which was stronger, the craving to burst into tears and plead for him to take her into his arms, or the trembling desire to strike out at him.

She did neither. He sat on the bed and she inhaled, drawing into herself as much as possible, keeping her eyes open and level with his. Inside she trembled with awareness of his clean, manly scent, his face and features, and the bronze of his hands against the white-laced edge of his sleeves.

"You're well?" he said.

"Nay, I'm horrid! I do not wish to be here, I—stop!"

He was reaching beneath the hem of her blue wool, sliding his hands along the length of her legs, calves, and thigh, to reach the hard mound of her stomach. Outraged, she tried to stop him, but she should have learned that no one stopped Tristan when he was determined.

Breathless, she grit her teeth to hold back her tears and glared at him in fury. He did not note her face though; he gazed upon her bare belly and moved his hands over it as he would.

"Don't!" she cried again, trembling.

He looked at her at last. "The child is mine."

"The flesh is mine!"

He smiled, and her heart caught at the sight of that smile, and then again she wondered with whom he had been smiling before, with whom had he laughed. And in all these months who had he charmed and seduced and touched and kissed and cared for?

"I felt him kick."

"He doesn't want you here, either!"

"But I am here."

"A bit late for any real concern, I believe."

He drew his hands away at last and turned, rising from the bed. "I didn't think that I would be the one you would be waiting for."

"You were the one who ordered my presence."

"But not the one you gave the passionate good-bye to in the chapel."

Good God, she had forgotten all about Guy. Forgotten that he had ridden with Tristan. Forgotten that he was a friend, that she should care desperately whether he had lived or died.

"You've had no other visitors?"

He spoke bitingly, mockingly. She answered in turn.

"If I had them, milord, I would not know. They could not have gotten past your guards."

"The King's guards, milady."

" 'Tis often one and the same."

"It's good to know where you're sleeping."

"Why should you know, when I do not?"

"Do you care?"

His back was still to her; his voice was casual. But she could suddenly not answer, and at last he swung back to her, something so demanding about his expression that she longed for a place to hide. Why was he doing this to her? If he did not care, he should just leave her be.

She lowered her eyes and tried to drag her gown back down over herself, and he laughed again, catching her hands then placing both of his own over her bare stomach again.

And his touch was light and gentle. Palms against her, fingers stroking. She closed her eyes, thinking how grossly distorted she was, how vulnerable he had made her, how he must be thinking that she was grotesque, ugly. She wished desperately that she could cover up, that she could at least be slim and trim so exposed.

"He moved again. You're wrong. He likes me, and he likes to be touched. He knows."

She opened her eyes. His head was bowed, but he was smiling still. And she trembled, admitting to herself that he gazed at her with a tender fascination now. He was making no attempt to humiliate her; he merely demanded, as was his way, to have what was his.

"He kicks strongly . . ."

There was pain in his voice. And a sudden, excruciating pain in his features. A tremor seared Genevieve's heart, and her fingers moved against the sheets. She wanted to touch his face so badly, to ease away the pain she did not understand.

She lifted her hand, but it fell flat at the sudden rapping at the door. Tristan pulled down her gown, smoothing it over her stomach, then reached for the covers, bringing them protectively over her.

"What is it?" he called out.

"Lord de la Tere! The King has been seeking you. He wants you in his privy chamber at once, your grace."

Tristan stood. He felt her eyes on him, and returned her stare, then offered her a deep, mocking bow. She glared at him, pale, her eyes sparkling like crystals.

"You'll excuse me?"

She did not reply. He left the room and closed the door behind him, then followed the liveried page down the twisting halls and corridors to the King's privy chamber.

What now? Tristan wondered. I will not go away again! I do not know how to be with her, but I do not know how to be without her. I must regain something that I have lost.

He stepped on in. Henry awaited him behind his desk, tapping his fingers against it. Tristan twisted his jaw and clenched his teeth together. Don't tell me I'm to ride again, I beg of you, Your Majesty!

He bowed, inclining his head warily. "Sire?"

"Tristan. I am grateful, you are aware, for your loyalty and service."

"Aye." Cautiously.

Henry stood. "I want you to marry Genevieve Llewelyn."

"Marry!" Tristan stared at him blankly.

"Marry, Tristan. I've told you before—it's a contract. Marry. Take her to wife."

Tristan shook his head. "I—I can't—"

"Well, you will. I've given you her holdings. I'll add to that the Treveryll estates and you'll be one of the most powerful men in the Kingdom."

"I—don't seek further wealth."

"You will do it because I ask it of you."

"Why?" Tristan asked in a whisper. Marry. He couldn't.

"Tristan! It's a contract! It's a way of cementing family bonds and loyalties. She is going to have your child. She came from a family of steadfast Yorkists. The white rose and the red."

Tristan stared at him. A contract. It was a contract only. No, marriage was love and . . .

He didn't dare think any further. He stared blankly as Henry picked up a pen and started writing, then looked at him again.

"Tristan, I command this—as your King. If you won't do it for my pleasure, I will have to take Edenby—and Genevieve —from you and give them elsewhere."

"She's pregnant! With my child!"

"Oh, many a man would happily claim your bastard for the sake of such a beauty and Edenby."

"Be damn—" Tristan began, and then he remembered he spoke to the King. Well he would be damned if anyone else was taking Edenby. Or Genevieve.

"Henry—there is one difficulty. The lady will refuse to marry me."

Henry looked up. "Will she?"

"Emphatically."

The King shrugged and went back to his work.

"You'll think of something, Tristan. Oh—I do think that this wedding should take place before the child is born. A boy stands to inherit, so you'll want him to be legitimate issue."

Tristan kept staring, blankly.

"That's all," Henry said.

Tristan turned and left.

The doors closed behind him. For a long while he stood in

the hallway, unable to believe that Henry was forcing his hand. He thought long and hard about Lisette. She was dead. Nothing could change that.

Genevieve would not want to marry him. But she had to do so, and then their child would be legitimate and she would be his undeniably. Forever. And if Guy so much as touched her, he'd have every right in the world to challenge him.

He felt lightened suddenly. He smiled, and then he began to whistle as he stepped down the hall. Genevieve would see it his way. He had the perfect plan.

Chapter
Twenty-One

"DON'T BE ABSURD—I know her!" Tristan told Jon. "She will never agree!"

He had gone to his friend first, finding him in the gallery playing chess with Lord Whiggin, Edwyna perched behind him to watch the game. Whiggin was a wonderful player, so Tristan had casually dropped a few hints to help Jon lose the game, and baffled, Jon had reproached Tristan. But as soon as he had risen, Tristan had looped an arm about his shoulder, excused himself to Edwyna, and muttered something to draw Jon out to the streets with him. Now they meandered along the docks. It was a clear, cold day, with just a hint of spring in the air. A mortar and pestle etched into a wooden sign indicated the chemist's shop at their left; beside that was a barber-surgeon's shop front and across an alley crowded with onlookers, where street urchins danced and a traveling minstrel sang the praises of the new Tudor King, there was an open forge, where the blast from the furnaces warmed the air.

"I still say it is well worth the attempt," Jon argued, rubbing his hands together. His fingers were cold despite his soft lambskin gauntlets, Edwyna's gift to him at Christmastide. "There's a tavern, let's make our way to it, shall we?

Some good ale might make the problem seem an easier one.''

Ten minutes later they were in a private room with a warm fire burning and an awestruck wench assigned to serve them. Tristan sat with his legs stretched out to the fire, one ankle crossed over the other, fingers laced around his pewter pint mug, eyes brooding upon the blaze. Jon was the animated one, still trying to convince him that all he needed do was ask.

"You tell her that you wish to put the past behind you. That for the sake of the child you must not tarry."

"Jon—she won't do it, I know."

"Any woman in her predicament would surely long to marry the father of her child. The Church! Bring up the Church!"

"Rather late, don't you think? I'm quite sure she knows what I had to say to our good Father Thomas at Edenby."

Jon swallowed down a draught of ale, slammed the tankard down, and threw up his arms. "Tell her that the King commands it!"

"Ah, but you don't understand, my friend. One obeys a King that one honors for political purposes. Fathers obey kings; daughters obey fathers. They do so in fear of loss. But Genevieve has nothing to lose."

Jon stared at him blankly, then rose to open the door and hail the young serving wench to bring more ale. He called out, then as he waited he turned back to Tristan.

"But your idea is madness!"

"Nay, it is not! Bribe the priest, and it is done. It will be easy to bribe the priest once he believes that he is doing the King's will!"

The girl came through the door then, balancing a tray with heavy new tankards. She set the tray before Tristan, leaning over, pressing her breasts high against her bodice. She was a pretty lass, well endowed and pleasingly plump, with merry brown eyes and bright red cheeks. He smiled at her idly, aware that she probably was considering what sum she might ask him for her favors.

Someday, Tristan mused, she would be fat! And those bright cheeks would fall to jowls . . .

And he was being cruel, he realized. At one time in his life he might have found her tempting for an evening; like as not, she knew a trade beyond that of serving ale well! It would have been nothing more than a night of drunken revelry, a simple easing of natural needs . . . she was attractive enough.

Yet all he could see when he looked at her now was a vast and unfavorable comparison to Genevieve. Just as it had been through all those long, long nights in Ireland, when he closed his eyes he saw her. Saw the beautifully slim construction of her face, the high cheekbones, the full lips defined and colored as if with an artist's brush. Her back, sleek and dimpled and evocative. Her legs, long and supple and slightly muscular, divinely shaped.

Genevieve . . .

He thought of her now, and not of Lisette. And as the wench continued to eye him coyly, prating on about the foodstuffs the inn had to offer, he felt a tremor seize him most suddenly, and he had to admit to himself something he had begun to realize with coming home, something that had taken full root in his heart outside of Henry's door, something that tore at him even now.

He did not just desire her, he needed her. He was taken with her spirit, with her voice and her words, her tenderness to those she loved. He admired her tenacity and her loyalty to those gone before her. All this time and he had not broken her, for she was too fine to be broken.

When he had returned from battle across the Irish Sea, it had not been to punish her that he had ignored her, but because he had not been able to still the raging war inside of him. It should not have been the gentle whisper of love that spoke to him now.

"Your grace?"

"What?" He shook his head slightly at the tavern maid, and Jon asked if Tristan were not hungry. He said surely. The wench promised him the sweetest food that could fill his mouth. She departed, and he stared at the fire grimly again.

So you love her, fool. You would bury the past and love her; and it is not Henry's command that you obey to marry her, but the dictates of your own desires. All this you have decided—when it seems possible that she would still plot against you, that she would dance most merrily at your deathbed. She met with Sir Guy in the chapel and he can be trusted just as far as he could be thrown in full armor! Idiot, don't love her . . .

He picked up the new tankard and drained it in one long, long gulp and then grinned at Jon, grateful for the sweeping warmth and the reckless dizziness that he felt. He never drank to excess; yet this day perhaps he would.

Jon slipped beside him again. "What if she manages to speak?"

Tristan laughed, a glitter to his eyes. "Oh, but she will not!" He recalled that day when Genevieve had so nearly reached the Sisters of Good Hope. "I will not give her the breath of a chance!"

There was suddenly riotous laughter from beyond the door and Jon got to his feet, curious. Into the common room he stared, where a meeting of one of the city's guild was taking place. A score of men ate and drank and laughed at the antics of a young musician, a boy not twenty, Jon was sure, but talented with the lute and with his tongue.

Jon stepped out into the room, calling to a burly man at a back bench, with the foam of his ale stuck full to his graying beard.

"What goes on?" Jon asked, and the man, seeing his dress and appearance and the coat of arms upon the brooch that bound the fine fabric of his mantle, stood quickly to speak to Jon. "Milord, the lad sings a song about women, most bawdy and amusing."

And Jon, having imbibed well himself, went forward to the handsome youth. The youth, too, hastened to sobriety to stand and bow at Jon's appearance, but Jon grinned and took him by the shoulder and bid him come along. Tristan looked up with surprise when Jon appeared with company, and the rough young lad blushed and bowed and said, "Your grace! I know not why I'm here."

"Oh, but, young fellow, we need your advice!"

"We do?" demanded Tristan, grinning at Jon. He stretched his feet out comfortably once again, and picked up his ale. "We do, then. So Jon, go forward! Let's see what this shrewd minstrel might tell us."

"His grace is a powerful man, my friend!" Jon told the boy. "The Duke of Edenby, the Earl of Bedford Heath. And they are not empty titles, for his lands stretch as far as the eye can see—he is a favored, battle-proven knight to His Majesty Henry VII. But he has a problem, too, you know." Jon paused, pouring the uneasy youth some ale and slipping it into his fingers. The youth drank deeply.

"A woman?" he asked.

"Aye, a woman." Jon agreed.

"Beautiful?" the youth asked.

"Like no other," Jon said.

"Young and fair?"

"Young and incredibly fair."

"Sweet and gentle?"

"As sharp as ever the thorns on any rosebush!" Tristan replied this time, laughing. He poured more ale, all the way around, and the boy forgot his lowly position with a sloppy smile and slid down to sit beside them.

"A rose among thorns!" he proclaimed.

"A white rose—where the world grows red!" Jon supplied.

"Ahhh . . ." The minstrel murmured.

"Now, I say—" Jon patted the young minstrel on the back. "I say that he should woo her sweetly. Say gentle words, and bid her be his bride."

"She will say nay," Tristan supplied.

The boy inclined his head in thought, and looked up smiling pleasantly. "I say, take her, milord! A fine knight, sweeping her atop his steed, racing off into the darkness to make her his own! Thus will she then agree."

"Nay," Jon said gravely. "He's done that already."

"Oh!" the minstrel said perplexed.

"He thinks to trick her, take her down the aisle on his arm, and when she would say nay, have none of it!"

"What if she will not walk?"

"Then he would carry her."

"Seems to me, milords, a risky scheme at best! But then I am but a poor lad, and I lack the understanding of this maid."

"So do we all," Tristan laughed.

The minstrel stood again, walking and pondering. "A rose among thorns, eh? A lady who has well met the great knight's— sword—yet says aye and nay where she will please, most arrogant! But if one would claim the rose, then one must carefully prune the thorns! Therefore I say try both the plea— and then the force! And consider always this, my lord! That which is most beautiful and best is most often the prickliest to subdue."

"Met his sword!" Jon convulsed into laughter. "Why, friend—she carries the seed of the blade!"

"And still says no!" the minstrel marveled.

"And still says no!"

"Why, your grace! I'd give the girl the boot of your palm, and have her aye or nay!"

Jon laughed and picked up his tankard. "To Genevieve, then! May she fall—by fair means or foul!"

And Tristan picked up his tankard, and the young minstrel did likewise. And soon he was singing uproarious lyrics, and the day seemed to pass with monstrous speed. They had eaten two great legs of lamb and consumed vast quantities of ale and seen that rosy cheeked wench happily seated on the young minstrel's lap before they took to the darkened streets, arm in arm, still singing.

Tristan agreed that he would talk to Genevieve first, and if that failed, Edwyna must be called upon to aid them. Surely she would, for she wished Genevieve well—and anyone with any sense would see this as the best for Genevieve.

"And I dare say that we'll need her—"

Jon broke off, frowning, fighting for sobriety. Tristan had gone dead still in the night, staring about the alley they traversed.

A cat shrieked; there was movement nearby. Rats? They toured the dock area by the thousands. More perhaps.

Tristan shook his head at Jon, sobering quickly. He indicated that they should walk again. The gates to the palace were still a distance from them, through many dark and narrow winding streets.

Then Jon heard it. Footsteps that followed their own. Tristan continued talking, but Jon was aware that he was careful to space his words so that they could hear.

They rounded a corner, and the footsteps suddenly came full force. Jon felt a swoop of air as they were rushed from behind.

With Tristan he was already turning, his sword unsheathed and raised high. A great, toothless brute in a dirty leather jerkin jumped forward with a knife, while a leaner, more dexterous fellow with a filthy woolen cape tore at Tristan with a battle mace.

The fight was over almost before it began, Jon and Tristan were so accustomed to wielding their swords. Yet while the two thugs lay bleeding in the alley, Tristan swore and reached down to them, trying to find a pulse of life in one.

"Thieves and robbers!" Jon complained. "What is this city coming to!"

Tristan let out an aggravated oath. "They're dead."

"Rather them than us! And scum who would murder for a purse—"

"I don't think they were robbers."

"Then what?"

Tristan rose, shaking his head. "I don't know. But a robber would not choose to accost two armed knights. He would prey upon a weak merchant or scholar or craftsman."

"An assassin then? But who would think to set us up upon the streets? Any man we know would issue a challenge!"

Tristan felt a little chill, remembering Genevieve's eyes. Would she—seek to have him murdered? She had tried the deed once herself, and had nearly succeeded. Could he believe it of her again?

She had been whispering with Guy in the chapel. Heatedly. Once before they had planned treachery together. Guy, he knew full well, wished him dead. How could he prove such a thing? Did he want to prove that the beauty who carried his child, who had become his obsession in life, wanted not his heart—but his head upon a platter?

Genevieve started, gazing upward at the sound of the pebble clattering against the glass.

She moved quickly to her feet, leaving Mr. Claxton's book on chess lying on the chair by the fire, and rushed over to look out into the small courtyard beyond her room. She could see a shadow there, and for a moment it seemed menacing and she shivered. Then she realized that it was Guy, and a little gasp escaped her.

Ducking back into the room, she slipped her cloak around her and hurried out the door to the courtyard. It was dark here, but candles from the open hallway leading to the King's chamber cast enough light so that one could see without tripping. Genevieve came out, carefully closing the door behind her; yet before she could speak, her open mouth was caught in a quick kiss and she had her back against the door, Guy's body pressed to hers, his hands on her shoulders—and his eyes upon hers with such open torment that she could not rail against him for all his foolishness.

"Guy! I am most heartily glad to see you well, but—"

"Ah, Genevieve! Genevieve! How it pains me to see you so!" He stepped backed rudely, as if her belly contained disease instead of an innocent babe. "But it will not be long now, I swear it. You will be with me."

Genevieve lowered her eyes. "Guy," she murmured wearily. "Tristan—"

"Tristan will be taken care of, milady!" Guy said, laughing curtly. "Ah, Genevieve, you are still so beautiful. I dreamt of you night after night. Thinking, yearning."

"Guy, please," she murmured nervously. She glanced up at the open hallway, praying that no one would choose to walk by. She was furious with Tristan for neglecting her, but she did not want him to hear that she had been talking with Guy again. And, before God, she did not want him to catch them together again!

"You needn't worry, Genevieve," Guy said bitterly. "Your lover plays in a tavern. He will not be back."

"Until late?"

Guy smiled. "He will not be back. Oh, Genevieve!" He touched her stomach and she felt like jumping back, though she didn't understand how a friend could make her feel so. "Pray that it is a girl, Genevieve. The King would be more likely give a father's holdings to a bastard girl. A son though could be frightening."

"Guy, what are you talking about?"

He shook his head, then laughed. "Although, God knows, the rutting stud might have left a dozen little bastards in Ireland."

She felt herself stiffen, as a steel blade of jealousy pierced her. She told herself that she was insane to be here—and she felt like bursting into tears. She could have sworn that Tristan wanted this child alive and healthy. That he wanted her. Or would want her again. He gave her so much of himself.

Yet he had never pretended theirs was an affair to last forever. He might well have bedded a dozen little Irish whores, and he would consider it his right and his business to do whatever he chose. She was merely a trophy of war. She had come with the castle—just like the furnishings and tapestries. But oh, God, how had she been so stupid after all the tragedy in her life to allow him to claim her heart?

"Guy—"

"Nay, love, don't look at me like that! I'll not hurt your babe, so mine must inherit. A boy . . . we can give to the Church! Your son will rise high!"

"Guy! Please, you are making no sense!"

He touched her cheek, and again he spoke raggedly. "He would have married you, do you know that? I've spies among the King's closest servants. The King admires you. He was forcing de la Tere's hand. If he did not marry you, Henry would have taken Edenby from him. Perhaps a threat only . . . but I couldn't take the chance."

"What?"

"The King demanded that Tristan marry you. Henry is even placing a dowry with you, greater than Edenby. Tristan will own as much land as the highest nobility. Henry planned on being very careful. Don't give your nobles power unless you know damned well they've reason to be completely loyal.''

She was shaking; she felt that she would fall. But when she opened her mouth to speak again, she gasped, falling silent instead. She heard something behind her. In her room. And no one entered there—not even the King!—without warning. Except for Tristan.

"Guy! Please! Get out of here. It's Tristan!"

Guy grinned smugly. "Nay, it is not!"

"Genevieve!" The call came from inside, a deep, demanding baritone. Guy started violently.

"I told you!" Genevieve hissed. "Go, please! Oh, for God's sake, Guy—he will kill you!"

He turned and fled across the courtyard, leaping up on one of the trellises to reach the arched hallway overhead. The door behind Genevieve moved; she gasped, leaning her weight against it, until she was certain that Guy was gone.

Tristan came out, shrouded in shadow—reeking of ale. She could not see his face in that shadow; she could only pray that he had not seen Guy.

"What are you doing out here?" he demanded.

"Nothing.''

"It's freezing out here.''

"I—was looking at the moon.''

"There is no moon.''

"Oh . . .'' She remembered Guy's words to her then, and she felt an aching torment begin to swell within her. "What business is it of yours!" she cried out, ready to sail past him, but he caught her and wrenched her against him, slipping one arm about her waist to hold her tight and using his free hand to stroke the mound of her stomach.

"It is completely my business, my love.''

"You're drunk!"

"Only a bit.''

"You're breathing on me.''

"Ah, yes. You would prefer that I do not breathe.''

"Tristan, damn you, let me go! You said you did not wish to inflict yourself on me last night—go wherever you were then, I pray you!"

"Nay, lady, last night was a curious exception. I am home. And it is cold—you will come in now."

Still his features were in shadow. She tried to wrench from him, then knew she would never succeed. She felt slightly ill. She ached to have him hold her with tenderness, not restraint. She had waited for him, wanted him for three long months.

And then she thought of Guy's words . . .

"In, milady!"

She rasped out a protest but she was off her feet and back inside and he was closing the courtyard door most firmly. Ignoring him, Genevieve walked over to the fire. Hmmph! And damn him, he had been drinking all day . . .

"I've something to say to you," he told her from a distance. She turned slightly, noted the sharp and wary fire in his dark eyes, and felt a sizzle of longing race through her. Oh, how she wanted him! His lips on hers, his hands stroking her. All the tender feminine softness of her own body against the sinewed maleness of his . . .

It seemed so long since she had really seen him. She just wanted to touch him, even if he were a roving cad. She looked back to the fire, hardening herself as a spark of pride and defiance came to the fore. Let him talk! Oh, the scheming blackguard! So the King was fond of her now . . .

"I have thought long and hard. For the good of Edenby and the future of our child, I will marry you."

"Oh, will you?" She was able to spin around, laughing.

"Three weeks from today. The banns will be cried. And I must make a trip to Bedford Heath."

"Oh. I thought, milord, that you would never marry?"

His mouth tightened and for a moment he did not reply. "Genevieve, you are very nearly delivered of an illicit child."

Her temper soared. If she'd had something to throw, she would have thrown it.

"Ah, milord! I hear that Ireland is nearly repopulated with Englishmen since your stay there! Run back to the enchanting green forests of Erin with your wedding proposals!"

"Genevieve—"

"Nay!" She stomped a foot against the floor, aching and near tears. "I'll not marry you! You killed my father, you stole my land! And one day, milord, I will have freedom—for my child and myself!''

''Genevieve—''

''You lying, rutting stud—rogue! I'll not marry you, I promise you that! The King commanded this, you fool! I will gloat most happily while he strips you of power!''

He did not show any anger. He arched a brow pleasantly—and started toward her. She felt his warmth long before he touched her, swept his powerful arms around her. She felt dizzy, so keenly aware of him that it took her a long time to find the strength to push away. Yet she could not escape, only stare into eyes darker than any midnight and totally determined.

''Milady, you will marry me three weeks hence.''

''Say what you will, milord. The wedding vows will not leave my mouth!''

''We shall see, won't we?''

''I tell you, I will not do it!''

''You may tell me whatever you please!''

For the longest time they held there, eyes at war, tension crackling heatedly between them.

And then Tristan hiccoughed, releasing her, swaying slightly, and gripping the mantel.

''Oh! You drunken, wenching lout!'' she cried, tears of fury and hurt forming in her eyes. Here he was demanding marriage, while she was caged in a room like a heavy brood mare and he was out drinking and philandering all day. She'd not have it; he wouldn't touch her, oh, she swore it!

''Wenching?'' he inquired politely, and then he started to laugh, and indeed, though he could hold his ale remarkably well, it was quite apparent that he was—drunk! He reached for her again and she let out a squeal and ducked to escape him, but she was hardly light on her feet and his hands found a hold upon her shoulders. The fabric of her robe came away in his grip, and she was left to trip and struggle with her gown. Laughing, he found his way to her, disentangling her by disrobing her; she found his eyes, heatedly, again.

''Nay, I'll not entertain you after you've spent the days drinking and whoring and—Tristan!''

She was in his arms, furious—comfortable. And he was staring down at her most cryptically, smiling warily. She banged a fist against his chest, but it just fell there and she lowered her eyes. "Tristan," she choked, and her words were but a breath, "I—cannot. I don't believe that I've many weeks left and . . ."

"Shush, Genevieve. I simply wish to sleep, and hold you and the babe."

He laid her tenderly down and doused the candles. She heard him strip and thought bitterly that she hated him, oh, she really did, for all that he'd done and for—making her so miserably jealous and hurt and indignant . . . and in love.

The sheets moved, and he was beside her. She felt all the wonderful heat of his naked body and all the strength in his arms as he pulled her against him, stroking her gently, tenderly.

Time passed, and he held her only.

"I'll not marry you, Tristan!" she warned him, her voice catching as tears rose that she had to swallow down quickly.

"Sleep, Genevieve."

Silence fell between them, until she was compelled to speak once again.

"I am glad that you were not killed, Tristan. I swear it. I was—anxious that you return alive. But I'll not marry you."

"Hush, Genevieve. Sleep."

She fell silent.

He brushed a kiss against the web of her hair. And wondered. Someone had tried to kill him that night. And if he was not mistaken, there had been a shadow in the courtyard.

Tristan spent the next few days mostly in the company of the King and his ministers. Despite foreign affairs, in which the King wished Tristan's opinions, Henry had also determined that Edenby might be granted a Royal Charter to form as a city rather than as a walled town and appendages. Tristan liked the idea; he thought it promoted growth and education and welfare for the artisans and farmers alike. Henry, he knew, was interested in having another city where certain of England's goods might be transferred abroad—with the assurance he would receive all his royal taxes.

Genevieve still refused to appear publicly. Curiously, though, he enjoyed their time together—even the sharp barbs of her quick tongue. She intended to win—but he was determined to be the victor in this battle, and enjoy its fight. He did not trust her; beyond that he loved her, and he had missed her, and he was quite content to lie beside her and stroke her at night, laughing with pleasure each time he felt the movement within her.

She had her defenses, too, he knew. He did not mention marriage again; he simply set the mechanisms he needed into action. She took care to warn him now and then that she would not marry him—he could force her into being a concubine, but never a wife. Nor did he deny her accusations, but merely frowned, wondering where she had heard such tales.

He hadn't been attracted to another woman since he had met her. Long before he had been able to admit in his traumatized heart that he was falling in love, he had known simply that she was all beauty and all magic—that anything else would pale in comparison. He'd barely seen another woman during the entire campaign.

There was one final trip he had to make. On a morning in mid-April he rose and kissed her where she slept still, curiously childlike in her blanket of golden tresses with her belly so distended. He stepped back ruefully, painfully, to tell her that he would be gone for a week or so.

He thought that something of misery danced through her eyes, but it was so quickly gone he resolved himself to the fact that she did despise him. The past remained alive in her heart.

"Don't miss me too much," he told her, and when she turned her back on him he was too tempted by the idea to plant a good smack against the rise of the rump to resist.

"Oh!" she cried, swinging back in outrage.

And like a satisfied alley cat, he simply smiled. "Fear not—I'll be back in time for our wedding."

He left her then, with no explanation because he could not explain it. He had not been home to Bedford Heath in nearly three years, and he knew he had to go back.

Jon and Thomas Tidewell rode with him. It was almost

exactly as it had been that day all those long months ago when they had come home to find carnage and disaster.

But the day remained serene, and night fell sweetly. Tristan saw that the fields were being prepared for spring planting, that thatch-roofed cottages had risen again to grace the landscape. Men worked in the fields, and a farm wife came running out to greet him and tell him that he had been missed.

That night he ate in the hall with Jon and Thomas, and all his servants greeted him kindly. The guard and the people came, the priest and laymen, the tenants and the artisans and the soldiers. With his steward and the captain of the guard and Jon and Thomas he went over his business affairs, and before the fire in his beautiful manor house he sipped a fine wine.

Jon and Thomas did not want to leave him, but he sent them to bed.

And all night he saw her: sailing about the dining hall and the gallery; sitting, sewing, before the fire, letting her fingers play over the harp, turning cards at the table, and smiling with elation when she won a game. He heard her whisper, and he felt her caress.

He trudged to the nursery and to his bedroom. He lay down where he had lain, when they had laughed and played together. He did not sleep but spent the night staring into the darkness, remembering.

The next day there was a memorial service in the chapel, and Mass was said for the souls lost. Tristan looked over the beautiful effigies carved of his loved ones in his absence, and he understood fully how Genevieve had felt on Christmas Day.

The artists had caught something of Lisette. Her relief was neither stark nor plain; her eyes were closed, but it looked like they might open at any moment, and her lips were carved in the beautiful semblance of a smile, as if she knew some secret. Tristan believed fervently that she rested somewhere in Heaven, and perhaps she smiled so sweetly in stone because she was beyond earthly pain, as he could not be himself.

He had no lack of business to attend to in the next few days. Bedford Heath had prospered because Thomas had seen to it, but Thomas had been in Ireland with Tristan on his last journey, and so there were months of accounting to be caught up and numerous decisions to be made. Tristan had thought that he would never come back, and he knew that he did not want to stay here. But the land was his; the title was his, the wealth and the manor and the rents were his. He was going to marry Genevieve. He would leave heirs behind him, and perhaps his son or his grandson would return and find his happiness here.

The priest warned him that his manor was considered haunted; Tristan disdained that information. Would that it were! Would that his father could whisper advice to him, that his brother could bluster and laugh, that Lisette could reach out . . .

It was not haunted, but he was. By coming back, he had purged some of that feeling from his heart. He was glad of Henry's order. He was going to marry again. Start over again. And here he had discovered in the gentle carving of Lisette's face that it was all right to . . . love again. He could not be a fool; his life could be forfeit. But Genevieve was going to be his wife, and he would tame her rather than break her and savor the fire until he dared to show the tenderness.

On the night that he rode back, he was later than he had planned. He saw the King briefly, then hurried toward the chamber where Genevieve awaited, his heart pounding out a staccato beat. Ah, but you are a ruthless fellow, he reminded himself. And you will succeed.

Jon and Edwyna met him in the hallway. Edwyna looked prettily flushed, and Tristan smiled secretively, aware that she had greeted her husband with tremendous—if quick—ardor. She caught his glance, and flushed again, and he laughed, and she began to whisper worriedly.

"Tristan, I'm sure she does not suspect! But she is so angry with you! I told her where you had gone, since you did not—" She cast him a reproachful glance. "But Tristan, her time has nearly come and she is distraught and therefore—"

"More shrewish than ever!" Tristan answered. "And you needn't whisper. Has she dressed? Is she ready?"

Edwyna nodded unhappily. "I have told her that we are

going into the City, that we will see no one with whom she is
acquainted. I told her that the establishment is one of the
King's favorites and that he has asked you specifically to dine
there.''

"Well then," Tristan murmured. "Let's get her, shall
we?''

"Perhaps you should go alone," Edwyna said.

"Edwyna!" Jon chastised her. "Will you quit acting like
such a frightened little goose! She will suspect something.''

"You'd send me after that shrew alone?" Tristan teased.

"Hmmph!" Edwyna protested. "Oh, I should not be a part
of this!''

"But don't you want your niece to be respectable and your
great-nephew to be legal issue?" Tristan laughed.

"Oh, all right! Let's go!" Edwyna said.

Together, they went for Genevieve.

"The two of you flirt and act like long-lost lovers," Tristan
warned them.

"I'll just act drunk," Jon offered.

Tristan opened the door to the chamber. He smiled as her
head raised quickly from her work. She was dressed—and she
looked beautiful. All his tenderness rose within him. Some of
her hair was twisted into elegant braids that looped through
the gold-jeweled headdress he had given her. Some of the
rich golden tendrils were free and curled and waved beneath it
like a train of shimmering gold. Her gown was girdled just
below her breasts, and the great sweep of her fur-trimmed
skirt hid much of her advanced pregnancy. She stood, and
conflicting emotions raced through her eyes like stardust; they
were blue and they were silver and then they were mauve,
and she wavered slightly. Tristan liked to think that she
considered approaching him, that she had missed him . . .

"Good evening, Genevieve."

"Is it, milord?"

"Oh, do be pleasant!" Edwyna pouted from the doorway,
her arms happily about her husband.

"Genevieve!"

Jon went to her, kissed her hands, complimented her

appearance—and smoothed the way. Tristan strode forward and took her arm and said impatiently that they must be off.

"Are we taking a carriage?" Genevieve demanded stiffly at his side.

"Nay. I'll not have you jolted. Your time is too close."

They quickly traversed the hall. The Earl of Nottingham saw Tristan when they passed through the long gallery. Tristan waved and they hurried along, out of the steps to the palace, past the night guards, out to the great gates. Genevieve's head was lowered, he saw, and her features flushed.

"You are well?" he asked anxiously.

"I am fine."

"You are—embarrassed by your condition!"

Her face blazed. "Aye!"

"You needn't be."

"I'll not marry you, Tristan."

"Henry could give you to a fat, ugly old lord!" Tristan warned direly.

"That would serve you right!"

"Ah, but you would suffer nightly!"

Thomas stepped up behind them, and Genevieve flushed again because he had obviously heard their words.

"And he could have liverish lips and belch in bed!"

"Thomas, can't you find a lady of your own to torture?" Genevieve wailed.

"Nay—for with Tristan as my liege, my time is lamentably limited!"

"When the babe is born," Tristan retorted, "you can have all the time in the world, for you'll have to return to the care of Bedford Heath. As soon as Genevieve can travel, we're going back to Edenby."

"Not 'we,' " Genevieve protested sweetly. "I'll belong to that fat lord with the liver lips."

"What a fate!" Edwyna shuddered, and they all laughed, and walked again.

But Genevieve looked up at Tristan, and though her fingers trembled in his hand and a great desire welled up within her. She forced herself to remember the battles, the invasion—and the fact that he used her still.

"I will not marry you, Tristan. And you'll not coax me into changing my mind by an elegant supper or special entertainment. I'll never give you that satisfaction, I swear it."

He merely smiled. Minutes later they came to a handsome building, made of stone. A liveried servant met them at the door, and Genevieve did not recognize the colors of the livery or the emblem emblazoned at the shoulder.

"Who owns this establishment?" she demanded.

"A friend of the King's," Tristan answered evasively, and they were ushered down a hall to a private dining room.

Genevieve paused at the table, a hand held against one of the massive, fine carved chairs as she looked about. Banners hung from the high ceiling, and the walls were paneled and decorated with various arms.

Tristan came to her, courteously taking her hand and pulling out her chair. "Sit, my love."

"I'm not at all your love," she retorted softly, "and I own to a great fear of sitting."

"Ah, but you must! And have no fear—I'll sit all the way at the other end of the table!"

She sat. Edwyna did the same, then the men. Instantly a host of servants—all in the same handsome livery of lime-green and black—came and went. Wine was poured, and they were offered a multitude of entrées, from candied eels to tender beef, from fish to fowl to rare, exotic fruits. The meal took time, and for all that there was to eat it seemed there was far more to drink, and Tristan, carefully watching Genevieve from his end of the table, was quite glad to see that she was nervous—and raised her cup frequently.

Edwyna kept up a steady chatter; Thomas and Jon laughed most frequently, too. Only Genevieve and Tristan were silent.

And then the time was upon them. Tristan nodded at Jon, and then came around for Genevieve, who commented to Edwyna that this place more resembled a private residence than any inn or tavern. Tristan grimaced over her head to Jon; he led her down the hall, but not to the door by which they had entered.

"Tristan, were we the King's guests?" she asked. "You paid no one for the food or service! And I've seen no other guests—and you're going the wrong way! This is not where we entered!''

But it was the door to the Bishop of Southgate's private chapel. Tristan opened it and urged her in, and despite the wine she had consumed, Genevieve was too instantly aware.

How could she not be? The bishop himself awaited them at the altar with two young acolytes at his side.

''No!'' Genevieve balked. ''No! Tristan, I'll not do this! Edwyna, I'll not! It will not be legal! You can't do this, you can't do this!'' She tried to twist from Tristan's hold.

''Damnit, Edwyna, she didn't drink enough!'' Tristan grumbled.

''What did you want me to do?'' Edwyna wailed. ''I could not pour it down her throat!''

''Come on!'' he swore to Genevieve.

She was simply incapable of losing a fight, gracefully or otherwise. Ranting and raving, she strove to kick him and pummel him with her fists.

''Genevieve, bound and gagged or on your own, you will marry me.''

''Dear, dear!'' said the Bishop coming forward. He was a gray-haired man with pleasant eyes and stern features. ''Child, you're expecting this man's wee babe. The King wishes you to wed. Be reasonable—''

Genevieve was not listening. She took a swing at Tristan but missed and caught the bishop in the chin.

Tristan caught her flying fist and apologized to the bishop over the sound of her protests—growing tearful now.

''I will await you at the altar,'' the bishop stated.

''Genevieve—'' Edwyna tried to plead.

''You—whoreson!'' Genevieve accused Tristan, her eyes wide as his arms clenched tight around and he lifted her, striding down the aisle. ''Bastard, rat, scum—''

His hand clamped over her mouth. Thomas, Jon, and Edwyna followed uneasily behind them. Tristan stood before the altar with Genevieve locked in his arms, his hand clamped like steel over her mouth. His shirt was ripped, his hair was in his eyes, and he was panting. He smiled. ''Proceed, please, Father. We are ready.''

And so the service began. The bishop read the marriage ceremony quickly—very quickly. Tristan was asked to swear the vows and he did most gravely.

Genevieve awaited her chance. Trembling, tears burning her eyes, she awaited. Tristan would have to move his hand for her to speak, and then.

"Genevieve Llewellyn . . ."

And he went on to state her parentage—returning her titles to her. "Do you . . ."

Never! Obey! Take to husband, cherish, and love?

It was time to answer. Tristan would have to let her go. His hand slipped from her mouth and she inhaled to shout out her definite and absolute refusal.

"I do n—"

His mouth clamped down over hers—just like the day when she had tried to summon the nuns for help! Covering her lips, devouring her breath. She struggled, she twisted, she slammed her hands against him. Tristan merely motioned for the bishop to continue. The bishop cleared his throat and did so.

Genevieve could hear the words, but they grew dim. Stars and then blackness appeared before her—now she couldn't hear words at all. She began to weaken.

He moved his all-consuming mouth from hers at last. She struggled for breath—and found herself receiving a host. Their wedding ceremony was complete down to the Mass now being said . . .

"No!" she gasped, and Tristan's hand clamped over her mouth once again. And then, as she struggled both to breathe and free herself, she was suddenly set down rudely on her feet. She swayed, not certain that she could stand. Tristan caught her, and for a moment she could do nothing but stagger for balance and air.

Then she was suddenly wrenched about—led back down that aisle and out of the chapel and to a desk. And Tristan was signing papers that the others had already witnessed.

"I'll not sign!" she shrieked, but ruthless fingers wound around hers, and protesting all the while she did sign.

"It's not legal!" she swore, breaking free of Tristan at last.

He didn't answer her. He was just staring at her. The bishop stepped forward, clearly angry.

"Milady, it is indeed legal! Why, I did hear you give your vow just as these other witnesses did. I assure you, my dear, you are most legally married."

"Oh!" Tears rushed to her eyes. She felt the swollen bruises on her mouth and the steel of arms on her as if he held her still. "Oh! I hate you, and Edwyna and Jon—and Thomas! You had no right, you had no—"

She broke off suddenly, feeling something new—like the touch of a knife against the small of her back.

"Oh!" It came out like a whisper, and then she gasped, confused and amazed as it seemed that a cascade of water came from within her to drench her. And she realized blindly that her babe was coming. Everyone was staring at her, she could see through a haze. Staring, unaware . . .

"Tristan!" She was going to fall, she knew; she needed him.

He came to her and picked her up just before the room could spin to blackness.

"Dear, dear," she vaguely heard the bishop say. "The marriage is quite legal—and not a moment too soon, so it seems!"

Chapter
Twenty-Two

"YOU MUST RELAX, Genevieve!" Edwyna implored her. "It—takes time to bring a babe into the world!" Tenderly, she wiped the beads of perspiration from Genevieve's forehead, trying to smile as she stared into great violet eyes that looked to her beseechingly for solace.

Genevieve had been frightened that she would deliver her infant right on the bishop's chapel floor! But that was hours ago now. Hours since Tristan had carried her here, to the bishop's warmest guest room, and laid her down. To sit beside her tensely, his jaw twisted and locked and his fingers so tightly entwined with hers that she had nearly cried out at the pressure. Still she hadn't wanted him to go. She had wanted to cling to him.

But a tall, slim woman with iron-gray hair and no-nonsense eyes had appeared. The bishop called her Katie; she was kind and competent, and she quickly had the room cleared of the men, including Tristan, the ornately decked bed stripped down to simple sheets and Genevieve dressed in a loose robe against the chill. Katie assured Genevieve that she was the eldest child in a family of twelve and that everything would be fine—she had been delivering babies for years. Chilled and shaking, Genevieve had stared at her, and she knew that her lip quivered lamentably, and she had whispered, "Will it—die?" And she'd had to wet her mouth to form words again. "I'm at least a full month early."

"Now God gives none of us guarantees, milady! But neither is there reason to assume you'll lose the wee one!"

That was hours ago—or was it days? She felt like giving way and just crying until she died, the pains came so quickly and so close, and so she swore instead. Two of the young housemaids had been summoned to help change linen and keep Genevieve warm, and so she tried to stay quiet to show some dignity.

But it was impossible when she felt that knives sheared again and again against her spine. She refused to scream, and so she grit her teeth and swore to Edwyna once more, ranting on and on.

"Oh, I shall never do this again, never! And to think that we women willingly partake in the act which brings us here! Edwyna, how could you—marry again, having known this! Be with that man when you were aware of what could come with it?"

Edwyna had to laugh. "You get over it, Genevieve, honestly. You will forget it."

"If you'd just give out a scream or two, milady, it might ease your spirit. And mind ye, lass, this has not been difficult. I believe the babe is coming soon," Katie said cheerfully.

And Genevieve looked at her with hope, but just then the agony constricted around her with merciless ferocity and she choked back a cry, tears spilling from her eyes as she wound her fingers into the torn sheets Katie had tied to the bedposts for her use.

"Milady, now you must push with all your might!" Katie commanded her. "Hold your breath, sit forward, and bear down hard!"

Genevieve did, straining, then lying back, panting and gasping.

"The next time," Katie promised. And in misery, Genevieve tried to nod. She looked at Katie.

"Does this mean he—lives?"

"Have faith," Katie told her.

"Edwyna!" She clasped her aunt's hand and held there, swearing again. "Oh, never! I'll never do this again . . . Tristan, oh, I'll rip him to shreds if he thinks to touch me ever, ever again!"

"You just married him, Genevieve."

"But I didn't!"

"Ah, but you did, milady!" Katie offered. "And the wee one will be an heir, noble and legitimate!"

Tight, suffocating pain welled in her again. She tried to hold it back. She felt the sweat break out all over her flesh in beads and she was freezing at the same time. Face sick, hair soaked, and in anguish as the pain squeezed and squeezed and she tried to listen to Katie and Edwyna, and could not. For the first time, she screamed. High and loud and long . . .

Tristan strode across the dining hall for at least the hundredth time, past the displays of pikes and armor, beneath the banners of the bishop's prominent family. Jon, standing near the fire, glanced at Thomas, and Thomas glanced at the bishop, and the bishop started to say something soothing, but Tristan erupted again with a groan, stopping at the mantel, dragging his fingers through his hair and staring at the fire.

"It's too soon, and whatever goes wrong—"

"Tristan, quit blaming yourself."

"And who am I too blame? Who dragged her here? Who half-strangled her to force words from her lips?"

"My son!" The bishop stood, pursing his lips together, bringing his fingers, prayer-fashion, to his chin. "You formed a union before God Almighty. You must not question Divinity!"

Tristan slammed a fist against the wall with a cry. Where had God been at Bedford Heath, and where was He now? What great sin had Tristan committed that God had seen fit to slay Lisette and her unborn child and now take this toll upon Genevieve, when . . .

"I did this to her," he breathed, and he sat before the fire.

Jon brought Tristan a glass of hot, potent wine, in one of the bishop's beautiful Venetian glasses. Tristan sipped it mechanically.

"You married her," Jon said softly. "It was the right thing to do."

"Surely! Surely!"

He was pacing again. The glass seemed to be in his way, and so he drained the wine and set it down. He crossed his arms over his chest and strode up and strode down. "I should have married her," he said thickly, "as soon as I knew. I should never have—"

Touched her? Loved her? Which had hurt her the worst? And when she had vowed with all her heart that she would not have him, he had dragged her here, forced this upon her. Now she lay upstairs and he could not hear a cry; he could only flex and unflex his fingers and try to pray to the God who had forgotten him that this child not die. Oh, God! Find mercy on me this time, let her live, and I'll not force her ever again . . .

And then her scream pierced the air, high and shrill and full of torment, reaching him through closed doors.

He was instantly in motion, bolting for the door. Jon tried to catch him, but he pushed his friend aside. Tristan took the hallway and stairs at giant leaps, bursting through the door.

He first thought that she was silent, that her lustrous lashes lay heavily over her cheeks, that she was white, oh, paler than the moon. Her hair was a damp tangle about her, and Katie smoothed that hair from her forehead. He had an image of her body, limp, on the bed, a sodden, bloody pool.

A keening groan escaped him, and he fell to his knees.

"Lord Tristan! You must be patient! We've still to bathe your lady and the wee lass and—"

"What?" He stared up at the bishop's housekeeper. The graying woman with the shrewd and gentle eyes touched his shoulder, leading him back to his feet. "Milord, she is well, exhausted merely. And the babe is a perfect little thing, howling like as if she was scalded, milord."

"She . . . lives!"

"They both live, Lord Tristan."

Tristan couldn't move then. His legs were weak and his stomach was doing somersaults. He couldn't even see anymore; the world was a cascade of shimmers and gray.

"Tristan, look at her! She's amazing. My dear Lord, all that hair! Dark as a winter's eve!" Edwyna was talking to him.

Something was stuffed into his arms. He looked down and saw in a pile of swaddling his . . . daughter. She was not fully cleansed; her hair was plastered against her tiny head, but Edwyna was right, it was tremendously plentiful for an infant. And she had little dark brows and a puckered face and a little fist that waved in the air suddenly as she opened a generous mouth and let out a screech of indignation and fury.

Tristan stared in joy and disbelief, fighting tears, finding incredible gladness. Ten fingers, ten toes, a plump little belly with its cord just cut, beautiful, beautiful flesh. "She is perfect!" he whispered. Almighty God! He prayed in silence, thank you, thank you, thank you.

"Aye, a bonny lass!"

He turned and saw Edwyna, smudged and sweaty but smiling, reaching out to take her again.

"Oh, Tristan! She is a beauty! Tiny but sound and such a temperamental little thing already! Oh, Tristan, look how lovely she is!"

Edwyna touched the babe, but Tristan felt tremors sweeping over him again and he looked past Edwyna to the bed. Katie had drawn a clean sheet high around Genevieve, and all that he could see was the pale almost translucent elegance of her fragile features and the loose tendrils of hair curling around her forehead. He handed his newborn to Edwyna without a word and strode over to the bed, kneeling at its side, reaching for her fingers, rising petallike over the hem of the sheet.

"Genevieve . . . ?"

Her lashes fluttered and her eyes opened on him and for a moment they went wide, then fell. And she shuddered and tried to speak, and it was a pained whisper.

"You wanted a son, I know. I am . . . sorry. I . . ."

Her voice trailed away, the effort to speak seeming to be too much for her now. Tears and exhaustion glazed her eyes, and he wondered if she really knew that he was there. He tightened his grip around her fingers and whispered tenderly against her cheek.

"A son! Milady, I wanted a living child, and a living wife. Genevieve! She is the most wonderful gift I have received in this life! She is perfect and whole and beautiful and—"

"Milord!" Katie urged him. "Please now, go and lift a glass with your friends to your new daughter, for we must bathe mother and babe properly. You are in the way!"

Genevieve's eyes were closed. Tristan nodded, then kissed her on the forehead. Tremors raced through him and he touched his lips to her flesh once again, reverently. He placed his cheek next to hers and he knew that she slept again.

"Thank you, my love," he breathed to her, and then he stood. He took the babe from Edwyna one more time, and he laughed when she howled again with outrage. He lifted her high and scanned her perfect little body again, laughing again with sheer joy as she howled and flailed tiny fists.

Edwyna smiled at the male crow of possession in his voice; then she reached for the babe.

"Tristan, please! Let me bathe her. Oh, I am a great-aunt! And I'm ever too young to sound so old! Give her to me, please. And Jon, what are you doing here? Get out."

Tristan swung around to see Jon slumped against the door frame, grinning out his pleasure. Thomas was just behind him, and the bishop was a more discreet distance away in the hallway.

"Will you all get out of here, please! Now I mean it!" Edwyna stamped a foot against the floor. "Tristan," she added more softly. "Genevieve needs some rest. Please, go get drunk or something." She rescued the babe from her father's arms, and a thrill of happiness swept through her. She had never seen a man so pleased with the birth of a daughter—in fact she had never seen a man so tenderly pleased with the birth of any child. "Go," she said with a smile. "Go get wantonly drunk!"

He grinned at her in turn, and walked past her. Edwyna met Jon's eyes across the room and they smiled together; then Tristan reached Jon and they looped arms and proceeded back downstairs. At the bishop's invitation, they did proceed to get rollicking drunk.

She was in love, and she was in awe, and she had never felt such a joy in her life.

Genevieve stared at her daughter on the bed beside her and marveled at her beauty. Surely no child on earth had ever been so precious. She seemed tiny, oh, so tiny! But splendid in every way. Katie had dressed her in an elegant little gown with fine smocking that had belonged to one of the bishop's little nieces or nephews, and though the gown was too big for her daughter, Genevieve was convinced that she was more than exquisite in it. Her absolute fascination with the baby had swept her far, far away from any thoughts of pain, and she felt lethargic and content. Nay, she felt like an angel surrounded by a gentle, mellow, almost heavenly glow.

She was still tired and sore but she could do nothing but smile, shyly and proudly, and think that she was indeed encased in magic, engrossed in love. She could vaguely remember the overwhelming exhaustion and what had at first been only vague wonder at what should come of all her misery. But when she had awakened, clean and refreshed, and Edwyna had handed her the baby, she had known instant adoration. Such a small, small creature! The babe's eyes were her father's—so deep a blue that they would never go light. And that hair, all that hair . . . dark, too. But the incredibly small fingers that had brushed her cheek were long and feminine, and, Genevieve thought, there is something of me in her, even if only my sex! And then the babe had gazed upon her and let off the saddest little cry, and Edwyna had laughed and told Genevieve that she was hungry. And when the babe had first tugged against her breast she had felt herself possessed for all time.

Genevieve was so rapt that she did not hear the door open and quietly close. And when he had come in, Tristan was loath to disrupt her. She was all in white, her hair washed and brushed, floating free like a cloud of golddust behind her head on the pillow. And his daughter . . . she, too, was in white, tiny and feisty, wiggling away beside her mother.

Mother stared at daughter, and daughter seemed to stare at mother, and both in that innocent white, so beautiful, so sweetly pure.

Tristan felt extremely awkward. He was afraid to walk forward, afraid to intrude. Yet the virginal blond beauty in white was his wife, and the babe was the fruit of their passion, their child, to be shared. Reminding himself that the child was his, he strode over to the bed.

Genevieve turned with alarm, as if she would battle anyone fiercely who thought to reach for her babe. She saw him then, and a shield seemed to fall over the delicate mauve beauty of her eyes. For a second her breasts ceased to rise and fall, as if she held her breath—and awaited some word from him.

He gazed at her, not knowing what to say now, wondering what she remembered of his words before. Then he looked from her to the baby, and sat upon the foot of the bed, leaning over to gently tough her check, barely larger than the thumb that caressed it with such tenderness. Instantly, her perfect little miniature rose mouth puckered into a noisy motion; startled, Tristan drew his hand back.

"She's hungry," Genevieve murmured, and a lovely flood of color came to her cheeks. She hesitated only briefly; then, loosening her gown, swept the baby to her breast.

Tristan laughed, and the tension eased from him as the tiny infant latched onto her mother's engorged nipple with a far less than ladylike suckling noise.

"She sounds just like a squealing little piglet!"

Genevieve cast him a condemning stare, but then she, too, chuckled softly, touching the fine dark hair on her daughter's head and conceding, "Aye, she's not a very refined eater."

Tenderness overwhelmed Tristan then. With a swift, graceful motion he stood, sweeping an arm around Genevieve to stroke the babe's hair as she nursed. Genevieve's head was bowed toward her daughter, and Tristan could not read his wife's feelings in regard to his arms about her. He remembered his vow, but knew he could not deny himself the simple assurance of feeling his daughter's life or his wife's warmth.

"We need to name her," he said softly. "The bishop intends to baptize her right away."

"Why?" Genevieve asked with alarm. "She is well and strong, Tristan, is she not?"

"Aye." He could not look down into the eyes that now searched his, for he felt responsible for the fear in her voice. "Aye, she is well and strong and beautiful. Any babe should be baptized in all haste, milady. What would you call her?"

He felt Genevieve's eyes widen on him. "I may name her?"

"Well, I should like to approve it."

Genevieve trembled, wondering if he cared little about the name since she had given him a daughter—and not a son. She felt the movement in her.

"Genevieve?"

"I did fail you. And to think, milord, of all you did to assure things for an heir . . ."

"What are you saying?" he demanded with annoyance.

"She is a girl," Genevieve coolly stated the obvious.

"Aye," he said with a softness that caught at her heart. "So lovely a lass that already she has my heart at her feet; my life with the greatest pleasure I would lay down for her!"

Genevieve dared not look at him, dared not believe that his pleasure could be so ardent, and so real.

"Katherine?" She whispered.

"Katherine. Katherine . . . Marie. Katherine Marie de la Tere. I christen thee, little one, ere the formality!"

Genevieve could feel his warm breath against her cheek and the firm power of the arm lightly over her. She was his wife—the sudden remembrance swept through her like fire, and she ached with it. She had fought it from pride, from honor—and from fear. It had come to pass . . . and they were now a family. I love you! she longed to shout suddenly, I love you, oh can't you see, I am afraid, and I know that loving so greatly brings about the greatest pain . . .

She laid her hot face against the cool pillow, and swallowed with pleasure as baby Katherine made a last frantic little tug against her nipple. Tristan laughed softly, using the baby's hem to clean the little drop of spilled milk off of her lip. "Katherine . . ."

Genevieve smiled, too, and closed her eyes. Her husband's

hand rested with casual intimacy upon her hip then as he smiled at their daughter. It seemed like the most beautiful moment of her life, and her eyes were closing again. She tried to flutter them open.

"Sleep, Genevieve," Tristan whispered to her, and again she felt the delicious rush of his breath against her cheek.

"I can't. She will need to be held—"

"And I can hold her very well, thank you, madam. Now go to sleep. You promised to obey me."

"I did not."

"Oh, but you did. Under duress, but the vow was made. Close your eyes and sleep."

Her eyes closed. She resisted the urge to draw the soft form of her daughter back to her side, and allowed the babe to go to her father. With a long yawn, she gave up the battle to remain awake.

Genevieve was to be the guest of the bishop for a fortnight—no one seemed to think she had recovered enough to move.

She quickly felt well enough herself, though she could admit to a weakness when she remained up and about too long. And in the days that followed she grew ever more attached to her daughter, ever more in love. Tristan was ceaselessly polite to her. On the second morning he brought her a gold and emerald locket on a velvet chain, a lying-in present, a husband's appreciation for a newborn child. Genevieve loved the locket. He had promised her they would have a miniature done of little Katherine, and she could wear it by her heart. He had kissed her on the forehead.

She longed for him to kiss her on the lips but he withdrew quickly, and the distance between them seemed to grow with the days that passed.

He could not be with her always; he was working on the charter to be granted by the King to make Edenby a city, and so he returned to the bishop's only by night. He did not sleep with her. She knew that it would be some weeks ere she healed well enough to behave as his bride, but she ached for his touch. The simple intimacy of being beside him, curling against him, feeling the casual and tender stroke of his hands. Battling now and then in verbal warfare perhaps, but touching . . .

Holding her baby by the window, delighting in her one afternoon, Genevieve felt the most horrible burst of panic. Had she become his wife—only to lose him completely? Things were going well, that she knew. He spoke of his business with the charter and of the afternoons he had spent with other knights on a practice field.

He also told her that he intended to finish some business at Court, return to Bedford Heath to settle last-minute things before leaving Thomas to manage his homeland, and then— once Katherine was two months old—they would travel back to Edenby. It sometimes surprised Genevieve that Tristan should be so much more attached to her home than his own, yet it was undeniably so. But then of course Lisette had died at Bedford Heath.

Genevieve looked forward to his visit daily. The bishop was a wonderful host; he was a grave man, pious in one way, worldly in another. Genevieve apologized for hitting him; he apologized for forcing the issue, yet told her that he was not wrong—and didn't she know it now? Was she not glad of the marriage for her beautiful little daughter's sake?

To that Genevieve could only flush and lower her head. She was glad, oh, aye! She'd die for this tiny life that trusted her so completely and claimed her heart.

But somehow she had lost Tristan. She was his wife. But now not only did he not love her, he did not even want her! Not to tease, not to claim, not to fight with passion, not to hold with triumph and laughter.

He was merely her husband—handsome, cool, ever-polite; the stranger who came with the darkness of night, held his child with love and laughter—and then spoke to her cordially of his schedule! She could not understand, and it hurt terribly. Oh, she had fought the ceremony! But no amount of fighting on her part had ever deterred him before. He'd always claimed what was his, when he wanted it.

She wondered if he blamed her for the early birth, for risking the babe, yet she dared not ask him. They had shared anger and hatred, tenderness and laughter. Whatever their emotions in the past, they had been filled with passion. But now there was a void, curiously created by the birth of the daughter they both so adored.

Henry and Elizabeth took time to come to the christening, and the King presented Genevieve with a grant of land for the baby. She was surprised and grateful. She did not reproach the King for forcing her into marriage—for Henry had probably known her heart better than she. "Katherine . . ." In a quiet minute alone, he whispered the name to her. "Not after another lady of such name? That beauteous ancestress of mine who came to be John of Gaunt's bride—after many years and children born between them?"

Genevieve smiled. "I have always loved her story, Your Majesty. It is a bitter-sweet romance."

"This Katherine shall have her pick of noble swains," the King promised her, and she kissed his ring; and then Tristan was there, and the King winked, and she was glad that they shared a secret.

But not even that night did Tristan stay with her.

On the morning of her fifteenth day in the bishop's manor, Genevieve woke to hear gurgling noises. She looked across the room to the window where Tristan, clad only in hose, tight breeches, and boots, leaned against the wall. Katherine, naked as birth, lay against his chest, batting against the muscled breadth of it with a tiny fist, and catching the crisp dark hair there between her fingers. Tristan, his handsome head bent to his daughter, was telling her about her fine future.

"You'll ride in a fine coach with four dappled mares, my love! Gilded it will be, in the finest gold. And the noblest lads in the land will come to your door, but you'll send them all out on their heels, my beauty! You'll wear soft velvets and softer silks, and diamonds in your hair . . ."

He broke off, suddenly aware of Genevieve's scrutiny. For a long moment their eyes caught and held across the distance, and Genevieve longed to speak, longed to reach her arms out and beg him to come to her, to hold her.

But there was a rap at the door then. Balancing Katherine

with exemplary grace, he rose to his feet and called out, "Enter!"

Glancing at Genevieve, he was cool and distant again. "Katherine did see fit to gurgle upon her dress and my shirt! Here's help, now."

Katie came in, bearing a gown and swaddling for Katherine and Tristan's cleaned shirt. It was blue velvet, and when he slipped it over his head and adjusted his scabbard around it Genevieve could think only that the color and style of the elegant Court garment lent itself beautifully to the bronze of his skin and the clean lines of his trim, muscular form.

Pained, she looked away from him, reaching to Katie for the baby, and laughing when Katherine immediately nuzzled against her. Katie promised her a meal in a matter of minutes, and then she would arrange milady's things for travel.

Katie left, and Genevieve silently watched Tristan while Katherine continued to whimper.

"She's hungry," Tristan reminded Genevieve sharply.

"We are going back to Court?"

He seemed to hesitate. "You are going back to Court. Jon and Thomas will be there should you need anything. I'm going to Bedford Heath. Genevieve, have a care. The babe."

She swept Katherine to her, turning her back on her husband to nurse the babe. She felt so very far from him.

"I would rather go home," she said.

"Not yet. You are not fit for the journey."

"I am very well, thank you."

"When I return, we will go home."

She fought the overwhelming sensation to burst into tears. What was wrong? What created the awful, aching void? Was it true that he had taken a dozen women in Ireland? Had he lost all desire for the one he chose to marry?

There was something of the old Tristan about him; he came around the bed—not willing to allow her to turn her back. He sat on the bed and stroked his daughter's hair. "I'm leaving in a few minutes, Genevieve."

"Oh, aye. And you'll leave me with Henry, you'll leave me with Jon, you'll leave me with Thomas."

"And what, milady, does that mean?"

She could not look at him; and she did not like the idea of his having the privilege to watch his daughter nurse. She pulled the covers up around the babe's face. She felt his sudden wrath, when what she sought was understanding. He caught her wrist and drew her eyes to his.

"You'll smother her!"

"I'll not!"

"If you're not fit for such a task—"

"Go on, go about your business. I will see to mine."

He stood angrily. "Edwyna will be with you, then." He held his anger in check, nodding to her briefly and curtly, pausing to kiss his daughter's head, but not the mother's. He strode toward the door. Genevieve choked back a little sob to stop him with a demand that sounded far more shrill than she had intended.

"Why am I always left to your watchdogs! Never trusted, never—brought along . . ."

She was never sure whether he heard the last, or nay. He spun quickly to answer her before she could finish.

"Because, milady, you cannot be trusted, as we all know well."

"I have your child!"

"Aye, and I wish to keep her!"

"I'd not take her from you!"

"I shall see that you do not."

"You married me!"

He paused, inhaling sharply, crossing his arms over his chest.

"Aye, milady. I married you. But you did not wish to marry me. I have documents that claim us man and wife, yet they are really nothing more than paper—are they? Paper that brought about extreme duress . . . and near tragedy," he added bitterly, his eyes lowering. But they quickly blazed into hers again. "I have to go, Genevieve. Jon is your friend, as is Thomas. See them as guards and keepers if you so choose. I leave you at Henry's Court, for I know that you are safe there, and cared for. Good-day, milady wife. Stay well, and I will return with all haste. Though I do feel I am the most detested of your—keepers."

He bowed to her, while she stared at him in stricken confusion. He opened the door, stepped out, and was gone.

Genevieve set the baby tenderly aside and raced after him. She reached the door barefoot and shivering, but he was nowhere to be seen.

Katherine set up a reproachful and outraged cry from the bed.

"Oh, Katherine!" Genevieve whispered, and, with tears stinging her eyes, she gave up the pursuit of her departed husband.

She walked back to the bed and scooped the baby into her arms, urging Katherine's trembling little mouth back to her breast.

The baby ceased to cry with a satisfied little gasp.

But Genevieve started up. She bit her lip to calm her sobs, and silent tears of confusion and loss streaked down her cheeks.

Chapter
Twenty-Three

"THOMAS, IF YOU'LL not take me, I swear that I'll find a way to go myself!"

Genevieve wasn't sure that she sounded imperious but she meant to be as persuasive as possible. Jon had managed to evade her and give her vague promises, and so tonight she had determined to accost Thomas.

It hadn't been difficult, she thought dryly. She'd had only to look in the hall to find him. It seemed that when she was not with Jon and Edwyna, Thomas hounded her footsteps. And when Thomas was nowhere to be seen, she could count on her aunt and Jon to be lurking somewhere near.

Katherine was soundly sleeping, in a cradle given graciously to Genevieve by Elizabeth of York. Thomas was in a mellow mood—created by warm mulled wine that Genevieve had carefully tended over the fire herself. She needed to strike now and not be deterred.

Thomas cast her an uneasy, skeptical gaze, idly shuffling a boot over the stone before the hearth. He finished his wine and nervously set the cup down upon the mantel, lacing his fingers behind his back.

Genevieve looked as determined as she had been when

she had held out against Tristan's cannons at the siege of Edenby.

She was like a mythical warrioress, thought Thomas, with that hair flowing behind her like a golden banner and flashing eyes that defied description. She was everything that a man could desire in a woman—soft and yet fierce. Determined and alive with spirit, yet so feminine that one was instantly touched. The little Lady Katherine was barely five weeks old, yet already her mother was as trim as a sylph and as seductive in appearance as she was in the lilting tones of her voice.

What was it that drove Tristan so hard he could not see the bounty that was his? Why, still, did the dark moods drive him, why did he need to cause her this suffering? Thomas reminded himself that she had once tried to kill Tristan—but he had slain many an admirable man himself in warfare. If that had been the root of the problem, Tristan should have forgiven her by now. The most curious thing was that Tristan loved her—of this, Thomas was certain.

"Thomas!" She was quite close to tears, to desperation, he thought. "I know that I am watched day and night, but I have escaped such situations before. Please, please, Thomas! He has been gone nearly three weeks."

Thomas grinned ruefully. "And he will be gone again, milady. He inherited an earldom; he was created the Duke of Edenby by our new King, and he is His Majesty's subject. You deceive yourself cruelly if you think he will never again be called to do battle against some pretender."

Genevieve walked over to stare down into the cradle. "I know that he will be called. But why, Thomas, did he have to go back to Bedford Heath again? You manage the estates as his steward, and you do miraculously well."

Thomas shrugged unhappily. He couldn't avoid her stare.

"Come on, Thomas, please! You owe me, sir! You were part and parcel of dragging me off to marry him!"

He groaned softly. "Genevieve, he went back because even some of his most trusted men, guards who are educated and level in their thinking, are growing convinced that his manor is haunted."

"Haunted!"

"Yes, well . . ." Thomas lifted his hands uncomfortably. "It was the scene of tremendous bloodshed and . . ."

"Please, Thomas?"

"I'm not at all sure—"

"Did he tell you that you could not bring me?"

"Nay—no one thought you would demand to go!" Thomas reproached her. "And truly, Genevieve, how can you? What of Katherine? Do you intend to leave her with a nursemaid? She is so tiny still?"

Genevieve breathed in and out sharply. "I can leave her with Edwyna and Mary. Mary says she knows the perfect young wet nurse, a carpenter's daughter who has milk aplenty to feed her own and mine."

Genevieve's return to their spacious chamber at Court had been improved by some curious surprises; Mary had come to serve her, summoned by Tristan. Even more touching had been the appearance of Sir Humphrey, who had told her that he had met with Tristan in Henry's chambers at Tristan's request and that he had been pardoned and forgiven. But these things did not quell her urge to go to Tristan and risk his anger. If she were to be his wife, she would not be cast aside!

Thomas watched her for a moment and sighed. Which would be better—explaining to Tristan that she had eluded him and ridden alone? Or explaining to Tristan that he lacked the strength of will to fight her?

Maybe she should come to Bedford Heath. It might be good for both of them.

He threw his hands up in the air.

"All right."

"Oh, Thomas, really?"

Her smile was dazzling. She raced across the room, threw her arms around him, and planted a kiss on his cheek. Thomas smiled, taking her hands in his and thinking, my God, if she looks at Tristan so, it is no wonder that he is so deeply in love.

"We leave right after sunup. You'll ride in a coach."

"Thank you, Thomas!"

*　　*　　*

In the end Jon and Edwyna decided to accompany them. Jon thought the whole scheme a grave mistake but would not let them go without him. Genevieve brought Mary along to help with Katherine, and they set out in something of a party atmosphere, the women inside the coach and the men riding ahead. It wasn't a leased vehicle, Genevieve discovered, but her husband's, with the single coat of arms of Bedford Heath blazoned on the doors. Jon explained that since the holdings were so close to London, the family maintained a coach in the City.

It was a beautiful, comfortable conveyance, and for the start of the trip Genevieve, Edwyna, Mary, and the baby were able to make something of an outing of it. It was spring, and the land was beautiful. As they left the bustle of London behind they saw farmers at work in their fields sowing seeds. Wildflowers covered the heaths and meadows, and the air was alive with butterflies and bees.

For a time Jon rode in the coach, his horse tethered to the rear, and for a time Thomas joined them likewise. They stopped for lunch at an inn, where the cream and the bread were fresh and the trout had been caught in the stream just moments before their arrival.

Back on the road sitting tensely beside Genevieve, Thomas said, "Here begin the outlands of Bedford Heath, milady."

Night began to fall, and suddenly the holiday mood was gone. Nervously Genevieve held Katherine to her chest, crooning softly to her. Night came swiftly. She could see little of the land but she could tell that it was vast. And as they rode they came upon more and more buildings. Farm cottages, where cooking fires sent warmth and light into the night. A cluster of homes and shops. The great stone walls of several manors rose in the distance, beautiful and dazzling with light at the windows, created not with the harsh gray slate and stone of Edenby, but with artistic brick and mortar.

Thomas cleared his throat suddenly and pointed across a vast drive and courtyard. "Tristan's house," he murmured. "He didn't stand to inherit, you know. His brother would have received the title and the bulk of the land. He had this place built about five years after the Battle of Tewkesberry."

The coach pulled up at last before before a graceful staircase leading to massive, carved doors. Thomas leapt from the
coach and adjusted the footstep and helped Genevieve alight.
While the others followed, Genevieve stepped back and stared
upward at the large, graceful building. It was not quite castle,
not quite manor, but a beautiful combination of both.

Then she frowned suddenly, for through paned windows on
the second floor she could see a shadow moving about. She
shook her head slightly, wondering why a shadow should
disturb her. There were surely people within the manor, any
number of them. Tristan should be within.

Then she realized that the shadow bothered her because it
seemed to move furtively and that a pinpoint of light seemed
to move with the shadow.

''Genevieve!''

Edwyna was calling to her. Genevieve turned to see that
the great doors had opened and that servants had come to
help. Thomas was speaking to a portly man in handsome
livery, and younger lads were coming to take their trunks.

Genevieve started up the steps, nervous now that she was
here. Yet it seemed she had little reason to fear her husband's
reaction to her arrival—he was not there.

While Jon gave the portly man at the door a ferocious hug,
Thomas laughed, introducing him to Genevieve and Edwyna
as Gaylord. Jon promised Genevieve that Gaylord would see
to everything that she might need. Gaylord, he said, had seen
them all through many a scrape as children. Genevieve smiled
at the lot of them, glad of the closeness, and instantly warmed
to Gaylord, though she was aware of his careful scrutiny of
her. He asked for the baby, and Genevieve started. Jon
assured her that Gaylord had held them all as babies. To
Genevieve's pleased surprise, her daughter liked old Gaylord
and cooed with delight as he began to carry her in.

Genevieve's hem snagged at the door and she paused with
a slight sound; Thomas chuckled and came back to loosen her
hem. She found herself staring over his head and into the
night, and then feeling a strange quickening of fear assail her.

Beyond the manor, right behind a group of outbuildings,
the forests began. And where the oaks began to tangle to-

gether, Genevieve saw another shadow. It carried a lantern, a small pinpoint of light, and moved most furtively.

"Thomas!"

"What?"

But the light was gone, disappeared into the trees. "I thought I saw . . . never mind." She decided not to say anything. If people were already murmuring that the manor was haunted, she probably shouldn't mention a shadow. At least not to anyone but Tristan. "Thomas, where is Tristan?"

"Still out settling a land dispute," Thomas murmured unhappily.

"He'll be back tonight?"

"Late, so Gaylord tells me. Which is quite fine by me! I shall have my head chewed off and spit out for this, you know. Come on, now. See the manor, as you are here."

He took her arm and led her to a grand, paneled entry. Off to the left was a dining hall and gallery; to the right were the great hall and the offices and kitchens. He led her to the great hall and she gasped at its splendor. Window seats with plush cushions were in abundance, and bright rugs from exotic lands warmed the floors. Tapestries and draperies elegantly adorned the walls, and great chairs lined the arched stone that surrounded the hearth.

"And he—hates this place!" she murmured.

Gaylord, studying Katherine before the light of the fire, gazed up at her unhappily. Katherine started to cry and Genevieve thought that the baby was hungry and fretful—it had not been easy to care for her properly in the coach. She smiled and took her child back from Gaylord.

"Good sir, perhaps you could show me where I might . . . bring my child."

"Milady," Gaylord said most respectfully. But she saw him glance at Thomas over her head as if for help, and she realized that Gaylord thought that Tristan might not want her here.

"Gaylord, I need a place to feed my baby," she said flatly, with the subtle tones of strong authority she had spent a lifetime learning.

He was up quickly, nodding to a boy in the back, directing her eyes toward the staircase. "I shall take you—"

"Nay, Gaylord, I shall do it. His lordship is probably going to hang me as it is," Thomas sighed.

"Thank you," Genevieve murmured. She smiled at Edwyna and Jon, and thought that they looked a little white, too. Jon wished her good-night, and she longed to call him a coward—he intended to be safely in bed with his wife before Tristan could return. But could she blame him? This was none of Jon's doing.

The second story of the manor was as elegant as the first. The rooms and hallways were separated by stylish arches, and a multitude of portraits hung on the wall. Thomas pointed out the library and a music room, all part of the master suite. Then he paused and pushed open a set of doors with heavy brass handles. Her heart fluttering, Genevieve preceded him in.

She stood there, surveying the elegant rugs on the floors and the rich, warming draperies at the windows. The bed was huge, with four heavy posters carved in a simple acorn style. Heavy damask hangings were gathered at each post, and only the lightest white gossamer trailed around the bed. It was not a feminine room, nor too masculine, but rather adorned to be pleasing to a man and a woman together. It was commonly the custom for married couples in such a household—even those who had wed by choice—to maintain separate personal quarters. But Lisette and Tristan had always been together, Genevieve surmised, with a tug at her heart.

"I'll send Mary up, and a lad with your things," Thomas offered. "Would you like a bath?"

Genevieve nodded. Aye, she wanted a bath! She wanted to feel fresh and she wanted to fill the water with perfumed oil. She wanted to know that her skin was soft and sleek, and enticing to the man who had turned from her.

Thomas started to leave her. Genevieve raised her eyes and they fell on the windows again. They were beautiful; each pane along the edge of the arches had been stained a royal blue. But she had realized suddenly that here, exactly here, was where she had seen the shadow and the light moving so furtively from below.

"Thomas! Wait. Are you quite sure that—Tristan is not here?"

"Well of course I am sure," Thomas replied somewhat impatiently. "Gaylord would not be mistaken. Why?"

She smiled uneasily and patted Katherine's back. "I'm sorry, Thomas. Never mind."

As soon as he was gone, Genevieve lay down with Katherine. While her baby nursed she continued to look around the room. It was so lovely, so warm, so inviting. She tried to imagine Lisette, and though she could not picture a face, she could sense the woman—graceful and supple, moving with a whisper of silk; a breath of gentle beauty where she sat at the dressing table. Genevieve thought again of the shadow and the light, and felt a chill. Then she dismissed it. She did not believe in evil spirits coming back to plague the living. Moreover Lisette had been good. Genevieve was convinced that the gentle woman would understand her, and be her friend, and certainly wish her no harm.

In time Katherine slept. Mary appeared, and boys came with a fine brass tub and buckets of hot water. Genevieve bathed long and nervously, praying that the steam would ease her spirit. What could Tristan do? she asked herself again and again. Send her away? Perhaps he would not be pleased to see her here, but surely he would want to hold his daughter.

Mary brushed her hair until it shone and curled and waved down her back. Genevieve instinctively clad herself in white, a nightdress of softest silk, with sheer laced overlays and pearled epaulets. Mary called down for the boys, and the bath was taken away and the room quickly righted. Then Gaylord came to show Mary her room in the servants' quarters above, and Genevieve was alone again.

She glanced at her beloved daughter, sleeping so sweetly upon the bed. She bit her lip. She had not thought to ask, and apparently neither Gaylord or any other member of the household staff had thought of finding a cradle for Katherine. She had not been expected of course, as Genevieve had not.

There was another arched doorway at the rear of the room

and Genevieve stared at it a moment, wondering if it might not lead to a nursery. Alone, she had always been content to sleep with Katherine beside her. But tonight she wanted Tristan to have no distractions.

She carefully picked up the baby and started curiously for the arch, aware that any bedding would need to be changed, but Tristan's staff were quick and capable here. Yet even as she thought this there was a tap at the door, and she hurried to it, anxious that Katherine not awaken now—the hour was growing late.

Thomas was standing there, grinning a little ruefully, a tray with wine and glasses in his hand. "I thought you might want something to . . . for the wait." he said, and she smiled because he knew how nervous she was.

"Thank you, Thomas, thank you, and come in. Please. I need your help!" Genevieve whispered.

Curious, Thomas followed her, setting the tray down on a table. Genevieve beckoned him toward the door, and he stopped suddenly unwilling to go farther.

"Thomas, is this a nursery?"

He didn't answer right away. Genevieve frowned, and tried the door. It slid open. "Thomas, bring a light, please." She stepped into the shadowy darkness, wondering if he would follow her or not. In a second he did, carrying a lantern.

"Genevieve—"

She had seen the cradle and she cried out with soft delight. Someone had prepared things for Katherine. She could smell the cleanliness of the sheets that lay in the fine new piece of furniture. And there was a table nearby, chairs, a trunk, all sorts of accommodations for a wee one.

Carefully, tenderly, she set Katherine into the cradle. Then she turned to see Thomas behind her, holding the light. The shadows fell over his face, betraying his ashen coloring.

"Thomas—"

"Step back, Genevieve." He inclined his head downward, indicating the floor.

She stepped back and looked down and saw the stain, large and dark, nearly beneath the cradle.

"She died here," Thomas said dully. "And Tristan found

her here. I suppose that someone prepared this tonight for
Katherine, but I don't know, perhaps you shouldn't . . .''

Genevieve found herself sweeping to her knees, touching
the floor, feeling pain streak through her for the unknown
woman who had once lived here, who died atop the cradle
where her child would have lain. She looked at Thomas, and
she must have appeared stricken, for Thomas strode to her
quickly, kneeling down beside her, lifting her chin.

"Genevieve, I do not know what to say to ease—"

"Perhaps, Thomas, you had best think of something
quickly!"

The voice came from the archway, harsh and menacing.
Genevieve's eyes riveted to the doorway and she rose with a
slight gasp. Tristan was home.

He was plainly clad in tight fawn breeches and knee-high
boots, a flowing white shirt, and rugged leather jerkin. He
leaned against that archway in a casual stance, yet Genevieve
did not think that she had ever seen such murderous fury in
his eyes. He moved with the silent, supple grace of a cat,
coming toward them, staring at Thomas, with his hand on the
hilt of his sword.

Thomas stood, facing Tristan.

"Draw your sword then, my lord! I have served you well
these many years—and your doubt of me is a keen insult
indeed. You know full well that there is nothing deceitful
here.''

Tristan paused in the center of the room, and his gaze
flicked to Genevieve. Then he sat down in one of the great
chairs, observing them still with the glitter of hell's fire in his
eyes, though he lifted a hand nonchalantly indicating Genevieve's dress.

"Are you accustomed to visiting my wife so?''

"Nay, I am not!" Thomas charged him heatedly. "I came
merely to explain—''

"You have no need to explain me to her!'' Tristan thundered suddenly.

Genevieve wanted to cry out; she could feel the violence
brewing between them on the air, and she could not believe
that Tristan could turn against Thomas.

"If milord—" Thomas spat out the title with chill formality, "you so wish to believe—"

"Stop it, Thomas!" Genevieve cried out, ignoring Tristan. Her heart sank and numbness filled her, but whatever she said, whatever wrath she brought down on herself, she couldn't allow the two of them to go on like that. "Don't you see, he isn't angry with you. He simply cannot forgive me—for not being Lisette!"

"Genevieve!" Tristan bellowed, his eyes narrowing.

She strode over to him, maintaining an arm's distance. "I am sorry, Tristan! But, God knows I—"

He rose suddenly, and in spite of herself Genevieve backed away, clenching her fingers tightly behind her back. His wrath was now directed at her, and not Thomas. He looked to his friend and still spoke curtly.

"What is she doing here?"

"She's your wife. She demanded to be brought. What could I do?"

Tristan stared at Genevieve again. She circled behind the cradle, anguished that nothing she could say mattered to him. "You lost a child," she said coolly. "But you have another, and if she is not the result of the alliance of your choice, it was your own doing, and you do owe her some consideration!"

He hadn't seen Katherine. Genevieve realized that he glared at her white-lipped, as if she had gone completely mad. She cried out as he came to the cradle and plucked Katherine from her nest of bedding without hesitance, swirling around to leave both Genevieve and Thomas staring after him.

"Tristan! She was tired, she was sleeping!" With a quick glance at Thomas, Genevieve raced after Tristan. She paused, knotting her fists at her sides, seeing him before the windows, the baby safe and still asleep, against his shoulder.

He didn't turn to look at them. "Thomas, if you'll excuse us, please . . . ?" he said coldly.

Thomas hesitated, casting Genevieve an uneasy glance. But he had no right to remain, to come between a man and his wife. He turned stiffly on his heels, and departed.

"What, in God's name, are you doing here?" he demanded in a hoarse breath when the door had closed.

Genevieve stared at his back blankly. Than her eyes fell to what should have been the seductive skirt of her soft sheer gown with hem done in pearls. She felt like laughing, and like crying.

"I really don't know," she said in soft but bitter return. His back remained to her, stiff and untouchable. She swung around, fighting tears and hurrying to the wine that Thomas had brought her. Silence reigned while she sipped it—along with a growing tension. Genevieve feared the glass would break in her fingers. She lashed out at him again.

"For God's sake, Tristan! Have pity on your daughter! The cradle is not tainted! Please . . . !"

For a second he remained there, stiff and straight. Then he strode back through the archway. Genevieve felt his coldness assail her, and she hurried over to the fire, anxious for warmth. She rubbed her hands together, then turned and cried out softly again, for he was back, watching her with such a brooding tension that she suddenly longed for escape.

His eyes did not leave her as he walked over to the table and poured himself wine. He drank it like ale in one swallow.

"What are you doing here?" he repeated hoarsely.

She didn't answer him. He could see a pulse beating against the soft flesh of her throat. And he could see far more. Her breasts, still enlarged, round and straining against the fabric of the nearly sheer bodice.

And the fire . . . behind her. It caught the rich and lustrous hues and strands of her hair so that it seemed to cascade like a glowing halo about her.

Every nuance of her form was outlined. The flare of her hips, the graceful, sultry curves, vital and beseeching to all in him that had longed for her.

She shouldn't be here; she shouldn't have come. He could not help his mood here; he was not free from the past.

He did not believe Lisette could come back—for by God, he would have ridden through the very gates of hell to drag her back.

He did not believe Bedford was haunted, yet he was wary

of something, and he could not bear Genevieve here. Perhaps he was afraid for her.

He'd sworn to God that he'd not touch her in force again. But neither could he resist her. Not in the tumult that he felt, seeing her in this room. He ached for her with a gnawing desire, a frantic pulse from deep in the core of his being. With a bitter smile, he set down his glass to accost her one last time.

"I repeat myself, milady! What are you doing here?" And he strode to her, aware of the brimming fire in her eyes. She did not speak; the sweet aroma of her scent and the subtle perfume of roses engulfed him, and he jerked her suddenly into his arms, forcefully taking her lips, plundering her mouth with no thought to resistance or denial. And when her arms came against his chest, he laughed, oh, bitter still, and caught her to him, near quaking at the feel of her flesh pressed so close, so long denied him. "It seems to me, milady, you've come for just one thing, and I could not well deprive you of it!"

"Tristan!" Genevieve shrieked, near tears as her feet roughly left the floor. He carried her across the room on long, hard strides and tossed her on the bed. Oh, how she had dreamed of a sweet reunion! Whispered words before the fire, his gentle caress. But this lover was a ruthless one, determined rather than tender, and she was frightened of him, for she barely knew him.

"Tristan!" She struggled to rise, but his hands were upon her, and her seductive white gown was tangled to the waist. He held her, fumbling with his own apparel, and ere she knew it she felt the smooth weight and hardness of his body against hers, ablaze with purpose. She stared at the taut rigor of his features and the driven chill in his eyes, torn and bewildered that there should be no mercy within him.

"This is why you came here?" he demanded curtly. "I can fathom no other reason."

"Tristan! Nay! Not—like this!"

He seemed not to hear her, and perhaps he did not, for she realized that in this place demons haunted the man. She tried to strike out, to little effect. His lips were hot on her throat, his hands rough against her tender breasts. And then she felt him, strong and hot, an alien shaft piercing into her. She screamed because she had not expected the pain. She hadn't known herself what care she would need the first time after Katherine's birth.

The sound of her cry, brimming with pain, tore into him. He wanted her with every vital thing within him, but he did not wish to hurt her. He drew from her, abruptly. For seconds she lay there like a wounded doe, eyes wet and shimmering, breasts rising and falling. She didn't move, not to draw a cover against him, not to sweep her skirts down.

And then she bounded from the bed and knelt before the fire, hugging her knees to her chest. He could see her shoulders shake and he could not bear it.

"Genevieve, why did you come?"

His voice was broken, like a cry or a whisper. And to Genevieve, still stunned by the hurt done her, it seemed an echo of all her own pain.

"You've hated me so long . . ." he murmured.

She cast back her head with an hysterical little shriek, and then she started to laugh softly, and her laughter was spiked with her tears. "I've hated you because—I love you. Hated and hated because I could not stand to love you. I am here . . . because I love you."

The words wrapped around him like shimmering rays of sunlight, like the softness of a white cloud. He could not believe them, but he had to savor them, and dared not think of anything else or analyze . . .

He had to go to her, to touch her, with tenderness and the greatest care, and he had to bury himself within her, lose the tension and the cares in the sweet web of her hair and the enthralling heat of her body. Bury himself deep within her, his shaft and his heart and his soul. Her voice, those words . . . like a silver thread they came to him, and entangled him, and drew him to her.

He rose, coming to the hearth, bending down beside her. Sweeping her gently into the all-encompassing strength of his arms. He kissed her forehead and her cheeks and he murmured things that were incoherent. And she clung to him, sobbing like a lost child. Then she began to whisper, and to whimper.

He stood at last, with his precious bundle in his arms. And when he carried her back she trembled still, and he promised that he would love her so long and tenderly that she would not feel the least touch of pain.

And that he did. Savoring each stroke, drinking in her flesh, taking her so far into the heady pulse of desire with the caress of his kiss and touch and tongue that she writhed in his arms, and came to him in fever, slick and wanton, a tempest of sensuality.

Came to him, bound to him, and filled his needs. Like a fire against a chill, like the crystal cool beauty of a spring against the heat. She refreshed him and gave to him, and he was suddenly whole again. No torments rose to haunt him, no thoughts, no past deeds. She was a soft and fragrant rose against the dust and dirt and death of the battlefield. She was everything in his arms, she was life.

And she loved him.

Chapter
Twenty-Four

THERE WAS A farm house in the near distance; fields with their earth fresh from the plow stretched out far and wide. In the pastureland newborn colts frolicked and played, kicking up their heels, racing like the wind, their tails high. Closer by, daffodils grew in great quantity, and the land seemed gold with them.

Above, the gnarled fingers of an old oak stretched out like webbing across the blue sky. Genevieve could hear the gentle melody of the tiny mill brook bubbling in the background, its melody delightful.

She sighed with contentment, clutching Tristan's fingers where they lay idly upon her shoulder and planting tiny kisses upon them individually. Then she chose to nibble upon them, and tease the calloused tips with lazy darts of her tongue.

"Uh-hum!"

He cleared his throat, body stiffening, and she gazed at him. Her head lay in his lap and against one raised knee; his back rested against the hardy spine of the oak. He smiled at her ruefully, tracing a damp finger over her lips and warning, "Milady, your heartless seduction can hardly, in all decency, be handled properly where we lie."

She flushed and reached to touch his cheek, smiling. "Do I seduce his lordship?"

"Aye. Be careful, lest you discover just what arousing a lord can reach," he returned, and she laughed again, springing to her feet, scampering down to the water to cool her feet. She shrieked gaily when he charged up behind her, slipping his arms around her waist and telling her she was a heartless hussy to abuse his senses so. She looped her arms around his neck and kissed him, dazzled by the feeling that spread through, fascinated by the tender care in his eyes . . . warmed and dizzied by the love she gave—and received.

He took her hand and they walked along the brook in companionable silence. In the days since Genevieve had come they had talked endlessly. Before the fire in the bedchamber Genevieve had tried to explain how she had never wanted to kill him. How she had sworn to her father that she would keep up the battle. She had told him how she had come to love him, bit by bit, and how the longing for him had made her ever more eager to escape.

"I didn't think that you could ever love me," she had said.

And he held her tenderly, saying that he hadn't wanted to love her, he had been afraid, and then so hungry for her, bewitched by her, that he dared not let down a guard.

And walking hand in hand through Bedford, Tristan had spoken about Lisette. For the first time the words had tumbled from him easily, and he was ever more able to put her to rest with each word spoken. He had talked about his father and his brother, and he'd even described that day they had ridden home, laughing about Thomas' sweet, productive, ugly, but much-beloved wife. She, too, had been slain.

Tristan pulled her hand suddenly and they came into the shelter of a little copse. He dragged her down beside him and gave her a long lover's kiss, then smiled into her eyes with a sigh. "We should head back. I'm sure Katherine is quite fretful by now."

But he didn't rise. He leaned upon an elbow on the soft damp ground and watched her. He was both tense and curious, but in a gentle way, and seeing him beside her so, chewing idly upon a blade of grass, Genevieve was again swept on a tide of her feelings. She loved him so much. The laughter that came so easily to his eyes now. The youth about him. He was so striking a man, and the power that had once been anathema to her was now stirring. Beyond the passion now, she had his heart, and it was an overwhelming gift.

She smiled, Tristan saw, her eyes going soft, and he could not help but feel a little stab of jealousy.

"Did you love him so much?" he asked softly.

"I loved him," she murmured, and her lashes swept over her cheeks. "Oh, Tristan! You would have liked him well. Axel was ever slow to judge and quick to listen. He had been to Oxford and he had been to Eton, and he loved poetry and music and language! He—he did not want the fight. He warned father that we should cede—that most of the nobility, English and Welsh, would keep clear of the battle. But father was a warrior, you see, and would keep his sworn loyalty. And Axel would be loyal to father. He was a brave man, bright and gentle and dear. Aye, I loved him." Her lashes raised suddenly, and she smiled ruefully at Tristan. "But never as I love you," she whispered. "I never felt the . . ."

"Lust?" Tristan suggested, and she blushed crimson.

"Nay, you scurvy knave! 'Tis not what ladies feel!"

"Oh, but it is. And I love my lusty lady, I swear that I do."

"You have no manners, milord!" Genevieve protested in mock horror.

"Manners, madam?" He caught her fingers and tenderly kissed her palm. "It has nothing to do with manners, I am merely a happy man. I would not be jealous of that poor boy slain in a fray that was not of his making."

"Jealous. Hmmph."

Tristan suddenly leaned over, anxious. "Genevieve, I swear my heart was haunted long but you have cleansed it. Lisette—"

"Oh, Tristan!" She touched his cheek. The breeze wafted above them and the trees swayed and the still brook gave out its melody. She thought she had never known such happiness. "Tristan," she told him earnestly, "believe me. I am not jealous of your past! I am glad of the love you shared with her."

He smiled and kissed her, and the heat of the kiss was such that Genevieve gave him a serious tap on the rump and when he rose above her, roaring in mock indignation, she managed to roll from his touch. "Nay, sir! You have more in way of explanation!" She teased at first, then grew serious, for the matter had wounded her deeply. "I hear tell that little Katherine might well have a dozen sisters and brothers over in Eire!"

"What?"

"So the rumor goes!"

"What?" Tristan stood, dragging her to her feet and staring at her quite seriously. "That's a lie! By the time I sailed the Irish Sea, I was so besotten with my lusting little Welsh wench that I could not go near another."

"Is that the truth?"

"Aye, and it is! Where did you hear otherwise?"

Where had she? And then she remembered—Guy. Guy had warned her about Tristan's behavior.

She lowered her eyes quickly, a little spasm of fear taking root in her heart. Tristan had slowly forgiven all those who had played treacherously against him. Even dear old Sir Humphrey now had leave to return to his home in Edenby.

But Tristan hated Guy. Genevieve was convinced that if the knight did not have Henry's protection, Tristan would have challenged him and slain him long ere now.

She looked up quickly, hating herself for lying but knowing that she must. She smiled. "I don't remember. It was rumor, my love, and rumor that tore at my heart."

He cradled her close against his chest. "Tear at thy heart no longer love, for my life lies in its tender recesses."

"Oh, Tristan." She looped her arms about his neck and kissed him, and though she longed to stay beneath the trees, she sighed and spoke, her tone muffled against his chest. "We must get back to Katherine."

"Aye, love, come then."

They hurried back through the brook and over the pebbles. By the old oak they donned their shoes; Tristan paused, looking out over the landscape.

"I am grateful that you came." He gazed her way with sly

humor in his eyes. "For more than the immediate gratification of lust!"

"Tristan—"

He laughed and hugged her. "Nay, but it is beautiful to me again, Genevieve. I never thought that it could be." He sighed. "We must return, though. I am very anxious to see Edenby granted a city charter. I just wish . . . well, I wish I could have solved something here. Lisette does not haunt these halls, nor does my father, but something is not right. Jon and I were attacked one night in the street in London—"

Genevieve let out a little shriek. "Tristan! You never told me."

He shrugged ruefully. "At the time I did not think that you would care. But—" He paused, watching her eyes turn their extraordinary violet color with her concern. He thought to tell her that the assailants were not mere thieves and that it had troubled him since; then he thought that he would not. It would only worry her.

"It was nothing, Genevieve. Rabble, quickly silenced. I don't know why I mentioned it now. Just . . . well, I wish I could have proven this 'haunting' was a trick of flesh and blood. Ah, well. Thomas will remain now and eventually the culprit will be caught. It frustrates me though not to solve my own dilemmas."

Genevieve hesitated, wondering whether or not to mention the shadows she had seen the night of her arrival. She had seen nothing since—and she didn't want Tristan thinking that she might believe in the ghosts.

Tristan whistled, and Pie—who had been munching springy grass in the copse nearby—trotted obediently to them. Tristan lifted Genevieve up into the saddle, then swung high behind her. She leaned against him as they rode with the breeze to return to the manor, savoring the heat of his chest and the beat of his heart.

Pie was taken at the steps to the manor by a young groom. Tristan caught Genevieve's hand and they hurried up the steps together. The door opened, and Edwyna—with a loudly squalling Katherine in her hands—accosted them quickly.

"Oh, thank God! Genevieve!" she remonstrated, but with

a smile. "This one is hungry, and her temper is even worse than yours!"

"I have no temper," Genevieve said with a little sniff as she took her daughter, nuzzling against her little neck, delighting in her baby scent. Katherine instantly whimpered and nuzzled her mother in return, seeking out her food supply.

"I'll take her up," Genevieve told Tristan quickly.

He smiled, the contented husband. "I'll be there soon," he promised, and thanked Edwyna for looking after their daughter and giving them precious moments of complete freedom.

Genevieve, halfway down the hall and nearing the stairway, paused when he suddenly called her back.

"Milady, have Mary gather your things tonight. We'll travel back to Court tomorrow."

Genevieve nodded and hurried on up the stairs. Katherine was growing more and more insistent.

The room was nicely warm. Candles gleamed from their sconces, and everything was in readiness for their return. The draperies on the bed had been drawn, and clean linen lain for the baby. Mary knew that Genevieve loved to lie down to nurse, and rest, and watch her baby's face in one. Crooning to her infant, Genevieve started to loosen her gown, walking toward the bed. Then she stopped suddenly, drawn to the windows by a curious speck of moving light just beyond the house.

She moved close to the window to watch, frowning. In the copse of trees nearest the manor she saw the light wavering— and a pair of shadows meeting in some secret tryst. She pressed closer to the window, squinting to see better. Katherine let out a cry, and Genevieve fumbled to bring the baby to her breast while not ceasing to stare out the window.

There were two figures. One man meeting another in the shadow of the trees. Something was exchanged. The one man seemed to hand over documents—the other seemed to receive some payment. They lingered together another moment, then parted.

Genevieve was stunned. She pushed away from the wall, opening her mouth to call to Tristan—

But then she paused. One of the men came out of the trees

leading a horse. He was elegantly dressed; she saw the reflection of a gold medal against the rich velvet of his shirt. She couldn't see his face. But his manner . . . his walk . . . the way he swung with easy grace upon the horse . . . she knew. Just as she knew the horse—a roan gelding with one solid white leg. The horse had come from her father's stables. It had been ridden out to the Battle of Bosworth Field by Sir Guy.

Her cry died in her throat. What was he doing? She should tell Tristan, but she couldn't. Tristan was unreasonable where Guy was concerned, and he would use any excuse to rid his world of Sir Guy.

Genevieve bit her lip. She owed Guy something for his care of her and his past loyalty. She couldn't tell Tristan. She would have to accost Guy herself and demand to know what was going on.

Worried, she lay down at last with Katherine. In time the baby fell asleep, and Genevieve moved her to her cradle. Then Mary came in, and they packed. When that was done, Tristan came up.

Genevieve could have spoken then—but then she was in his arms, and she hadn't said a word. And for good or ill, it quickly became too late to speak.

They had barely returned to Court before Genevieve had her chance to accost Guy, or rather Guy to accost her, as it came to pass. Their first night back among Henry's retinue, the King summoned Tristan for a meeting with the Lord Mayor of London. Anne was in Genevieve's chamber for some time, playing with her little cousin—Anne was entranced with Katherine. She told Genevieve that her mother had said that Tristan had given Genevieve a baby. Perhaps, Anne said, she might ask Tristan if he would give Edwyna one, too. Genevieve laughed and suggested that it might be much better if Anne asked Jon to give Edwyna a baby.

Mary came to take Anne to her mother and stepfather and on to bed. Genevieve stood over her daughter's cradle, cooing softly to her, when the door opened suddenly.

Genevieve swung around with a smile, certain that it was

Tristan. It was not. Guy stood there. He quickly glanced into the hall, then closed the door behind him.

"Genevieve!"

"Guy! I want to talk to you! What—"

"Genevieve!"

She could not finish. He rushed to her and wrenched her into his arms, running his fingers over her hair and holding her tightly. She tried to push him away, growing desperate, afraid to shout lest someone come. How had he gotten in? And then she knew of course. Tristan no longer had her watched day and night.

"Guy! Stop it! If Tristan finds you here, he'll kill you!"

"He won't come. He is with the King, and I have men who will warn me of his approach. Trust me, my love, I shall not get into a tussle with him now and destroy all my hard work. Genevieve, Genevieve, the time is right. I have laid my plans well, and he shall crash to a swift downfall."

"Guy, please, cease this—"

"We'll be together at last."

"Guy! Stop this madness! Guy, he is my husband. That is our child. All wrongs have been redressed in this. And now! You are going to tell me—"

"Don't you see, love?" Guy shook his sandy head with a charming, rueful smile. Genevieve thought fleetingly of the way things had once been. Of the days when she and Axel and Guy had ridden to the hunt, when they had laughed in her father's hall, when they had all been so wonderfully young and innocent of the wars. "It will not matter that you've married him! When he is dead, it will not matter. When that noble head is sprung upon the block, he will stand between us no more!"

Horrified, Genevieve drew back. "Tristan! His head upon the block! Never. Oh, Guy, what have you done? Tell me! I saw you, you know. I saw you at Bedford Heath! Guy—"

He started to laugh and he flung himself back upon the bed and stared at her lasciviously.

"Documents, Genevieve! Oh, bless these fratricidal Plantagenet heirs! Edward and Richard and Henry—and then Edward and

Richard all over again. My God, they used the same names over and over again, generation after generation.''

"Guy! What are you saying—''

He pounced up upon an elbow excitedly. "Letters, Genevieve, of conspiracy.'' He laughed again, so pleased with himself. "It was so easy to hire my spy! A clever man, really. His brother was killed in Tristan's spree of vengeance, after the debacle at Bedford Heath. He was quite glad to take my money—and become the 'ghost' of Bedford Heath. He was serving in the kitchens, you see, so he had easy access to the place. And lo and behold—imagine! A complete correspondence with half a dozen Plantagenet heirs! Addressed to the Earl of Bedford Heath and signed by the Earl of Warwick and others! Genevieve, don't you see? It's perfect! These letters were from a past generation, when Edward would be king, but seen now they make it appear that the Earl of Bedford Heath—the noble Tristan de la Tere!—is plotting treason against the King with his Yorkist contenders! Once I have discovered how to bring these letters carefully to light, Tristan will be no more, milady. You'll be free. And the King will give me Edenby—and you.'' He sprang to his feet and slipped his arms around her with such fervent joy and vigor that Genevieve, stunned by his information, could barely control him.

"Guy! Stop! Listen to me, and listen well! You can't do this! It is madness!'' She trembled. Henry knew that Tristan was loyal to a fault. Or did he?

Her blood raced hot and cold. She had to stop Guy. Henry loved Tristan, surely! But it was true, too, she thought with a sinking heart, that Henry could be as nervous as a cat when it came to contenders for the throne. He didn't want mass bloodshed, but when he was forced to it he could be ruthless. If he did believe that Tristan, someone he had trusted so fully, had turned against him, he might be merciless.

"Genevieve, I love you. I have loved you forever. I will love you forever. I have wanted you for a lifetime. And now I will have you. Your father will be avenged, and Axel will be avenged. Your honor will be avenged, and I will love you still, dearest, despite the taint of his touch.''

"Guy!" She stared at him incredulously. She wasn't sure if he was mad or touchingly endearing. He was so anxious, so concerned, and so pathetic in his desire. "Please, I do not want my honor avenged! You must cease this madness. Listen to me, Guy! You are my friend, my dear, dear friend! I'd not want to see you hurt, ever. But I am sorry that you love me; I cannot love you. Oh, Guy, can't you see? I am married to him now, and I love him and I wish only—"

"Genevieve! Genevieve!" He shook her, smiling at her ruefully and with a special tenderness that might have been reserved for a misled child. "I know that you are afraid, and I cannot blame you! My poor love! It will come right! I swear it. I will take care of everything."

"No, Guy—"

He pressed his lips against her, cutting off her words and her breath. She twisted her head, and he did not notice, for he abruptly released her, hurrying toward the door, "Soon, my love, soon!" he vowed.

"Guy—"

The door closed behind him. "Wait!" Genevieve raced after him into the hallway. He was already gone. Behind her the baby started to cry. Genevieve came back into her room and swept Katherine into her arms, crooning to her. She was so nervous herself that the baby kept crying, and she forced herself to try to be calm. At length Katherine slept again, and Genevieve put her down to pace the room in a fever. What could she do? Tell Tristan? But Guy would die, and his death would lie heavy on her heart—and between them—for all the years to come.

Do nothing? Let Guy produce these letters, and trust in Tristan's allegiance to the King? But what if . . . what if Henry were to drag Tristan to the Tower? Tristan would have enemies, as all men of power did. And perhaps those enemies would remind Henry that once upon a time Tristan de la Tere had been a Yorkist through and through.

"Arggh!" With a cry of misery she ceased her pacing and knelt upon the floor, biting hard into her knuckles. It came to her suddenly that Guy had these letters of which he spoke in his possession. Genevieve had seen his lackey hand them to him in the copse. She had seen Guy ride away with them. Back to London? Back to his quarters at Court? If she could search his accommodations, she could steal the documents back—and destroy them. Guy would be powerless to hurt Tristan, and Tristan would never know that his enemy had sought to destroy him.

It was foolhardy, but she was desperate. Her mind made up, Genevieve quickly rose and slipped into the hallway. Breathlessly she scurried down to the servants quarters, where Mary was billeted with a number of ladies' maids. The girl was half-asleep, but at Genevieve's urging she came back to remain with Katherine.

Genevieve then hurried along the corridors, her heart pounding as she realized that she did not know where to go. Turning and twisting through the maze of corridors, she came upon a guard and asked where the knights might be lodged, Sir Guy in particular. The guard directed her, and she then prayed that Guy would not be in his quarters and that he did not share them with some snoring friend!

She found the room and quickly scanned the hallway before hurrying in.

She closed the door and leaned against it, quickly surveying the space within. All was neat. As yet there was no fire, and it seemed very cold. There were a number of trunks and a cot and a plain writing desk with a single lighted candle upon it, burning out a small flame. Genevieve's heart quickened anew; Guy would be back any minute.

She pushed away from the door and frantically tried the desk; she could find nothing. She sat back, frustrated, then plunged into the first of the trunks and found nothing but gauntlets and leather jerkins and hose. Again she paused, frustrated and frantic, then plunged into the third trunk, growing reckless. She tossed out breeches and shirts and boots and still came upon nothing. Her fingers raked across the bottom of the trunk and then she knew! Probing and probing and probing, she found the latch to the false bottom and pulled upon it. She fell back as it gave, and then she cried out softly in triumph, reaching for the ribboned and rolled letters.

She stripped away the ribbons and unrolled the parchment

to scan the words quickly. A chill swept over her. Dear God, Guy had been right! They were letters to the Earl of Bedford Heath from Yorkist factions, gratefully accepting his aid! Tristan was not that Earl of Bedford Heath—surely it had been his father when Edward was about to go forward to Tewkesberry all those years ago.

But the letters could very possibly bring Tristan to the block now.

There seemed to be some movement in the hall. Genevieve stuffed the letters quickly down her bodice and hastened to right the trunk. She sprang up and ran to the door, cracking it to check the hallway. She slipped out and began a quick walk along the corridor. The candles in their sconces seemed to burn a wavering beat. Her shadow was huge against the wall, and she could hear the staccato beat of her footsteps too loudly.

"Halt!"

At the sudden command she panicked, certain that Guy had returned. If he caught her, he would retrieve the letters. He would perhaps even use that moment to bring them to light.

She started to run.

"Halt! In the name of King!"

It wasn't Guy; it was just a guard, and the letters were secured safely in her bodice. She breathed deeply, slowing, yet spinning with alarm to realize that the guard had kept running when she had stopped. He slammed against her and she fell, rolling on the hard stone floor. Her head cracked against the wall, and a dizzying pain swept through her.

"Milady—"

Someone was reaching to assist her, demanding to know why she had been running. Genevieve tried to rise, then heard a horrible tearing noise, and realized that the letters were spilling out of her bodice.

And there were suddenly sounds. The hall, so silent before, was alive with movement. Footsteps, many of them, running, coming closer and closer, then stopping all around her.

"What's this?"

The letters were wrenched away from her. Genevieve

blinked, trying to dispel the dizziness of her fall, trying to think.

"How dare you?" she demanded with her best, most imperious tone. "Sirs! Where lies gallantry? I am the Countess of Bedford Heath and Duchess of Edenby and you've no right to so accost me! I—"

"My God! Look at this, Anthony! Why, these letters are treason!"

"She is in a conspiracy! The King must see these!"

"Lady of Edenby! She is a Yorkist! She has always been so—she fought Henry when he landed."

The accusations were coming at her fast and quick and through the haze that spun before her eyes. At least ten of the King's royal guard stood grouped around her.

"Nay! They are no treason—" she cried. "They—"

"They implicate Lord de la Tere!" someone said.

And then another stepped forward, looking at the letters, staring keenly at Genevieve. Genevieve knew him vaguely. One of the Sir Nevills—a member of a vast and powerful family, ever anxious for more and more power. They, too, had a connection with the Crown.

"Sir—" she began, but he cut her off crudely, his eyes narrowing with sharp and pleased appraisal.

"Madam, I charge you with 'high treason'! Take her to the Tower! I shall accost his grace de la Tere immediately!"

Sir Nevill turned around. Genevieve felt herself grasped roughly by both arms. She jerked herself free, tears that she would not allow to fall stinging her eyes.

"I shall walk! Do not touch me!"

And she did walk, but her heart was tremulous with terror and her knees would scarcely hold her. The Tower. Prisoners were held in the Tower for years on end; prisoners left the Tower to lay down their heads upon a block.

And Sir Nevill was going after Tristan. With all the letters in his hands. And they would drag Tristan off and . . .

Katherine! Was she crying? Did she fuss, had she awakened, did she miss her mother? Did she need her, did she hunger? Oh, God, if not now, in time she would awaken.

Katherine! Oh, what would become of her precious and innocent babe if she and Tristan were both taken to the Tower?

Genevieve stumbled. One of the guards reached with strange courtesy for her arm, but she jerked it back, blinded by her tears. She tried to hold her head high and turn to the man with dignity.

"Could you—" She had to start over; she could find no voice. "Could you find the Lady Edwyna, wife of Sir Jon of Pleasance, and see that she tends to my daughter?"

"Milady!" This guard was of the kinder sort. He bowed most courteously to her, and someone was sent.

Then the corridors seemed to stretch and stretch until they exited by the rear and came to the river Thames. A boatsman was hailed.

Genevieve could hear the constant slap of the water against the boat. She could look up and see a million stars dotting the sky. The moon was out, high and full.

It was better to look up than across the water.

She could hear the oars pound the water. Slowly, surely, rhythmically. She swallowed, and she fought her nausea and her panic, and she tried not think, not to find reproach; yet the bile rose in her throat and she could not help herself. What else could she have done! She'd had to try to destroy the letters! Else Tristan would have faced the charge of treason anyway, or Guy would have died a bloody death and Tristan might have been charged with murder . . .

Tristan. Where was he now?

Tristan stared with cold fury across the King's privy chamber to Sir Nevill. He hadn't said a word to the charges against him—indeed he had not moved. He remained where he had been when Nevill had burst in upon them, sipping a chalice of the King's finest Bordeaux, his stance casual before the fire.

"As you can see, Your Majesty—" Nevill continued to Henry, seated at the table before the newly signed charter which would make Edenby a city, "—these letters are awful and horrible proof—"

"That my father and family and I fought for King Edward at the battle of Tewkesberry," Tristan interrupted disdainfully at last. Eyes boring into Nevill's, Tristan came from the fire past Henry's clerks and stood beside the King, pointing down to the letter. "See here, man! The Earl of Warwick is a ten-year-old boy! This is not the penmanship of a ten year old—"

"Rubbish!" Nevill swore. "Letters would be written by his clerics—"

"And this! This which now claims me guilty of treason. If you would care to search the records, Your Majesty, you would know that penmanship to belong to Edward III!"

Henry pushed the letter from him, staring at Nevill. "I don't need to make reference to past documents; I've studied many. This is Edward's writing. The parchment is old and frayed, and a blind man might well tell that this is no new missive but an old and fading correspondence. Sir Nevill! Where did this come from?"

Nevill appeared both surly and unappeased, but directly questioned by the King he could not back down. "They were on the person of the Duchess of Edenby, Sire." He bowed toward Tristan. "My Lord de la Tere's Yorkist wife."

Tristan stiffened and his blood boiled. Genevieve!

The room swam black in his anger, denial, and bitter admission. Genevieve . . . she had come to Bedford Heath. She had whispered—and he had fallen into sweet seduction, into love. He had fallen as he had fallen before. Into her sensual web. Into the golden allure. In the heat . . . into the fire.

She had betrayed him again—whispering not just passion, but love. Lying with him again and again in ecstasy's abandon, searing his heart and soul and sense and—making him believe. Seducing him, compelling him, until he could die, drown gladly in the perfume of her sweet scent.

The pain was harsh agony within him, a knife wound that rendered him weak. Yet before Nevill he could not falter. She was his wife. Their war had always been a private one. She was Katherine's mother . . . nay, he could not falter before Nevill!

His features stayed rigid, cold, and ruthless. "Where is my wife?"

"On her way to the Tower."

"I signed no warrant!" Henry roared.

"Your Majesty! I saw treason—she is a Yorkist!"

Tristan ignored Nevill and turned to Henry. "Your Grace, I would go retrieve what is mine, and deal with it as I see best."

Henry sighed, watching Tristan.

"Perhaps you judge too harshly," he said, studying the man.

"Nay," Tristan said bitterly. "She has betrayed me again. Yet it is my concern. I beg your leave to take her from Court. Our business is done, and I would keep her in my own tower, by your leave."

The King nodded, and Tristan strode from the room.

"Oh, God!" The whisper escaped her because Traitor's Gate—like the jaws of death—loomed suddenly before her. Genevieve could not control the shivering inside of her.

The constable was waiting the boat's delivery on a dock damp with moss and slippery with water. Her heart started to thunder, and she thought that she would not be able to stand, that she would faint and fall.

"Halt, ahoy there!"

The command came from behind. Genevieve whirled in the rocking rowboat.

Another boat approached, with Tristan standing tall within it. His mantle flowed behind him. Blessed God, he wore no chains! He held papers in his hand, papers he gave with cool propriety to the constable as his craft drifted to the step and he leapt upon it.

"The lady is not your prisoner, sir, but is to be delivered unto my keeping."

The constable scanned the note with the King's seal upon it and nodded.

"Milady?"

One of the guards reached for Genevieve's hand to help her from the boat to the step. She looked at her husband. His features were in shadow, but his expression was harsh. And as her foot fell upon the slick step, she felt the heat of his anger, which reached out in the night to sweep over her in waves. He did not touch her but surveyed her coldly.

But he was there to retrieve her! He was not under arrest!

"Madam!" he said hoarsely, through tight-clenched teeth, and bowed his head, indicating the other boat. She tried to step into it and she stumbled. He caught her elbow, and she feared that he would wrench away her arm. Steeling herself against the pain, she bit into her lip to keep silent, and he released her to allow her to sit.

Silence cold and dark fell over them as the boatsman pushed away from the steps, and they left Traitor's Gate behind. A breeze swept up, and again Genevieve heard the constant lap of the water against the wood of their craft. She wanted to talk; she wanted to throw her arms around Tristan and cry out her fear and her anguish and tell him how desperately grateful she was that he had not suffered.

She opened her mouth, but it was too dry for sound. She looked at him and knew that she faced a stranger. Fear danced through her like the reflection of the stars against the moat and then the Thames.

"Tristan . . ." At last she spoke his name as they neared the shore. It came as a croak, dry as brittle leaves. And she got no further. He leaned precariously across the seat to grip her chin in a painful vise.

"Not now, madam. I will hear it all, later!"

She did not attempt to speak again until the hired boat had brought them to the shore and a wretched long walk had returned them to their room.

Seated on the bed, anxiously rocking Katherine's cradle, Edwyna jumped to her feet at the sight of them.

"Genevieve!" She hugged her niece, talking frantically. "Genevieve, Tristan! Oh, I was so heartily worried. I—"

Tristan pulled Edwyna from Genevieve, bringing her to the door. "Find Jon," he told her curtly. "Tell him we go home in the morning. Ask him to go to the King for our papers and to formally request our leave."

Edwyna nodded miserably. Tristan closed the door.

And Genevieve stared at him in heartache and misery. She could not fathom his fury, and so she gave out a desperate little cry and came hurriedly to him, whispering his name and bringing her trembling fingers to his cheek.

She never touched him. The back of his hand came hard against her cheek, and she was flung carelessly back to the bed by the force of it.

"Nay, madam!" He thundered. "Never again! Never again will I fall for your beauty or your lies, and never again my own desperate desire! I love you—so you whispered, and whispered well, and I—stupid fool, who had already felt the iron of your treachery against my skull, fell into the sweet seduction of your willing arms and supple thighs. Why should you come to Bedford Heath? For love. Bah! You were there seeking some means for my downfall, but you missed your mark on this one, lady! The King is not stupid, and he knew the charge of treason false!"

Aghast and incredulous, Genevieve stared at his steely countenance as he stood over her, untouchable, unreachable—the iron warrior upon the field of battle. Her cheek throbbed from his blow and yet the tears that came to her eyes were not of pain. He thought that she had stolen the documents! That she had searched his records and his books and his home . . . and thought to see him imprisoned.

That she had lied. That her love, admitted so painfully, had been nothing but a lie.

"Tristan!"

There was such pain to her cry, such agony, that it gave him pause. He faltered. He wanted so desperately to believe her. To reach out and hold her. To love her tenderly and bathe away the tears and hold her to him in naked tenderness . . .

Nay! Again and again she deceived him! With beauty and grace and evocative allure. What fool of a man could fall not once but again and again to the drumbeat in his loins and ragged tempest in his heart.

"Lady, you've played the traitor against me one time too many!"

"Tristan, I did not!"

"Then what?" he perched beside her. She cringed when he reached for her shoulders, wrenching her up to face him. He shook her and her head fell back and he was met by those incredible eyes with their lying glitter of tears once again. "Then what?"

She laughed, and she cried, and she laughed again.

She could accuse Guy—and he would slay Guy. Yet not even that would save her from this awful wrath, for he would merely think that she had conspired with Guy.

There was no help for her.

"Tristan, please—"

"Tell me, Genevieve!"

"I—cannot."

He hurtled her away from him and she lay upon the pillow, dazed. And then Katherine began to cry, fretful and hungry.

And with that cry Genevieve felt her breasts sting, heavy with her daughter's delayed meal. She was so weary! She could barely turn, barely force herself to face Tristan to rise to go to her daughter.

But Tristan was up. Like a tiger, his energy was restive and explosive. Distraught, Genevieve still assumed that he would take the babe from her cradle and bring Katherine to her.

He did pluck her from the cradle. And then he started for the door.

Genevieve lost her inertia. She sat up, then sprang up in growing alarm, for he was opening the door with their daughter in his arms.

"Tristan!" She raced for him, and paused when he turned to her with incredibly cold eyes. Tears streaming down her cheeks; she did not try to touch him, but reached out her arms in beseechment.

"Tristan, what are you doing?"

"Lady, you are not fit to raise her."

"She's my child!"

"And mine, madam."

"Tristan! Good God! You could not be so cruel! Oh, please, God, have mercy, you cannot take her from me!"

He stood, ruthless and unrelenting. She could not see for her tears. She fell on her knees before him, her head bowed. "Oh, my God, Tristan, please, do with me what you will, but don't—don't take her from me!" Her voice broke—and she was broken.

And Tristan stared down at her, at the beautiful blond head bowed before him. More than anything he wanted to believe! He wanted some miraculous excuse that would prove her innocent. He wanted to cradle her into his arms—he loved her with all his heart and wanted her more than ever. It was as if a part of him were being slowly severed away.

His eyes misted and he could barely see. Her fragrance cascaded around him. She was a cloud of golden beauty, pleading at his feet.

Katherine sobbed loudly.

Tristan inhaled, clenching his teeth tightly together. He reached down for his wife's hands and drew her to her feet.

He returned his squalling daughter to her arms and heard her fervent, broken words of gratitude.

For a moment he stood there. He watched as Genevieve brought the babe to the bed, and lay with her. He watched the baby latch onto her mother's swollen breast, and tremors shook over him with the tender beauty of a sight that had never failed to touch him.

Then he turned and left, slamming the door shut with a finality more chilling to Genevieve than any words he had ever spoken.

Chapter
Twenty-Five

"A TOAST!" MR. Crowley, master goldsmith, cried out, raising his glass. "A toast to the city of Edenby. And to her founder, my friends, our liege lord, his grace Tristan de la Tere!"

There was a pleasant shower of accolades as the merchants and artisans in the hallway raised their libations in salute. Tristan, seated at the head of the long table in the great hall, stretched out his legs and shoved the last of the papers toward Sir Humphrey, smiling. He had decided that gentleman would be the best choice for mayor. Sir Humphrey had a manor right on the boundary line of the new city; the people knew him and they loved him. He had been a fighter and he had worked among them. He was liked and he was respected.

"Thank you, gentlemen," Tristan said. He lifted his own glass. "And may we all prosper!"

Griswald appeared, and the sound of that old man clearing his throat seemed a cue. The citizens of the newly founded city of Edenby set down their various tankards and glasses and began to file from the hall.

All but Sir Humphrey, who hovered by the fire. Tristan ignored him, lifting a booted foot to set upon the chair beside him and stretching out to sit with more casual comfort in his chair. He lifted his glass idly and drained it, warily awaiting Sir Humphrey's next comments—which he was sure would be some plea on Genevieve's behalf.

It was.

"You have done well here, Tristan."

"I thank you, sir."

"And you have shown great mercy to your vanquished enemies. You have returned my home to me. Tamkin is quite pleased with being your official steward, a free man now to work for you at his choice. The Lady Edwyna and Jon are blessed with rare happiness. All that—"

"All that I will listen to has been said," Tristan interrupted impatiently. Go no further, old man! he thought broodingly. He scowled and poured himself more wine. Talk, talk, talk! What could be said? Three times in the fortnight since they had been home he'd gone to see Genevieve. Three times he had stayed near the door, arms crossed rigidly over his chest lest he fall to the desire to reach for her. Three times he had asked her for some explanation.

And three times she had bowed her head in silence.

So the Lady of Edenby was his prisoner once more, confined to her room, and Tristan had taken up residence in the master's chamber.

Yet he often wondered bitterly if his life were not far more wretched than Genevieve's, for he had barely slept. He paced, and he ached, and he wanted her. He dreamed of holding her. Yet it was not surrender that he wanted, but love—and love had betrayed him again and again.

He stared into his wine and mused with simmering heartache and anger that she had been in his blood like an obsessive fever since he had first set eyes upon her.

He slammed his wine glass down so suddenly that the fragile crystal threatened to shatter. He threw his feet to the floor and stood, determined to be free of her.

Ignoring Sir Humphrey he strode to the bottom of the staircase. "Jon! Jon! Come down here, will you!"

A moment later Jon came down the stairs eying Tristan

curiously—for he had not heard so light a tone in his voice for a long while.

"Come, Jon! Young Mister Piers has opened an inn just at the new city limit. Let's go and drink his ale and start him on a fine opening of trade!" He turned to Sir Humphrey. "Would you join us, sir?"

"Nay, I think not," Sir Humphrey said sadly.

"Tristan—" Jon began.

And Tristan slipped a comradely arm about his shoulder. "I've a yearning to get drunk. Wonderfully, rip-roaring drunk."

"Drown your sorrows," Jon muttered heatedly.

"Drown them, nay! Merely saturate and drench them, Jon. Find solace in some ale—and mayhap in a willing and eager young wench, who knows? Come!"

Tristan waved idly to Sir Humphrey and called out to Matthew for their horses.

Jon followed hastily. Seemed 'twould be one of those nights when it would be best to stay close to Tristan and temper his mood where he could.

He glanced at Sir Humphrey. "Tell my wife, for me, sir, if you would, that I am desperately trying to catch the tiger's tail."

Sir Humphrey nodded. Tristan's long strides were already taking him out; Jon followed him quickly.

"If you'll not talk to Tristan, I still cannot see why you will not talk to me!" Edwyna complained, exasperated. Genevieve was pacing again, like a wild creature in a cage. Edwyna sat with little Katherine on her lap, thinking of what a beauty the child would grow to be—with Tristan's coloring and her mother's delicate features. She watched the baby with a special, glowing wonder now, for she believed that she would give Jon—and Anne!—the baby they so wanted before the fall harvests were in. And she argued blindly with Genevieve because she could not bear to see both her niece and Tristan so wounded and terribly at odds.

"I can't talk to you, Edwyna," Genevieve said with a soft sigh. "You would think it your duty to tell him—"

"I am your aunt! Flesh and blood!" ·

Genevieve smiled a little wanly, and paused to look at Edwyna directly. "And, nay, I am sorry, I cannot trust you in this, for you'll insist upon doing what you think is right. You cannot help me, but you can cause great calamity."

"Genevieve! Don't you understand?" Edwyna began.

"Aye, I understand," Genevieve said wearily, and she ceased her pacing to curl up at the foot of her bed. "He thinks that I went to Bedford Heath to find some such evidence against him. I did not, though, Edwyna, I swear it!" She laid her head back on the bed, close to tears, and disgusted with herself for her lack of strength. But she was not only heartsick and desperate—she was tormented by morning sickness again. She wondered what this new pregnancy would mean to Tristan—if anything.

Oh, it had to mean something! They could not go on like this, could they? She shivered and hugged her arms to her chest. Edwyna had told her that he and Jon had ridden off together. That he had been imbibing large quantities of wine and was in a wild mood. Had he truly finished with her, then? What did men want of their wives but heirs? Possibly this child would be a boy—and then he wouldn't need to care if he ever came near her again . . .

"Genevieve, I swear by God most holy I'll not betray you in this!" Edwyna promised her softly. "You have to speak on it, you are eating away at your soul and sanity in here!"

"I'm going to have another child," she blurted out.

Edwyna was silent for several seconds. "He will be pleased, of course. But . . ."

"It will not make him forgive me," Genevieve finished bitterly on a little note between a cry and a laugh. "Oh, God, Edwyna! What—"

"Tell me," Edwyna said serenely.

"Edwyna, you'll go to hell if you're lying to me, you know!" Genevieve promised her severely. "Honestly, it could make matters all the worse."

"Let me hear it, please."

And so Genevieve, glad to be able to talk about it, told Edwyna about seeing Guy at Bedford Heath and how she had planned to accost him herself. "Edwyna, can you understand? He was father's man, he was Axel's friend. I could not let him be killed if I could save him!''

"Please, go on,'' Edwyna said grimly.

"Well, at Court he came to my room. And he started on and on about how he loved me and how he had solved everything. He started telling me about these letters he had stolen. And so . . .''

"And so you decided to steal them back. But the guard got suspicious and chased you—and found them.''

Genevieve nodded unhappily.

"Tell him!'' Edwyna exclaimed in a fair temper.

"I can't! He'll merely think that I was in league with Guy!''

"You should have told him from the time that you saw Sir Guy on his property.''

"Maybe,'' Genevieve said dispiritedly. She moved back to her bed and sat. "Maybe. But still, oh, I don't know! I—''

Genevieve broke off, staring open-mouthed at her door— which had just opened. To her utter amazement, the object of her conversation stood before her.

Sir Guy. In a black cloak and cap, with even his hose dark, and his velvet shirt a dusky gray beneath it. He stood there for a moment, poised, his sandy hair curling over his forehead in minor disarray. He smiled slowly at Genevieve.

"I've come for you, love. I've come to rescue you.''

Seconds passed in which she was too stunned to speak. Her mind seemed to work so slowly!

Her hand fluttered to her throat. How had he got in? Young Roger de Treyne was supposed to be her guardian. Where had Roger gone?

Fear and anger rose in Genevieve. "Guy,'' she said coldly, "what are you doing here? Didn't it occur to you that I might have talked to Tristan? I am sure you heard that I had an evening's excursion through Traitor's Gate.''

From the chair Edwyna made a little sound, and Genevieve realized that Edwyna was seeing things much more quickly than she. Understanding. Knowing the import of Guy being able to stand there—inside Genevieve's door.

"I was sorry,'' Guy whispered. "Ah, Genevieve, what a

fool thing you did! But you didn't give my name to your husband. Else he'd not be gone without you now—and you'd not be awaiting me here.''

"I'm not awaiting you!" Genevieve cried out, jumping up. "I nearly lost my head over you, Guy!"

He strode to her quickly, and though Genevieve backed away he caught her to him. "Come on, Genevieve! We've got to go now!"

His touch hurt. His hold on her was a painful grip, and she felt a rising panic. "Guy! I do not want to go with you! I am Tristan's wife! I—"

She broke off because he shook her with such cruel vigor that she had to gasp for air and then stare at him, incredulous again.

"Guy!"

"I love you, Genevieve! I wanted you—"

"Guy, you were my friend! You were Axel's friend! I never loved you, you couldn't have presumed—"

Next she broke off because he was laughing. And because his eyes were filled with terrible malice. "Genevieve, you are with me or against me! Edenby was to be mine—"

"What?" she retorted, straining against his grip. He wasn't a weak man; he was practiced at arms, and his power was almost as great as Tristan's. Desperately she looked over his head to Edwyna. Edwyna was sitting very still, her eyes wide, her hand protectively covering little Katherine's head. Edwyna shook her head slightly, and Genevieve felt a new rush of trembling fear. She understood the look in Edwyna's eyes. Go carefully—this man will hurt you. Hurt—all of us.

"Guy! I was never to marry you—"

"So much, Genevieve. I'd lie awake nights and imagine how it would be here. I'd lie on the bed and you'd stand before me and toss your clothes aside and crawl atop me—"

"Guy! I was never promised to you! I loved Axel—"

"Are you coming with me, Genevieve? I wanted Edenby, I wanted Edenby badly. And still one day I might have it. We'll meet up with other Yorkists in Ireland. One day they'll rise against Henry. And perhaps then we'll come back here.

Perhaps they'll allow me to hack Tristan de la Tere's head from his body.''

"Oh, Guy! Don't you understand! I love him! I will not go anywhere with you! Go! Quickly. Before he comes home. Before the guards discover you! Listen! I love him. Freely. I—''

She screamed, crashing to the floor, when he hit her. She gathered herself up again, stunned. And he took a step toward her, staring down at her in a maddened wrath.

"You will come with me. Willingly. You little bitch, I will have you—'til I tire of you and your arrogant ways! Little fool! 'Twas no Lancastrian knight killed Axel on the battlefield! I killed him! And I killed old Edgar.''

"Oh, my God!" Genevieve breathed.

He smiled charmingly. "And I'll kill again and again, Genevieve. I'll kill you—rather than leave you to him. I'd much rather you come along with me.''

Genevieve took a deep breath and screamed as loudly as she could.

He kicked her in the ribs. Edwyna chose that moment to leap from the chair, but before she could reach the door a stranger with a drawn knife appeared to block her way. Edwyna backed up into the room, sheltering the baby against her chest. She spun to Guy, her lips quivering. "Where, where—''

"Oh, little Anne? Why she is fine. Locked in with Mary and that other little serving slut.''

"Sir Humphrey?" Edwyna asked, wetting her lips.

"Bleeding on the floor," Guy said distastefully. "And that old man Griswald . . . well, he might live. The rest of the mewling servants here were easily cowed. A number of them are in the tower. And that de Treyne lad, well he fought but we caught him from the rear, eh, Filbert?''

"From the rear," the man at the doorway grinned.

"There are a host of guards outside these walls—'' Genevieve threatened, but Guy seemed undisturbed.

"We'll be gone before they can be summoned. Edwyna, give me the brat.''

"Nay!" Edwyna screamed and tried to race from Guy.

Genevieve rose to her feet, swaying but determined. She lunged at Guy like a she-cat, but he turned with a snarl and slapped her hard to the floor again. His hands fell on the baby. Edwyna screamed again, but the man at the door left his stance to rip at her hair, jerking her backward, and Katherine fell into Guy's arms. The baby cried now, aware of the tumult in the room.

Genevieve scrambled to her feet again, crying out and pouncing toward Guy. But he managed to stop her with a few subtle words.

"I'll slit her throat, Genevieve, and I'd most gladly slit the throat of his child. She should have never filled your belly. Now, my grand Lady Genevieve! You'll put on your cloak and go outside and you'll sweetly ask the stable boy for your cloak."

"I am a prisoner here!" Genevieve spat out at him, yet she was in terror, for he held her squalling child, and she had little doubt that he would do as he threatened. Oh, God! She had never imagined the truth! Her father had not died in battle—he had been slain by his own man! And Axel, dear Axel. Oh, God, Guy had been murderous and unscrupulous and insane all along—and they'd never seen it!

"Nay, milady, you needn't fear. When we rode I talked casually to the boy, telling him that perhaps you would ride with me. And he just smiled—you see, my dear, your husband did not care to tell the common rabble that he and his bride were at odds once again!"

What could she do? There was no help from within the keep walls. Perhaps in the courtyard she could scream and rouse the guard, and they would know that a true traitor was in their midst.

"I'll—I'll come," she said. "Please, just give my baby to Edwyna and I—"

"Nay, milady. I will carry the child. And if you do not smile as sweetly as a ray of sunshine to all around you, I will snuff out her odious life in a second's time."

"You bastard! You vile snake, you are spit on the ground—" Edwyna said suddenly, snarling into action. But as she started for Guy, he struck out hard; Edwyna was thrown against the bedpost and fell to the floor in a silent heap.

Genevieve cried out and rushed to her aunt, kneeling down in anxious fear. Oh, she breathed at least. "Edwyna, dear Edwyna—"

Genevieve screamed as Guy tugged ruthlessly on her hair.

"She is alive—leave it at that. Get your cloak. We're going."

Trembling, Genevieve dug out a light summer cloak. She slipped it around her shoulders and gazed down at her aunt's fallen body again.

"I can kill her before we leave, Genevieve. Perhaps I should. You won't doubt me then."

"I am coming," Genevieve said. She marched past him. Outside her door she stopped with a horrified gasp and rushed to the fallen body of Roger de Treyne. Blood carried a trail across his forehead, but, oh, bless the saints! It appeared that he, too, still had breath in his body.

"Get up!"

Guy wrenched her to her feet. Katherine started to wail and Guy compressed his lips in a snarl. "I can really make her squeal, Genevieve."

She lowered her eyes quickly and let him lead her to the stairs. Katherine still sniffled in his arms, but she sensed her mother's presence and did not scream. Perhaps she knew that her life depended on quiet.

In seconds they were out of the hall. From a distant parapet, a guard saluted. Genevieve could hear laughter from the rows of shops within the walls.

Matthew came to her, and she smiled and told him that she would ride with Sir Guy. He smiled in return and said he would quickly bring the horses.

Oh, Matthew, Matthew! Can none of you see that this is wrong! The sun shone so strongly while they waited! The air seemed so warm with the summer and the sky so blue. Voices dulled to a lazy chant and she could hear them so clearly, as clearly as the terrified beating of her heart. Tristan, I love you, she thought. I love you so much! With all my heart! And yet I was so foolish! Please, please believe that I did not run away with him!

Edwyna would tell him the truth, she assured herself. Pray to God he would believe it. And he would come for her, oh, surely he would . . .

But would he reach her? Or would Guy abduct her in truth and take her captive to Ireland's shores? Or tire of the quest and slay her and Katherine, as he had so many others.

She almost cried out, feeling his powerful hand on her arm and knowing that he could throttle her baby in a second. And just when she thought that she could not stand any longer Matthew returned with the horses.

"Milady!" he said, leading the mounts from the stable. He made his hands into a mounting platform for Genevieve and she swung unto the horse he had brought her, a bay mare.

Guy swung onto his mount easily, even with little Katherine in his arms. Genevieve feared that she would choke, watching him mount his horse with her baby. He could drop her! He could trample her beneath the horse's hooves . . .

"We'll just ride in the forest for awhile," Guy said pleasantly to Matthew.

"Aye, Sir Guy!"

"Run ahead and tell the guard to open the gate, boy," Guy said, and he tossed Matthew a coin.

"Aye, sir!" Matthew agreed. He stared at Genevieve with a peculiar smile, then ran ahead. Guy chuckled very softly and Filbert made a snickering sound behind them.

"Genevieve, my love . . ."

Guy gave her mare's rump a smack, and the mare trotted obediently alongside him. In seconds the guards at the main gate waved down to them, and they were quit of Edenby. Once again Guy smacked her horse's rump, and she cried out as they raced southward along the jagged terrain that rimmed the sea.

Katherine began to scream freely in tears at last, and Genevieve urged her mount purposely closer to Guy's. Guy, scowling, slowed.

"Please, Guy, give her to me! I can cry out no longer, I cannot give an alarm, please, give me my daughter—"

Guy passed the baby to her with a frightening abandon. "Take her! And shut her up! Now!"

Genevieve held her baby close. Guy dismounted from his horse to loop the reins over the mare's neck so that he could lead her and so that Genevieve could have no control. Katherine continued to scream despite her mother's arms.

"Shut her up!" Guy bellowed.

"She's—hungry."

"Then feed her!"

"I cannot feed her before you! We must stop, I need a place—"

Guy laughed, and the sound raked along her spine like a score of needles.

"You'd best feed her before me. I'll not stop until we're far, far away."

"Tristan will come after you."

"Tristan will be busy." He smiled at her so pleasantly then that she instantly knew a whole new rash of unreasoning fear.

Then he pointed behind them. She had to stare for several seconds before she realized that a billow of smoke was rising into the summer air.

Genevieve gasped. "The castle! It's—"

"Burning. On fire." He started to laugh again. "I told you, Genevieve, if I cannot have what I want, then no one else may have it." His tone roughened and he stared at her with a cruel and malicious curl to his lip. "I'd rather destroy it."

"You've killed them!" she choked out. "All those people, trapped within—"

"Maybe a few got out. Pray for them, Genevieve. And ride!"

Matthew knew that it was wrong. Lady Genevieve had smiled— but she looked as if she would burst into tears at any moment. Aye, Sir Guy had come to Edenby before—with the King's men, to boot—but it was still wrong. Why, when the lord and lady had come from London, terse as they were with one another, they'd both been gentle with that wee babe. The lady would hardly trust the child to her new husband's arms—so why allow this knight to take her upon a horse so?

He didn't think on it long—thankfully. Certain that something was wrong, he tore into the great hall. And lo and behold, the old knight, Sir Humphrey, lay on the floor, moaning. And from the kitchen there came a noise as to wake the dead.

And he could smell it. Smoke.

Matthew raced outside, screaming for help. In seconds guards were rushing about the place. He took the stairs two at a time. He nearly tripped over the man near the landing, but bent to him instead.

Roger de Treyne came to with a groan.

"Fire, sir, fire!" Matthew warned. And Roger needed to hear no more. He stumbled to his feet swearing. While Matthew rushed on up the tower stairs, Roger stumbled into the Lady Genevieve's chamber. The curtains were ablaze, and the bedclothes had caught.

And the Lady Edwyna lay at the foot of the bed.

Roger hurried to her. The fire crackled and spread while he bent, dizzy himself, and swept her into his arms. He raced out just before one of the ceiling beams crashed down to the floor with a terrible shower of sparks and deadly force.

He did not stop until she was outside, moaning and gasping for air. Then she gazed at him, eyes glazed, and her face all smudged.

"Anne! My daughter. Oh, my God, Roger—"

"Milady, milady, the wee one's 'ere!" Matthew cried, leading out little Lady Anne along with Mary and Meg and a host of the household servants. Anne sniffled and pitched herself into her mother's arms; Edwyna rocked her, shivering and whispering, "My baby!" over and over again and then she suddenly stared at Roger. "Genevieve! He's taken Genevieve! We've got to summon Tristan and Jon and—"

"I'll go now," Roger said grimly.

"Nay, wait!" Edwyna cried. "He might not believe you, but he must believe me!"

Roger stared at her, confused.

"That she did not go willingly," Edwyna said softly, and Roger nodded.

"I'll get the horses," Matthew said.

And Edwyna, finding strength, took command. "Oh, bless us, Sir Humphrey! You are well. See that everyone makes it out. Griswald, account for everyone! See that the fire is stopped. Anne, oh, Annie my love! You take care of Mary, she is crying and scared! Little one, I'll be back soon."

Matthew had the horses; Roger was ready for her. With Matthew's help she swung into the saddle.

It was no good. He could drink until the stars ceased to shine at night, and it would still be no good. He could smile at buxom tavern wenches and try to tell himself that the merry promises in their eyes could heal his burning flesh, but it could never be true. He could laugh and joke and tease and swig ale until the end of time, and it would not still the longing in his heart. Only one wench could heal him, with her love like balm, like scented oil and potent wine.

Go to her! He told himself. The cry was in his heart and in his soul: Go to her, take all her sweet beauty into your arms.

He slammed his tankard down suddenly. Jon, morose beside him, looked up quickly.

"Tristan—"

Tristan stood and threw coins upon the table. "Let's go home," he said softly. And Jon gazed down from his eyes, relieved. He didn't know what had brought about the change in Tristan, he was simply glad of it.

He rose, too, and called out a thank-you to the saucy wench who had served them—disappointed now to see that her quest for the sport of a noble lord seemed lost. And lost it was. His mind made up, Tristan was heading for the door.

But they did not reach it before it was suddenly burst inward.

"Edwyna!"

At the sight of his wife's smudged face, Jon scrambled desperately forward, heedless of the tankards and trenchers that fell in his wake. "Edwyna, my God! Roger! What is the meaning of this?"

"What in God's name happened?" Tristan demanded tersely from behind him.

Edwyna spoke quickly and gravely.

"Sir Guy. He has taken Genevieve and Katherine. He set fire to the hall, but that does not matter now, Tristan." She watched his expression. "Damn you, Tristan! This was no plan, no conspiracy! Guy stole your papers, and Genevieve tried to steal them back so that you would not kill Guy or go to the Tower. Oh, and worse, much worse. He is mad, Tristan, he must be—and he has been! Genevieve's father did not die from a battle wound—Guy killed him, as he killed Axel, so that he could have Genevieve. And he has her now, Tristan, and—" She broke off with a little sob. "—and the baby! And some of them are out, but he knows this territory. Tristan, you have to find her. He'll hurt her. She'll fight him—you know how she fights!—and he'll kill her or the baby! And she cannot ride as he'll make her, she'll lose the new one—"

"When?" Tristan thundered out. "Who is he with? How many men?"

"Not an hour. One man. Filbert, he called him—"

Tristan swore in a loud raging cry. "Filbert! The man was a servant at Bedford. My God, I will kill him! If he touches her, if he harms her or Katherine—"

He did not finish the thought. He was out the door with a savage stride, and indeed fury and anguish laced his eyes so that they burned with the sure and primitive fury of hell's fire. In seconds he was up on his enormous piebald.

Roger and Jon exchanged glances and raced after him, mounting their horses in bold, desperate leaps.

But they could not keep up with Pie, for he raced with the wind, and his master's great heartbeats sounded along with his hoofbeats.

A cry could be heard on the air. A battle cry, hoarse and chilling and terrible, and far older than any war created by kings of Lancaster or of York.

Chapter
Twenty-Six

GENEVIEVE WISHED THAT they would not ride so close to the sea; the path that they followed moved terrifyingly through dense foliage which would suddenly break—and they would be high above the water on the ragged cliffs. This was her country, she tried to tell herself. She knew this land as well as Guy did. But it helped little. She still rode in continual agitation, terrified that her mare would lose her footing and that she and the animal and Katherine would fall down the steep rock to knives of death below. For herself she was so weary she did not know if she might not welcome the quick grasp into oblivion, but for Katherine . . .

Indeed as night came and Guy continued to force his hurried scramble northward, her despair and exhaustion were such that only thoughts of Katherine, sleeping sweetly in her arms and unaware of their rigors in that tender nest, kept her going and clinging to life.

Filbert rode behind them. Guy dropped back suddenly, and Genevieve bit her lip, wishing he would not, as they were high upon a cliff and the trail was narrow. He smiled in the growing darkness, and she knew that he was amused by her fear. She did not speak to him but stared at him through narrowed, watchful eyes.

"Take heart, love. We're stopping soon."

She did not reply.

"Up ahead. There is a group of caves that run deep and long. One could be lost among them for days."

She knew where she was. As children, they had called the caves the devil's pits, and she knew that they ran deep and forever along the sea. Rebels had come here in days gone by; the Celts had run from the Romans to hole up here, and the Angles had run from the Saxons, and the Saxons from Normans and Jutes.

She lowered her head suddenly. He had meant to scare her, yet he had given some small hope. She knew the caves—he had forgotten that she was a Llewellyn, child of this rugged place even more than he. With just the smallest head start, she might escape him.

She had to keep believing—or else go mad. As it was, she had spent the day in tormented prayer. If only she could know that God had spared Edwyna and Anne and the others from the fire. But things must have gone badly or Tristan would now be in pursuit of her. Oh, God, most surely, he would come! If not for her, then for Katherine . . .

Guy moved ahead; to her relief they took a sharp turn inland, away from that dangerous precipice. They came to a clearing before the first of the gaping caves, and Guy dismounted, pulling her mare forward into the cave. Filbert followed, lighting a torch, then using that torch to set ablaze a stack of kindling—obviously prepared at an earlier date for this occasion. Guy had planned and waited carefully, she realized sickly. He had waited for Tristan to leave Edenby before he had burst in upon her.

Guy stared at Genevieve. He did not glance at Filbert as he spoke. "Guard the entrance here. And do not disturb me."

Silently Filbert slunk out of the cave. Watching Genevieve, Guy grinned. "What do you think of my love nest, milady?"

"You're are grievously ill, Guy."

"Nay, I am feeling exquisitely healthy. And virile. You will discover just how sweetly so."

He reached for her, and without jarring Katherine, Genevieve could not fight his hold. She landed on her feet with the baby clutched to her, and his arms around her waist. For a moment faintness overwhelmed her. This seemed the final horror. If he touched her, she would willingly throw herself from the cliffs; she simply could take no more.

Then she thought, like one drowning, that she must fight—else she would give way to the cold clamp of the water. She jerked away from him.

"Get your hands off of me!"

He laughed, but released her. He was not ready yet to prove his point. "Genevieve, you are so arrogant! It charms me, it fascinates me! And—it will change."

He stepped away from her, pulling things from his leather saddlebags. He had packed, she realized with disbelief, as if they were lovers on a picnic. He had a skin of wine and loaves of bread and large wads of cheese, which he laid out on a cloth before the fire.

Then he sat by it, and waved an arm for Genevieve to join him. She did not, but stood, cradling her child, staring at him.

"Get rid of the brat, Genevieve, and sit beside me."

She told him in most certain terms what he should do to himself. With a grim smile, Guy retorted that he did intend to do just what she suggested—but that she would be involved.

"Such language, milady! Do you whisper such things to your Lancastrian knight in the heat of passion? Did he teach you those words and when to use them to increase the thrust of his blade?" She stared at him coolly, her face and stance so scornful that he started to his feet. He laughed when she backed away.

"Now, Genevieve. While she still sleeps and sets up no noise. Take the blanket there and set her to sleep. For if she cries when I do not wish to be disturbed, I will see that she is silenced."

Genevieve swung away from him before he could see the tears of horror, fear, and revulsion in her eyes. She dragged the blanket from the leather satchel he had indicated, and took Katherine as far from him as she could, settling her into a little niche in the rock where the cave stretched farther into the maze of gaps and holes and darkness.

She stared into that darkness and thought that perhaps this was her chance; she could snatch Katherine to her breast again and run. But if he caught her, she knew beyond a doubt that he would kill Katherine then and there, and make her watch.

A better chance would come, she thought. She had seen that he carried a dirk strapped about his ankle. If she could but lull him along for a few minutes, she could slip that dirk from the strap and she would not hesitate to shove it into his gut.

She came back and sat beside him. He handed her the wine, and she sipped it, watching him. He offered her bread, and she took it for whatever strength it might give her in a fight.

He watched her with a satisfied smile.

"Do you know, Genevieve, what we will do when we are done?" She remained silent, and he leaned upon an elbow to stare at her; and he did so with such a smile that for a minute she thought she must have imagined it all. Here was the handsome, easy-going, sandy-haired knight who trudged along at Axel's side. A dozen times they had ridden out to the woods and drawn a blanket over the cool earth to enjoy a spring day and nibble bread and cheese and fruit and drink wine. This was Guy, laughing, joking, quick to tease, quick to excitement when they spoke of tournaments and jousts.

Her stomach pitched and rolled. He was insane, or so totally ruthless and power hungry that it was all the same. He had murdered her father. In the heat of battle he had slain not the enemy, but his best friend.

"Do you know, Genevieve?" he asked her softly. And he stretched to touch her chin with the tip of his finger.

"You're going to rape me," she said contemptuously.

"Oh, nay, Genevieve. Nay, nay, nay! You, my love, are going to come to me. You will create my dream in this dusty cave—you will bring gold to it, my love! You will stand and you will smile down at me as you have smiled down at him. That smile which alone brings a man to full brink! And slowly, seductively, you will cast your clothing aside until you stand before me in your hair only. And you will let it cascade all over me . . . all over my body.''

"You are sick!''

He chuckled softly. "You will do it. Because if you do not, I will skewer Katherine right through the heart.''

Genevieve looked quickly away, loath for him to see the desperation that filled her. Dearest God! To think that she had suffered for this man! That she had cast herself into realms of misery lest Tristan should slay him! How eagerly, now, would she see him bleed!

"You killed my father!'' she whispered.

"That did not bother you, milady, when you believed him slain by de la Tere—you cozened to him quick enough, milady, believing all that blood upon his hands.''

" 'Twas battle, not murder!'' she cried, and then she quickly lowered her gaze from his, waging a terrible inward battle. If she had any hope of securing that knife, she had to take him somewhat off-guard. Still she could not bring herself to touch him, nor even to tease.

Her heart pounded. Ah, that night so long ago when she had been so terrified of Tristan! When she had first brought him into the hall. Even then, when treachery was their hope and their plan, she had known a quickening from a gaze, a simmering inside. She had hated his arrogance, but she had admired the strong clean lines of his face and she had known that she faced a true knight, bred in honor and gallantry. Time had taught her that the noble strength of his face was true, and time had taught her love as she thought that she could never learn it. And now it seemed as if she would never see that face scowl or smile again, or hear his voice, in a tender whisper or raging roar. She would never have a chance to fall upon her knees and trust in his love enough to tell him the truth, to speak when he demanded her trust . . .

Oh, God.

She closed her eyes and swallowed as a convulsion shook her like an icy blade of death. She opened her eyes and looked at Guy, and forced herself to chuckle.

His brows arched high. "You laugh, milady? I am glad of your humor."

"I was thinking of the irony—Guy. Ghosts abounding in Bedford Heath—and here, far away in the wilds of Wales—is that ghost! I'd have never imagined it." She leaned forward, carefully. "Guy! My father, dying—telling me that I must not surrender. Oh, he never knew! And then you—coming up with the plan to kill Tristan and his men. And then you asked for my hand so gallantly! Like a true knight, you went off to battle; but ever the opportunist you saw Richard's cause lost—so you leapt to Henry's side. How bitter for you to discover the castle retaken! You are a chameleon! Remarkable. You change colors at will!" She was close. So close. Almost atop him, and he was staring in her eyes.

Then!

She reached for the dirk, and it slipped free in her hand, and she had it against his stomach ere he could breathe. He stared at her still, apparently still amused; she heard him inhale sharply and watch her now with wary respect.

"Put it down, Genevieve."

"Nay, if you move I'll—"

"Genevieve . . ." He gazed past her shoulder, and he was smiling now. Slowly, panic seeped into her at that smile. "Turn, milady," he suggested.

"Don't you move!" she hissed, and wedged the blade closer to him. But when she turned it was to see that Filbert had crept into the cave. He stood, smiling, back in the little cranny above Katherine; in his hand a hunting knife gleamed like fire.

"Oh!" Genevieve whispered. And Guy took that opportunity to wrest at her hand. Instinct drove her to keep her fingers clutched around the dagger, but Guy twisted and she was suddenly swung beneath him; she stabbed at him fiercely, but the blade slipped against the dirt and stone of the floor, doing no damage. Guy slapped her hand and the dirk flew from it. He straddled over her, holding her still, and for good measure he slapped her face so hard that bells seemed to ring and reverberate in her head. Like a wild beast, she flailed against him and caught his face with vicious scratches, and his throat, but he caught her fingers then and leaned so close to her she really feared that she would be sick. She gasped for breath and felt the warmth of his as he bent to her in sudden fury.

"Your last chance, Genevieve! One more move and he kills her!"

"Nay!" she cried out, shuddering, trembling. Guy smiled, jerking his head to send Filbert to his post outside. "Now, you bitch, we do it my way! And make it good, my lady!"

He stood suddenly, jerking her to her feet, shoving her roughly. She stumbled, and nearly fell, but he caught her, wrenching her up. "Now, Genevieve! Or so help me I will kill her before your eyes—and slowly, so that she will scream! And you can go mad if you so choose, for I will let you die slowly in a pool of blood then, too!"

"Stop!" she shrieked, shoving him away. "Stop!" She was near hysterically mad then, she thought, and she whipped her cloak from her shoulders, tossing it down. Then she stood, trembling, so terrified that she could not seem to move.

"Now!"

"I despise you!"

"She will die."

"Nay!" Shrieking, Genevieve stooped to take off her shoes. As Guy had ordered; she did it slowly, praying for any time that she could buy.

"I shall retch all over you!" she swore.

"I suggest that you do not, milady."

She stripped away her hose, and surely her speed pleased him, for she took an inordinate amount of time. And she felt his eyes on her, viciously evil.

She turned away from him, to look once more upon her sleeping child before entering into hell. She turned slowly, then froze.

Katherine was gone.

There was no blood upon the floor. No sign of violence. The baby was gone, as if she had simply slipped into the darkened void of a netherworld.

"Damned bitch!" Guy suddenly swore, and she felt a rush

of wind as he came for her, clutching at her shoulders, rending fabric from her back. Genevieve did scream then, in fierce fury.

Then she heard a roar like the pounding surf, like a wolf at bay. It sounded like thunder in the cave, and when she gazed into that darkened space again there was no void.

There was Tristan—savage, splendid, all supple motion and graceful power. Where Guy's hand had lain upon her body there was nothing but the wind which came in the wake of Tristan's fury. He leaped on Guy, landing hard, and they were locked in bare-handed combat. Genevieve cried out in astonishment and fear, looking anxiously to the entrance lest Filbert attack Tristan's back. No one entered the cave, but when she turned quickly back she saw Guy's hand reaching out . . .

He lay beneath Tristan, and Tristan's hands were at his throat. Yet his fingers reached and reached for the dirk . . .

"Tristan!" she screamed. "The dirk!"

Guy had it and stabbed fiercely, but Tristan twisted away. The blade did not penetrate his heart but tore into the flesh of his thigh instead.

Guy seized the advantage, shoving the weight from him. He caught the dirk again, yet did not attack Tristan, for that knight's fury was such he knew he could not win.

He staggered up—and caught Genevieve, wrenching her to him by the hair. Tristan, about to tackle him again, was caught up short by the strangled sound of her cry; Guy inched the dirk below her breast, its point at her heart.

"Stay back, de la Tere."

"Tristan!" Genevieve cried. "Take Katherine—"

"Back off!" Guy shouted. And he began to edge out of the cave, dragging Genevieve with him.

She could hardly breathe, his hold was so tight around her. Her bare feet scraped the ground as he dragged her out of the cave.

Genevieve was dimly aware that they passed Filbert's body, that he lay dead outside the cave. Then blackness nearly blinded her, she was so short of breath. Still she could feel the rocks cutting her feet and the point of the blade drawing a trickle of blood from her flesh.

Tristan was following them, his eyes locked with Guy's. They were nearly at the edge of the cliffs. They would all go over, she thought; the three of them would pitch to their deaths upon the jagged rock. Genevieve was almost beyond caring.

"Let her go! Face me. Fight for her!" Tristan thundered out.

"Back off!"

Genevieve could hear the waves far below, like a lulling melody. Guy just kept backing away, dragging her along. She felt rocks shuffle beneath her bare feet, heard them tumble off the cliff edge—far, far below.

"Get out of here, Tristan, or I'll throw her straight over the side, I swear it! You get away from me and give me a horse, and I'll just take her for a little safeguard. You've got your brat back. Take her! You don't want Genevieve. You don't need her. She's in with me, de la Tere! Can't you see that? Your precious little wench has been with me from beginning to end. She's been mine, Tristan, when—"

"Free yourself, Genevieve!" Tristan railed, and for a split second she merely stood, bewildered. She didn't understand the sound, the whistle in the air. She had barely seen Tristan move.

But he had moved. He'd snatched his dagger from the sheath at his calf and sent it flying in an arc so clean and smooth that it was barely motion, just that whistle . . .

Striking Guy's shoulder.

She heard his cry, and slammed her elbow into his ribs. His hand grabbed desperately at the hilt of the knife protruding from his flesh. But he did not release her! One arm remained firmly around her as he fell to the earth. She screamed, staring over the brink with horror at the whitecaps so far below, shining in the moonlight. She was entangled with Guy, and halfway over, clawing at the ground.

"Genevieve!" Tristan shrieked. She heard him running, running to her, to where she lay entangled with Guy.

Guy's fingers clutched for her, winding around her. Then

those fingers released their death grasp as Tristan came upon them.

"Genevieve!" Tristan screamed again above the pounding of the surf and her own heart. She was entranced, horribly entranced with the call of that surf, too terrified to move.

Then she heard them, scuffling beside her, throwing up clouds of dust and pebbles. Stunned, she watched as the men rolled closer and closer to the edge, their legs dangling over it . . .

Then there was a scream—long, wretched, filled with the knowledge of death. And in that awful darkness, Genevieve started to scream, too. She saw the body hit the rocks. She saw it bounce and fall and bounce again, like a rag doll. And she saw it hit the surf at last, and be swept away with the tide.

Genevieve screamed and screamed until warm arms enfolded her and carried her away from that precipice of blood and death.

"Tristan!"

She could barely whisper his name as she stared up at him, and then she whispered it again and again. And she looped her arms around his neck, but that was not enough. She had to touch his face again and again, sobbing as she felt the sheer wonder of it beneath her touch.

"Tristan . . ." she choked it out. And he shushed her with a kiss as he carried her back to the cave.

"Katherine!" she whispered. "Oh, Tristan—"

"She's in the cave, my love. With Jon. I would not let him leave her."

"How—?"

"Edwyna is not far behind. I dared not attempt to attack Guy upon the cliff path as it was so narrow and so close . . . Jon and Roger and Edwyna caught up with me there. Edwyna knew of the caves and described them to me. We could not rush in . . . not when he had you both."

"I nearly died when I saw her gone. Thank God—"

"I saw your face. I could not let you wonder long."

"Oh, Tristan!"

They were just outside the entrance to the cave and he

paused, looking down at her. Shadow and firelight and moon-light all played on his dirty, dusty features; yet he had never appeared more noble, nor more fine. She began to tremble in his arms, ridiculously near sobs now that she was safe with him.

Her voice was scarcely a whisper as she rushed desperately to say everything at once.

"Tristan, I did not . . . Guy lied! I didn't know—Tristan! He killed my father. And he killed Axel! He killed them—and we all believed them slain in battle! He killed them, and then he swore to be my friend and oh, God, Tristan I swear, I only protected him out of some sort of loyalty because—"

"I know," Tristan interrupted her quietly, smiling tenderly.

"You—know?"

"I was a fool, my love. I was afraid to trust you. Will you forgive me?"

Tears welled behind her eyes as she looked at him, shaking as she stroked her knuckles over a bruise on his cheek.

"I—forgive you? Tristan, had I warned you from the start, at Bedford Heath, that he was furtively up to something—"

"Hush, my love."

"But my silence proved so dangerous. Oh, my God, Tristan, I still shudder to think . . . Katherine . . ."

"And you." He smiled and brushed a kiss across the top of her head. "This hair, this form, this voice, this soul. My jewel, my love, my life." His voice grew tender, and he rested his cheek tensely against her head, drawing her to his chest. "But fear came so hot and close upon those dragon rocks that I can do naught now but thank Almighty God that he has given us a chance to live, and love again."

"Oh, Tristan—"

"Excuse me, but can this wait!"

They both started and Tristan turned, and there stood Jon, gingerly holding Katherine, who cooed curiously and giggled and beat her tiny fists against his face.

"Katherine!" Genevieve cried joyously, and she struggled from Tristan's hold to reach Jon and snatch her infant joy-ously to her.

"She's quite—wet," Jon remarked.

"Oh my darling, precious love!"

Genevieve's tears spilled, finally, over the babe—so that all in all they were quite drenched. Tristan came and put a protective arm around them both, reminding Jon with amusement that he'd best come to terms with small, wet wriggling bundles.

"Umm," Jon agreed pleasantly. And then he suggested that they get the horses, since Edwyna and Roger were surely beside themselves with worry by now. He gazed toward the body of Sir Guy's henchman and murmured that they should bury it quickly. Tristan told Genevieve to get her things and wait; but she could not go back into the cave, so he brought out her shoes and cloak, and wrapped it gently around her shoulders. Genevieve waited feeling very little remorse while they buried the body of her tormenter; with a smile she cradled the baby he would have pierced through the heart.

Genevieve did not ride back on the mare; but with Katherine in her arms, she rode before Tristan on Pie. Down the cliff, they came upon Roger and Edwyna, and Genevieve and her aunt clung together, crying all over again and both telling one another how very frightened they had been.

Then once again they all started out for home, for Edenby.

It was hours before they saw the waning moon rise over the walls and parapets of the castle. Daylight was coming, slowly peeping out from the clouds, while a full moon remained as if it wished to wink at the sun and tease it.

Roger and Jon and Edwyna were quite a bit ahead by then, and Edwyna held the baby. Tristan's hands rested over Genevieve's on the pommel, and they were both weary yet curiously content at Pie's slow, lazy gait.

"It burned," Genevieve murmured, "but no one was killed. We were blessed, my love."

"Aye, we were blessed." He nuzzled her head. "But what shall I do now, love? I have no walls behind which to hold my errant, wild rose of a wife."

Genevieve smiled, rolling her head against his chest to glance up into his features. "You have needed no walls to hold me, milord, for a long, long time now. There are delicate chains about my heart that tie me to you forever."

He chuckled softly. "Chains! Aye, silken webs and delicate whispers. Long was I your captive, lady, ere you were mine!"

"Oh, Tristan! Milord, do I love you!"

"And I, you, milady."

"Home," she murmured contentedly, caring not that her home was a rubble of ash. Edenby was more. It was the wild beautiful sea, and the cliffs, and the people. It was a city now. It was what they would make it. It was their future. "We'll have to rebuild."

"Aye."

"And enlarge. And, Tristan, I was ever so impressed with Bedford Heath! May we have those glorious windows?"

"Whatever you wish, my love."

"And those wonderful rugs, especially for the nursery. And we will really need a schoolroom. And wonderful, warm guest rooms so that scholars from all over the world will come to us, and stay with us. And musicians! And—"

"A schoolroom?"

"Aye! Annie must learn things other than needlework. And Katherine will be a most intelligent girl, I'm sure of it. And Jon and Edwyna could have a son this time, and . . ."

"And?" His arms tightened around her.

She smiled, and then laughed. "You knave! You already know."

"Well, Edwyna did blurt out something. I thought you might care to tell me, though."

"We could have a son this time," she whispered.

"Aye, we could," he said, and he reined Pie to a halt, and allowed his arms to sweep fully around her so that he could kiss her long and deep and with a sweeping tenderness. At length he drew from her, and he smiled, and together they looked out again. Aye, the castle had burned. But the stone stood, as tall and proud as ever. The air was clear and the sky was blue above the charred but noble foundations of Edenby.

"Tristan, look at how the sun dazzles upon the parapets!" Genevieve whispered. "I feel the most incredible happiness; yet I wonder if I should?"

"Aye, love," Tristan murmured. "Happiness must be taken

and cherished when it comes.'' He wrapped his arms around her and hugged her gently, pulling her back closer in to his embrace, cradling his hands beneath her breasts. ''As for me, Lady of Edenby, I, too, am incredibly happy. More pleased than I had ever dreamed possible. Indeed, lady, you do please me again, and again, and again.'' ·

''Knave!'' she charged him, laughing.

''Aye—but most adoring, ever revering, bewitched and beguiled husband as well. A red rose of Lancaster, madam, most earnestly seeking to entwine with the white rose of York. England united . . . our house united.''

''In truth, do you think?'' Genevieve whispered. ''Have the wars really ended at last?''

''Ours have, my love,'' he said firmly. ''Our house is one.''

She smiled, content. ''Aye, Lancastrian lord! This white rose then casts her thorns aside forever!''

Tristan grinned and nudged Pie forward, and as they came near the gates he whispered softly in her ear.

''Come, love, and please me, and where we have no bed of our own this night, still we'll lie forever in a bed of roses, soft and aye! plucked of those demon thorns—forever.''

The sun climbed high above the cliffs and rock and walls of Edenby as they made their way forward; and the sky came gloriously alive in shades of gold and crimson with the coming of the new day.